STONE UNTURNED

STONE UNTURNED

LAWRENCE WATT-EVANS

A Legend of Ethshar

WILDSIDE PRESS

Dedicated to Jeffry Dwight & Steve Ratzlaff
for twenty years of making me feel at home on the net.

Published by Wildside Press LLC.
www.wildsidepress.com

PROLOGUE

Zerra the Ageless was relaxing on her balcony one afternoon, enjoying the warm weather and a glass of fine Shularan wine, when a scrap of paper tumbled down out of the sky and landed in her lap.

She stared at it, startled, then sighed and set her glass down. She picked up the paper, unfolded it, and read: "Bring your carpet to the home of Erdrik the Grim, on Old East Avenue in the south end of the New City, as soon as possible." The signature, of course, was "Ithinia."

Zerra gazed up at a clear blue sky and felt the gentlest of breezes, faintly scented with the spices for which the city was named. A bird called somewhere in the distance. It was, she had to admit, a fine day for flying. She got out of her chair, picked up her glass, and went inside.

A moment later, she emerged dragging a heavy roll of carpet. She dropped it with a thud, pushed her chair all the way to one end of the balcony to make room, then unrolled the rug.

It filled the entire depth of the balcony, the hem on one side brushing up against the wall and threshold, while the other touched the uprights in the railing. About fifteen feet long, its gold and green silk shone in the afternoon sun. Zerra seated herself cross-legged in the center, settled in, took a deep breath, then said a single word, "*Soorgeh.*"

The carpet rose gently, lifting a yard or so above the planking, and Zerra commanded, "*Maweyat ooday mannumeya!*"

The fabric rippled.

Zerra raised a hand and moved it sideways; the carpet turned in the same direction and floated over the balcony railing, over the garden behind her house. Satisfied that Varrin's Lesser Propulsion was still working properly—it was due to be renewed soon, so it might be getting quirky—she sent the carpet soaring upward, into the warm, clear air above the rooftops of the Wizards' Quarter, then westward, across Arena to the centuries-old district still called the New City.

A moment later she let it settle down to just a few feet above the hard-packed dirt of Old East Avenue. Ithinia of the Isle, senior Guild-master of Ethshar of the Spices, waited there, standing very straight in her customary white robes. Other people, some of them more junior wizards, paused to watch the flying carpet, but no one dared approach. Zerra was sure they were more intimidated by Ithinia than by the carpet.

"What's going on?" Zerra called, still seated in the center of the rug.

"We finally got into Erdrik's house," Ithinia called back, stepping nearer to the carpet's edge. "Using Kandir's Impregnable Sphere." She pointed to the tall black house across the street, where the iron-bound front door stood open.

Zerra tilted her head. "It was that easy?"

"No. It wasn't easy." Ithinia frowned. "We had to strip away about fifteen different wards and protections first, and then we had to use Lirrim's Rectification to repair the hole we made, but the Impregnable Sphere was what finally got us inside."

"Was Erdrik in there?"

"No. He's gone. Not a trace of him. And we can't find any portals or tapestries or Transporting Fissures or anything else that might tell us where he went. The whole house is awash in wizardry, but none of it obviously involves transportation—at least, none that we've found and identified. I don't think he was transported away; I think he probably had a spell go wrong, and it killed him."

"Really? He was a very good wizard."

"He was a *powerful* wizard, certainly," Ithinia acknowledged, "but I'm not sure I'd call him a *good* one—he was reckless and arrogant, and he probably got sloppy."

"Maybe," Zerra said.

"Well, whatever really happened, we are going to *tell* the over-lord that we think a spell went wrong and killed him," Ithinia said. "And if Erdrik ever *does* turn up alive, I think we may arrange a little accident of our own. I'm tired of cleaning up his messes and apologizing to the overlord and paying Erdrik's taxes for him. I'd have happily killed him long ago myself if I was sure I could do it without wrecking the entire neighborhood. Two centuries of his abuse is more than enough."

"Fine," Zerra said, raising a hand in surrender. "He's gone and you're glad, and the Guild's reputation here should be better in the future, if a little less terrifying. But what am *I* doing here? You said you wanted my carpet; what for?"

"Because the *next* step, my dear Zerra, is cleaning out this nightmare house as best we can. It's *full* of magic; it makes my own house look like an empty shed. And a lot of it is bloody *dangerous* magic; we're probably going to be clearing traps for months. He's been accumulating clutter for more than two hundred years, and we can't leave *all* of it in there. The worst of it needs to go. And I don't want to parade some of it through the streets—I want to fly it away, safely out of everyone's reach. And that, of course, is what *you* do."

That was true. Although Zerra had trained in a variety of magics, like every other wizard, she found she made a comfortable living renting out her services as the pilot of a flying carpet. It was safer than operating the usual wizard's shop. She did keep her hand in with various other spells when the opportunity arose, but did not bother with a proper storefront or workshop or even a signboard—word of mouth kept her comfortably employed.

There were other wizards with flying carpets, of course, but she was the only one in Ethshar of the Spices who *specialized* in operating one.

That still left a major question, though.

"Fly it *where*?" she asked.

"Well, some of it is going to my place, and some of it to that Guild warehouse in Eastwark, and *some* of it, I think, we may want to just drop into the ocean a hundred miles offshore. Or maybe entirely over the edge of the World."

"I've never flown over the edge," Zerra said. "I'm not sure I can."

"Well, maybe you won't need to. We've only just begun sorting through it all."

"And what are you going to do with the house when it's been cleaned out? It still has all those protective spells. I can feel them. Can you shut them all down?"

Ithinia sighed. "Probably not," she said. "I think the Guild is going to have to buy this place from the overlord, after he claims it for unpaid taxes, and keep it closed up. It won't be empty, by any means. You'll be hauling out the worst of the mess, but we won't move everything; I don't think we could, even if we wanted to. It may *never* be safe."

"I see." Zerra looked up at the house, a towering stone monstrosity that looked thoroughly out of place among the graceful mansions and walled gardens of the New City. "How much do you think you'll need me and my carpet?"

"Far more than I'd like. And before you ask, yes, the Guild will pay you, at our usual almost-generous rates."

"In gold, or silver?"

"Gold."

Zerra dipped her head in the seated equivalent of a bow.

"In that case, Guildmaster, I am at your disposal. Where shall we start?"

CHAPTER ONE

MORVASH OF THE SHADOWS

22ND OF GREENGROWTH, YS 5238

Morvash of the Shadows leaned over the rail, ignoring the glares of the crewmen who obviously wished passengers would stay below, out of sight and out of their way, while the ship maneuvered up the Grand Canal into the heart of Ethshar of the Spices. One advantage of being a wizard, though, was that no one was going to actually *order* him to move, so he was able to stay where he was and watch.

The warehouses of Spicetown slid by to starboard. Stretching a little and peering forward, he could see the yellow walls and red tile roof of the overlord's palace. Judging by the shouted orders and the men hauling ropes, though, the ship would not be going that far.

Indeed, a moment later the first mooring line was flung to a waiting dockworker, and the ship's forward motion slowed to a stop. Morvash watched with interest as that first rope was used to haul a much larger, heavier rope, which was then secured to a bollard at the end of a wooden dock. A second line quickly followed, then a third and a fourth; when those had been pulled tight, securing the ship to the dock, two more were added. That seemed unnecessarily thorough to Morvash, but he assumed the sailors knew what they were doing.

Once all six lines were secured, men ran the gangplank out, and the bustle on the deck shifted focus. Most of the sails had been taken in before venturing into the crowded waters of the canal, but now the remaining canvas was furled and various parts of the ship's superstructure were secured or rearranged. To Morvash, it all seemed to be happening very quickly; he supposed the sailors had done it all hundreds of times and knew exactly what was going on, but Morvash had no idea what all the complicated actions were for.

Morvash turned his attention to the dock just as a carriage came rattling to a stop on the heavy planks. He squinted to see better. The coach was painted in his family's colors, maroon and silver, so it was *probably* his uncle's.

He straightened, turned toward the stern, and called, "May I go ashore now?"

The captain stood on the afterdeck, keeping an eye on his ship and crew, but now he glanced down at the wizard. "Please yourself," he said.

Morvash nodded and made his way to the gangplank.

His feet had just landed on the dock when the carriage door opened and a man stepped out, a man considerably fatter than Morvash remembered his uncle to be, and with gray hair rather than black—but it had been a long, long time, and the face looked familiar.

"Morvash?" the fat man called.

"Uncle Gror?" Morvash picked up his pace, and the two men met and embraced midway between the ship and the coach.

"Welcome to Ethshar of the Spices!" Gror exclaimed. "You've grown!"

"I would hope so," Morvash said. "I was eight the last time you saw me."

Gror laughed. "And here you are, a grown man and a wizard! It's been too long."

"You *could* have come to visit us," Morvash said. "My mother and Uncle Kargan would have been glad to see you." He did not mention his father; Gror and Morrin had never gotten along very well.

"Oh, I've seen all I need of Kargan," Gror said, slapping Morvash on the back. "He's here every year, and all he does is complain about the prices."

"I can believe it," Morvash replied. "But when was the last time you saw my mother, or my brothers?"

"Far too long ago, I admit," Gror said. He looked at the ship. "How was your voyage? Do you have luggage?"

"The journey went well enough," Morvash said. "We had calm seas, and I frightened off some pirates near Shan with a simple pyrotechnic spell."

"I don't suppose the captain saw fit to pay you for defending his ship?"

"Of course not. But I did eat better after that."

"And your luggage?"

"I'm afraid there's a lot of it—possibly more than will fit in your carriage. Shall I hire a wagon to have it brought to the house?"

"Oh, I'll have my staff fetch it. Just tell the captain."

"I think that would be the purser's concern, but I'll tell someone."

"I hope there won't be any serious pilferage."

Morvash laughed. "Uncle, I'm a *wizard*! Nobody steals from a wizard. I've drawn runes on every case, just to be sure."

Gror looked intrigued. "What sort of runes? What do they do?"

Morvash leaned close. "Nothing," he whispered. "But they *look* like magic, and that should be enough."

Gror smiled. "Well, *I* certainly wouldn't meddle with a wizard's belongings if I saw mystic runes on them. Come on, then, let's get home."

Morvash started to say something about it not being *his* home, but he caught himself. It *was* his home now, at least for the moment.

Instead, he turned back to the ship and called out his farewells to the captain and crew.

* * * *

Half an hour later the carriage rolled through the elegant gates of Gror's mansion on Canal Avenue, in the heart of the district called the New City. The mansion's wrought iron gates depicted a pair of dragons; the house itself was of fine yellow brick, with broad windows, white-painted trim, and a red tile roof. It was not very different from the overlord's palace in style, though of course it was much smaller. It blended nicely with its neighbors. Morvash looked up at the facade and frowned; except for the bright colors, it seemed rather plain, with no turrets or gargoyles. In fact, most of the buildings here seemed pale and insubstantial compared to the architecture of his native city, Ethshar of the Rocks—carved wood and pastel brick and painted plaster, instead of the dark, solid stone structures of home. It probably came of using materials readily to hand; after all, his home city was called Ethshar of the Rocks for a reason, while this Ethshar of the Spices was built on clay and sand.

"It's big," Morvash remarked. "Is it all just for you?"

"Well, me, and four footmen, and a housekeeper, and a cook, and my driver who is also my gardener. And sometimes I bring a friend home for the night."

"Why so many servants?"

"To take care of the place, of course."

"But why do you need such a *big* place?"

"To impress customers. Honestly, that's all."

One of the four footmen opened the carriage door while another held open the door to the house. Morvash climbed out first, then waited for his uncle to lead the way.

"I hope you'll like living here," Gror said, as they crossed the forecourt. "As I understand it, you're planning an extended stay?"

"Yes," Morvash said. "Uncle Kargan…well, he and Mother think it would be unwise to show my face in the Rocks or Tintallion for the foreseeable future."

"Your father is still unhappy with you?"

Morvash nodded.

"Is it as serious as all that?"

"I don't really know," Morvash admitted as they climbed the steps. "It seems to be. But honestly, Uncle Gror, I didn't have any choice. Doing what they wanted would have been a violation of Wizards' Guild rules, and I swore to obey the Guild law—I can be killed if I break it."

"Did you tell Morrin and Kargan that?"

"Of course!"

"I suppose they thought you were just making excuses. I know Kargan had really been looking forward to having a wizard in the family."

Morvash stepped past the footman into the hall, planning to reply, but once he was inside the house he stopped dead. "By the gods!" he said.

Gror smiled at him. "Impressive, isn't it?"

"All these *statues*!" Morvash said, staring.

"Lord Landessin collected them," his uncle said. "The whole house is jammed with statuary of one sort or another."

The entry hall certainly was. All four corners held niches displaying full-sized sculptures of beautiful women, and the walls between were covered in shelves, niches, and alcoves holding an assortment of other pieces—stone dogs, metal birds, wooden deer, and men, women, and children of every description in a huge range of sizes and materials.

"Who's Lord Landessin?" Morvash asked. "A customer?"

"No, no." Gror waved away the suggestion. "He's dead, I'm afraid, and I'm leasing this place from his estate. His heirs didn't want to live here, and there aren't too many people who want to rent something like this, so I got a good deal. Lord Landessin's collection came with it." He waved at some of the statuary. "It impresses some of my clients. You know it's good for business if they think I'm ridiculously wealthy; it lets them feel as if they're dealing with an equal, and that I must know something about quality. Naturally, I don't tell *them* that all these things came with the house, or that I don't own the place. Actually, I have an arrangement with Landessin's heirs that if any of my customers take a fancy to any of the sculptures, I can negotiate a sale and keep a 25% commission."

"Where did he *get* them all?"

Gror turned up an empty palm. "His niece told me that he spent most of his life roaming around the World, buying every sculpture or carving he could. He had inherited a fortune and held some position in the overlord's government that required extensive traveling; the niece was a little vague about the exact nature of her uncle's duties, but apparently he spent years at a time in the Small Kingdoms or the Baronies of Sardiron, and always returned home with dozens of new statues."

Morvash considered that as he looked at the shelves and niches. "Do you think he was a spy?" He had visions of secret staircases or hidden rooms.

"Probably nothing quite so crude as that, but I suspect he did indeed represent the Hegemony's interests in some clandestine way." Gror smiled and patted Morvash on the back. "Come on, lad, and I'll show you the rest of the house. You'll want to see where you'll be sleeping, I'm sure."

"Of course, Uncle. Lead the way!"

Gror led, and Morvash discovered that the displays of statuary extended from the marble-floored entry hall through a grand parlor, a gallery, a dining hall, and a ballroom; the only part of the main floor not decorated with sculpture was the kitchen alcove. Presumably the lower level that held the kitchens proper and the cellars was also free of ornament, but Gror did not show his nephew that. Instead he led the way upstairs. A white marble figure of a boy in a broad-brimmed hat adorned the lower end of the bannister on the staircase leading up from the ballroom foyer to the guest quarters. A shrine to Unniel stood at the top.

Morvash's room, just off the landing, was as crowded with statues as the rest of the mansion. A forbidding life-sized figure in black granite stood at the foot of the bed, glowering down at the embroidered coverlet.

The idea of having that thing watching him while he slept did not appeal to Morvash. "Would it be all right if I moved that one?" he asked.

"*I* don't mind," Gror said. "And Lord Landessin's niece didn't say anything to the contrary. As long as you don't damage it, I suppose you can put it wherever you please."

Morvash contemplated the statue for a moment. Why would anyone carve such a thing? It clearly represented a female magician—a warlock, perhaps? Or a demonologist? Whatever she was meant to be, she was no beauty.

Then another thought struck him. "Uncle, why are you renting? Why didn't you *buy* a house?"

Gror grimaced. "Because I still hope to go back to Ethshar of the Rocks someday, Morvash. Even after all these years, this city isn't home; it's just where I work. We needed *someone* we could trust completely here, and I got the job, but I didn't *want* to come here. Besides, I couldn't afford to *buy* a place like this!" He gestured at the huge bedchamber, the brocade draperies, the elegant walnut furniture, the dozens of assorted statues.

"But—won't the family *always* need someone here? How can you ever go back?"

Gror turned up a hand. "Oh, one of the younger relatives might decide that it would be exciting to work here in Azrad's Ethshar—up until he married that magistrate's daughter, I thought your brother Ilzan might be interested. Or the war in Tintallion might end, which would put us out of the arms business."

"Not *completely*, would it?"

"Well, maybe not, but without the war we probably wouldn't

need to have a full-time agent here, funneling weapons from the Small Kingdoms, and I think I could relocate my other business back home."

Morvash was suddenly uncomfortable with the reminder of just what his merchant family mostly sold. To distract himself, he reached out toward the granite statue. He tugged at its shoulder and discovered it was heavier than he had realized; he could not budge it.

"That one's pretty solid," Gror remarked. "I don't know who put it by the bed, or why anyone thought that was a good place for it. You'll need help if you intend to move it by hand. Can't you work a spell to transport it somewhere?"

"Maybe," Morvash said, eyeing the figure. It was probably meant to be a demonologist, he thought. Now, why would anyone want a statue of a demonologist? A pretty girl he could understand, and of course gods and goddesses were useful, but a rather ugly demonologist? And why carve it out of such dark granite? It was extraordinarily detailed work, especially for such a hard stone, and a lighter-colored material would have displayed the workmanship better.

"Where do you want your luggage, when it arrives? Shall I have everything sent up here?"

Morvash turned. "Most of it is my tools of the trade, Uncle. Is there a room somewhere I can use as a workshop?"

Gror frowned. "I can find something, I suppose, but you aren't planning to run a wizard's business from this house, are you?"

"Well, I want to do *something* to earn my keep," Morvash answered.

"Yes, of course you do, and I'll be glad of your services, but… there's no need to rush, is there? Take your time, get settled in first. Oh, is there anyone you need to talk to? Anyone from the Guild, I mean?"

Morvash turned up a palm. "Not really. It would probably be polite to eventually tell the local Wizards' Guild official that I'm here— Guildmasters, we call them. But I don't have to formally report in or anything; the Guild doesn't work like that."

Gror nodded.

There were a few seconds of awkward silence, and then Gror said, "You must be tired, and probably hungry, if the shipboard food was the usual sort. I'll go see to your luggage while you rest, and then we can have a little something to eat. Would you like to join me in the parlor, or have something sent up?"

"Oh, I'll be down in a few minutes," Morvash said. "I'm not so tired as all that, and after being confined to the ship, I'm glad to stretch my legs a little." Morvash gave the granite statue an uneasy glance; its presence was another reason he was not eager to stay in this room.

"Good, good! I'll see you in a few minutes, then." With that, Gror turned and left, closing the bedchamber door behind him.

Morvash turned back to the statue of the demonologist. He frowned, then crossed to the windows and pushed back the brocade drapes, letting as much light into the room as he could. He went so far as to hook the draperies over nearby furniture or statuary, to expose as much glass as possible. Sunlight spilled across the parquetry. Then he slowly and carefully approached the granite figure, studying it closely. A horrible suspicion was growing in him.

The statue's face was unbelievably realistic. The nostrils went so deep into the stone that Morvash could not see their end, even with the additional light provided by a quick fire spell. The hair was flawlessly accurate in its texture. A small pimple was half-hidden by the hairline.

Surely, no sculptor carved in such detail. Morvash knew the truth even before he drew the silver dagger from his belt and touched the enchanted blade to the demonologist's cheek, but the faint blue glow that indicated the presence of residual magic confirmed his fears.

This wasn't a true statue at all. This was a living woman who had been turned to stone. Morvash had no idea who it was, or why she had been petrified, or when, or by whom, but this was a real person.

Or it *had* been, anyway. Whether the spell was reversible was another unanswered question. There were reversible petrifaction spells, and irreversible ones, and Morvash did not know how to recognize which had been used, or even whether there *was* a simple way to tell.

He sighed. It appeared he was going to be busy for awhile, figuring out just what the situation here was, and what, if anything, he could, or should, do about it.

He definitely wanted to do *something*. He did not want to sleep in the same room as a petrified demonologist.

He glanced around at the other statues and carvings, and he remembered the hundreds of other sculptures jammed into the house. Most of them were probably exactly what they appeared to be, examples of a carver's art, but where there was one enchantment, there might well be others.

He had some research to do.

CHAPTER TWO

DARISSA THE WITCH'S APPRENTICE

Darissa strolled up the row of stalls and displays, taking in the sounds, sights, and smells, and sensing the thoughts and moods of the merchants and customers. Most were fairly relaxed, focused on the business of buying and selling. The farmers generally seemed to look on this market day as an excuse to avoid the heavy labor that was their usual lot. Craftspeople tended to be slightly more anxious—if their wares didn't sell, they might starve during the coming winter. Farmers could always eat their own produce.

The folks who had come down from the castle were a varied lot. Some were just happy to be out in the fine weather, looking over the various wares offered for sale, but others had been unable to put aside their other concerns. Darissa picked up worries about the possibility of war, though she discern no details, and several more personal issues weighed on various minds. She could hear the thoughts of a man working himself into a fury—he suspected his wife was unfaithful; elsewhere, a woman was trying unsuccessfully to convince herself that nothing was wrong with her pregnancy, the baby being so quiet did not mean anything, and the cramps were perfectly normal...

Darissa frowned. She should attend to that one. Those cramps were *not* normal for late in the fifth month of pregnancy, and witchcraft might be able to do something about the situation. She stopped walking and craned her head, trying to pick out the source of the thoughts.

She sensed a man's happy appreciation of the sight of a pretty girl—common enough, but not helpful. It drowned out the other thoughts. She turned, and suddenly found herself face to face—or really, until she looked up, face to chest—with a young man. He smiled down at her.

"Looking for something?" he asked.

"A pregnant woman," she said, without thinking. "But the pregnancy may not be very obvious yet." Only after the words came out did she realize that *this* was the man who had been admiring someone—and that someone was her.

"Ah," he said, glancing at the crowd. "Do you know what she's wearing? Tall, short?"

Darissa shook her head. "I don't know what she looks like at all."

He cocked his head to one side. "Then how do you know…well, why are you looking for her?"

"Something's wrong. I want to see if I can help her."

"How do you know?"

Darissa did not look at him; she was trying to spot the mother to be. "I'm a witch. I heard her thoughts."

"You're dressed as an apprentice."

"Fine, I'm an *apprentice* witch. Do you see her or not?"

"A moment." He straightened and gazed out across the crowd, and Darissa found herself envying his height—he was looking over everyone's heads, while she could not even see over his shoulders. "Bergan!" he shouted. "My banner!"

"What?" She looked up at him again, startled, and finally registered that he was not merely taller than most men, but impeccably dressed and coifed, with strong features.

"Your highness!" came an answering shout. Darissa turned to see where this reply came from and saw a man in the king's livery unrolling a blue and gold pennant.

"People of Melitha!" the tall man roared, in an amazingly powerful voice. "I am Prince Marek, and I ask any woman here who is with child to present herself to me, here and now, that I may reward her for adding to the kingdom's prosperity and strength!"

The normal chatter of the market quickly died as people turned to look at the prince, or at one another. Then, as Prince Marek lifted a fat purse from his belt, women began to step forward. Darissa stood beside him, watching, as they made their way through the crowd to the waiting nobleman.

As women approached, Marek shook their hands, handed each a

silver bit, said something encouraging, and glanced at Darissa, not necessarily in that order. It was the fifth recipient, a thin, pale woman in shabby clothes, who was tensed against cramps or other pains.

Darissa hesitated, glancing at Marek. What should she do?

Marek caught her glance, and Darissa sensed his thoughts as clearly as if he had spoken: *Is she the one?*

Darissa nodded.

"Ah," the prince said, not releasing the hand of this mother-to-be. "Mistress, could I trouble you to wait here for a moment? There is another matter I would like to discuss, once I have finished my task."

"I…of course, your highness." The woman looked startled and confused, but did not argue. Darissa sensed that she was too involved in other concerns to resist the prince's request.

"Then if you would please stay with this apprentice, I will be right with you."

"Yes, your highness." The pale woman attempted a curtsey, but had obviously never learned to do one properly and almost fell over when she tried to bob back up. Darissa reached over and caught her.

Marek smiled at them both, then turned his attention back to the crowd and continued handing out coins.

"If you'll forgive me, Mistress, I believe you may need my services," Darissa murmured to her charge.

"Oh, I'm fine," the woman replied weakly.

"No, you are *not*," Darissa said firmly. "I'm a witch's apprentice, a few months short of journeyman, and it's very clear to me that you are *not* fine. You and your child are, in fact, in great danger."

The woman had been half looking at the prince, and half down at her own belly, but at this she focused her entire attention on Darissa.

"Are you sure?" Her expression hardened. "I…I mean, how do I know this isn't a trick? How do I know you don't want the child yourself, to sell to the wizards for their spells?"

Darissa had seen how the woman looked at Marek, and quickly improvised, "Do you think I would be allowed in the prince's company if I were as vile as that? I promise you, I want only what's best for *you*."

The prince had apparently been listening. He turned and added quietly, "I put my full faith in this apprentice, dear lady. Please, do us all a kindness and allow her to tend to you. My footman, Bergan, will be happy to assist you in any way."

Darissa was suddenly aware of a sharp pain in the woman's abdomen. She reached out to steady the woman. "Please, let me help you," she said.

The woman's face, pale to begin with, had gone white. She nodded, and Darissa threw an arm around her waist and led her from the market toward her master's cottage. She was vaguely aware of the prince's footman, Bergan, following them.

* * * *

It was clear to Darissa and her master, Nondel of the Oaks, that they had been just in time. Without their intervention, Darissa was fairly certain that Alasha, as she called herself, would have been dead by nightfall. As it was, they were unable to save the baby—it had already been dead for some time, Nondel said, and even if it weren't, the poor misshapen thing would never have survived its birth. The mother had developed a severe infection; it took hours to stop the bleeding, heal the injuries to Alasha's womb, and soothe the mother's anguish enough to let her sleep. Nondel did most of the magic, drawing energy from Darissa when his own reserves were depleted, but both of them worked hard to keep their patient alive.

When it was done, when all three adults had been cleaned up and the tiny, pitiful remains of the unborn infant wrapped up and put safely aside until the mother was able to attend to them, Alasha lay unconscious in Darissa's own narrow bed, in the back of the cottage. The master gave his apprentice a nod and said, "Well done, girl. Well spotted."

"Thank you, Master," Darissa said. She glanced at the window, and saw the slanting light of late afternoon; the market would be largely deserted by now, the prince and his man back at the castle.

It had been very kind of him to draw the pregnant women out that way. Darissa was fairly sure he only did it to impress her, in hopes of getting into her bed—that had certainly been the trend of his thoughts when she first noticed his presence—but still, it was kind. He could easily have relied on his royal status to sway her; it undoubtedly worked on plenty of women without the aid of extravagant acts of charity. Further, he had continued to hand out coins, staying true to his promise, rather than following Darissa under the guise of helping see Alasha safe. His presence would have been a distraction while the witches worked.

I should, she thought, send him a message to let him know his actions were appreciated. She could just leave a word with one of the castle guards; a small spell of persuasion would ensure that the guard would pass it on promptly.

"Excuse me, Master," she said. "I have an errand."

Nondel cocked his head. "You're tired; can't your errand wait until you've rested?"

"I think it would best be done quickly, Master."

He smiled. "The easier to get him out of your thoughts, eh? As you please."

Darissa had been a witch's apprentice for more than five years, plenty of time to become accustomed to the lack of privacy, so she did not offer any denial, nor even a blush. Instead she smiled, and headed for the door.

As she opened it, she felt the pleased thoughts of someone outside, but still, she was astonished to find Prince Marek leaning against the big oak beside the front walk. He straightened at the sight of her.

"Is she all right?" he asked, his expression grim.

"She lost the child and much blood," Darissa replied, flustered.

"But she'll live?"

"She should recover, yes, your highness."

"Does her husband know anything of this yet?"

"I...I don't know. I don't think so." Darissa was annoyed to realize she had given the baby's father no thought at all.

"Someone should inform him as soon as possible."

"Yes, of course," Darissa agreed. "I'll see to it."

The prince suddenly smiled, the grimness vanishing. "Good!" he said. "Now that that's out of the way, I'm Prince Marek, third son of King Terren of Melitha. I don't believe I got your name." He held out his hand.

"Uh..." Caught off-guard by the abrupt change in demeanor, Darissa stared stupidly at the hand.

His smile broadened. "I doubt even the most eccentric parents would name a daughter Uh, and it's hardly a good name to attract business. I know witches don't go in for the fancy names wizards prefer, Domididulus the Over-Endowed or whatever, but Uh?"

"Darissa," she managed. "I'm Darissa the Witch's Apprentice, your highness."

"And were you on your way to tell the poor thing's husband what happened? Perhaps I could walk with you."

"No," Darissa admitted. "I don't even know where he is; I didn't think to ask."

"Then why *were* you coming out here, when you're obviously exhausted and in need of rest?"

Darissa grimaced wryly. "I was going to the castle, to leave you a message."

"Me?" The prince looked inordinately pleased. "Were you really?"

"Yes."

"What sort of message?"

"Just…just a thank you, for your kindness in helping me find Alasha in the crowd."

"Oh, that? That was nothing." He waved it aside.

"But the money…!"

"Money? Oh—that's right! You cost me better than two rounds of silver, didn't you?" He turned up an empty palm. "That's nothing. I'll charge it to the royal treasury."

Darissa felt a brief surge of resentment at the idea that two rounds of silver were "nothing." Spent carefully, that would be enough to feed her for half a year. But Marek was a prince; to him, it *was* nothing.

Still, she said, "You didn't need to give it all out. You could have stopped once we'd found her."

"Oh, no—that would hardly be fair!" He appeared genuinely shocked. "I'd promised every expectant mother in the market a silver bit, so every one must have her coin. A prince's word is good."

Darissa stared up at his broad face and saw no hint of sarcasm or dishonesty. He seemed to truly believe what he was saying. If she had not been so very tired, she could have used her magic to verify her impression.

"I'm sorry I couldn't follow and help with the woman—Alasha, you said? But I had to finish distributing the money. By the time I finished, you were gone. Bergan gave me directions when he returned, but when I got here you were inside with the door closed, and I had no excuse for intruding. So I waited."

Tired or not, Darissa *had* to know whether that was the truth, and stretched out her perceptions enough to see that it was. This man, this prince, had been waiting here for *hours*.

"Why?" she asked.

"Why what?"

"Why did you wait? You didn't know Alasha, did you?"

"No, I regret to say I did not—but I was waiting for *you*, Darissa."

She stared at him and did not need to ask why this time—she could feel his desire, his intense interest in not just her body, but her face, her manner, her desire to help a stranger without any promise of payment. He *admired* her. A *prince* admired her—her, Darissa, the long-nosed orphan girl with no patience for primping and posing to please men.

He was staring at her. "You're tired," he said, before she could think of a response. "This isn't a good time."

"No," she agreed. She was not sure *any* time would be a good time for this.

"I could come back tomorrow," he said.

She shook her head. "No," she repeated. "I'm an apprentice. My time is not my own."

He frowned. "I could talk to your master, but that wouldn't be fair. Why don't you just come to the castle, when you have the time and the inclination? Or rather, *if* you have them—I don't mean to assume anything. If you never come, I will deeply regret it, but I will respect your decision. I *hope*, though, that you will see fit to visit. Or if you prefer, send an invitation for me to join you somewhere. Perhaps meeting on neutral ground would be advisable, until we know each other better."

"Perhaps it would," she agreed.

"Then I'll be off and let you rest. Before I go, would you like me to take a message to Alasha's husband?"

She shook her head. "She didn't tell us his name, and she's asleep—I won't wake her to ask. I appreciate the offer, though."

"You can't take his name from her sleeping thoughts?"

Darissa shook her head again. "No, I can't. There may be witches who can—in fact, I'm sure there are—but I'm only an apprentice."

"All right," he said, nodding. "I do need to go, but may I send a man to serve as your messenger when she wakes?"

She stared at him. "You're a prince," she said. "You can do anything you want."

He smiled crookedly. "Ha! Haven't known many princes, have you? But I can send a messenger." He bowed. "Get your rest, dear apprentice, and I hope I will see you again soon."

With that he turned, waved to her, and strode off toward the castle.

She watched him go, unsure what to make of him. In truth, she had never known *any* princes before; yes, the Small Kingdoms were awash in petty royalty, but she was a peasant farmer's daughter and a witch's apprentice, not someone who had business with kings or princes.

At last, as he vanished around the corner of the tavern at the top of the street, she turned and went back inside, where she fell into her bed.

* * * *

When she awoke the next morning, the whole encounter seemed almost like a dream. She was surprised to look out front and see an older man in royal livery waiting by the oak—obviously the promised messenger.

Not long after that, Alasha stirred. Soon Darissa and Nondel were able to ask her what family she had, and who they should inform of her condition. Nondel wrote up a note, and Darissa took it to the messenger with instructions.

He nodded and accepted the folded paper. "And you, Mistress," he said. "Do you have a message for his highness, Prince Marek?"

"What?" She stared blankly at him.

"I was ordered to ask, Mistress. Do you have a message for the prince?"

She blinked, considered for a moment, then said, "Not yet. But stop by on your way back to the castle, and I may have something for you."

He bowed. "As you please, Mistress." Then he turned and trotted off, Nondel's note in his hand.

Darissa watched him go. What might she want to say in her letter to the prince?

CHAPTER THREE

MORVASH OF THE SHADOWS

23RD OF GREENGROWTH, YS 5238

Morvash did not bother with any of the sculptures other than the more or less life-sized humans. He knew people could be transformed into pretty much anything, but why do that and *then* petrify someone? It didn't seem reasonable. Wizards were perfectly capable of being unreasonable, of course, but Morvash felt he had to draw the line *somewhere*. Lord Landessin's collection was simply too vast and varied to inspect every single item.

Even with that limitation, it took almost an entire day to locate every such statue, and to check each one for residual magic. It did not help that Uncle Gror did not actually *use* all of the estate he rented, so that there were rooms, passages, and even outbuildings about which he could tell Morvash nothing.

In the end, Morvash counted thirty-two sculptures, representing thirty-three individuals, that caused his *athame*, his wizard's dagger, to glow, including the granite magician and two of the four women in the entry hall. To his relief, about two hundred other life-sized statues on the property did *not* show any sign of having ever been alive—figures of stone, wood, metal, and pottery that his dagger indicated were no more than they appeared.

Still, it was disturbing to realize that thirty-three people were on display, trapped in stone. The *most* disturbing of them, the one that was responsible for the uneven count, was hidden away in a sort of marble grotto in the garden behind the house, and depicted a young man and a young woman in what might politely be called an intimate embrace, or a compromising position. They were not in the sort of elegant pose that artists use for erotica, with graceful lines displaying the female's curves and the male's muscles. They were in an earthier position. The woman—a girl, really—was on her back, with her knees drawn up to her chest and her head raised as her blank stone eyes stared perpetually at the man's belly. Her mouth was open as if panting. Her partner was kneeling between her legs, leaning forward over her, one hand grabbing her shoulder, the other occupied elsewhere. His eyes were closed, but his mouth was also open; Morvash thought it was more of a moan than a pant. He could almost smell the sweat. Neither wore any clothing whatsoever, nor were there any artfully-placed draperies or fig leaves to obscure the details.

Had the wizard responsible for this petrifaction timed it deliberately, or had he caught them in this position by accident?

Assuming, of course, that it *was* a wizard. Morvash didn't know of any other sort of magic that could turn people to stone, but he couldn't rule out the possibility that demons or other magical beings might be capable of it. He was no expert on petrifaction—in fact, he didn't know how to cast any spells that would turn anything to stone, nor any spells to undo a petrifaction. Until arriving at Lord Landessin's mansion the day before, he had never seen a statue he knew to have once been alive. He had no way of knowing which of the thirty-three victims were truly dead, and which might be revived. He did know that both reversible petrifactions and irreversible ones existed, but he was not entirely clear whether those categories corresponded exactly with fatal and non-fatal.

He couldn't be sure his athame's reaction would be the same with both living and dead victims; it might be that some of those two hundred that showed no evidence of magic *had* been living people once, and the lack of reaction simply meant they could not be saved. In any case, he had thirty-three people who *might* be restored by the appropriate spell.

In addition to the lovers, the beauties from the entry, and the probably-a-demonologist, there were assorted men and women ranging in age from a boy who could scarcely have been old enough for apprenticeship to a gaunt old man with a waist-length beard—seventeen more boys and men, eleven more women and girls. Except for the lovers, all were at least partially clothed, allowing Morvash to guess at their occupations, stations in life, and how long they had been stone. Most appeared to have been wealthy, but not all; Morvash suspected one oddly-garbed young woman had been a burglar who broke into the wrong house.

And one of them, a fine figure in gleaming yellowish alabaster, had unquestionably been either a wizard or someone pretending to be one. He was tall and thin, with a face that Morvash judged to have seen at least half a century, and he wore elegant robes that had been frozen forever as they swirled about his ankles—he appeared to have been turning quickly, as if to face his attacker. His expression, beneath the brim of his pointed hat, was one of angry disdain, as if he had been interrupted by someone unworthy of his attention.

Morvash carefully catalogued all thirty-two statues, noting what kind of stone each one was, what clothing each wore, and each one's apparent age at the time of enchantment. He tried to estimate how long each one might have been petrified from the styles they wore, though in several instances their attire simply didn't have enough detail to judge. In any case, Morvash was no expert on the history of fashion. There were a few where he could not place the victim's garb in *any* familiar realm or century.

He also recorded how brightly his athame responded to each victim, and whether the glow was some color other than the usual blue. He did not really know what this information might signify, but he thought it might eventually prove useful.

When he finished, he joined his uncle in the dining hall, where Gror chastised him mildly for missing supper. The remaining soup and meat had gone cold, but Morvash ate some anyway, filling out his meal with bread, cheese, and honeyed pears.

"What have you been *doing* all day?" Gror asked, as Morvash ate.

Morvash swallowed the bread he had been chewing. "Studying Lord Landessin's collection. Uncle, did you know that several of those statues were once living people?"

Gror had been sipping wine, and almost choked. "They *what?*"

"More than thirty of them are people who were turned to stone," Morvash said.

Gror set down his glass. "How can you *tell?*"

"I'm a wizard, Uncle. I can tell. And magic aside, some of them are simply beyond the skills of any ordinary sculptor. Surely you must have suspected that?"

"I…oh, very well, I admit I wondered about some of them. I suspected. Though I found it hard to believe that anyone would have sold them to Lord Landessin in such a case—wouldn't they be selling their own friends or family?"

"Or their victims," Morvash suggested. "He may have bought them from the magicians who enchanted them."

"I hadn't thought of that," Gror admitted. "That's…rather unpleasant. But it isn't as if there's anything to be done about it."

"Well, that's the thing, Uncle—there might be a way to turn some of them back."

Gror had started to reach for his glass again, but now his hand fell away. "There might?"

Morvash nodded. "It depends which spells were used on them."

"That's…that's very interesting."

"I intend to revive them, Uncle—at least, the ones I can."

Gror frowned. "Are you sure that's wise?"

Morvash was startled. "How could it not be?"

"Well, some of them may have been turned to stone for a *reason*."

"*What* reason?" Morvash demanded. "Uncle, the magistrates don't turn people to stone; these people were enchanted by their enemies, not because they had committed any crimes." Even as the words left his lips, Morvash remembered the badly-dressed girl he thought might have been a burglar, but he thrust that thought aside. The penalty for housebreaking was twenty lashes, not petrifaction!

"Well, maybe they never got to the magistrates—maybe the Wizards' Guild got to them first."

Morvash shook his head. "The Guild doesn't petrify people who break its rules; we just kill them."

The directness of that reply seemed to startle Gror. He hesitated for a second or two before saying, "Still, *someone* turned these people to stone, and whoever it was must have had *some* reason. That must be a difficult spell, I would think."

"There are several spells they could have used, Uncle, but all of them are fairly difficult, yes."

"Well, do you really think it's safe to bring back to life people some wizard thought deserved such a fate?"

"I think it's entirely possible they were all simply innocents who were in the wrong place at the wrong time when some wizard decided to try out his latest spell."

Gror frowned as he thought about that. He picked up his wine again, turned the glass so that it caught the candlelight, then lifted it and drained it in one long, slow drink. Then he set the glass down and looked at Morvash.

"You said you're going to turn them back?"

Morvash nodded. "I have to, Uncle. I can't leave them petrified."

"Oh, you *could*," Gror said. "But I can't convince you to leave well enough alone?"

"I don't think so, Uncle. I'm sorry."

"So you know the spell to revive them? I suppose it involves a bunch of exotic ingredients…"

"I *don't* know it, Uncle. I'll need to do some research."

"You will?" Gror frowned, toying with his empty wineglass. "What *kind* of research?"

"I'll need to learn the spells that can reverse petrifaction," Morvash replied.

"Spells? Plural?"

"I'm not certain, but I believe so."

"I suppose they're difficult, too?"

"Yes, I think so."

"Is that safe?"

"No."

Gror stared at his nephew for a moment, considering this blunt reply. Finally he asked, "Why can't you just hire a wizard who already *knows* the spell you want, and have *him* turn them back?"

Morvash let out a long breath and looked down at his plate before answering, "Professional pride, mostly. Cost, too, though."

"It's cheaper to learn it yourself?"

Morvash nodded.

"What will it cost?"

"Oh, I can't put a price on it in coin. I'll have to earn it."

"What? Why?"

"That's how the Guild works, Uncle—if I need to learn a spell from another wizard I can trade one of my own spells for it, or I can pay for it with labor, but I can't pay cash. We aren't allowed to buy and sell the knowledge of how to perform spells."

"Why?"

Morvash turned up an empty palm. "I don't know, Uncle. Some of the Guild's rules don't make any obvious sense, but they're still the rules. There was probably a good reason for it a couple of hundred years ago."

"And how will you learn it, once you have the formula?"

"I'll practice it until I can work the spell reliably."

"But it won't be reliable at first?"

"Probably not."

"So you're proposing to experiment with dangerous magic you don't really know, here in my home? In a mansion I am responsible for, but do not own?"

"Well...yes."

Gror slowly shook his head. "I don't *think* so," he said.

"Uh...what?"

"Morvash, I can't stop you from doing whatever you please—you're a grown man and a journeyman wizard, and I'm not your father or your master. But I *can* forbid you to do it *here*. You're going to need to find your own place. I don't want you blowing holes in the walls, or turning my guests into spiders, or whatever."

"But...but this is where the statues are!"

"You'll have to take them somewhere else to cast your spells on them."

"But..." Morvash stopped. He had been going to say that Lord Landessin's family might object to seeing their property carted away, but if he succeeded they would be losing the statues anyway, and his uncle had said something about the heirs giving permission to sell off parts of the collection. He bowed his head. "Very well, Uncle. I can see the logic in your position. I'll find another place."

"Thank you," Gror said. He smiled sadly. "You know, I do appreciate that you're trying to do the right thing and help out these enchanted unfortunates, but I hope you haven't underestimated the risks."

"So do I," Morvash replied.

"What's the next step, then? How do you go about learning the spells you need?"

Marvash had not really thought that through yet. "Well, I'll have to ask around until I find a wizard who can teach me," he said.

"There isn't some spell you can use to find the wizard you need?"

Morvash smiled wryly. "Actually, there *is* such a spell—in fact, there are several such spells—but I don't know any of them, so I'll need to do it the old-fashioned way and ask other wizards."

Gror nodded, then paused. "How do you go about that, when you're new in town? Do you just walk along Wizard Street asking the shopkeepers at random?"

Morvash pursed his lips. "Actually, I…well, I was thinking I would ask people I knew back in Ethshar of the Rocks, but that won't work, will it? I'm forbidden to go back. So I may have to do exactly what you suggest. I may do better, though, by talking to the nearest Guildmaster. He probably knows."

"Ah. You said you would want to let him know you were in town, as I recall. Who *is* the nearest Guildmaster?"

Morvash sighed. "I don't know. But I'll find out." He looked down at his empty plate, then wiped his fingers on his robe. "I could go do that now, in fact."

"At this hour?"

"Why not? It's unlikely he'd already be asleep."

"You would know better than I. But how will you find him?"

Morvash waved a hand. "I'll manage. I have a spell that should serve." He declined to explain further.

* * * *

A few minutes later he was strolling down Canal Avenue.

He had refused to explain because he found his method slightly embarrassing. He did not, in fact, have an actual *spell* that would locate a Guildmaster. Instead, he planned to use his athame's natural sensitivity to wizardry. He had his hand clamped tightly on the hilt, and as he walked, he felt for the faint tingling that indicated the presence of magic. That would, sooner or later, lead him to a local wizard who could advise him.

Not all wizards were sensitive to the presence of other magic, but he had discovered early in his apprenticeship that he had an inborn talent for it. He had cultivated it ever since, doing what he could to enhance his athame's inherent response, even though his master had thought it was a waste of time. One reason to do his exploring in the evening was that darkness made it easier to see the glow when his athame reacted to nearby magic.

He had headed down the street to the north simply because going downhill was easier, and it was only after he had gone a block or two that he realized—if he remembered his lessons about the city's geography correctly—that the Wizards' Quarter lay in the opposite direction, to the south. Or maybe the southeast, but certainly not north. Undoubtedly wizards lived throughout the city, though, or at least in the wealthier areas, so after a moment's hesitation, he continued as he had been going.

There were few other pedestrians about, even though the streetlamps were lit; the weather was unseasonably cool, and most people clearly preferred to stay indoors. That suited Morvash. The people he did see did not pay any great attention to him; he drew a few glances, but nothing more.

One of the green-skinned, froglike little creatures called spriggans followed him for a few yards, but when he turned and shouted at it, it fled into an alley and did not pursue him further.

After another block, he sensed something ahead and to his right. He hoped it wasn't just some wealthy merchant's talking gatepost or animated teapot. He picked up his pace.

If it was a rich man's toy, it was a very powerfully enchanted one; the awareness of nearby wizardry grew stronger as he continued down Canal Avenue, and by the time he turned right he was sure that he was approaching the locus of multiple spells. He thought he might have passed some minor magic along the way, but if so, those enchantments had been drowned out by the massive concentration of power ahead.

He wondered what street he was on; he had not yet learned his way around Ethshar of the Spices, and no one seemed to use street signs here. Not, he reminded himself, that they were common back in Ethshar of the Rocks, either, though there were a few here and there.

He crossed another north-south street, one narrower and not quite as steep as Canal Avenue, then spotted what must be his destination. It was a gray stone house near the end of the north side of the next block, and two gargoyles were perched on the cornice at the top of the facade.

That might not have been definitive; after all, even though he had not yet seen any others in *this* city, back in Ethshar of the Rocks a great many of the larger houses and other buildings were ornamented with gargoyles. *These* gargoyles, though, had turned to look at him. Apparently they were as sensitive to his efforts at detection as he was to their inherent magic.

Nor were the gargoyles the only magic he felt here. That gray house *reeked* of magic. Morvash smiled; any place fraught with *that* much wizardry had to be home to a Guildmaster. He would be able to report his presence in the city and inquire after anti-petrifaction spells all at once. He picked up his pace, pushing his athame back into its sheath as he reached the unknown wizard's house.

The gargoyles watched him, but remained at their posts. They said nothing as he stepped up to the door and knocked.

Immediately after knocking he noticed the bell-pull; embarrassed, he decided to wait and see whether anyone had heard his knock.

Someone had. A voice like nothing he had ever heard before, reminiscent of stone grinding on stone, spoke from somewhere above him.

"What do you want?"

Startled, Morvash looked up to find one of the gargoyles had moved from its perch to crouch almost directly above him. It peered down, wings spread.

"I'd like to speak to the Guildmaster," he said, hoping that he had not misjudged the situation.

"Who are you?"

Morvash smiled. This *was* a Guildmaster's house! "My name is Morvash of the Shadows," he said. "I wanted to introduce myself and bring a certain matter to his attention."

The gargoyle shifted and folded its wings. "Maybe you have the wrong house. My Guildmaster is not a 'he.'"

"Ah! My apologies," Morvash said. "I used a spell to locate the nearest Guildmaster, and did not concern myself with the details. I would very much like to bring my concern to *her* attention."

The gargoyle shook itself. "I will let her know you are here, Morvash of the Shadow."

"Shadows, plural. Yes."

"You wait."

Morvash did as instructed and waited as the gargoyle withdrew onto the roof, out of sight.

Morvash looked around at the surrounding homes. This was clearly a wealthy neighborhood, but he saw nothing to indicate any of the other residents were magicians. What should he make of that? He glanced up at the remaining gargoyle; it was watching him. He read nothing in its stony expression.

Then, just as he was beginning to wonder how long he should wait, a woman in a white robe door opened the door and said, "I'm Ithinia of the Isle, the senior Guildmaster. Come in."

Even back in Ethshar of the Rocks, Morvash had heard of Ithinia of the Isle. She was said to be one of the half-dozen most powerful wizards in the Hegemony. He had not expected to find anyone quite so famous, but he was not about to say anything about that. He did not want to risk offending her.

Morvash bowed and followed as the woman led him into the house.

CHAPTER FOUR

DARISSA THE WITCH'S APPRENTICE

Darissa had not really expected to hear anything more from Prince Marek; she had written a brief polite letter expressing her gratitude for his assistance and thought that would be the end of it. Yes, he had taken an interest in her, but surely it had only been a passing fancy. He had almost certainly moved on to some other girl.

She was astonished, therefore, to see him once again leaning on the oak. At the sight of her he straightened up.

"Darissa," he said. "You didn't say when you might come to the castle."

"I didn't… I'm an apprentice. My time is not my own." She knew this was misleading at best, since Nondel did not care what she did with most of her time, but she could think of no other excuse. She had not thought for a moment that the prince would really care whether he ever saw her again—she knew well that men could be intensely interested in any pretty girl they happened to notice, and then forget about her once she was out of sight. She had assumed that she had been just such a whim for Marek, but here he was.

"I would not have thought Nondel was such a tyrant," Marek remarked.

Darissa stared at him. He knew her master's name, though she was fairly sure she had not mentioned it. Had it been in her letter, perhaps? He was also suggesting he knew Nondel's reputation, and from what she could feel of his thoughts, that was the truth.

He was watching her, and she could feel his lust—but also concern and gratitude and warmth and a host of other emotions that far outweighed simple desire. He really *cared* about her. He even *ad-*

mired her. And his intentions were about as honorable as could be asked of a healthy young man.

She glanced back at the door of the house. She had no particular duties or obligations at the moment; she had already attended to her basic morning chores. "I could… Perhaps this afternoon…" Then she took a deep breath. "Or right now, if Nondel doesn't mind."

His face lit up in a smile. "That would be wonderful!"

"Let me ask," she said, ducking back inside.

Nondel was standing in the front room, and before she could say a word, he said, "Go ahead. It never hurts to be on good terms with the royal family."

Darissa blinked and nodded, then turned to go—but as she did, an uncomfortable thought struck her.

Technically, it *could* hurt to be on good terms with the royal family, if carried far enough. It was forbidden for any member of any royal family to personally perform magic; that was one of the handful of edicts of the Wizards' Guild that applied to people who were not members of the Guild. There were a few special cases where magicians could hold power, as they did in Klathoa, but those were all in places where there *was* no royal family.

Legally, the Wizards' Guild had no authority to tell other people what to do, but pragmatically, they were *wizards* and could do pretty much as they pleased. There were undoubtedly limits to what rules they could enforce without provoking violent opposition, but most people agreed with them that combining political and magical power was dangerous, so that particular demand was widely accepted, and no one would protest too loudly if a magic-working king was assassinated by some sort of spell.

Or if a witch was prevented from marrying into a royal family. Even if that prevention was lethal.

But it was obviously far too soon to be thinking about such things. And she had no reason to think Prince Marek would ever want to marry her. He was more likely to consider her a brief indulgence before he married some surplus princess to cement an alliance.

She didn't find that idea especially unpleasant. One of the biggest advantages of being a witch—one she had never considered before starting her apprenticeship, since she had not yet hit puberty at the time, but which she had come to greatly appreciate—was that her magic could prevent any sort of infection and keep her from getting pregnant. A dalliance with a handsome prince could be enjoyed for its own sake, without any great risk.

Of course, even that might be getting ahead of herself. They had hardly met and had yet to really get to know one another.

She smiled at Prince Marek as she emerged from the house. "Lead on, your Highness," she said.

He smiled in return and offered his arm.

The castle was, of course, located atop the highest hill in central Melitha, but since Melitha was located on the broad coastal plain of the northwestern Small Kingdoms, that was not saying very much. It was, in fact, the *only* real hill in the kingdom, rising a good fifty or sixty feet above the surrounding farmland; legend had it that the kingdom's name, which derived from the Old Ethsharitic word for "struck by lightning," had originally applied only to the hill, as its height had made it a prime target for storms blowing in from the Gulf of the East.

Now, of course, the castle had various magical spells and devices defending it from lightning; kings could not use magic themselves, but they were always free to hire wizards or other magicians to serve their needs. These protections had allowed Melitha's rulers to build a very impressive fortress, one that towered over the capital.

As Darissa and Marek approached, the young witch looked up at it appraisingly.

From the foot of the hill the curtain wall was largely hidden by the surrounding homes and shops, but the battlements rose a story or two above the rooftops, so that they could see the turrets and crenellations that adorned the structure. The keep was, in turn, mostly hidden by the curtain wall, but its slate roof and corner turrets were visible.

And the central tower rose up from the keep, thrusting at least a hundred feet into the air, its strange metal cap gleaming in the sun. Darissa didn't know what sort of magician was responsible for that shining summit, but it was known to have great protective powers. Lightning had reportedly struck it any number of times, but it remained completely undamaged, and since its completion lightning had never hit any other part of the castle, nor the surrounding town— it seemed to somehow draw all the storm's power into itself, away from the rest of the kingdom.

Darissa wondered where all that power *went*; as a witch, she knew that natural energy was never destroyed, only absorbed or dissipated or transformed.

She had seen the castle many times before, of course; when the leaves were off the trees the great tower was visible from Nondel's kitchen window, and she had spent plenty of time in town. She had never been inside it, though. She allowed Marek to escort her into town, past the market and up Castle Street, past the bakeries and wine shops to Castle Square.

She had been that far before, but now the prince led her up the right-hand stair to the raised platform above the inner end of the square, where half a dozen soldiers in the king's livery were standing guard—or standing, at any rate; they did not seem to be particularly attentive about guarding anything.

All of them simply watched as she and Marek walked up the steps; no weapons were drawn, no challenges issued. As they reached the top step, the nearest guardsman nodded politely and said, "Good morning, your Highness."

"The same to you, Arra," Marek replied. "Is your wife feeling better?"

"Somewhat, your Highness. I'm sure she'll be fine in another day or two."

"Let us hope so." He glanced at Darissa, and she knew he was wondering whether he should ask her to take a look at the sick woman. She shook her head slightly. If the soldier wanted to hire a witch, he was free to do so, but she did not want to intrude. He did not sound particularly worried about his wife, and she sensed that he did not want to trouble the prince with personal problems.

The guards were stepping aside, clearing a path to the stone bridge that led across the dry moat to the castle gates. Marek strolled on, and Darissa followed.

The bridge was broad, but Darissa ambled over toward one side to look down at the fifty-foot drop onto jagged rocks. Then she hurried to catch up to Marek, who waited for her with an amused smile.

"Enjoying the view?" he asked.

"Yes," Darissa said, smiling back.

The gates stood open, and the two walked into the passage beyond, where half a dozen more guards snapped to attention at the sight of Prince Marek. The prince smiled. "Relax," he said. "It's just me."

Then the inner doors swung open, and they emerged into the castle courtyard, where a couple of dozen people were going about their everyday business. Marek waved to a few, but led the way across the yard and up the steps to the keep entry without stopping.

Darissa took it all in with interest—soldiers drilling with their spears, a girl gathering eggs from a chicken coop, three young boys chasing each other across the sparse grass with much shrieking and giggling, an old woman hanging laundry out to dry. The clotheslines the old woman was using were longer and more numerous than Darissa had ever before seen in one place and held a wide variety of fabrics.

Marek noticed her interest. "You've never been here before?" he asked.

"No," Darissa said. "I never had any business here."

"So it's all new? What would you like to see, then? The great hall? The armory? The tower?"

"I...don't know. What would you suggest?"

"Well, probably not the armory," Marek said, looking around the courtyard. "You don't strike me as someone with a fondness for weaponry, though you might appreciate the workmanship that goes into some of it. But the best pieces are on display elsewhere, so if you're only interested in the workmanship I don't think the armory is our best choice." He looked up. "The view from the top of the tower is spectacular, but it involves climbing a lot of stairs—unless you can fly up there?"

Darissa grimaced. "I can levitate a little, but it's just as tiring as the stairs would be. Maybe even more so."

"Well, I wouldn't want to tire you out, at least not when you've just arrived, so perhaps we should leave that for later. The great hall, then?"

"Won't... Isn't the king..."

"Oh, my father is probably holding court there, yes. Why should that stop us? We won't bother him."

"All right," Darissa said, feeling slightly overwhelmed. Three days ago she had never spoken to a member of the royal family, or come within twenty feet of one, and here she was with a prince casually talking to her about intruding on the king's court!

"Fine!" Marek smiled broadly. "This way."

Darissa had expected him to lead her through the grand ornate portal at the top of the steps, but to her surprise he gestured to a small, black door on one side. "This way," he repeated.

She followed him into a dim little room lit by a single arrow slit. "Let me take a look," he said, leading her to a heavy wooden door on the opposite side. A small hinged panel was set in the door at about the level of Darissa's face. Marek opened it, then had to stoop to peer through.

"Well," he said, as he gazed at whatever lay beyond, "there are half a dozen petitioners, and some of my father's officers, but I don't see Dad, so we won't be committing any terrible breach of protocol if we walk in unannounced. Come on." He slid back a bolt and swung the door open—not wide, just enough for the two of them to slip through.

The room beyond was the largest enclosed space Darissa had ever seen, but she was well aware that she was not an experienced traveler. It might well be quite ordinary by royal standards. Still, it seemed huge to her—over a hundred feet long, she was sure, the barrel-vaulted ceiling easily twenty feet up. She could not readily judge the width because it was not a simple rectangle; there were pillars and galleries, nooks and niches, along every side. A cluster of people stood around a long wooden table midway down one side, beneath a dark balcony; a handful of others were seated at desks here and there.

And in an alcove at the far end sat a dais, and on the dais stood a big gilded chair, the seat upholstered in dark red velvet—the king's throne, surely. It was unoccupied.

Light poured in through half a dozen high windows, but there were dozens, perhaps hundreds, of lit candles arrayed along either side, as well; dust and smoke danced in the sunlight above, and the air smelled of hot wax and polishing oil.

"Shall I introduce you to some of these people?" Marek asked quietly, gesturing toward the nearest desks.

Darissa shook her head. This was not somewhere either a peasant or a witch belonged. She felt terribly out of place.

Marek looked disappointed—or, rather, *felt* disappointed. Darissa realized she was sensing his disappointment with witchcraft, rather than through anything she saw on his face, as he had hidden his emotions very effectively. This was his home, after all, and he wanted her to like it.

"Maybe a few," Darissa said, relenting. "But it's all a little overwhelming."

"Well," Marek said, his disappointment dissipating, "there's my sister—you don't mind meeting *her*, do you?"

"Your sister?"

Marek grabbed her hand and tugged.

Darissa's first instinct was to resist, but she did not want to cause a disturbance, and Marek was a *prince*, so resisting him would be… well, it might not be a good idea. He had been very pleasant to her so far, and everyone seemed to like him, but still, he was a prince, a member of the royal family. He wasn't accustomed to being disobeyed, and he had the authority to have her thrown in a dungeon if he chose. She let herself be led along one side of the great hall.

"Hinda!" Marek called. He kept his voice low.

A tall woman in a flowing wine-colored velvet dress, who had been standing by a pillar and watching one of the desk-bound officials writing, turned. She said nothing, but watched as they approached. She watched Marek at first, then as they neared turned her attention to Darissa.

"Marek," she said, her eyes firmly fixed on Darissa. "Who is this?"

"Hinda, may I present Darissa the Apprentice? And Darissa, this is my sister, her highness Princess Hinda of Melitha."

Darissa did her best to curtsey in the proper fashion, but was not sure how well she had done it. Nondel had not taught her royal protocol.

Hinda nodded in return. "Apprentice," she said.

"Yes, your Highness," Darissa replied. She did not intend to admit to being a witch unless asked directly, so she did not answer any implied question—and in truth, she was not sure whether Princess Hinda *cared* what sort of apprentice she was.

"And what brings you to Melitha Castle?"

"Prince Marek," Darissa answered.

"Well, yes." She turned her attention to her brother.

"She was helping a sick woman in the market," Marek said. "I was moved by her kindness."

"Your brother is too modest," Darissa added quickly. "He helped, as well—he and his men."

The princess did not look impressed. "Who was this woman? Your mother?"

"No, your Highness. A stranger."

Hinda gave a slight nod that ended with her nose in the air. "I see."

"I doubt it," Marek said. "I can't imagine you troubling yourself about a sick woman."

"If you mean I prefer not to interfere in other people's business, you're quite right. Let her own family attend to her. I take it she's well now?"

"No," Darissa said. "But she'll live."

Hinda looked startled. "Oh," she said.

"She lost her baby, though."

"She... Oh." Hinda looked slightly abashed. "Apprentice...midwife, then?"

"No."

Before Hinda could ask any further questions, Marek had one of his own. "Where's Dad?"

Hinda glanced at the throne. "Taking a moment to refresh himself. He should be back any time now. So you brought your new friend to meet the king?"

"I brought her to see the castle." He glanced down at Darissa. "Our father is one of the sights here, so I thought he should be included in her tour. Don't worry, I'm not going to interrupt anything; I know that's none of my business."

"It *could* be your business," Hinda said. "After all, if you marry the right princess you might eventually wind up on a throne somewhere."

"Well, Dad has yet to find a suitable bride for me, and I think any princess who stands to inherit a throne can do better than a third son, in any case. No, I plan to let my elder brothers look after the kingdom's affairs."

"Leaving you free to chase after cute little apprentices."

Marek's expression hardened, and Darissa could feel that Hinda's words had hurt him more than he wanted anyone, even himself, to know.

"Look," Darissa said, pointing. "Is that the king?"

As she had hoped, her question distracted the royal offspring from their conversation as they both turned to see.

"That's his herald," Marek told her, as the new arrival in the fancy white and gold tunic took up a position at the foot of the throne and raised a banner.

"My lords and ladies, and citizens of Melitha!" the herald announced, his voice somehow filling the immense room. "His Majesty, King Terren of Melitha!"

Everyone who had been seated rose.

"Excuse me," Hinda said. She turned and hurried away.

Marek stood where he was and told Darissa, "Well, that's my sister. And there's my father."

Darissa did not dare reply. Instead, following the example of everyone else in the room except Hinda and Marek, she went down on one knee as the king, in his red and gold velvet robes, marched into the hall.

CHAPTER FIVE

MORVASH OF THE SHADOWS

23ʳᵈ OF GREENGROWTH, YS 5238

Morvash settled back in the chair and smiled at the white-robed, strong-featured woman who sat across from him. This was Ithinia of the Isle, the city's famous senior Guildmaster.

"It's a pleasure to meet you," he said.

She ignored the pleasantry. "Why are you here?"

"Well, partly just as a courtesy," he said. "I have recently relocated to Ethshar of the Spices, and wanted to let the Guild know my whereabouts."

"Fang said you gave your name as Morvash of the Shadows. Journeyman?"

"Yes."

"Who was your master?"

"Avizar of the Blue Eyes."

Ithinia nodded. "You said 'partly.' What else?"

Ithinia seemed to prefer directness, so Morvash did not waste time on background details. "I'm staying with my uncle, Gror the Merchant, who rents the late Lord Landessin's mansion, and I've noticed that several of the statues in his possession are enchanted people, rather than carved stone. It seems to me that restoring them to life would be the right thing to do, but there are two serious obstacles to that."

"*Several* of them? How many is that?"

"Thirty-three people. At least. I didn't check any of the animals, and there may have been some cases where the petrifaction was so complete I couldn't detect it."

Ithinia stared at him silently for a few seconds, then said, "Thirty-three?"

Morvash nodded.

"You're certain of that?"

"As certain as I can be."

"How many statues does your uncle *have*?"

"Lord Landessin was a collector. There are hundreds."

Ithinia considered that, then asked, "Is there any record of where these statues came from, or who they might have been?"

Morvash hesitated, then admitted, "I don't know. Uncle Gror doesn't know anything about them, but I haven't talked to Lord Landessin's family."

"I would suggest finding out as much as you can before restoring them to life. Some of them may be dangerous."

"But they were turned to stone! If they were criminals, the magistrates would have had them flogged or executed, not petrified."

"The wizards who petrified them may have been acting in self-defense. Hadn't you thought of that?"

"I…well, no, not really." Morvash frowned. "I suppose I didn't."

Ithinia smiled indulgently. "You're young and idealistic. I understand. You see an apparent injustice and you want to put it right, and for many of these people, that may be what they deserve. But perhaps not *all* of them."

"Perhaps not," Morvash admitted. He remembered the young couple, and added, "But for some, I don't see how they could possibly have done anything to justify it."

"You know, I've turned a few people to stone myself; I know more than one petrifaction spell."

Morvash was startled, but recovered quickly. "But you didn't just *leave* them like that, did you? You didn't let them wind up in someone's sculpture collection."

"No, I didn't. All right, then. We'll come back to that in a moment. For now, though, you said there were obstacles to your plan. What obstacles?"

"Well, first, I don't know how. I can't afford to hire someone to restore them, so I need to learn a spell that will do it."

"You may need more than one; not all petrifactions are alike."

"Oh, I know *that*, Guildmaster. And I know I'll need to earn every spell. I was hoping you could advise me as to who might be able to teach me."

She nodded. "I think I can do that. I could do it myself, but I don't have the time; I'll find someone else who knows the relevant magic. Learning it may take years, though." She sighed. "What's the other obstacle?"

Morvash paused, caught off-guard by the suggestion his project might take years; he had been thinking in terms of a few sixnights. Then he recollected himself and said, "I need a place to work. My uncle doesn't want me working magic in his home; he's afraid a spell could go wrong."

"Your uncle is a sensible man. I fail to see, however, what this has to do with me or the Guild."

"I was hoping the Guild might have a place available where I could experiment."

"And why do you not simply rent or buy your own shop?"

"Because I don't... I need a workroom, not a shop. And I was hoping to avoid the delay finding my own place would entail. Leaving these innocents petrified..." He swallowed. "I mean, I suppose they're unaware of their situation, but they may have friends and family who miss them."

"They aren't necessarily unaware," Ithinia said. "It depends how they were petrified. Fendel's Superior Petrifaction leaves its victims conscious, though they can then be put to sleep with other spells."

"Oh," Morvash said. "*Oh.* Then we really... I must..." He stopped in confusion, overwhelmed by the thought of all those people trapped in utter isolation for *years*, unable to move.

Ithinia seemed undisturbed. "I agree that it would be considerate to restore them to life. I would advise you to be careful in doing so, though—some of them may have been transformed for good reasons. And I am not yet convinced the Guild should supply a place for you to do this, instead of leaving it to you to obtain a place of your own."

"All right," Morvash said. "I'll find a place. Ah...do you have any suggestions? Are you aware of any suitable vacancies?"

"As I'm sure you understand, shops in the Wizards' Quarter are in high demand..."

"I don't *need* a shop," Morvash interrupted. "Just somewhere to practice my spells."

"Oh?"

"I work for my uncle. I don't need to sell spells. But he won't let me experiment in his home, so I need a workroom. It doesn't need to be in the Wizards' Quarter."

"Ah. I did not understand the situation. Perhaps we can help you after all." She frowned slightly, and tapped her mouth with a finger. "As it happens, the Guild has a house we would like to dispose of. Might you be interested in buying it?"

Morvash had not expected that. "Buy? I had only meant to rent."

"I suppose we could rent it to you. That might be just as well, really. Giving up control completely could be rash."

That did not sound very reassuring. "What sort of house? I don't have a great deal of money."

"Oh, I think we can come to some sort of agreement—and some of these people you intend to rescue may be both wealthy and grateful; we'll have to see how that works out."

"That would be wonderful," Morvash said.

Ithinia nodded, then rose from her chair. "Be here tomorrow around mid-morning, but don't knock—I'll have our agent meet you out front."

Morvash rose as well, following his host's lead. "Thank you!" he said.

"I'll give her a list of wizards who may have spells you can use to unpetrify these people."

"Thank you!" Morvash repeated.

The Guildmaster escorted Morvash from the parlor to the front door, and as she opened it she said, "Be careful."

"Yes, Guildmaster," he said. Then he stepped out onto the street. He glanced up at the shadowy eaves, and saw the two gargoyles peering down at them. One of them, the one who had spoken to him, was apparently named Fang. That seemed appropriate, as it had four immense fangs; he wondered how it spoke as well as it did with those things in the way.

He also wondered whether those creatures had originally been human—had Ithinia transformed them? She said she had petrified people...

"Ellran's Immortal Animation," Ithinia's voice said, startling him. His gaze fell back to its usual level, and he saw that the Guildmaster had not yet closed the door.

"I never heard of it," Morvash admitted.

"It's an eighth-order spell; not many people can perform it." She glanced up, then back at Morvash. "It will bring anything to life—won't work on anything that's already alive, but stone, brick, metal, wood, bone, cloth, it will affect any of those."

He wondered whether she had guessed his suspicions. "That's amazing," he said. "Why 'Immortal,' though?"

"Oh, well, that's one of the potential drawbacks," Ithinia said. "Once you bring something to life with this particular spell, it can't be killed. Ever. By anything. If you break it into pieces, each piece will still be alive. That can be inconvenient. The wizard who taught it to me had a big jar of shattered bits hidden away, and the way they kept moving was…disturbing. I have a small jar of powdered pottery myself—a certain individual created a nasty little monster he sent to attack one of his enemies, and we intercepted it and smashed it, but we couldn't kill it. Fortunately, ceramic dust is fairly harmless even when alive." She looked up once more. "I love my gargoyles, but I doubt I'll ever use that spell again."

A dozen questions popped into Morvash's head—had she ever smashed one of her own creations? How could she be *sure* there wasn't a spell that could kill them—a reversal or restoration spell, perhaps? What would happen if he tried Ellran's spell on one of the petrified people? What if he brought some of Lord Landessin's *other* statuary to life?

But it was an eighth-order spell. He had never managed anything above fifth order, and was not comfortable even at that level. And he had no business asking the Guildmaster nosy questions.

"Good night, Guildmaster, and thank you for your help."

"Good night, journeyman," Ithinia said. Then she finally closed the door.

He headed around the corner, and south on Canal Avenue.

At breakfast the following morning he explained the situation to his uncle. Gror, despite not being a wizard, had heard of Ithinia of the Isle, and told Morvash that her house was on Lower Street.

"I didn't know the address," Morvash admitted. "I found it by magic."

Gror nodded. "You didn't know who she was?"

"Not until she introduced herself. I was just looking for a Guildmaster, any Guildmaster."

Gror frowned. "So she's helping you?" he asked. "A virtual stranger, and one of the most powerful people in the city agreed to help you?"

Morvash nodded.

"Why?"

"Just helping out a Guild member, I think. And it's not as if she's teaching me anything herself; she's just giving me a few names and a referral on a house."

"Hmph."

Morvash did not let his uncle's distrust trouble him; Gror was a merchant, not a wizard. Wizards cooperated with one another, while merchants competed. He finished his meal, tidied up, and then set out for Ithinia's home.

Canal Avenue looked different in bright morning sun, and was significantly more crowded, so that Morvash almost turned onto High Street before catching himself and continuing another block to Lower Street. He had remembered the house as being at the end of the first block, and was momentarily puzzled not to see the distinctive gargoyles, until he realized that he had missed another cross-street in the dark, and the house was on the north side of the *next* block.

He thought Fang was watching him as he approached, and was so focused on the gargoyles that he didn't notice the woman waiting for him until he was only a few yards away.

She was not young—at least Uncle Gror's age, Morvash judged. She was wearing a white tunic and dark blue skirt, very conservative, and had her waist-length hair pulled back and tied at the nape of her neck. She had spotted him before he saw her, and was waiting for him to come close enough to address without shouting. He hurried to oblige.

"Morvash of the Shadows?" she asked.

"Yes," he acknowledged, stopping a few feet away. "And you are…?"

"I am the Guild's agent. Call me by any name you like. Alir would be fine."

"Ah," Morvash said, slightly taken aback. "Alir, then."

"I was told to give you this list of wizards who may know the spells you seek." She held out a rolled paper; Morvash accepted it, then hesitated, unsure whether he should look at it immediately, or save it for later.

"I have also been instructed to show you the Guild's vacant house on Old East Avenue."

Morvash tucked the paper in his belt, then looked at Alir again. "I look forward to seeing it."

"Then follow me." She turned, and marched around the corner onto the street paralleling Canal Avenue one block to the east. Morvash followed. As they walked he let his hand fall to the hilt of his athame and adjusted it slightly, muttering a brief incantation.

The agent appeared to be human, and not an illusion or homunculus, but he could sense magic around her—protective spells, most likely. That was no surprise.

They walked steadily southward up the slope; after the third major cross-street the avenue began curving gently westward, toward the very peak of the hill that marked the end of the New City district. They had proceeded perhaps two hundred feet around the curve when the agent stopped and pointed ahead, to the right.

"There," she said.

The house she indicated was tall and dark, very unlike its neighbors. Where most of the mansions on this part of Old East Avenue were white or red or yellow, half-timbered or built of brick, this one was black stone, with deep-set windows and with turrets and small gargoyles adorning the roof-line, though he saw no sign these gargoyles were animated. A few spriggans were staring at the house from across the street, but none went near it.

Morvash smiled at the sight of the dark stone walls; the house reminded him of home. "Tell me about it," he said.

The agent coughed, clearly surprised by his smile. "They say it's about two hundred years old," she replied. "A wizard called Erdrik the Grim built it not long after the Great War, when the New City was still actually new. It was the first house on this block."

"Did he use magic to build it?"

"I don't know," the agent admitted. "He certainly used enough magic after it was built, though."

"Was he from Ethshar of the Rocks, by any chance? It looks something like the architecture there."

"I don't know that, either. To be honest, nobody seems to know much about him—or if they do, they haven't told *me*. He wasn't originally from Ethshar of the Spices, and he was already extremely rich and powerful when he came to the city, but that's about everything I know. He wasn't very friendly, from what I hear. In fact, he appears to have been quite the recluse, as well as a troublemaker. Half the time the neighbors didn't know whether he was still here, and when they did it was usually because he was fighting with someone, or disturbing everyone with magical lights and noises."

"Well, I suppose that's all ancient history," Morvash said.

"Uh…not *that* ancient. He lived here until eleven years ago last Rains."

Morvash had been gazing up at the four-story tower on the south corner; now he turned, startled. "Eleven years ago?"

"That's right."

"But you said he built it two hundred years ago?"

"Well, he *was* a wizard," the agent said.

Morvash nodded. "What happened to him?"

"I don't know."

Morvash was starting to become annoyed at the woman's ignorance. Ithinia had sent her to show him the house; shouldn't she know more about its history? "Well, did he die? Is that why it's available?"

"I don't know; they didn't tell me. All I know is that the Wizards' Guild says he's gone for good and left no heirs, so after ten years all his possessions, including the house, went to either the Guild or the tax collectors. The taxes have all been paid, everything's settled, so the Guild owns the house. They would like to sell it, but because there's still magic in it, they'll only sell to a wizard. And there aren't any interested wizards at the moment, so Ithinia is willing to let you rent it."

"They think there's still magic in it?" Morvash looked up at the gargoyles. None of them were moving, but now he wondered whether any of them might be animated after all.

"A wizard lived here for two hundred years; what do *you* think? And they *know* there's still magic in it. You'll see."

Morvash had no answer for that. Instead he said, "Shall we go inside?"

CHAPTER SIX

DARISSA THE WITCH'S APPRENTICE

15TH OF HARVEST, YS 5199

Darissa refused to let Marek introduce her to the king, even though she could sense that he was disappointed by her reluctance. She could tell that he was not at all intimidated by His Majesty—but then, why should he be? To him, the king was merely his father.

She, however, was terrified at the prospect of such a meeting. A prince was one thing, a king another. She knew of too many cases where witches had wound up in deep trouble for their dealings with royalty. Kings had a habit of thinking it would be very useful to have a courtier who could sense emotions, tell truth from lies, detect poisons, heal minor injuries, and do all the other magic witches could do. While it could be profitable to cooperate with such requests—or demands!—it could also lead to deeper and deeper entanglement in politics, with a very real risk of angering more powerful magicians, such as the Wizards' Guild.

And refusing royal commands—or even requests—was equally dangerous. Marek seemed harmless enough, and had asked nothing of her, but he was merely a relatively minor prince, third in line for the throne and likely to drop back in the succession when his older brothers started siring sons of their own. He was not a reigning monarch.

Her brief encounter with Princess Hinda had confirmed her reluctance; she had sensed a very different personality than her brother's. Hinda was harder, more selfish; her heart was colder. Darissa was very glad Marek had not told his sister that Darissa was a witch.

They did stay long enough to hear the king listen to a petition requesting an unsafe bridge be rebuilt, but then Darissa slipped away.

She had not insisted Marek accompany her; in fact, she had not even told him she was leaving. He had reluctantly stopped trying to convince her to meet his father, and the two were merely standing side by side when she stepped back and headed for the door.

She used just a little bit of magic to keep her departure from being noticed by anyone else, but Marek realized immediately and was just a step behind when she left the great hall. The spell was not strong enough to block someone who was already very aware of her presence.

He said nothing at first, but once they were out in the courtyard he asked, "Is there anything else I can show you? The family apartments, perhaps?"

She smiled. "Isn't it a bit soon to be inviting me up to your room?"

"Oh, I…" Then he saw her expression and caught himself. "Ah, you *knew* I didn't mean it like that. I see this witchcraft thing has its advantages—you know my intentions, probably as well as I do myself."

"Better," Darissa said with a grin.

He grinned back, but the smile quickly faded into an expression of intense interest. "Really?" he said. "How is that possible?"

He was quick; she had expected him to take it as a mere joke. If he was going to take it seriously, then she would answer his question seriously.

"For all of us, no matter who we are, there are things we don't want to admit to ourselves," she said. "We hide them so we can tell ourselves we are good and unselfish, with only the very best motives. But with a little effort the right sort of witch can see those, even when they're hidden."

"Oh, now that raises *several* questions," he said, carefully not directing their steps toward the royal apartments. "Does *everyone* do this, hide things from themselves?"

"Everyone *I've* ever met, at any rate, and my master says he's never found an exception."

"And what about you? Do *you* do it?"

She nodded. "Yes. And yes, I can use my magic to sense my own hidden motives, but it's much harder than sensing anyone else's, because part of me is fighting it."

"What about your master? His witchcraft is stronger than yours, isn't it? So can you sense what *he* wants to keep hidden?"

Darissa grinned as she looked up at him. "You ask good questions! Maybe you should have been a witch yourself."

He smiled back. "Maybe, but I was born into the wrong family for that. You haven't *answered* my good question; are you going to?"

She turned up an empty palm. "It's complicated," she said. "He can hide things from me if he consciously tries to, but sometimes I can tell he's hiding something, even if I don't know what it is. Sometimes I sense things he doesn't know are there; other times I don't. And he's my master, so I don't pry. In fact, I don't generally pry into *anyone's* mind; people have a right to privacy. But sometimes, as you saw, I overhear things in the market, and sometimes I see things through windows, and sometimes, whether I intend it or not, I know people's thoughts. When I'm talking to someone it's hard *not* to know the thoughts behind the words, and I don't usually worry about it. And as for people's moods, their strong emotions, what's heavy on their minds, I can't avoid sensing that, any more than I can avoid seeing their faces. My master gives away less than most people—it's as if he's whispering instead of shouting—but I can still sense *some* of what he's thinking and feeling, whether he wants me to or not."

"It *is* complicated!"

"I told you it was."

"You said this was something the *right sort* of witch does; is there a wrong sort?" They were about to walk into a wall, and he turned left. She turned with him.

"Oh, yes," she said. "Different witches have different specialties. Some know everything there is to know about herbs, for example, but have no idea what's going on in any head but their own. Some can open locks, or purify water, or any number of other skills, but can still be as easily fooled by a misleading expression as any ordinary person."

"And you?"

She smiled crookedly. "My specialty is moods and thoughts. Nondel has made his living by seeing what people want and finding a way to satisfy them, and that's what he's teaching me. If someone comes asking for a love potion or a prophecy, we'll see why they want it, and what we can do instead."

"You can't just give them love potions and prophecies?"

She shook her head. "Witches don't make love potions, not really. That's wizardry, or maybe sorcery, not witchcraft. There are some herbal things…but they aren't true love potions. And prophecies—well, there *are* witches who can see into the future a little, or sometimes more than a little, but *we* can't do it, Nondel and I, and I'm not sure it counts as actual prophecy. A theurgist would be better for prophecy. But if someone comes to us asking for a love potion, we'll see why he wants it, and try to find a way to help him."

"You do real healing, though."

"Yes, we do. And other magic. But knowing what our customers are thinking and feeling is our most important skill."

"Interesting!" He looked up, just short of walking into a clothesline, and stopped. Darissa stopped as well.

"Have you ever heard of Klathoa?" Marek asked.

"Of course!" Darissa guessed that every witch in the Small Kingdoms knew about Klathoa, the tiny realm forty or fifty miles to the west of Melitha where there was no king or queen or royal family, and witches ran everything.

"I begin to see how they manage without any of the usual trappings of government," he said. "If their rulers always know what everyone wants, and who is dissatisfied, that would make it much easier to keep everyone happy."

"I suppose it would," Darissa agreed.

"Have you ever considered moving there, so that you could be a member of the ruling class?"

"Oh, I'm happy here in Melitha. It's where I was born," she replied. "And my master tells me that the witches of Klathoa are really very limited in what they can do, living in constant fear that the Wizards' Guild will decide it was a mistake to leave them in power."

"That might be true," Marek acknowledged. Then abruptly changing the subject, he pointed to a door in the courtyard wall, just behind the clotheslines. "This is the laundry; would you like to see that, perhaps?"

She laughed. "Why not?"

And in the end, it proved very interesting. She had never seen anything like the castle laundry before, with its steaming vats and scores of drying racks and hot, swampy air. It was far more elaborate than the simple washtub she and Nondel used.

But then, some of the clothing and linens in the castle were far more elaborate than anything she and Nondel had!

The laundry workers—mostly women, but with a few children of both sexes helping out—did not seem especially surprised to see the prince; in fact, he greeted several of them by name, which prompted Darissa to ask, once they were back outside, "Do you go there often?"

"Oh, not *that* often. Maybe once a month."

"Once a month? Why?"

"Well, in the winter I like to stop in there because it's always warm. And the rest of the year it's a cheerful, busy sort of place, and I enjoy that. I've known some of the women there since I was a little child, I used to hide there when my parents were angry with me, and I like to stop in and say hello to them sometimes. In the summer, if it's really hot, I try to remember to bring them something cool to drink—something that won't stain, though, if they spill it on my father's robes, so it's more likely to be lemonade than beer."

"Do your brothers go there, too?"

Marek let out a laugh. "By the gods, no! They would never stoop to such a thing. That's one reason it was such a good hiding place."

"But *you* go there."

"Darissa, I'm the king's third son and fourth child. Nobody cares what I do. I'm never going to be king, and I'm not particularly valuable on the marriage market, so I can do what I please, and I don't need to worry about preparing for my future reign. My brothers are always studying diplomacy and statecraft and military matters, from swordplay up to grand strategy; they're constantly being sent to visit other kingdoms, to negotiate treaties and court suitable princesses—especially Terren, though now that he's married to Indamara he doesn't do the courting part anymore. Evreth needs to be ready if anything happens to Terren, so he gets included in all the studying and training and diplomacy, and now *he* does all the princess-courting, though to be honest I'm not sure how interested he is in women. I'm not important enough for that—well, not usually, not yet. If Evreth marries the right princess and gets into the line of succession somewhere else I'd move up, so I am expected to keep up with the family business in *some* regards, and now that I'm old enough to command some respect I'll probably be sent on an embassy or trade mission every so often, should the occasion arise, but mostly I'm left to my own devices. I was never watched over the way my brothers were—or even my sister, as poor Hinda is expected to marry when we need to cement an alliance, and not when, or to whom, she pleases. When our mother was alive she used to keep an eye on me, but since she died—well, Dad is too busy being king, and the courtiers prefer to keep themselves with more important or profitable tasks, so I'm generally left to myself."

Darissa might have expected a prince to resent being ignored, but instead she could tell that Marek was *happy* about his situation. He liked the freedom from obligation.

He glanced at her face, and guessed what she was thinking. "Yes, I enjoy my situation," he said. "I have the best of everything. I have the advantages of royalty without the responsibilities."

"But…don't you ever feel a little useless? Meaningless?"

He smiled at her. "I try to make myself useful," he said. "I wander around Melitha getting to know my father's subjects, and seeing what they need or want, and then I try to see that my father provides it. I act as what the diplomats call a minister without portfolio, filling in wherever I see a need."

"What does your family think of this?"

"Oh, I don't think they even realize I'm doing it. Father originally thought that I should join the army to keep myself busy, but I convinced him I was unsuited to it."

Something about the way he said that prompted Darissa to ask, "*Are* you unsuited to it?"

"Well, not physically. Father thinks I'm hopelessly clumsy and would probably cut my own nose off if I ever tried to use a sword, but that's what I want him to think. Mostly, I don't *want* to be a soldier. All those rules and regulations! And I don't want to hurt anyone; I suspect that if I ever got into a battle I wouldn't be very effective simply because I'd be too reluctant to kill the enemy."

"*That's* hardly a bad thing!"

"In an ordinary person, of course not, and even in a king it's far better than being eager to kill people, but in a soldier it's really less than ideal."

"In a war, I suppose it is, but we aren't at war."

"Not at the moment, but we're probably about due."

Startled, she looked up at him. She remembered that she had been sensing worry about a war in the market just before Alasha's pain distracted her, though she had not recognized a cause for this concern. "Due?" she asked. "Is there a schedule?"

He smiled wryly. "Very nearly," he said. "Generally speaking, we fight a war every twenty years or so, and it's been eighteen since the Treaty of Ressamor."

"But how…why does that happen?"

"Well, it's because…several things." He gestured at another door. "Would you like to climb the tower and look at the view? You can see almost all of Melitha from up there."

Darissa thought at first that this was an attempt to change the subject, but something told her it was more than that. "All right," she said.

They made their way through a few more doors and passageways to the foot of a great stone staircase, then started climbing.

"By the standards of the Small Kingdoms," Marek said as they climbed, "Melitha is a good-sized country—not one of the largest, but probably bigger than average. But as I said, you can see almost all of it from the top of this tower; it's not much more than twenty miles across in any direction, less than fifteen in most. There probably aren't more than fifteen thousand people here; we haven't done a census in fifty years, so no one knows exactly. We have eight immediate neighbors—Kanthoa, Elankora, Ressamor, Tal, Bhella, Hollendon, Trafoa, and Eknera. None of them like us all that very much, though just how little varies." He nodded politely at a pair of courtiers hurrying down the stairs past them; the two bowed in exchange, one of them so deeply he almost tumbled down the stairs.

"Your Highness," the other said, as he straightened up. He glanced at Darissa, but said nothing to her before continuing his descent.

"I've been to Trafoa," Darissa said. "The people there were friendly enough."

"Oh, I don't mean the common people," Marek said, as they rounded a turn onto the next upward flight. "I mean the ruling families, because that's who decides whether or not to go to war. My family has not endeared itself to our neighbors. We're respected, unlike some I could mention, but we aren't well-liked."

"Oh."

They did not speak for the next several steps; then Marek continued, "In the last big war, Melitha was allied with Elankora against Kanthoa and Eknera—my mother was from Elankora, so we had a solid connection there. We won a great victory, and took away some of their land—I'll point it out to you when we reach the top. Almost thirty years earlier we and Bhella won a war against Hollendon, and took a piece of *their* territory—I can't point *that* out, though, because it's too far away; it's Melitha's southwestern corner now, and pretty much the only part of the country you can't see from here. A generation before that, we lost our old southernmost land to Bhella—that was why our alliance with them caught Hollendon off-guard and let us win that one quickly."

"It sounds very complicated," Darissa said; they were four flights up now, and climbing took most of her breath.

There was a soldier standing guard at the next landing; he snatched up his spear and snapped upright when he recognized the prince. Marek nodded to him. "Elzen," he said. "How's the baby?"

The soldier smiled. "Doing fine, your Highness. Fat and happy and growing like a vine."

"Good! Keep a good watch."

"Of course, your Highness." He nodded at the prince, and then at Darissa. The witch could sense that he had no idea who she was, but anyone with the prince was welcome, without question.

Then they were past.

At the next landing there were windows on three sides; they had climbed into the tower itself. Darissa paused to catch her breath and looked out one of them.

Marek stood behind her, looking over her shoulder at the castle roofs and the green horizon beyond. "Beautiful, isn't it?"

Darissa made a wordless noise of agreement. She was still a little short of breath. They were about six stories up, without counting the hill the castle was built on; that was higher than she had ever climbed before. Marek did not seem troubled at all; he clearly got more exercise and climbed more stairs than she did.

"That's east," the prince said. "Seven or eight miles out—you can see about that far from here, I think—is the border with Ressamor. You'll have a much better view from the top."

Darissa did not reply.

"Shall we continue?" Marek asked, gesturing toward the stairs leading up. A little reluctantly, Darissa nodded.

They were now above the main part of the keep, where only the tower extended; the stairs wound their way around the outside of a square, with wooden floors every fifteen feet or so dividing the central space and providing access to windows on every side. A strange round metal column ran down the center of the tower, no more than half a foot in diameter; Darissa had no idea what it was, or what it was for, as it did not appear to be supporting anything.

"You may wonder," Marek said, as they continued upward, "just why we would fight wars. Why is it worth the pain and bloodshed and risk to maybe transfer a few dozen farms from one kingdom to the next?"

"I assume..." Darissa said, struggling for breath. "I...young men like to fight..."

Marek smiled. "If that was all there was to it, we'd build an arena and stage fights to first blood. We wouldn't need to kill anyone, or burn any crops or homes."

"Then..." Darissa was mostly focused on reaching the top without embarrassing herself, but she had enough energy to be surprised, and a little confused, by Marek's speech. Did anyone really *know* why the Small Kingdoms fought so many wars? She had always assumed that there were many different reasons, not a single basic cause. But she had never studied history or politics, while Marek's education had concentrated on little else.

"Why?" she asked.

"When we get to the top," Marek said.

The rest of the climb was silent except for Darissa's panting, but at last they emerged into the room at the top of the tower. The walls here were more glass than stone, and supported a high wooden ceiling; the room was uncomfortably warm and smelled of varnish and dust. A rather startled young soldier was sitting in a wooden chair by one of the dozen broad windows; recognizing Marek, he leapt to his feet. "Your Highness!" he said.

"Hello, Debren," the prince replied. "Relax; I'm just showing Darissa the view."

The soldier relaxed. "Yes, your Highness."

"Do you know *all* the soldiers in Melitha by name?" Darissa asked.

"Most of them," Marek said. "Not all of them."

Darissa stared at him for a second or two, and saw that he was not joking, nor did he take pride in this knowledge; it was just a fact.

"There are only a couple of hundred," he added.

Darissa blinked, then turned her attention to the windows.

The view was spectacular, as expected. The land stretched out in all directions, flat and green and speckled with houses and barns until it faded into the hazy distance. A few roads wound their way across the landscape, spreading out like the veins in a leaf, and there were small streams sparkling here and there, but most of the countryside was broken into squares and rectangles of various shades of green and brown. She had to deliberately look down to see any of the town below; simply looking out sent her gaze past the streets and shops to the surrounding farms.

To the east the land rose into gentle hills; as she looked in that direction Marek came up behind her and pointed. "Elankora," he said. "That dark spot on one hilltop? That's Elankora Castle, about fourteen miles from here, where my mother was born." He moved his finger to the right. "That's Ressamor. We can't see the town from here; it's almost twenty miles, beyond the first hills." He moved on to the southeast, and told her that the stone wall in that corner of the tower blocked the view of Tal. Directly to the south Darissa could see nothing but flat farmland. "That's almost all Melitha," Marek told her, "but right at the horizon is Bhella. You can't see Hollendon at all; the southwest corner hides it completely, and even if we had a window there I'm not sure it would help—that's the most distant of our borders."

They moved on to the west, where Trafoa lay; Darissa tried to spot her family farm, where she had been born and raised, but was not certain she had identified it correctly. She reminded herself that sometime she should go see how her Aunt Inria and her cousins were doing. She had relinquished any claim to the property when she was apprenticed to Nondel, but they were still her family, and the farm was still where her parents had lived and died.

Then came the north, for Eknera and Kanthoa. Eknera Keep was no more distant than Elankora Castle, Marek said, but was not on a hilltop and lay at a less convenient angle, so he was unable to point it out. "Sometimes you can see the smoke, though," he said. "Especially in winter."

Debren had resumed his seat, and now Marek turned and indicated the soldier. "His job," the prince said, "is to watch the borders, take a good look around every quarter-hour or so, and let us know if he sees an army approaching. That's the main reason we have this tower—to give us warning. We're fortunate in that our entire country is flat and open; in the hill country of the east, or the southern forests, whole armies can hide behind hills and trees and go undetected until they're dangerously close."

The mention of armies reminded Darissa. "You were going to tell me why the Small Countries fight wars."

"Yes." Marek waved at the view from the windows. "What do you see out there?"

"Farms," Darissa said immediately.

"Exactly. Farms. Every bit of Melitha is farmed. We have no forests or mines or seacoast, no woodcutters or hunters or miners or quarrymen or fishermen or saltpans. Most of our neighbors are the same—not Elankora and Ressamor, but even there, it's *mostly* farmland. That means that the money that built this castle, and that keeps my family wealthy and pays for our army, comes from taxing farms, or taxing the tradesmen who sell to the farmers. Now, that means that we want our farmers to be healthy and successful, so that they can keep on paying those taxes. We can't tax them too heavily, or they won't be as productive—or as happy, and if they're unhappy they won't be as willing to pay the taxes, and we'll need more soldiers to collect them, and we'd have to pay those soldiers, which would mean even *more* taxes. And after a certain point, the peasants would rise up and kill us—or we'd kill them, and dead people don't pay taxes any more than rebels do. So over the two hundred years my family has ruled Melitha, we've learned just how much we can tax a farm family to get the best results. It's pretty stable, and everyone seems reasonably happy with it—ask Debren, here; his family runs a farm over that way, but they had four sons, so the younger ones looked for other work."

Debren turned up an empty palm. "No one likes paying taxes, but they aren't a hardship." He pointed to the southeast. "That's my family's place, right there."

Marek nodded. "And the other kingdoms around us operate the same way, for the most part."

None of this was really news to Darissa; after all, she had lived on her family's farm until a month after her twelfth birthday, when she first came to Nondel's cottage. As a child she had not paid much attention to taxes, but she saw the king's men come around each autumn, share a beer with her father and uncle, and collect a handful of copper coins. She had heard her parents and her aunt and uncle gripe about the taxes, but never very seriously. She did not really see what this had to do with fighting wars, but she did not interrupt.

"Now," Marek said, "if all our money comes from farms, and we want more money for some reason, we know it's not a good idea to raise taxes significantly, so our only other choice is to acquire more farms. But Melitha is *full*; there's no more land to farm. So we have to get it from somewhere else. And our neighbors aren't about to *give* us any land, so we have to *take* it. The farmers themselves don't generally care much—they pay about the same taxes, whether it's to us or Bhella or Eknera. But the royal families of those other kingdoms, *they* care very much. They want the money, too. So they fight for it, and that means a war." He sighed. "That last war, when we allied with Elankora to fight Kanthoa and Eknera—that happened because my grandfather made some bad decisions, and lost a lot of money paying magicians for a scheme to grow trees in the air, so we wouldn't need to buy so much wood. It was a stupid idea, and it left us so far in debt the only way out was a successful war. Which we fought."

Darissa winced. "Grow trees in the *air*?"

"Something like that. I was just a baby, I don't know the details. Anyway, we picked a fight with Eknera and Kanthoa over an imagined slight, and took the Northangle district from them, and forced them to pay our debts. The actual fighting didn't even last a sixnight, but the peace negotiations took more than a month, even though my father says everyone knew how they would come out. We've been fine ever since, so *we* don't want a war, but sooner or later one of our neighbors is going to need money and decide we're a good place to get it." He crossed to the left-hand window in the north wall and pointed. "That's Northangle over there..."

Then he stopped. He blinked, and stared.

"Debren, come here," he said.

Debren had been gazing wistfully toward his family farm, but he hurried to the prince's side and peered into the distance. Darissa heard him suck in his breath.

"What is it?" she asked.

"I'll raise the alarm," Debren said. He dashed to one corner, tugged at a rope Darissa had not previously noticed, then ran for the stairs.

"*What is it?*" Darissa cried.

"An army," Marek said, pointing. "There. On the border with Eknera—there are men with banners marching." He swallowed.

"We're at war."

CHAPTER SEVEN

MORVASH OF THE SHADOWS

24TH OF GREENGROWTH, YS 5238

Once past the iron-bound front door, the house's interior appeared alarmingly cluttered. Making room for the thirty-two statues might be a challenge, Morvash thought.

Or perhaps he could bring them one at a time, and transform them individually. That would be slower and undoubtedly more expensive, but it might be safer.

Whatever had happened to Erdrik the Grim had clearly not involved packing up and moving all his belonging elsewhere; from the entryway Morvash could see books, papers, and paraphernalia on all sides, as well as carvings and small statues in numbers that Morvash would have found surprising if he had not already become acquainted with Lord Landessin's collection.

Erdrik also seemed to have been inordinately fond of chairs and tables, at least some of which were animated—half a dozen came trotting into the foyer to greet Morvash and his guide. Alir shooed them away, and led Morvash into the parlor, where another half-dozen chairs were milling about.

A fire leapt up on the hearth as they entered the room. The flames smelled incongruously of cinnamon; in fact, the entire house had a faint odor of spices.

By this point it was very clear to Morvash why the Guild would not sell the house to anyone but a wizard. He was a little surprised the entire thing hadn't been destroyed, or at least gutted.

Behind the parlor was a dim dining room, lit by a single small window; polished brass and oiled wood gleamed dully, but at least it was not crowded. A big table occupied the center of the room, beneath a brass chandelier, but there were no chairs; Morvash supposed they had wandered off to join the herd in the parlor and entryway. A sideboard held a few modest platters and a brass bowl, but nothing more. The walls were a dark wood Morvash could not identify.

Beyond the dining room was a sloping stone passageway down to a huge stone-and-brick kitchen that Morvash was not sure was in normal space; it did not seem to match any part of what he had seen of the house's exterior. Two kettles, one copper and one some sort of glazed ceramic, waddled back and forth across the black iron stove-top, while something rattled inside one of the drawers, and a mustard pot with painted-on eyes peered over the top of a cabinet. Several objects elsewhere on the very full shelves were moving about, as well.

"I take it Erdrik specialized in animation spells," Morvash said.

"I wouldn't know," Alir answered.

"It seems obvious."

"Well, he certainly did a lot of them, I agree," she said, "but remember, he lived here for two hundred years. You can accumulate a lot of things in that much time."

Morvash nodded, but he was not really paying attention; he was looking around the kitchen. There were no windows, and no lit candles or lamps were visible, but it was well-lighted anyway; that seemed a very useful trick, and Morvash wondered whether he might learn the spell that made it possible.

He turned, and noticed a door beside the passage connecting the kitchen to the dining room. He opened it, expecting a pantry, and instead found a short, narrow stair leading down into darkness. He conjured a fingertip flame and walked down, to find himself in the cellars beneath the main part of the house. He took a quick look, but saw nothing of any interest. Stone walls, a floor that appeared to be carved from the bedrock on which the city stood, beams close enough above him that he could not stand up straight, a dozen thick stone pillars—a very ordinary empty cellar, remarkable only in its lack of dust. Half a dozen large barrels, suitable for beer, wine, or water, lay on oaken frames along one wall, but the sound and feel when he rapped the wooden sides made him think they were all empty. He could sense no particular magic here, certainly less than he had felt on the floor above.

There was plenty of open space if he wanted to try some of his experiments down here, but some of the statues would not fit down the narrow stairs or under the low ceiling, and the lack of any natural light was not encouraging. He returned to the well-lit and welcoming kitchen and stood for a moment, taking another look around.

The ceramic kettle on the stove butted the copper one with a clang, distracting him, and triggering a new line of thought. This house was *full* of animated objects; would that hinder attempts to restore petrified people to life? Or might it actually help, having all that magical energy around?

"What happened to Erdrik's book of spells?" he asked.

"I have no idea," the agent replied. "It isn't included with the house, if that's what you were thinking."

"All these animated nicknacks—why weren't they sold off?"

"I believe the more obedient ones *were* sold off," Alir said. "The ones that are still here wouldn't take orders from anyone, or were otherwise uncooperative. Maybe they'd listen to Erdrik, but they mostly ignored everyone else. And some of the furniture that isn't obviously animated was left here just in case it had some other sort of spell on it." She waved at some of the cluttered shelves. "There were protective spells on some of this that nobody thought were worth removing, since it all looks like ordinary kitchen supplies—though they did try to clear out anything obviously dangerous." She grimaced. "And the cleaning out work was interrupted by events elsewhere. They might have removed more, but once they stopped getting started again was difficult, and no one ever got around to finishing the job."

That made sense. It also meant that the animated things might be a nuisance—but he wasn't planning to *live* here, at least not permanently. He would just try out his experiments in magic, and if he had to he could set up wards to keep the various magical trinkets out of the way while he was working.

Looking around, a thought struck Morvash. A place with this much lingering magic should be overrun with spriggans, but he had not spotted a single one since they entered the house, and even the ones on the street, though obviously interested, had been staying well clear. Perhaps there were wards that actually kept them out, though no one back in Ethshar of the Rocks had known of any spells that would reliably do so.

"Why aren't there any spriggans?" he asked the agent.

"That's a good question," she replied. "If you find out, please tell us."

Morvash considered that. Not having the little pests around would certainly make his experiments safer. The animated furniture might be inconvenient sometimes, but it would be much less of a nuisance than spriggans.

He also realized that everything he had seen so far appeared clean—he could see no dust or cobwebs anywhere, even though the house had stood empty for years.

"Is there some sort of cleaning spell?" he asked. "It hardly appears to have been abandoned for so long.

"I believe there is a sprite of some sort that dusts everything. My understanding is that the Guild was unable to catch it easily, and decided they might as well leave it." She cleared her throat. "I mentioned before that the task of cleaning this place out was interrupted. That interruption was the appearance of Empress Tabaea, and once things were back to normal there was enough lingering damage elsewhere to deal with that no one ever got around to coming back here. We really don't know *what* might still be around."

Morvash nodded. He had only been a child at the time, but he remembered how much of a fuss there had been about Tabaea's brief conquest of Ethshar of the Sands even among the ordinary people of his own city. There had even been confused stories that it had some connection to an assassination attempt on Wulran III, the overlord of Ethshar of the Rocks, that happened at about the same time. Morvash could easily imagine it would have disrupted the normal course of business for magicians here. "Let's see the rest of the house," he said.

There were two workrooms on the ground floor—or at least, if they were not both workrooms, Morvash had no idea what the second one was for. There were two large pantries that, going by the remaining labels, had apparently once held magical ingredients, but now held only dozens of empty shelves and drawers. In fact, the entire work area was bare, especially when compared to the crowded front rooms—beyond workbenches and a single three-legged stool, there was no furniture. One workroom's floor was black stone, the other battered wooden planks, and neither had any rugs or carpets. Apparently any clutter that had once been there had been removed, either to the front rooms or elsewhere; the Guild's people must have done this part of the house before Empress Tabaea showed up. As he had seen elsewhere, there was no dust, nor any sign of spriggans.

Returning to the front hall, the grand staircase with its elaborately-carved balustrade led to the second floor, which consisted of a splendid wood-paneled gallery overlooking the street, a large sitting room, a vast bedchamber, and some much smaller bedrooms and closets; a smaller stair led to the third story, where Morvash found four more bedrooms, another workroom, and a storeroom half-full of crates and barrels. There was no visibly animated furniture on either of these upper levels, nor was there any of the other clutter that filled the front rooms downstairs; closets and drawers and shelves and cabinets were largely empty, save for some clothing in a wardrobe, and a single large chest that held towels and bedclothes, both in the master bedchamber. From the robes in the wardrobe it appeared Erdrik had been tall and thin and fond of dark fabrics.

An even smaller stair, a spiral this time, led from the third story up into a tower that gave a fine view of the courtyard behind the house from one side, and a view down the street from the other, as well as a good look at the half-dozen splendid little gargoyles scattered around the rooftop. A set of shelves held several devices Morvash did not recognize, and neither the table nor the two armchairs on this uppermost level appeared to be animated.

Morvash did not actually see any of the gargoyles move, but as he started back down the spiral stairs he thought one of them was in a slightly different position than when he came up.

There was plenty of space for statuary in the house, really; the upper stories were nowhere near as crowded as the ground level. The gallery on the second floor was particularly promising.

"All right," Morvash said to the waiting agent as he descended from the tower, "this will suit me well. What are the terms for allowing me to use it?"

"A round of silver a month, and reports on anything you learn about the things Erdrik left here. You are not to keep any secrets about anything you learn in your research into petrifaction, either."

That was not quite as generous as Morvash had hoped, but it was not at all unreasonable. "A round?" he asked, just in case it proved negotiable.

"Yes. Ithinia was very clear."

Morvash sighed. That did not sound negotiable. "Done," he said. "When can I begin my work?"

"Immediately, as soon as you sign this agreement in your own blood."

"Blood?"

"It must be binding by more than mere law."

"It's a geas?"

She nodded.

"Let me see it."

She handed over the document, and Morvash read it carefully.

Whoever had written it had understood how magical compulsions worked, and had tried to be reasonable, qualifying most of the demands with phrases like "when circumstances permit," "without undue hardship," and "to the best of his ability," since a geas that made impossible demands could have very nasty, even fatal, effects. The most inflexible terms had nothing to do with paying the rent or maintaining the property—in fact, that monthly silver round seemed like more of a suggestion than a requirement—but concerned keeping Guild secrets, informing the Guild through the local Guildmasters of any significant discoveries he made, and preventing ("to the best of his ability") magical mishaps. He was to report anything he learned about what had befallen Erdrik the Grim—in fact, that was given a fairly high priority. Obviously, despite their alleged certainty that he would not return, the Guild had no idea what had become of him.

He could sense the magic that had gone into preparing the agreement; this was no ordinary rental contract.

"I'd rather use ink," he said, when he had gone through the entire document.

"Ithinia wants blood."

Morvash sighed again, and pulled the silver dagger from his belt. He used the point of the blade to prick his finger, and scrawled the six runes of his name in blood at the bottom of the last page. It was not particularly neat or legible, but it was close enough to his usual signature to be magically binding.

Alir took the contract with a satisfied smile. "It's all yours," she said as she rolled it up.

"Thank you," Morvash replied.

She tucked the contract under one arm, and then handed him a ring of keys. "This is all the keys that were found here. *This* one," she said, indicating the large, ornate piece of black iron she had used to let them into the house, "fits the front door, and has been enchanted to deactivate all the external wards the Guild could find. All the others you use at your own risk."

"Does anyone know just how much risk there really is?"

"No. The Guild removed or deactivated or destroyed everything they could that they *knew* was dangerous, but no one knows how much they missed, and there were some spells they couldn't understand or defeat. So be careful."

Morvash sighed, already regretting that he had signed the lease in blood. "All right," he said.

"I'll be going, then. Good luck!" She turned before Morvash could reply, and headed down the stairs to the second floor. She seemed to be in a hurry, and he belatedly realized that she was uncomfortable and eager to be out of the house, despite whatever protective spells she bore.

CHAPTER EIGHT

HAKIN OF THE HUNDRED-FOOT FIELD

8TH OF LONGDAYS, YS 5231

Hakin was awakened from his nap by someone's scream, followed by a man's voice shouting. That was not particularly unusual in the Hundred-Foot Field, but he rolled over, away from where he had been nestled at the foot of the city wall, and pushed aside one corner of his crude tent to see what was happening.

All he saw was the near wall of Green Abia's hut, and a few feet of dried mud, but the shouting was louder now, as other voices joined the first, and there were more screams, as well. Hakin got to his knees and leaned out to peer around the corner of Abia's shack just as half a dozen people came running past, obviously fleeing from something.

That was a bit worrisome. Was the city guard clearing the field for some reason? That hadn't happened in Hakin's lifetime, but there were stories about it, and it would explain the shouting and fleeing. The screaming did not seem to fit, though. Hakin snatched up his pack and got to his feet as several more people ran past, all of them heading east, in the direction of Southgate; if he had to make a hurried departure, he did not want to leave any of his meager belongings behind. Then he moved along the wall of Abia's hut and looked around the next corner to see what was happening.

Ordinarily, this stretch of the Hundred-Foot Field was thickly inhabited, with a few narrow paths winding around dozens of makeshift shelters and campfires. Now, though, most of the fires and tents and shacks had been trampled flat, and the normal crowd of ragged inhabitants had vanished; only a single figure was marching across the packed earth toward Hakin. He stared.

Although it walked upright, that figure was clearly not human.

Just what it was Hakin was not entirely certain, though he could make a guess. It stood easily seven feet tall, with glossy black skin and huge pointed ears, and it had four arms, rather than the customary two. Hakin could see no sign of hair anywhere, but it did have fangs and horns.

Hakin thought he would give five to one odds that this thing was a demon.

But other than scaring away the regular inhabitants, what was a demon doing in the Hundred-Foot Field?

Obviously, none of Hakin's neighbors had thought it was safe to ask. Demons, after all, were ridiculously dangerous; ordinarily no one but a trained demonologist would have anything to do with them.

But ordinarily they didn't come marching through the Hundred-Foot Field, and while the creature's features weren't fully human, Hakin thought it looked confused, as well as angry. It was slowing down, looking around at the field, as if it was searching for something.

It wasn't just on an uncontrolled rampage, then. It might, Hakin thought, be running an errand for a demonologist. In fact, it almost *had* to be there at a demonologist's command—everyone said that demons couldn't enter the World unless summoned.

Maybe it could use some help—and maybe if it got some, not only would it stop terrorizing the field, but a demonologist somewhere might owe Hakin a favor, and it never hurt to have a magician in one's debt. "*Hai!*" he called, stepping out from behind Abia's hut. "What do you want here?"

The demon stopped and looked at Hakin, and when he saw the fury in those slanting yellow eyes the boy wished he hadn't spoken up. He was hesitating, debating whether to turn and run, when the demon said, in a rough and inhumanly deep voice, "I seek Karitha the Demonologist."

Hakin considered that for a moment, then said, "I...I don't believe I know her." His voice only shook a little.

The demon growled wordlessly, a sound like slow thunder. It took a step toward Hakin.

"I might be able to help you find her, though," Hakin hastily added, resisting the urge to step back. There was no need to let the demon see how frightened he was, and he was fairly certain that the demon could catch him if he ran, especially with the city wall to the south, preventing him from going more than a few feet in that direction.

"How?" the demon demanded.

"Well, I know my way around the city," Hakin said. "I make my living running errands for hire, and that often involves finding people. Tell me who this Karitha is, and why you're looking for her."

"She is Karitha the Demonologist. She summoned me and set me a task, and I have completed it; now she must set me another, or dismiss me, or if she will do neither, I will kill her—but first I must *find* her."

"Yes, I can see how that would be necessary. Yes. Um."

"If you cannot assist me, then go away. If you hinder me, I will kill *you*."

"I have every intention of assisting you!" Hakin protested. "But I don't know enough yet. I don't know this Karitha, but if you give me time I might be able to find her for you. Tell me more about her; where does she live?"

"She dwelt on Magician Street, on the northeast side, in the fourth shop south of Warlock Street. But *she is not there* now!"

Hakin cringed as the monster bellowed this final angry sentence. The demon glared at him, then raised a clawed hand.

"Wait!" Hakin said, holding up his own much smaller and less-intimidating hand. "So you came here looking for her?"

"Yes."

"Why here?"

"People hide here."

"People hide lots of places."

The demon did not bother to answer that. It took a step forward, bringing it close enough for Hakin to see faint wisps of steam rising from its back. A burning metallic smell reached him that he guessed was the demon's own odor.

"Wait, wait!" Hakin said, both hands held up before his chest. This time he could not prevent himself from taking a step back. "You said she set you a task—what was it?"

"She sent me to slay Wosten of the Red Robe."

"Ah," Hakin said. "And did you?"

"Of course! I could not return to Karitha until Wosten was dead.

See, his blood is still on my claws." It held up a handful of talons stained reddish-brown.

Hakin did not manage to completely suppress a shudder. "How did you find Wosten? How could you be sure you killed the right man?"

"I had his scent," the demon replied. "There was no mistake. I slew Wosten of the Red Robe."

"So you hunt by smell? But you can't smell Karitha?"

"Yes. Her scent leads nowhere. She is not dead—I have consulted the masters of the afterlife, and they have not received her soul—and yet I cannot smell her. Her odor lingers in her home and in the streets of the Wizards' Quarter, but it is hours or days old; there is no fresh trace."

"So ordinarily, you can smell anyone? How close do you need to be?"

"I can track a human scent across all the World!"

Hakin cocked his head slightly. He was not sure just how the sense of smell worked, but he knew that nothing natural could smell a person from a hundred leagues away. Demons weren't exactly natural, and this one obviously wasn't talking about "human scent" in the same way an ordinary person would use the term. Assuming it wasn't exaggerating, it probably wasn't using scent in the usual sense at all, but some sort of demonic magic that served roughly the same function.

"You don't know of anything that could hide a person's scent?"

"No!"

"Then it must be magic."

The demon's eyes narrowed. "What kind of magic?"

"I don't know," Hakin said. "Not yet. But perhaps we can find out."

"We?"

"Well, yes. Unless you think you can figure it out without me."

The demon considered that, and the glare of those yellow eyes seemed to dim slightly. It lowered its claws. "I am unfamiliar with any magic but my own," it said.

Hakin displayed an empty palm. "I'm no magician, either, but I can ask questions."

The demon stared at him. "Why?" it asked.

"Why what?" Hakin replied.

"Why would you help me? I am a demon. By Ethsharitic standards I am a monster, a killer, a creature of evil. Why would you help me?"

"First off, so you won't kill *me*," Hakin said, stating the obvious. He tried to think quickly about everything he had ever heard about demons, in hopes of understanding a little of how this one thought. He intended to stick to the truth, since some magical creatures could tell a lie when they heard one, but that still allowed for some variation in how he slanted it. "Second, so you won't kill anyone else who might happen to get in your way while you go smashing about looking for this Karitha. But third, maybe I can get something for myself out of this. Karitha might think it's worth a few bits to have her demon returned to her."

"Ah," the demon said. It nodded once. "Greed. Good. I understand greed. Where do we start?"

"The Wizards' Quarter seems like the obvious place," Hakin said. "We can talk to Karitha's neighbors—or did you already try that?"

"I did not. You are the first human I have conversed with since I tore out Wosten's throat."

Ignoring the unwanted image of Wosten's death, Hakin found it slightly surprising that no one else had tried talking to the demon—but only slightly. Most people had probably fled at first sight of it. He wasn't entirely sure why he hadn't fled himself. "The neighbors it is, then. Magician Street, you said?"

"Yes. Near Warlock Street."

"Then we'll head that way." He pointed north, toward the city beyond the Field.

"Good," the demon said, turning.

"Perhaps we should introduce ourselves," Hakin said, as he, too, turned.

"I am Tarker the Unrelenting, a demon of the First Circle, of the original ordering. You are Hakin, called Hakin of the Hundred-Foot Field, son of Nerra the Skinny Whore and Chend the Navigator."

"I...what?" Hakin, who had taken a single step, stumbled. "How did you know that?"

"I have your scent," the demon said, as it walked toward Wall Street.

"You know who my *father* was?" Hakin said, running to catch up.

"Yes. Chend the Navigator." Tarker marched on as it spoke.

"But *I* didn't know that! My mother said *she* didn't know that!"

"I am a demon of the First Circle. I have your scent."

"But that…that…I didn't know demons could do that!"

"We can."

"You…but…" Hakin swallowed, closed his eyes for a second, then opened them again. "Is he alive?"

"Who?"

"Chend the Navigator."

"Yes."

"You're sure?"

"Yes."

"Can you tell me—"

The demon marched on without looking at him. "I am not interested in answering your questions," it said. "This does not concern me."

Hakin could hardly argue with that. He wondered whether there was any way he could *make* it the demon's concern.

He also wondered whether the demon was telling the truth. He knew gods never lied, except by omission, but to the best of his knowledge demons were under no such restraint. It could be that every single word this demon had said to him was false.

Maybe if he knew more about it, he could tell. He had heard that demonologists knew a great deal about the demons they summoned; maybe Karitha, if they ever found her, could tell whether this thing could be trusted.

Right now, though, Karitha was missing—but they were heading toward the Wizards' Quarter, and there were other demonologists who lived and worked there.

He ran up to the demon's side again and said, "You said your name was Tarker?"

"I am Tarker the Unrelenting."

That was not a difficult name to remember. Hakin thought that when he had a chance—perhaps when this was all done, and the demon was gone—he would want to do some research. He had never had any interest in demonology, which seemed to focus on greed and violence, but it suddenly had a certain appeal. He wanted to know more about this Tarker, and about Chend the Navigator.

Assuming, of course, that he lived long enough to do anything. Walking around the city with a demon, harassing magicians, was probably not going to enhance his chances of surviving into adulthood.

Not that he was *walking,* exactly—the demon's stride was much longer than his. Hakin was running hard to keep up with the monster as it stalked up Widow Street, sending pedestrians fleeing in all directions.

As he ran, he wondered what he had gotten himself into. Who was this Karitha, and why couldn't the demon find her? The demon said it could smell her anywhere in the World—did that mean Karitha wasn't in the World? There were stories about gods and wizards being able to travel to other places; had one of them taken Karitha somewhere?

The obvious way to leave the World was to die, but Tarker said Karitha hadn't died. Did the demon really *know* that? Who were the masters of the afterlife it had mentioned? Hakin had never heard about anything like that before. He knew that not all souls went the same place—in fact, some didn't go anywhere, which was where ghosts came from. Did these masters really keep track of *all* of them? What about souls that were captured or devoured? Hakin had heard plenty of stories about *those* when he huddled around the campfires on chilly nights.

Karitha might be dead, and her soul lost or destroyed. Or she might have been transported to another world. Or she might still be alive and well, right here in Ethshar, but hidden somehow. Tarker said it could track a human scent anywhere in the World, but what if Karitha wasn't human anymore? What if she had been turned into, say, a toad, or a rat?

That was something he should ask Tarker about, when he could catch his breath and get within earshot. The demon was half a block ahead of him, and Hakin was starting to have trouble keeping his legs moving.

They were past South Street, though, which meant they were more than halfway through Southwark, more than halfway from Wall Street to the Wizards' Quarter.

What if Karitha had become a warlock? Hakin had heard someone say once that the gods couldn't see warlocks; maybe demons couldn't *smell* warlocks. Gods and demons were related somehow, weren't they? Could demons perceive warlocks? That was another question for Hakin to ask.

Or maybe he shouldn't ask *any* questions. Maybe he should just turn around and go back to the Hundred-Foot Field, where he belonged. Tarker didn't seem to be very concerned about his inability to keep pace.

But he had said he would help, and he really, really didn't want to make a demon angry. It wasn't as if he could hide; the demon had his scent.

He took a deep breath and kept running.

CHAPTER NINE

DARISSA THE WITCH'S APPRENTICE

15TH OF HARVEST, YS 5199

Darissa followed the prince down the stairs; her own much shorter legs could not match his stride, so she gathered her magic and lifted herself off the stone steps, floating down a few feet behind him and a few inches in the air. Levitating upward was exhausting, but gliding *down* was not hard at all.

By the time they were halfway down she could hear pounding feet and shouting voices below them. Elzen, the guard they had passed on the way up, was nowhere to be seen.

At the bottom of the stair half a dozen soldiers had formed into two lines facing another man, presumably an officer from his somewhat fancier uniform. "Captain Korl!" Marek called. "Have you seen either of my brothers?"

The officer turned, recognized Marek, and saluted. "No, your Highness. I've been collecting the household guard." He turned to his men. "Has anyone seen Prince Terren or Prince Evreth today?"

"I thought Prince Evreth was on a mission to Shulara, Captain," one of the men in the back row said.

"He is? I hadn't heard that," Marek said.

"It…might have been confidential, your Highness."

"Ordinarily I would ask why *you* know about it, Molvir, but right now I think we have more urgent concerns," Marek replied. "No one's seen Terren?"

No one spoke up, so Marek saluted Captain Korl, told him to carry on, and hurried onward, Darissa at his heel.

"Prince Marek," she called as they rushed down a corridor. "Your Highness!"

He stopped dead, and turned to look at her. "*You* don't need to call me that," he said.

Baffled, she said, "But *everybody* calls you that!"

"You aren't everybody; you're Darissa, and please, call me Marek. At least, in private."

"I...all right."

"Now, what is it?"

"Should I go home? It seems to me I can only be in the way here."

He looked around thoughtfully, then nodded. "You're right," he said. "You should go. We can't have magicians involved in a war, and you'll probably be safer if you're somewhere else."

She could feel honest regret in his thoughts. "I'm not worried about my safety," she said. "I just don't want to be underfoot."

"Well, whatever your reasons, I am sorry to say that yes, you should leave. I can send a soldier to escort you..."

"Oh, please, that's not necessary. I can find my own way. Your soldiers all have responsibilities right now, I'm sure—as *you* do."

"Of course." He hesitated, started to reach for her, then drew back. "Go. Take care of yourself, and be safe. Tell anyone who you speak to that we are at war with Eknera, and quite possibly with other neighboring realms, as well. We'll need to see..." He broke off in mid-sentence, frowning. "Go," he told her. Then he turned and called to a passing soldier, "Saldan! Has anyone taken Debren's place on tower watch? Are there sentries posted yet?"

Darissa took a second to look at him, at his strong features and fine shoulders, then turned and, guided by her witchcraft, headed for the exit into the courtyard.

The yard was full of running, shouting people; the children who had been playing earlier were nowhere to be seen. Darissa did not try to make sense of it, but continued on through the tunnel and over the bridge across the moat. The doors were still open, and no one tried to interfere as she walked through them. The guards in the passage who had been so casual before, and so deferential to Prince Marek, were now alert and on edge, staring out across the market, eyeing everyone suspiciously. They watched her pass, but said nothing; people coming *out* of the castle were not their problem.

The guards at the top of the stair, though, did stop her. "State your business," one of them said, as he blocked her path with his spear.

"I'm going home," she said. "I'd just be in the way up here."

"Who are you?"

"I'm Darissa the Witch's Apprentice."

"She came in with Prince Marek," said another guard—Arra, Marek had called him when they arrived, perhaps an hour before.

"Does His Highness know you're leaving?"

"He does," Darissa said. "He's busy with preparations for war, and sent me home."

"She could be a spy," one of the other soldiers suggested.

"If the Eknerans sent any spies," Darissa said, "wouldn't they either want them to report back before their army started marching, in which case I'd have left long ago, or to stay and find a way to get news to them from inside the walls? This would be a stupid time for a spy to leave."

The guards considered that, but one of them said, "You might have sent messages before the army marched, but stayed on until the war began in case you found more to report, and you're leaving now so you won't be stuck inside during a siege."

Darissa started to reply, then stopped as she realized that scenario made sense. "That's a good point," she said. "I hadn't thought of that. But I'm *not* a spy—I'm a Melithan, born and raised. I don't speak a word of Ekneran. What can I do to prove it?"

"She *wasn't* in the castle until today," Arra said. "At least, I never saw her before today. And she did come in with Prince Marek."

"All right," said the soldier who seemed to be in charge. "Where do you live?"

"Down there, just outside town," she pointed. "My master is Nondel the Witch."

"Fine," the commander said. "We'll let her go, but Pergren, escort her home and talk to this Nondel, see if he seems honest. Then get back here."

Pergren nodded, and trotted down the steps at Darissa's heels. She did not want to keep him from his post, so she did not tarry in the market or stroll the streets looking for anyone who might need her help; instead she marched straight home, where Nondel confirmed her identity. Pergren covered the essentials in a few minutes, then turned and hurried back up the slope to the castle.

"What's going on?" Nondel asked, the instant the soldier was out of earshot.

"We're at war," Darissa explained. "There's an army marching this way from Eknera. Marek was showing me the view from the big tower, and we saw them crossing the border."

Nondel's expression, already serious, turned grim. "War?"

Darissa nodded.

"You aren't old enough to remember the last one, are you?"

"I was born six months after the peace was signed."

"Then you don't know what it's like."

"Not first-hand, no, but I've talked to plenty of people who remember it."

Nondel shook his head. "Hearing about it is not like living through it." He sighed. "We'll need to stay out of sight as much as we can, but be ready to heal the wounded."

"Why do we need to stay out of sight?" Darissa asked, puzzled. "I would have thought we should be out where wounded people can find us."

"No," Nondel said. "Using magic to fight a war is absolutely forbidden—it's the *one* thing all the Small Kingdoms have agreed on, even Klathoa. If we're seen anywhere near the fighting, people will think we're helping our soldiers, and we'll be hanged by whichever side catches us first."

There was a moment of stunned silence. "I knew magic was forbidden, but I didn't realize it was like *that*," Darissa said, ducking back into the house.

"Oh, yes. Everywhere in the Small Kingdoms," Nondel said, following her inside. "Of course, the Hegemony of the Three Ethshars uses magic when they fight, but that's different—they're the heirs to the old military, and the Great War was fought with magic on both sides, and besides, who is going to argue with them? They rule more than half the World. I've also heard that the pirates of Shan on the Sea use magic, but they're pirates, whatever they may claim. Around here, from Fileia to Skaia, military magic is strictly outlawed, and any witch seen anywhere near the fighting will be killed, just to be sure. Even in Klathoa, the witches don't fight."

"That's…" Darissa had originally intended to say "ridiculous," but then she reconsidered. "That's terrifying," she said.

Nondel nodded. "The one good thing," he said, "is that this war probably won't last long. There aren't any natural defenses on this plain. We'll have a network of alliances, the armies will face off, and either it will be clear who has the advantage and the other side will sue for peace, or if it isn't obvious there will be a battle to determine who has the advantage, and the loser will surrender."

"Really? It's that simple?"

"It's not...that isn't simple," Nondel said. "That part about the network of alliances is important. Melitha undoubtedly has treaties with all its neighbors, but so does Eknera—you *did* say it was Eknera that's invading, didn't you?"

"Yes."

"Well, both sides have treaties and alliances, both open and secret, and now we'll see which government will honor which treaties. Eknera and Melitha are at war, yes, but Kanthoa and Trafoa border on both of us, and each now has three choices—no, five. They can join in the attack, join in the defense, remain neutral, or support one side or the other with money and supplies but not actually fight. Or really, they could attack *both* sides, if they think that's more promising. And meanwhile our other neighbors, Elankora and Ressamor and Tal and Bhella and Hollendon, could join in on either side, either invading Melitha themselves or providing us with troops and supplies, and Eknera's other neighbors, Yolder and Mezgalon and...I think it's Valamon, could join in. And that could spread—there have been wars that dragged in dozens of countries. If the mountainous areas get involved, or even just forested ones, it could turn ugly for them, because fighters can *hide* in that terrain, and set up ambushes and barricades and so on. Mountain wars can drag on for years."

"But...how do we know..."

"We don't, not until all the armies show up and we see who's facing off and who's cooperating. There could be a few sixnights of maneuvering before the alliances are all in place. And even then, someone might switch sides—though that's dangerous, as after the war no one will trust a ruler who did that."

"Oh." Darissa looked up at the castle.

"When did the Eknerans cross the border?" Nondel asked.

Darissa took a moment to locate the sun and estimate. "Maybe an hour ago?"

"And the Melithans haven't yet marched out to meet them? That's bad. They're probably at least a mile into our territory by now, and it's always better to fight on the *other* side's lands, because wherever the armies are, crops and houses get burned or trampled."

Before Darissa could reply they heard distant shouting from the direction of the castle.

"That's probably our soldiers getting ready," Nondel said.

"This is ridiculous!" Darissa said. "All those people are going out there to fight, and some of them will be killed, for *what*? Marek said it's all just about who collects which taxes—is that true?"

"I suppose that's most of it," Nondel said, "but for the ordinary soldiers there's a chance to do some looting, and some fighting, and maybe come home a hero. And for the kings and princes, it's partly a matter of family pride. Eknera was on the losing side in the last war; I suppose the current king wants revenge." He frowned. "Who *is* the current king there?"

"I have no idea," Darissa said. "Is it the same one Melitha defeated eighteen years ago?"

"I don't know. That was King Manrin, and he was getting old and eccentric last I heard. Perhaps he's become delusional, and thinks he's fighting monsters. Or if they've changed kings lately, the new one may want to prove himself in battle—that's something some kings do, to show they're strong leaders."

"I know Trafoa has three princes ruling jointly," Darissa said. "I don't know about Eknera."

"That's right about Trafoa; I'd forgotten."

"It's three brothers. Their father didn't die, he disappeared, and he hadn't named an heir, and nobody really wanted the oldest to be the new king, including himself, so they set up a royal council. I had it explained to me when I visited there with…with my father six years ago." The final phrase caught in her throat, as she remembered how her father had died a few months later.

"I heard about it when they first set it up, in…5190, was it?"

"After the last war, so we don't know which side *they'll* take."

"*Someone* probably knows—King Terren isn't an idiot, he'll have sent envoys and spies, so he probably has a pretty good idea. But *I* certainly don't know."

"How bad is this going to be?" Darissa asked. "There are old stories about sieges, and towns being burned, and massacres…"

Nondel shook his head. "I don't expect it will be *that* bad; as I just said, King Terren isn't an idiot, and I don't think any of our neighbors are *that* angry with him. It should all be settled in a month or so. I hope." He shivered, even though the afternoon air was warm. "Let's go inside."

"Yes, master," Darissa said, and followed him inside.

CHAPTER TEN

MORVASH OF THE SHADOWS

24TH OF GREENGROWTH, YS 5238

Morvash did not rush back downstairs when the agent left, but continued exploring, rapping on the barrels in the storeroom as he had in the basement, checking drawers for false bottoms or hidden compartments, and otherwise acquainting himself with his surroundings. He started planning where to put his thirty-odd statues, and using his arms to measure which doorways might cause problems in moving the statuary around.

The gallery would be the obvious place for most of the statues—maybe all of them. It was almost certainly big enough, if he counted the large alcove at the north end, and it had open access to the grand staircase, so anything that could get through the front door and could be hauled up the steps would be easy to install there. Anything that did not fit through the front door might be brought in through the big gallery windows, if he could get it up high enough off the street. If he had misjudged and could not fit all thirty-two statues across the front of the house, the last few could go in the passage beside the staircase. He could transform the sitting room into the workshop for his experiments, to avoid carrying anything magical between levels. It should all work out.

When he returned to the ground floor he was mobbed by chairs; at least half a dozen came bumping up against him, apparently wanting to be sat upon. He would need to restrain them somehow when bringing in statues, he thought. It was a good thing that they seemed to be unable to climb stairs, or to fly.

He pushed through the clustered furniture and slipped out the front door, careful not to let any of the chairs out onto the street; then he locked the house with the big key, tugging and pushing to make sure the latch was secure.

He had his new workshop—and more than that, really; except for the annoying chairs, he liked this place, and looked forward to spending time in it. For one thing, though the agent had assured him that the Guild had removed everything really dangerous that they could find, and the spell ingredients had indeed been stripped out of the workrooms, what were all the papers and books and devices and statuary in the front hall and parlor? He intended to take a good look through those. There might be some very interesting items.

And the statues—were any of those additional people in need of rescue from petrifaction? He didn't remember any life-sized ones.

He walked slowly back toward his uncle's house, lost in thought as he made plans. He would need to obtain a great many ingredients, he was sure, and either buy or trade for several spells; this project might prove very expensive indeed. His family would not like that. It would be very useful if one of the statues turned out to be someone rich and grateful.

A couple of spriggans followed him for a block or two, but he paid no attention, and they quickly got bored and vanished.

He reached the dragon gates of the late Lord Landessin's mansion and walked in. He was not quite at the steps when the front door swung open, a footman stepped aside, and Uncle Gror appeared.

"*There* you are!" he said. "How did it go?"

"I've rented the house," Morvash replied. He gestured. "It's over that way, just a few blocks away, on Old East Avenue."

"Old East..." Gror frowned. "What does it look like?"

"It's black stone, with a tower and gargoyles."

"*That* place? Seriously?"

Startled, Morvash said, "What place?"

"The old wizard's place? It's supposed to be haunted by ghosts he trapped."

Morvash blinked. "I don't think it's haunted," he said, even as he realized he might not have noticed if it was. It *might* be; the Ethereal Entrapment was a real spell, fourth or fifth order, that could confine ghosts to a small area, and Erdrik could easily have known it. Whether it would still be effective eleven years after Erdrik's disappearance was another question entirely, and it was more likely that any alleged haunting was a misinterpretation of all that ridiculous animated furniture bumping about.

"But it *is* the one? The one built by a hermit wizard who hasn't been seen outside in years?"

That did sound like Erdrik.

"He hasn't been seen in years because he vanished eleven years ago," Morvash said. "One of his spells may have gone wrong, or maybe he just left, but he's not there."

Gror frowned. "But then who did you rent it from?"

"The Wizards' Guild. After he disappeared they claimed it and paid all the taxes, so as far as the overlord is concerned, the Guild owns it."

"And you rented it from them."

"You didn't want me working here!" Morvash burst out.

"I didn't want you *experimenting* here," Gror corrected him. "I was worried about my safety. But Morvash, if you're renting that monstrosity, I'm worried about *your* safety. What if that hermit comes back? He had a pretty nasty reputation."

"The Guild says he's not coming back."

"How do they know?"

"Oh, really, Uncle," Morvash said, stepping up toward the door, wishing he was as certain as he sounded. "Magic, of course."

"Of course." Gror sighed and moved aside to let Morvash into the house. "So what happens now?"

"Now I move all the enchanted victims over to the other house," Morvash said, "and start trying to learn spells that might bring them back to life."

"Did the hermit leave any of his magic behind?" Gror said, as he followed his nephew inside.

"He left some magical things, but nothing useful, so far as I can see. His name was Erdrik, by the way."

"Was it? If you say so." The footman closed the door behind them.

"I'll need a lot of supplies," Morvash said, looking up the stairs. "And all those statues—not the carved ones, just the ones that used to be people."

"So you'll be trying out your spells on them, until you get it right?"

"No—at least, I hope not. I plan to learn the spells I need first; I don't want to risk killing any of those poor people when I'm trying to save them."

"How are you going to test them, then?"

"I don't know," Morvash admitted. "I haven't gotten that far yet. I'll find a way."

"Maybe you could buy a slave to test spells on."

That idea had a certain cold-blooded logic to it, but Morvash shook his head. "I'm not going to buy a slave," he said. "It wouldn't be… I'm not going to."

"Why not?"

"Slaves are people, too, you know."

"But they're people who don't have anything left to lose," Gror persisted.

Morvash closed his eyes, then opened them again. "Look, Uncle, I'll find a way to test my spells, but that's still a long way off. At this point I don't even know what spells I'll need, let alone how any of them work, or how difficult they are, or how dangerous. I may be able to test them on stray dogs. Right now, though, what I need is a way to get all my stuff to Erdrik's house."

"Morvash, my boy, I'm a merchant; moving things is what we *do*. I'll get your things over there. You just sort out what you need and have it ready to go."

"Thank you, Uncle! But there's…some of this…" His voice trailed off.

"What is it, Morvash?"

"This is going to be expensive, Uncle. I'm paying the Guild's rent in silver, and I'll need to acquire exotic ingredients, as well as all the normal living expenses. It's going to take all my money; I can't spare anything for you."

"Morvash, you're family. You're my sister's son. And you're a wizard. I know you won't use your magic to kill anyone, or make us magical weapons we can sell, I heard all about what happened in Tintallion and your Guild rules, but you can do *some* magic for us, can't you?"

"Of course!"

"Protective spells? Or some showy little spells just to show people we have a wizard on the payroll?"

"I can do that, yes…"

"Then we'll be fine! You'll earn your keep, and enough to pay all your expenses. Eventually."

Morvash did not like the sound of that last word—and not just because of the word's meaning, but because Gror's voice acquired a bit of a hard edge as he said it.

"I'll try," he said.

"You'll be fine," Gror said, slapping his nephew on the back. "You'll do just fine, you'll see." He turned away. "I'll go see about rounding us up some reliable transportation for all the statuary."

Morvash stood in the front hall and watched him go.

"I'll be fine," he said to no one. "Eventually."

CHAPTER ELEVEN

HAKIN OF THE HUNDRED-FOOT FIELD

8TH OF LONGDAYS, YS 5231

"This is her home?" Hakin asked, looking at the shop on Magician Street. The sign did indeed say KARITHA, SUMMONER OF DEMONS. The windows were hung with black curtains and held no displays.

The curtains were closed, and the door was locked.

"This is where she dwelt," Tarker confirmed. "Her scent is everywhere here. She summoned me to this place from a room at the back. But she has not been here for hours."

Hakin glanced around at the dozens of people and spriggans on the street. Most of them were watching Tarker—to say they were staring at the demon would not be an exaggeration—but they were all staying well away. In fact, the spriggans seemed to vanish completely if Tarker looked in their direction; there were fewer of them every time Hakin looked.

Hakin suspected that in other parts of the city a demon's presence would attract much louder, more excited attention, but this was the Wizards' Quarter, where magic was relatively commonplace. These people were giving the demon a wide berth, but not screaming or panicking or calling for guards.

He turned back to the closed door of the shop. "You're sure of that?" he asked. "Could she be hiding somewhere inside, with magic masking her scent?"

Tarker growled. "She is not here."

"Well, we should look inside, just to be sure, and to see whether there are any clues to where she went."

"I went inside when I first sought her, after killing Wosten of the

Red Robe."

Hakin frowned, and tried the door again. "But it's locked. Was it locked before?"

"Yes."

"Then how did you get in to look for her? You didn't break the lock; can you walk through walls?"

"There is another door."

"Oh? Show me."

Hakin was completely unprepared for what happened next. The demon's upper left claw flashed out and grabbed the front of his tunic, twisting it until Hakin thought the worn fabric might tear; then the monster picked him up by his garment and sprang upward.

Hakin was too startled to see just how Tarker managed it, but somehow the demon found places it could set its feet and its free hands, and climbed the front of the building as easily as Hakin might climb a front stoop. In a couple of seconds it had carried Hakin from the street to the rooftop, where in half a dozen strides it bounded from the front of the house to the back. Then it leapt over the edge, and landed with a loud thump on a balcony.

"Here," the demon said, releasing its hold.

Hakin staggered slightly as he got his feet under him, then looked around.

They were on the second floor, overlooking the courtyard behind the house where several small gardens, marked off by a variety of low fences, were scattered around the neighborhood's shared well. Clotheslines were strung higgledy-piggledy from porches and poles, and laundry hung from most of them. A few charcoal stoves were smoking here and there, adding to the cacophony of odors.

Given where they were, most of the houses surrounding the courtyard presumably belonged to magicians, but it did not look or smell noticeably different from any other neighborhood's back court that Hakin had seen in his travels around the city—not that he had seen many. He had lived in the Hundred-Foot Field almost as long as he could remember, never in an ordinary house; he had only seen such courtyards when he had been hired for an errand that took him to one.

Still, if there was anything to distinguish this from the others he had glimpsed, it was not obvious.

He turned his attention from the courtyard to Karitha's house.

The balcony was perhaps six feet deep and twenty feet wide, with two windows and a door opening onto it. All were closed, though the shutters were not. Hakin crossed to the door and tried the latch.

It opened easily—and why shouldn't it? They were not on ground level; if he had not had the demon's assistance Hakin would have had a hard time getting to this balcony. What's more, what sort of idiot would try to rob a *demonologist*? Far less dangerous targets abounded, and while demonologists were certainly reputed to handle plenty of gold, most of it supposedly went to pay the demons for their services, and the rest would undoubtedly be well hidden and well guarded. The front door was locked to keep out customers and curiosity-seekers when the shop was not open for business, and the back door was probably locked to keep out unwanted neighbors, but locking the balcony door would not seem necessary.

The youth swung the door open and looked in; he did not cross the threshold immediately, since there might be magic guarding it.

Beyond the door was a workshop of some sort, not the bedroom he would have expected at the rear of an upper story. The floor was bare planking, with no carpet or tiles, and a circle about eight feet in diameter was gouged into the wood in the center of the room; runes and other symbols were everywhere, drawn—rather sloppily, Hakin thought—in charcoal and several colors of paint, or in some cases carved, like the circle, into wood. The whole place smelled of smoke and candle-wax.

"That is where she summoned me," Tarker said over Hakin's shoulder.

The youth nodded. "Are there any traps here? Is it safe to go in?"

"The wards are broken," the demon replied.

Hakin was not *entirely* sure what that meant, but he stepped cautiously through the door, into the workshop.

Tarker followed close behind; its bulk blocked out much of the daylight. Hakin tried not to let that frighten him as he walked across the room to the door on the far side.

The door led to a corridor and a stairwell. "Hello?" Hakin called.

There was no response.

It took no more than a quarter hour to search the house thoroughly, from attic to cellars. Except for the workshop and some interesting storerooms in the cellar, it was very much like any other Ethsharitic shopkeeper's home. The demonologist's closets and pantries were fairly full, which implied that she had not planned a long trip.

Tarker had followed him as he wandered through the house. The demon had said nothing, and had not done any searching of its own; apparently it was certain of Karitha's absence and felt no need to verify anything.

There were no signs of any pets; Hakin had gotten an impression somewhere that most magicians kept a cat or dog around. He considered saying something to Tarker, but when he turned to look at the demon he realized that there were probably good reasons for a demonologist not to have any small animals around. The barking of a startled dog, or the hissing of a cat, might provoke an unfortunate response.

"You're right, she's not here," Hakin said at last, when he had been through the entire house twice. "Let's go talk to the neighbors."

Tarker growled. If it had intended the sound to include any words, Hakin could not make them out. A wisp of smoke rose from its nostrils.

The next question was whether they should leave through the front door, onto the street, or the kitchen door, into the courtyard— Hakin had no intention of leaving by way of the balcony. He considered for a moment, then chose the street.

He did not ask the demon's opinion. If Tarker had anything to say, it would undoubtedly say it without prompting. Hakin led the way through the parlor and out onto Magician Street.

It was well into the afternoon; the sun was nearing the western rooftops and painting window glass with golden fire. The street was neither crowded nor empty. Most people who had business somewhere had arrived there by now, and the rush to get home before dark would not begin for another hour or so, but there were always a few people out and about. Hakin ignored the people gawking at the demon as he chose a nearby shop more or less at random.

The signboard simply said ANDURON, WARLOCK—no fancy titles or extravagant claims, no explanatory images. The door was unlocked and had a bell hanging above it, so Hakin did not bother to knock before walking into the shop.

Tarker had to stoop and pull in its shoulders to fit through the door, but it followed the youth inside.

Anduron, it seemed, was a tall, thin man of middle years; he had been seated by the hearth, reading a book, but he put it aside and rose to his feet immediately when the door first opened.

"Greetings," the warlock said. "I am Anduron the Tall. How can I help you?" His eyes widened at the sight of the demon, and his nose wrinkled slightly, perhaps at Tarker's peculiar scent.

"Actually," Hakin said, "we're looking for a neighbor of yours—her name is Karitha."

"The demonologist?" Anduron's eyes fell to the youth, and he turned up an empty palm. "I haven't seen her lately." He did not sound at all concerned about this. He looked past Hakin at his companion again, and added, "I take it this…entity has business with her?"

Hakin nodded. "It can't go home until she releases it, and it can't find her."

"I'm sorry; I haven't seen her."

"She's missing," Hakin insisted. "Tarker, here, would know if she were anywhere in this area."

"I wish I could help, but I really have no idea where she is."

Hakin got the distinct impression that the warlock did not much *care* where she was, either.

"Did she have any particular friends who might have known what she had planned?" Hakin asked.

"Not that *I* know of."

"Did you know someone named Wosten?" Hakin asked. "Wosten of the Red Robe?"

"The wizard? Certainly. He lives on the corner two streets…" He started to point.

"He is dead," Tarker interrupted, speaking for the first time since they entered the warlock's shop. Its voice seemed to shake the entire room.

Anduron started. "He is?"

"I slew him," Tarker rumbled.

"Ah," Anduron said, looking at the demon and keeping his tone noncommital. "I see."

"Karitha the Demonologist summoned me, and commanded me to kill Wosten of the Red Robe. I tore out his throat. Now I seek Karitha so that she might release me."

"Ah. Yes." The warlock was visibly uneasy now. "Well, I knew she and Wosten didn't get along; I was going to say that if you thought Wosten was her friend then someone had misled you badly."

Hakin concluded that Karitha the Demonologist had not been well liked. If one of her closest neighbors could name her enemies but not a single friend, that did not exactly demonstrate great popularity.

"She *is* a demonologist," Anduron said, before Hakin could ask another question. "She was probably killed by one of her demons."

"No," Tarker growled. "I would know." Despite Hakin's earlier concern, it appeared that *this* demon, at least, had no problem seeing or hearing warlocks.

Anduron gave Tarker another quick glance, then shuddered and returned his attention to Hakin. "I don't know what happened to her, then."

"Have you heard *anything*?" Hakin asked. "Even a hint?"

"Have you smelled her?" Tarker demanded.

"No," Anduron said. "I'm sorry. I can't sense her, if that's what you mean."

"Is there any magic you can do that might find her?" Hakin asked.

Anduron shook his head. "Warlockry is not the magic you want for something like that. Warlockry is for moving, making, and breaking, not for finding or knowing." He frowned. "You say Wosten is dead?"

"Yes," Tarker rumbled.

Anduron glanced uneasily at the demon again, then turned back to Hakin. "Shouldn't someone do something about that? Inform the magistrate? Or the wizard's family?"

Hakin looked up over his own shoulder, then turned up an empty palm. "That might be a good thing to do," he said, "but it's not my place to do it. I never met the man, and I haven't seen that he *is* dead; I've only heard this demon tell me so."

"But still…"

Hakin interrupted the warlock. "I don't think I've made the situation clear," he said. "I'm not here about Wosten, and for myself, I don't care about Karitha. I'm here because I promised this demon I would help it find Karitha, and I did that so that it would not go rampaging around the city looking for her. If you want to report the crime to the magistrate, go right ahead. If the magistrate wants to capture and punish the demon for Wosten's murder he's welcome to try, but I doubt he'll manage it. If he wants to find and punish Karitha, that's fine, too, so long as he lets us know where she is; Tarker, here, may well save the overlord's government the trouble of hanging her."

"If she is hanged, she will be dead and I will be free," Tarker growled.

"Ah," Anduron said again. "I see."

"So you don't have any idea how we can find Karitha?" Hakin asked.

The warlock shook his head. "I really don't."

Tarker growled, but Hakin raised a hand. "There are plenty of other people we can talk to," he said. An idea struck him. "And maybe we *should* see what really happened to poor Wosten."

"I tore his throat out," Tarker interrupted, before Hakin could finish.

"Yes, I know," Hakin said. "But maybe he cast a spell on Karitha, and that's why you can't find her. Maybe we can find some clues at his place."

"That's a good idea," Anduron said.

"Thank you," the youth answered. "Now, could you direct us to Wosten's…"

"I know where it is," Tarker said, before Hakin could finish the request.

"Of course you do," Hakin said. "I should have realized that. Then we'll be going, Anduron. Feel free to tell the magistrate, and please, do let your neighbors know we're looking for Karitha, and that Tarker, here, is already getting irritable about not being able to find her. I don't know how long I can keep it from smashing things."

"Ah," Anduron said once more. "I'll tell them."

With that Hakin rose, and followed Tarker out the door into the street. He trotted after the demon as it led the way to the dead wizard's workshop.

CHAPTER TWELVE

DARISSA THE WITCH'S APPRENTICE

16ᵀᴴ OF HARVEST, YS 5199

The Melithan army, under the command of Crown Prince Terren, had met the invading Eknerans and halted their advance some five miles from the border—approximately halfway to Melitha Castle. The two roughly equal forces had stopped a hundred yards apart, and had not clashed immediately, but had instead set up improvised defenses on either side of a cornfield. The local farmers had formed a sort of militia that helped with these preparations and carried messages, but they clearly intended to leave the actual fighting to the professionals.

News reached the capital quickly—a runner could easily carry word from the front to the town in under an hour, after all, and sentries in the castle tower could see the situation for themselves—so everyone was aware of what was happening, if not the reasoning behind it. Some of the Melithans wanted to know why there had not yet been a battle, but these hotheads were generally shouted down by the parents and siblings of soldiers, who wanted their men to come home safely. Most people wanted to see everything resolved without bloodshed, with the Eknerans retreating without a fight.

Darissa was very much in this latter category, though she realized it was unlikely. She was further concerned because no one seemed to know what had become of Prince Marek since she had last seen him. King Terren was in the castle, sending and receiving emissaries, overseeing preparations for a siege, and making patriotic speeches. Prince Terren was commanding the army, while his wife, Princess Indamara of Pethmor, was organizing domestic matters at the castle and ensuring that the army had the supplies it needed. Prince Evreth was now known to be out of the country on a secret mission of some sort. Princess Hinda was said to be arranging for an evacuation of the town should it be necessary.

But no one seemed to have word of Prince Marek—or if they did, it was not reaching Darissa.

Various non-combatants had been fleeing the area; the foreign traders who usually made up perhaps a third of the market's vendors had all vanished. Other foreigners, though, had been arriving in ones and twos, on foot or horse or mule, and vanishing into the castle. Rumors as to who these strangers might be abounded, but the most common theory, and the one Darissa thought the most likely, held that they were emissaries from neighboring countries come to discuss alliances—or to discuss what bribes would keep them neutral.

Some of them did not *look* much like royal emissaries, though. Following Nondel's instructions to stay out of sight, Darissa had not gone up to the market since the invasion, but she watched the people passing the house. She was not making any particular effort to feel their thoughts, but she was not shutting them out, either, and she could sense caution, concern, fear, eagerness—a variety of emotions, often in the same individual.

From a few, though, she sensed nothing at all. Usually, in her limited experience, that meant a magician of some sort. That worried her; why would magicians be arriving during a war? Wouldn't that violate the Wizards' Guild's ban on using magic to fight?

Or perhaps they were not here to *fight*, but to perform other magic for the king, magic that he thought would be acceptable to the Wizards' Guild.

In fact, one tall, unusually straight-backed old woman with an intimidating face and expression, who marched past Nondel's house two days after the invasion, appeared to *be* a wizard; perhaps the king was consulting a Guild representative as to just where the boundary between acceptable and unacceptable fell. The woman wore a loose, dark blue gown and a matching broad-brimmed hat, and had a leather bag slung over her shoulder as she strode up the hill at a pace that Darissa knew she herself could not match without running.

At supper that night Nondel did not eat much; he was clearly worried.

"Is there anything I can do for you, Master?" Darissa asked.

He shook his head. "Not without risking our lives. I'm worried because the battle hasn't happened yet. The Eknerans wouldn't just walk in without a plan—either they thought they could win an open battle, or they wanted to negotiate terms, or they had some sort of strategem planned. If they wanted a fight, it would have happened by now. If they wanted to negotiate, we'd be hearing about it. That means they have a scheme, and they're waiting for something, and I'm worried about what it might be."

"Another neighbor invading us, perhaps?" Darissa suggested.

"It could be," Nondel agreed.

"Is there anything we can do about it?"

"Us? Absolutely not. We're witches. We can't get involved."

"But we're Melithans!"

"We're witches *first*," Nondel told her.

"We can't do anything even if we don't use magic?"

Nondel grimaced. "Be honest with yourself, Darissa," he said. "Can you do *anything* now without magic? Without sensing what the people around you want? Without seeing the secrets they want to hide? Without knowing what's around you, even when you can't see it?"

"Ah…" Darissa had not really thought about that, but it was true; she could no more stop using magic than she could stop her other senses. She could close her eyes, and block her ears, but she would still smell the air and feel the ground beneath her feet, light would penetrate her eyelids, muffled sounds reach her ears; even if she did not allow herself to use that information consciously, it would affect her actions. Similarly, the information her magic gave her could not be completely suppressed or ignored.

She was not merely someone who used witchcraft; she was a *witch*, and could not be anything less.

She spent most of the evening trying unsuccessfully to read, and worrying about Marek instead. Why did no one seem to know what happened to him? When she last saw him he had been organizing the castle's defense, but all the more recent reports said that was being handled by regular officers and Princesses Hinda and Indamara.

But why, she asked herself, did she care so much? Yes, he had been kind to her—and to everyone else around him—and he had clearly been interested in her in pretty much every way a young man *could* be interested in a girl, but really, she scarcely knew him, yet she could hardly think about anything else.

She thought she knew what love was, since she had seen it in so many other people's hearts in the five years since her witchcraft began to blossom, and she recognized that this *felt* like love, but could she really be in love with the prince? It seemed so irrational. He was tall and handsome and gentle and thoughtful, but he knew nothing about witchcraft...

But he had wanted to learn, and wasn't there more to her life than her magic?

She finally put the book aside and went to bed, still unsure what she felt, or what she *wanted* to feel.

She was awakened by shouting outside; startled, she rolled out of bed and grabbed her apprentice robe, tugging it on. A moment later she found Nondel in the kitchen, staring out the window toward the castle.

"What's happening?" she asked.

"More fighting," he said. "*Real* fighting, this time."

"The Eknerans attacked?"

He smiled crookedly. "No," he said. "Not the Eknerans, though I wouldn't be surprised if they're fighting too."

"What?"

"Bhella. Bhella invaded from the south—presumably this was all arranged with the Eknerans, where they would lure our army north, and the Bhellans could then march in from the south."

Darissa felt suddenly cold. "So there's a Bhellan army on the way?" She had heard stories about Bhellan soldiers; they were said to be far more than normally vicious, and prone to raping and pillaging.

"No," Nondel said, still smiling. "Because the moment they crossed our borders, just before dawn, a Talite army invaded Bhella behind them, and there's a rumor that Trothluria is involved on our side, as well. I understand the Bhellan army turned back."

Darissa had to think for a moment to remember where Trothluria was—somewhere to the southeast, beyond Tal.

"So this is the network of alliances you were talking about," she said.

"So it would appear, yes." He turned away from the window.

"How did you hear about it all?"

"I talked to the neighbors," Nondel said, nodding toward the door.

"I'll…" Darissa began, but Nondel cut her off.

"We may be at war, but you are still an apprentice with chores to do," he said.

Darissa stopped and bowed her head. "Yes, master," she said.

Something over an hour later, after Nondel had gone out on an unspecified errand, Darissa returned the broom to the cupboard and went to the front door. She stepped out onto the path, and saw several people hurrying up and down the road.

She recognized a neighbor's son and called, "Heremin!"

The boy, a lad of eleven, stopped and looked at her. She beckoned to him. "What's happened?" she called.

He glanced up the hill toward the castle, then turned and came up the path to meet her.

"There's a battle going on," he said. "Our army's fighting the Ekerans."

"Who's winning?"

"Don't know yet," he said.

"What about the south?"

"Oh, the Bhellans crossed the border first thing this morning, but word is that the Talites and Trothlurians went marching right up to Bhella Castle behind them, so they turned back."

"Is there fighting?"

"Don't know."

"Have you heard anything about Prince Marek?"

"Oh, they're saying he's the one who brought the Talites and Trothlurians in on our side! He's supposed to be due back at the castle any time now."

That was wonderful news, and Darissa let out a sigh of relief. "What about Prince Evreth?"

"Don't know—haven't heard about him. But Prince Terren's leading the fight against the Eknerans."

"Yes, I knew that. Thank you." She gave him a copper bit as a thank you for the news, then watched as he dashed off. Once the boy had rounded the corner, she went back inside.

There was a battle under way—or more probably two of them—but Marek was safe, and it sounded as if the war was going well. She headed into the kitchen with a smile on her face.

The rest of the morning and half the afternoon passed in a blur, with people running and shouting outside while Darissa stayed indoors, practicing her witchcraft and talking with Nondel. She kept listening for the shouts of joy that would follow a great victory, or the warning shouts if the enemy had defeated the army and was approaching the town, but neither one came.

At last, though, when the sun was low in the west, a knock on the door came, and she hurried to answer it.

It was a messenger in the king's livery. "Darissa the Apprentice?" he asked.

"Yes," she said.

"Your presence is required at the castle immediately."

"But...I'm a witch. We're at war. Is that allowed?"

"Your presence is *required*, Mistress, by royal command." She could feel that he did not know anything beyond his orders, and that he had been made to understand they were urgent. Further argument would upset him without accomplishing anything.

"All right; let me grab my shawl and tell my master."

"Be quick about it."

"Of course." She ducked back into the house, found her shawl, and called into the kitchen, "I've been ordered to the castle. I don't know when I'll be back."

"What? But..." Nondel emerged, wiping his hands on the dishrag.

"Be safe, Master," she said. Then she ran out, wrapping the shawl around her shoulders.

The square below the castle was crowded, but much of the crowd seemed to be people milling around, unsure of what was happening; their massed uncertainty and worry washed over her. Many of them were strangers, people she had not seen in town before. "What's going on?" she asked her escort.

"They've come to get away from the fighting," the messenger told her.

"What's been happening? Are we winning?"

"I don't know, Mistress. Stay close." He pressed forward, trying to get through the throng to the castle.

Darissa decided she could help with that—getting her into the castle could not really be considered part of the war, could it? She nudged the minds around her, and a path cleared ahead of the messenger just a little more quickly than would be natural.

She crossed the market, and hurried up the steps and across the moat on the messenger's heels, the guards and others moving out of their way. Beyond the tunnel and courtyard they entered the keep through an unfamiliar door, where the messenger led her through a series of rooms and passages until at last she found herself in a small room with a single door, a single window, a single table, three chairs, and a single occupant.

She was not really surprised to see that it was Prince Marek. He rose at the sight of her, and for a moment she thought he was going to embrace her, but he caught himself just short of wrapping his arms around her.

"Darissa!" he said. "Thank you for coming."

"You didn't really give me a choice," she replied.

"You're a witch," he said, smiling. "You don't need to do anything you don't want to."

"That isn't always true, but...yes, I wanted to see you again. How are you? How is the war going? I understand you're a hero of the southern front."

He waved the notion away. "I did what my father asked," he said. "Evreth had laid the foundations years ago."

She could see that he meant it, and was not feigning humility—his brother Evreth *had* laid the groundwork for the alliance with Tal and Trothluria, and all he had done was implement the plans that had been prepared.

There was a dark undertone to his thoughts that troubled her, though. "Where *is* Prince Evreth?" she asked.

"Probably somewhere in Ressamor. We don't know exactly."

"So he's still cementing alliances?"

"We certainly hope so!"

"It sounded to me as if we had a clear edge in this conflict."

Marek's expression turned somber. "We did," he said, "but...Darissa, my brother is dead."

"What?" Her hand flew to her mouth. "You just said Evreth... You mean Prince Terren?"

Marek nodded.

"What happened?"

"The battle, of course. Earlier today. The Eknerans launched their attack this morning, and our men fought back, but we were expecting them to try to break through our lines and move on the castle, or to attempt to flank our troops and…well, they didn't do anything we expected. They went after my brother—all their best men went straight for him and his personal guard. They lost ground everywhere else, some of them broke and ran for the border, but they got through his guards. The officers who reported to us said they think the plan was to capture him and ransom him back, but he wouldn't surrender, he just kept fighting, even when he had been separated from his company. They say he personally killed at *least* three men, and injured half a dozen more, that his sword was soaked in blood clear to the hilt, but he couldn't hold out forever, and his men couldn't get back to his side in sufficient numbers to help him in time. He bled to death—died as he was being carried off the field."

Darissa's hands trembled. She could feel Marek's grief, the horror and sense of loss he felt at his brother's death.

"We won the battle," Marek said, his voice unsteady. "The Eknerans put everything into trying to take Terren, and we tore their lines to pieces everywhere else. They fled back across the border in complete disarray once they realized they didn't have a captive prince to bargain with. But Terren is gone."

"I'm so sorry."

"General Tobul took command, and chased the enemy back to the border, and tried to parley, but the Eknerans wouldn't talk to him. They won't surrender. My father wanted to settle this quickly, so as to minimize long-term resentments, but…" He sighed, and did not finish the sentence.

"I don't understand," Darissa said. "They're defeated, aren't they?"

"Well, we *thought* so, but they aren't admitting it," Marek said. "Hinda and I think there are three possibilities—either they don't realize yet how badly hurt they are and don't know that the Bhellans turned back and won't be coming to help them, or they have some other surprise in store that we don't know about that's going to save them, or they're just desperate. Or crazy, which can sometimes come to the same thing. And I think that third one is the most likely."

"Why would they be desperate, though?" Darissa asked. "I hadn't heard that things were so very dreadful in Eknera. I've been talking to the neighbors, and I heard that the old king died last year and his nephew took the throne, and not everyone was happy about it, but... is that connected somehow?"

Marek glanced around, then closed the door to the corridor. "King Manrin didn't just die," he said quietly, leaning close to Darissa. "He was murdered. Assassinated. By his nephew, who is now reigning as King Abran III." His voice was cold and flat.

"You're sure?" Darissa did not really need to ask; she could feel Marek's certainty.

"We're sure."

"Do the Eknerans know that?"

"Some do. For most of his people it's just a nasty rumor, but there are some people in the castle, and in the royal family, who know what happened. It's hard to keep secrets when people have enough money to pay magicians for the truth."

"So...I'm not sure I really understand yet. What does this have to do with the war?"

"Abran needed to prove himself," Marek said. "He needed to show that he would be a better king than his uncle was, that he would make Eknera stronger and richer and happier; if everyone agreed that he was doing a good job, nobody would ever act on those nasty rumors about the old king's death. But if he *isn't* a good king, there are plenty of people who want to see him pay for his crimes. He has a cousin who is next in line for the throne, or there are nobles who could set themselves up as an oligarchy." He sighed. "We knew all about this, my family and I—you don't stay in power if you don't know what your neighbors are up to. But we didn't interfere because it isn't our business, and anything we did or said would just make his position stronger, because we're Eknera's natural enemy. We don't have any alliances to invoke; no one from our family has married into theirs for a hundred years, my father has no personal friends in their court, and there aren't any strong commercial bonds. So we let him take the throne, and left it to the Eknerans to sort it out among themselves."

"But then he invaded," Darissa said.

Marek nodded. "To strengthen his position at home. A quick victory over Melitha that would restore the territory they lost eighteen years ago, and maybe a little more, would make him look good—especially compared to his uncle, who lost that land in the first place."

"He *murdered* his own uncle—I still can't quite grasp that."

Marek turned up an empty palm. "It happens," he said. "But at any rate, he's fighting for his life—if he doesn't win this war, he's done. At best he'll be seriously weakened, his authority critically damaged, and at worst he'll be hanged as a traitor and a regicide. So he won't surrender."

"I understand," Darissa said. "But I don't see what this has to do with you, or me."

"It involves me because I am a prince of Melitha, and I am now second in line for the throne. My responsibilities have changed. I'm going to be helping my father to win this war and avenge my brother, even if it means completely destroying Eknera and probably bankrupting Melitha in the process. I'm not going to be able to wander freely about town any time soon. I can't waste my time courting you properly."

Darissa was surprised by just how much those words hurt. "So you summoned me here to say goodbye?"

"What?" The prince looked shocked. "Oh, *no*, beloved. Quite the opposite. I've summoned you here to *stay* with me. I love you, and I want you at my side always."

Now it was Darissa's turn to be shocked. "But…we barely know each other!"

"I know you well enough to know I don't ever want to be apart from you again. Stay, please, Darissa. I won't force you—I may be a prince, but you're a witch, so I don't know whether I *could* force you, and in any case I never would. If you don't want me, then my heart will be broken, but I will accept it—but I hope you *do* want me.

"Will you stay?"

"You can't marry me," Darissa said. "I'm a witch."

"I know. I'm so sorry. But I can't let you go, either, not until *you* tell me I must. We can make the terms whatever you like, so long as you stay with me, here in the castle. And once the war is over and Abran III is gone, we can go wherever you like. Evreth is still ahead of me in line. Indamara may be carrying Terren's child, if we're very lucky. They won't need me after the war. But they need me *now*, and

I need you. What do you say?"

Darissa hesitated, then said, "I'll stay. For now."

CHAPTER THIRTEEN

MORVASH OF THE SHADOWS

Morvash watched as the flying carpet drifted closer to the open gallery window, then beckoned it forward. The woman operating the carpet gestured, and it swung around, aligning with the casement, and surged into the gallery.

Once inside, Morvash directed it to the spot where three large men were waiting, and the four of them carefully maneuvered the last statue off the carpet and into its assigned spot in the gallery.

As soon as it was off, the wizard piloting the carpet swung her craft around and sailed back out the window. When he was satisfied with the placement of the statue, Morvash walked across and closed the casement. Once the latch was secured he reached for his purse, and paid off his three hirelings, thanking each of them warmly and giving each a silver bit beyond what he had agreed. His uncle had, as promised, provided these men, a wagon, and other necessities for the move, and Gror had thought that would be sufficient, but Morvash had insisted on asking Ithinia to find him a flying carpet for moving the statues. The thought that if he relied on ordinary muscle someone might drop one of them down the stairs and break off pieces had made him shudder.

Ithinia had sent this wizard, Zerra the Ageless, and her carpet had been extremely useful. She had said something about having been there before—apparently she had been involved in the partial clean-out when the Guild first claimed Erdrik's home. She declined to give any details, though.

Morvash had allowed three days for transferring everything to Erdrik's house, but in fact, largely thanks to Zerra, they had completed the job in two—or rather, two days and a night, as he had thought it best to move the statue of the nude couple under cover of darkness. Now all thirty-two statues were arranged on the second floor of his rented quarters; thirty-one were lined up in the gallery and hallway, mostly elbow to elbow along the back wall, facing the windows, but a few along the front between the big casements, or in the hallway opposite the stars.

The last statue, the young couple, was in the north alcove, where it could not be seen from the street.

Morvash followed his workers down the stairs and out onto the street, where the carpet swooped down to shoulder height.

"Is that everything?" its pilot asked.

"Yes, it is," Morvash answered. "My thanks to you, and to Ithinia."

Zerra turned up a palm. "Your uncle paid me. But you still owe me a favor," she said. "I'll probably collect it someday. For now, though, farewell." She gestured, and the carpet rose swiftly to rooftop level, then turned southeastward and vanished into the gathering dusk.

Morvash watched her go, then turned and re-entered the house. He shooed aside an inquisitive chair, then paused.

He was hungry, and the kitchen was just down the passage, but there was no food to be had there. He had not yet had time to stock it, and if Erdrik had left anything edible behind it was long gone, though whether it had been the Wizards' Guild or rats and other vermin or the house-cleaning sprite that got it, he could not be sure.

The nearest real market, so far as he knew, was Southmarket, a good half-mile to the south; to the north there was a grand plaza in front of the overlord's palace, which was a little closer, but that wasn't a proper market with farmers and fishmongers. The New City did not have a market of its own, nor even a decent selection of inns and taverns; the homeowners here generally had enough money to have their supplies delivered.

He would definitely need to fill the kitchen with groceries, but he was hungry *now*. Uncle Gror's place was only a couple of blocks away. Unpacking and organizing his new home could wait.

He turned and walked back out the front door, locking it behind him, and headed around the corner to Canal Avenue.

When he stepped through the dragon gates he found Uncle Gror waiting for him in the forecourt.

"How did you know I would be coming back?" Morvash asked, after an exchange of greetings.

"I didn't," Gror replied, "but I know *I* always forget something, so I thought you might, and if you didn't—well, it's a lovely day, and I was enjoying the weather."

"I forgot food," Morvash admitted. "I don't have a thing to eat yet at the new place."

"I think I can feed you once more. Come on." He led the way inside.

Over dinner, the two men discussed the future. "You'll still have time to work for the family?" Gror asked.

"Of course!" Morvash replied. "I told you. Anything you need."

"Anything that doesn't involve violating Guild rules, or killing people you don't think deserve it."

Morvash grinned wryly. "Well, yes. Anything I have no moral or legal problem with. For one thing, Uncle, I'll still need the money."

"So the Guild isn't paying you to turn these statues back into people?"

"No." Morvash shook his head. "The Guild doesn't care. Officially, anyway. I have the impression that Ithinia thinks it's a good idea, but that's speaking for herself, not the Guild. And she thinks there are some serious risks involved."

"She's probably right. After all, someone went to the trouble to turn these people to stone; even if it turns out *they* aren't dangerous, the wizards who petrified them might be annoyed at having their magic reversed."

Morvash stopped, a morsel of fish halfway to his mouth. "I hadn't even thought of that," he said. "I mean, I know some of the *victims* might not be the nicest people in the World, but I hadn't thought about the people who changed them."

"Well, now you have."

"Now I have," Morvash agreed. "I was already planning to have spells in place to protect me from the victims, but I hadn't thought about defending against their enemies."

"More magical preparations you'll need, then."

"Yes." Morvash sighed. "This project looks bigger and more

complicated all the time. It could be *years* before I finish it."

"Could you hire a helper, perhaps? Would that speed things up?"

Morvash put the fish in his mouth and chewed thoughtfully. "The problem there," he said, "is that I'd need to worry all the time about revealing Guild secrets. That would put too many limits on what a hireling could do for me."

"An apprentice, then?"

"I'm only a journeyman. I can't take on an apprentice until I'm rated as a master, and that's going to be *at least* another three years— the minimum as a journeyman is six years, and I'm only halfway."

"And you can't hire another wizard? A younger journeyman, perhaps?"

"I don't know anyone in this city. I could ask around, I suppose— but why would anyone want to sign on for something like that? I can't pay much, after all. In fact, I'm not sure how I can pay *anything*."

"You said something about wanting someone to test your spells on."

"Yes, eventually, but…"

"Morvash," his uncle interrupted, "I know you want to do everything nicely, without hurting anyone, or even *inconveniencing* anyone, but you need to be realistic. You can't do everything by yourself."

"Yes, I know…"

"I'm buying you a slave," Gror said. "It's the only thing that makes any sense. You can use him as your helper, and if you need a test subject, he'll be there, and you can use your magic to make sure he doesn't run away or reveal any secrets."

"Uncle, I…"

Gror held up a hand. "I know you don't like the idea, but remember, people who wind up as slaves are generally in a terrible position to begin with. You'd be keeping him from starving, or being worked to death by a mine owner, or some other horrible fate."

That was true enough. Morvash hesitated.

"I'll try to find you someone reasonably young and healthy, but don't expect too much. I won't have much to choose from, and anyone good-looking, especially a girl, is going to go for more than I'm willing to pay."

This was all unfamiliar territory to Morvash; he had never seen a slave auction, had hardly ever seen a slave. There were probably fewer than a hundred in the entire city of Ethshar of the Rocks, most of them condemned criminals, and they were generally confined to the most dangerous and unpleasant jobs, such as reinforcing the sea wall below the Fortress. He understood that here in Ethshar of the Spices they were somewhat more common, but he had yet to encounter any in his brief stay.

He knew that some wizards did use slaves as test subjects, but he had never liked the idea, and had never thought well of the wizards who resorted to this.

But it *would* be useful, and his uncle's arguments had some substance. And when he was done he could free the slave, along with the restored former statues.

There was still the question of what this slave would be like. "I don't know what your choices will be, Uncle, but I'd prefer not to have a violent criminal to worry about."

"You're a wizard; you can handle a mere thug."

"Yes, I *can*, but I would rather not *need* to."

"I'll see what I can do. But you'll accept, then?"

"As long as it doesn't come out of my pay."

"One reason I'm doing this, my boy, is to save you time, so you can devote more of your efforts to *our* business, rather than this project of yours."

"Thank you, Uncle. I think." With that, he turned his full attention to the grilled fish.

In the end he stayed the night at Uncle Gror's rented mansion, ate breakfast there, and then headed for Southmarket to stock his pantry.

Once the kitchen was fully supplied he once again left Erdrik's house, bound this time for the Wizards' Quarter in pursuit of the ingredients he would need for his spells. He also carried the list Ithinia's agent had given him, so that he could find people who could teach him what he needed to know.

One of the most useful bits of information he acquired that afternoon had nothing to do with magic; it was simply the existence of the notice boards outside the Arena. He stopped off on the way from the Quarter back to the New City, and read the various advertisements and requests until the fading daylight told him it was time to get home for supper.

That board, he saw, would be helpful if he needed to hire anyone. He could find laborers if he needed to move any of the statues again, and he could do it without troubling his uncle. He could also find suppliers who would provide the ingredients he needed for his spells.

He had thought that eating alone in the rented house might feel somewhat melancholy, but the animated furnishings prevented that; it was hard to work up a proper gloominess when a warm copper kettle was brushing against his shins, like a cat wanting to be petted, and a sugar bowl was running full-tilt back and forth from one end of the table to the other, in constant danger of sliding off and smashing itself on the floorboards but somehow always catching itself at the last instant and dancing back from the edge. It never even spilled any sugar.

When he had finished his meal he made his way to the stone-floored workroom, which he had chosen as his laboratory, at least initially. If he got to the point of testing spells that might affect normal stone, like the slabs in the floor, he told himself he would take his work somewhere else—probably upstairs, closer to the statues.

He set up a journal to record everything he did, and began sorting out possibilities. His preliminary studies had taught him that the most common reversible spell for turning someone to stone was Fendel's Superior Petrifaction; there were two well-known ways to undo it. One was a spell called Javan's Restorative, an eighth-order spell that generally returned damaged things to their natural healthy state; Morvash was only a journeyman, and any eighth-order spell was beyond his present abilities. Perhaps if he devoted himself exclusively to working on this single spell he could master it in a year or so.

The other method was theoretically much, much easier, but in practice almost impossible. Casting Fendel's Superior Petrifaction required a glass vessel; if the vessel could be found and shattered, that would break the spell on everyone ever enchanted using that particular tool.

Finding the right cup or goblet or bowl, though, would not be easy—though thinking about it, Morvash wondered whether it might not be easier to find each of those vessels than to master an eighth-order spell. He had never yet succeeded at anything above fifth order, and was only really reliable up to about third order.

Perhaps Fendel's Divination could help him undo Fendel's Petrifaction; the Divination, itself a fifth-order spell, would provide a magical and absolutely truthful answer to any question.

Whether that answer would be *useful* was a whole separate issue, though; any question that could be misinterpreted probably would be. Answers might be misleading, or simply unintelligible—many wards or protective spells would cause the Divination's answer to appear in obscure languages, or awkwardly-sized runes. Even magic not intended to defend against it might cause the Divination to misfire in some way. If the spell was done correctly the answer would always appear, and would always be truthful, but that did not mean it would be readable or helpful.

Morvash did know another divination, a mere third-order spell, but he was not sure how helpful it would be. The Spell of Omniscient Vision could show him anything, in any place and at any time, but you needed to know precisely when and where you wanted to see. You couldn't just say, "Show me when this person was turned to stone," you needed to specify, "Show me the upstairs front room of the fourth house from the north end of the east side of Arena Street, two hours before sunset on the fourteenth day of Icebound, in the Year of Human Speech 5210, looking south from the back corner," or whatever the location you wanted might be. You would then see a few minutes of images of that time and place—but you would not hear or smell anything; it was vision only. And if your target was dark at the time, well…

He did not see how that spell was going to help. Fendel's Divination, though, would be easier to master than Javan's Restorative.

Further complicating matters, he could not be sure the same spell had been used on all the victims. Even if it had, even if every one of the thirty-three victims had been enchanted with Fendel's Superior Petrifaction, tracking down a couple of dozen glass goblets that might be scattered across the World, perhaps in the possession of wizards who did not *want* their spells reversed, would be challenge worthy of a storybook hero.

And of course, *finding* the glass vessels might not be enough. Vindictive wizards had long ago found ways to defend such tools—embedding them deep in blocks of concrete, for example, and then sinking the concrete in the harbor.

Javan's Restorative might be difficult, but it was a known difficulty, where locating and breaking the glasses was a mystery that he might never be able to solve. And the Restorative should reverse *other* petrifaction spells besides Fendel's, as well. In theory.

But maybe there was a third way, or a fourth. Maybe there was some low-order spell that would do what he needed. He had heard of something called Lirrim's Rectification that was supposed to be fairly easy, though he didn't know any details. That should be investigated.

There was something called the Spell of Reversal that could undo petrifaction under the right circumstances, but it was far too late for that, even if he knew how to perform it, which he did not; supposedly that one could practically reverse time and undo anything, but only going back half an hour or so, and all the statues had been stone far longer than that. And he had the impression it was a very high-order spell, possibly higher than Javan's Restorative. But was there some way to alter time itself that would make it effective?

Or perhaps an animation spell would be better than nothing; that could bring the victims back to life, even if they would still be stone instead of flesh.

So many possibilities! So many questions! It would help, he thought, if he knew more about who the statues had been, and who had enchanted them, and how, and why. With that in mind, he went upstairs, lamp and notebook in hand, and went through his catalogue of the thirty-two statues, checking it against the collected statues and adding additional notes about every detail he could.

He hoped he had not missed any other petrified people among Lord Landessin's collection of sculpture—or at least, none who might be saved. He knew there were petrifaction spells that were completely irreversible, and that anyone enchanted with *those* was dead, their stone remains no more alive or magical than any pebble on the beach.

The possibility that there were more victims among Erdrik's belongings had also occurred to him, but a quick look did not reveal any life-sized statues of humans among the clutter on the ground floor, so he put that aside, at least for the moment.

Finally, though, he decided there was nothing more he could do that night. He would return to the Wizards' Quarter in the morning and ask some more specific questions.

And, he thought, he might talk to a few magicians other than wizards. Ordinarily wizards did not hire other varieties of magician, both as a matter of professional pride and because the Wizards' Guild did not approve of any sort of mixed magic, but Morvash thought it might be useful to talk to a witch or a theurgist—theurgists were good at healing, which might be applicable somehow, and at obtaining information, which should *definitely* be useful, while witches could sense things no one else could. It was said that some witches could hear thoughts, and Ithinia had said that some of the statues might still be conscious, so perhaps a witch could communicate with some of the victims and learn more about what had happened to them. That might help him find some of the glass vessels used in the spells that petrified them—assuming they hadn't been sealed up securely and thrown in the sea.

He knew the standard wizard's approach would simply be to study and practice until he could perform Javan's Restorative, but Morvash hoped to find a faster, more innovative, and frankly, less boring approach. He would try out every idea he had, and see which ones held promise.

And he would start in the morning, but for now, he decided, he was going to bed.

CHAPTER FOURTEEN

HAKIN OF THE HUNDRED-FOOT FIELD

8TH OF LONGDAYS, YS 5231

From the front Wosten's shop looked perfectly normal, albeit closed in the middle of the day. One blow of Tarker's fist broke in the locked door, though, and when Hakin stepped inside he found the interior of the shop anything but normal. The front room was not too bad, but the room beyond, where Wosten had worked his spells, was a horrific mess.

The demon had not exaggerated in saying it had ripped out the wizard's throat. Most of the wizard lay face-down on his workshop floor, but a few pieces and most of his blood were spread across his workbench and the walls. Those were almost lost in the splinters and plaster dust, though; Tarker had obviously come in through the roof on its previous visit. The wreckage somehow made the sight less ghastly.

The room smelled very strange; Hakin had no idea what the odor was. It was slightly sweet and acrid, but beyond that unlike anything he had ever encountered before. Sunlight and distant birdsong spilled through the gaping hole in the ceiling.

"Why didn't you use the door?" Hakin asked.

"The door bore a protective rune," Tarker growled. "No one who wished the wizard harm could pass it."

"But you just now smashed through it!"

"I wish him no further harm."

"Why didn't anyone *hear* anything when you broke in to kill him? It must have made a tremendous crash!"

"Some heard."

"Then why didn't they *do* anything?"

"He was a wizard."

Hakin stared at the demon for a moment, then decided that was probably enough of an explanation. He had not had very much experience of wizards, but he supposed it made sense that their neighbors would become accustomed to strange sights and sounds. He looked around the workshop.

A fat leather-bound book lay open on the workbench; blood was spattered across the pages, but Hakin could still read some of it. He was slightly startled to see that it was written in plain Ethsharitic, and not some arcane language he never saw before.

The caption at the top of the displayed page read, in large swooping runes, "Zaneyil's Aerial Servitor." That was followed by a short list of ingredients and a string of symbols Hakin did not recognize; the fact that they were half-hidden by blood did not help.

This was obviously Wosten's book of spells; Hakin had never seen one before, but he had heard that every wizard had one. And the fact that it was lying open on the bench, with no protective spells to keep him from reading it, probably meant that Wosten had been working a spell when he died—probably Zaneyil's Aerial Servitor, whatever that was.

"What was he doing before you killed him?" Hakin asked, as he tried to make out more of the text. The spell required powdered dove bone, it seemed, and an eagle's wing-feather, and something that *might* have been dragon's blood—or possibly mandrake blood, or something else entirely; that line was half-hidden by a smear of *human* blood. There was an annotation in a different handwriting saying that the spell appeared to be a seventh-order binding, whatever that meant.

"Standing where I slew him, speaking to himself."

Hakin skimmed down the page, past various incomprehensible preliminaries, and frowned. The spell appeared to create a creature made out of air. "Are you sure he wasn't talking to a...a sylph?" He was unsure whether he was pronouncing the word correctly; he had never heard it before, and the runes were ambiguous, if he was even interpreting them correctly through the spots of dried blood.

"I saw nothing alive but the wizard."

"It says here that sylphs are invisible."

"I saw nothing."

"You wouldn't have seen a sylph if it was invisible."

"I see many things humans do not."

"Maybe sylphs aren't one of the things you can see, though."

"I smelled nothing, and heard nothing, beyond the wizard."

"What was he saying?"

"He said, 'Is it done? Did the powder work?'"

"I think he was talking to a sylph. To an aerial servitor he had made with this spell." He pointed at the book.

Tarker did not answer; it simply stared at Hakin.

"He was *working magic* when you killed him," Hakin explained. "And whatever that magic was, maybe it's why you can't find Karitha."

Tarker still said nothing.

Hakin sighed. "We need to find out more about this spell. Maybe he turned Karitha into a toad or something."

"I would still smell..." the demon began. Then it stopped, and for the first time since Hakin had met it, it hesitated and looked uncertain. "I *think* I would still smell her," it said.

Well, that answered his earlier unasked question, Hakin thought. "Maybe we can find out, if he did," Hakin said. "We need to talk to another wizard, one who knows this spell."

"Find one."

"I will," Hakin said, "but it may take awhile. I never heard of this spell before; it may not be very common."

"Start trying," the demon growled.

"Fine!" Hakin said. "I didn't *ask* to be your assistant, you know."

Tarker just glowered at him.

Hakin looked around. "Did Wosten live alone?"

"I smell no one else who spent much time in this place."

"What about family?"

"Wosten of the Red Robe was the son of Dereth the Butcher and Reska of the Curly Hair."

Hakin had not expected that specific a response, but then he remembered how Tarker had identified his own ancestry when they first met. "Where are they?" he asked.

"Dereth the Butcher is dead. Reska of the Curly Hair is about two miles that way." It raised a claw and gestured in what Hakin thought was a northwesterly direction.

"Two miles—not in the Wizards' Quarter, then?"

"No. Two miles that way."

That was a possible lead to finding out more about Wosten, but not a very promising one; Hakin thought they would do better talking to the neighbors here in the Wizards' Quarter, and it would certainly involve less walking. "No wife or children?"

"I smell no one else who spent much time in this place," Tarker said again.

"Did Wosten have an apprentice?"

"I smell no one else who spent much time in this place," the demon repeated.

Hakin hid any annoyance at the monster's response and asked, "Maybe a journeyman?" He glanced at the corpse. He had been thinking of Wosten as an old man, but he realized that was just because he was a wizard in a red robe; the body on the floor did not look bent or withered with age, the splayed hands were not lined or bony, and Tarker had said the wizard's mother was still alive. "Or his former master?" Wizards probably learned most of their spells from their masters, so whoever Wosten had taught, or the person who had taught him, were the most likely to know about these aerial servitor things.

"I can smell a human's bonds of blood," Tarker said, "and the presence of anyone who has been here within the past three days, and traces of anyone who lived here in the past few years, and sometimes other connections, but who served whom, or who taught whom? I have no way to know that."

That gave Hakin a better understanding of the demon's limitations, and let him know that he was going to have to do some things the ordinary human way, rather than relying on demonic magic. He looked around the workbench for more clues.

There was a green earthenware jar next to the book; a cork blocked its mouth, but appeared loose, slightly crooked, not pushed in tight. Hakin carefully lifted the cork, ready to jam it back in if anything started to emerge.

Nothing did. He leaned over carefully and peered into the jar. It was mostly full of what appeared to be grayish-brown powder.

Hakin was not about to touch that, but he wondered whether it had anything to do with the wizard's last words, as Tarker had reported them. Was this the powder that the wizard asked about? Or was it powdered dove bone for the spell he had been preparing?

The jar was not labeled. Hakin looked at the shelves above the workbench and the dozens of jars they held; most of *those* were labeled, though many of the descriptions were cryptic abbreviations. Half a dozen other jars of various sizes were lined up along the back of the workbench; the smallest, a glass one, was labeled "M Dragon ae. 5." It held a few drops of dark red fluid.

There were some small bones, and an assortment of feathers, scattered around the workbench, as well; Hakin could not tell whether any of them were eagle feathers, or whether they came from wings or tails or crests. A tripod held a small cauldron; a brazier underneath it was half-full of fine gray ash.

None of that told him anything. He looked at the book again, and for the first time noticed a small scrap of paper serving as a bookmark. He reached for it carefully. When his fingers touched the book he froze, waiting for something terrible to happen.

Nothing did.

Cautiously, moving very slowly, he lifted the pages to see what the paper had been used to mark.

The name of this other spell was Illam's Powder Preparation, described as a fifth-order facilitation. It required a cauldron suspended from an iron tripod, and nothing of the sort was mentioned on the page for Zaneyil's Aerial Servitor, so Wosten had presumably used this, too. The only other ingredients Hakin could make out in a long jumble of abbreviations and mystic symbols were ground rice and goat's hoof.

What the spell actually *did* was completely unclear.

They needed to talk to a wizard.

Hakin let the pages fall back, and turned to Tarker. "Come on," he said, "we're going to talk to the neighbors."

Tarker growled.

Hakin took that as assent, and led the way back out to the street.

Wosten's house and shop stood on the south side of Wizard Street, at the north end of Potion Street. That meant the most immediate neighbor was the next house to the east on Wizard Street; west of the house was Potion Street, and the shops across the street would not share a courtyard or alley with Wosten's.

Hakin paused; did Wosten's home have a back door at all? With its corner location it might not.

But he decided it didn't matter; his neighbors would still know something about him. Hakin turned east, and found a signboard reading SALDA OF DEEPWATER, MASTER WIZARD. He had never heard of Deepwater, and had no idea whether it was a neighborhood in Ethshar, or a village somewhere else in the Hegemony, or one of the Small Kingdoms, or what, but that didn't matter, either. It was a wizard's shop, and they needed to talk to a wizard. The door was closed; he shooed away a spriggan and knocked. The spriggan glanced at Tarker, squeaked, and fled.

The wood twisted under Hakin's knuckles, and the door opened with a remarkable creak, almost as if it was trying to speak.

"Hello?" Hakin called.

"Come on in," a woman's voice replied. "I'll be right with you."

Hakin stepped in, and found himself in a small parlor. Four upholstered chairs and half a dozen small tables were arranged around a spiral rag rug. Uncertain, Hakin stood on the rug, not taking a seat.

Tarker followed him into the room, turning its shoulders sideways to clear the jamb, and ducking to fit under the transom; the front door slammed loudly back against the wall, though Hakin had not seen the demon touch it.

Three of the little tables skittered away from the demon and huddled in the far corner of the room, startling Hakin. Until then, the youth had not realized they were animate.

"Well," the woman's voice said, as its owner stepped into the room through a door at the back, "what can I do for you?"

The speaker was a little below average height, a little heavier than ideal, clad in a blue robe with waist-length black hair trailing down her back. She had a little too much nose and chin to be called pretty, but was not really ugly, either. She could have been around thirty.

Then she caught sight of Tarker, and stopped in her tracks. "Oh," she said.

"We were hoping you could answer a few questions about your neighbor, Wosten," Hakin said.

She kept staring at Tarker as she said, "What sort of questions?"

"I should probably tell you that he's dead," Hakin said.

"I tore his throat out," Tarker said.

Hakin wished that the demon weren't quite so fond of telling people that. "Yes," he said. "It did."

"Why?" the wizard asked, taking half a step back toward the door from which she had just emerged. Her eyes stayed fixed on the demon.

"Because it was ordered to by a demonologist named Karitha," Hakin explained.

"Her? I know her." From her tone of voice, Salda had not *liked* Karitha.

"I don't," Hakin said. "But she summoned Tarker here, and ordered it to kill Wosten, so it did, but when it went back to be released, she was gone. It can't find her. And it can't go home until she either releases it, or dies."

The woman considered this for a moment, then asked, "So who are *you*? What do you have to do with this?"

"I'm Hakin of the Hundred-Foot Field. I'm trying to help Tarker so it can go home before anyone else gets hurt."

"All right," she said. "That sounds good. What do you want from *me*?"

"We're trying to figure out what happened to Karitha. Tarker says it would know if she were dead, and that it could find her anywhere in the everyday World, but there's no sign of her anywhere. It looks as if Wosten was in the middle of a spell when he died, so I was thinking that maybe you could tell us something about that—could he have enchanted her somehow so that Tarker can't find her?"

"I have no idea," the woman replied, still warily eyeing Tarker. "I don't know anything about demons, and I don't know what Wosten was up to."

"Is there maybe some divination you could do?"

She shook her head, one quick jerk. "I do animations and love spells, not divinations."

Hakin sighed. "His book of spells was open to something called Zaya...no, Zaneyil. Zaneyil's Aerial Servitor."

"Oh, I know *that* one! It's an animation, sort of. I was the one who taught it to Wosten."

"Is it something that could hide Karitha from her demons?"

The wizard's mouth opened, then closed again. She frowned.

"Well, not obviously," she said. "It brings a piece of air to life—a sort of living wind—and the creature it makes then has to obey three commands. After that it's free and can't be controlled anymore; usually they just vanish, but sometimes they decide to explore a little before they fade away, and go around blowing people's hats off and that sort of thing. They're pretty harmless—just a breeze, really. But if Wosten gave it the right commands, it could have done something to Karitha."

"Like what?"

The wizard turned up an empty palm. "Like *anything*. The sylph—that's what the air creature is called, a sylph—can't carry more than a few ounces, so it couldn't have carried Karitha off or anything, but if Wosten got clever, I don't know what it might do."

"There was another spell bookmarked," Hakin said. "Illam's Powder Preparation."

The wizard blinked, and for the first time she looked directly at Hakin, rather than Tarker. "Really? That's pretty smart; I hadn't thought of that."

"Thought of *what*?"

"Using a sylph to carry Illam's Powder. Of course, I can't work Illam's myself, I've never learned it—it's common for animators, but I couldn't get it to work."

"What are you talking about?" Tarker growled.

The wizard cast the demon a startled glance, then explained, "Illam's Powder Preparation lets you put a spell into a magical powder. Then when you want to use the spell, you sprinkle the powder on whatever you want to enchant and say a magic word—that's one of the reasons I can't use it, I can't *pronounce* the confounded word. It isn't any language I know. Anyway, when you say the word, whatever spell you put in it is instantly cast on whatever you sprinkled the powder on. That can be very handy, much faster than making a spell from scratch, but you need to have the powder ready beforehand, and it takes *days* to make the stuff. But you can make enough in a batch to cast the spell maybe a dozen times, if you're careful. And lucky."

"So…what does this have to do with the aerial servitor thing?"

"Well, I'm just guessing, really, but I think Wosten might have made up a batch of powder, and then ordered the sylph to go sprinkle it on Karitha, and then say the magic word—sylphs can't talk above a whisper, but it wouldn't need to, the magic word doesn't have to be loud, a whisper is plenty. So that let him cast a spell on Karitha without going anywhere near her, and she wouldn't have seen the sylph coming, and it could probably have gotten past any protections she had in place—I mean, a sylph is just *air*, and the powder is a pretty fine dust, so it would go right through most defenses. That would take up two of the three commands—I wonder what he did with the third one?"

"I don't know," Hakin said. "So you think Wosten cast a spell that way, and the sylph used it on Karitha while Tarker was on its way to kill Wosten?"

"That would be my guess, but it's just a guess."

"It sounds like a good one to me," Hakin said, giving Tarker a glance. He could not read the demon's expressions; its emotional gamut seemed to range from annoyed to furious, without many other options. "So what spell would have been in the powder?"

"Oh, it could be *anything*—literally anything," the wizard said. "Any spell Wosten knew, from setting her on fire to making her fall in love to turning her into a tree squid. He could have cast her into another universe, or sent her to the lesser moon, or stood her on her head and set her spinning. *Any* spell he knew, any spell at all, could be in that powder."

"*Anything?*"

The wizard nodded. "Is there any of the powder left to test? Or was there another bookmark?"

"I didn't see any more bookmarks," Hakin said. "There was a jar of powder, but I don't know whether it was the magical one or some other ingredient." He looked at Tarker for confirmation.

The demon growled.

Hakin hesitated, thinking. He did not really want to go back into Wosten's blood-spattered workroom, where the wizard's corpse still lay, to check for bookmarks or magical powders, especially since the powder might still be active and might do to him whatever it had done to Karitha. "Did Wosten have any family?" he asked. "Any former apprentices? A former master?"

"Oh, yes, of course! They should be notified." She bustled into the room, apparently over her wariness of Tarker's presence. "I think his master is dead, but a year or two back he had an apprentice named Inza, and his mother lives over in Spicetown somewhere." She pointed in about the same direction Tarker had. "And the magistrate should be informed—I know they don't like to get involved in magical feuds, and no one's stupid enough to try to arrest the demon here, but they'll want to know." She opened a cabinet Hakin had not noticed. "You take your demon back to Wosten's place and see what you can find, and I'll see about telling the proper authorities."

Hakin opened his mouth to protest, then closed it again.

"Come on," he told Tarker. "Let's see if we missed any powders or bookmarks."

CHAPTER FIFTEEN

DARISSA THE WITCH'S APPRENTICE

21ˢᵀ OF HARVEST, YS 5199

The war would not *end*. King Abran would not surrender.

Darissa knew that wars could drag on for months or years, even in the Small Kingdoms, and of course the Great War had lasted centuries, but here on the open plains of the northwestern Small Kingdoms, most wars were over in a few days—the armies would march out, alliances would be revealed, battles would be fought, one side would have a clear advantage, and it would all be over quickly. She had never before been in a war herself, but neighboring countries had fought in her lifetime, and often the wars were over before she had even heard they were begun. She had assumed this war would follow the same pattern.

But Abran would not surrender.

Melitha's army had laid siege to Eknera Castle; the Ekneran army was largely dispersed, captured, wounded, or dead. Bhella had made terms with Melitha, Tal, and Trothluria—the Bhellans had gotten better terms than they expected, thanks to Melitha being busy elsewhere and wanting a quick settlement, and King Derath seemed more relieved than upset at the defeat. A regiment of Talite and Trothlurian volunteers was serving under Melitha's General Tobul in the siege, and two of Eknera's other neighbors, Yolder and Mezgalon, had joined in as well, all of them clearly wanting a share of the eventual booty. The town of Eknera was occupied, and the townspeople were fairly cooperative—Abran had not been popular with his own people. Bribed locals had shown the invaders where the hidden tunnels into the castle were, so that the siege was more complete than usual.

But Abran would not surrender.

Prince Evreth had still not come home, but it was commonly believed that he had been responsible for bringing Yolder and Mezgalon into the fight, and keeping Eknera's traditional ally, Kanthoa, out. King Terren had made several visits to the besieging army, as well as performing his usual duties at home. Princess Hinda had taken charge of logistics, making sure that all the combined armies were fed and equipped, and that the wounded were attended to quickly.

And Prince Marek was given the unhappy duty of planning his brother's funeral, which took place five days after the battle. The pyre was built in the castle courtyard—not from ordinary firewood, but from exotic perfumed woods brought from Vectamon, or Lumeth of the Forest, or even Sardiron. Six theurgists were present, gathered from six different kingdoms, as well as a troupe of ritual dancers from Kushin, to ensure that the dead prince's spirit would be guided safely and painlessly to the afterlife. Melitha's own court musicians were joined by the famous Falea the Sweet-Voiced, brought all the way from Pethmor, in performing the customary threnodies.

General Tobul was only able to put in a brief appearance before returning to Eknera, and Evreth was not there, but the rest of the royal family was present for the entire spectacle. Poor Princess Indamara was too overcome to speak, but the others all said their piece, acclaiming Prince Terren as a hero.

The crowd in attendance included virtually every important person in Melitha, and many Darissa did not think were from Melitha at all. She recognized a few as people she had seen arriving in the kingdom when the war first began, but she still did not who they were or why they were there.

Darissa found the whole event somewhat excessive, but did not admit that to anyone, most particularly not to Marek.

She had been assigned a guest chamber on the third floor, but by the night before the funeral she and Marek had abandoned any pretense that she would actually use it; she had moved into Marek's own apartments. Other than that she tried to stay out of sight as much as possible, and when Marek insisted she accompany him she did her best to stay in the background, using her magic to further discourage unwanted attention.

She was not there to participate in the castle's normal life—if anything in wartime could be called normal—but only to be with Marek, to comfort him over the loss of his brother and over the ongoing disaster of King Abran's war. Melitha was winning, there was no question about that, and would eventually annex more Ekneran land and collect reparations from the Eknerans, but in the meantime men were fighting and even dying, men and women had been called away from their normal labors to support the army, and the royal treasury was being depleted rapidly to pay for it all, and Marek felt himself partially responsible. Darissa could feel it—somehow, irrationally, a part of him felt that because he had been the one to first see the Ekneran invaders the war was his fault.

He knew that was nonsense—Darissa could feel *that*, too—but that did not make the guilt go away. He could not control his unconscious beliefs; even witches had trouble with that, and ordinary people rarely attempted it.

And then there were his feelings toward his dead brother. He had loved Terren, but he had not always *liked* him; they had been so very different. Terren had devoted himself to the role of king-to-be, to seeing the broad landscape, the entire kingdom, while Marek had never worried about the grand outlook, preferring to see the people of Melitha as individuals—friends, not subjects. The two brothers had spent little time together, and when they did it had usually been with other members of the family around; they had both gotten along better with Evreth than with each other.

Especially after the death of their mother, Queen Larsi, three years earlier, the brothers had drifted apart, and Marek felt guilty about letting that happen.

Darissa had not known *any* of this a sixnight earlier; it all came from staying with Marek as he prepared to say goodbye to Terren forever. Not all of what she learned came from her magic, by any means; on half a dozen occasions she found herself listening as Marek let his feelings pour out in words. She gave him someone he could speak to freely, a luxury he had never really had before. He had sometimes been able to share his emotions with friends or even his siblings, but always with a certain caution, a certain reserve; with Darissa he held nothing back, and half these private conversations ended with him weeping in her arms. He himself, she sensed, had not known how much he was holding back.

And Prince Evreth's absence hurt Marek, as well. He did not say *that* aloud even to Darissa, but she could feel it whenever Evreth's name came up. He thought Evreth should be there, that he should have abandoned his endless diplomatic schemes to come home for the funeral.

All through the long afternoon of Terren's cremation, Marek was secretly hoping Evreth would show up; from her corner at the back, behind the courtiers, Darissa could feel that, could see Marek looking at the entry port, wanting to see Evreth there.

Prince Evreth did not come. The long ceremony dragged on and on until the pyre was nothing but coals gleaming in the twilight, and at last the mourners scattered. Marek refused to follow his father and sister to supper in the great hall, preferring to retire to his chambers and continue his mourning fast.

Darissa saw that, and made a detour before following him upstairs, making sure that the kitchen staff would always have something that could be readied quickly and delivered promptly should Marek change his mind. She had a footman post himself outside the prince's door, ready to take a message to the kitchens—or anywhere else—should the need arise.

And she also made sure that *she* had plenty of food—boiled sausage and bread and cheese and stout beer—that she could take up with her to Marek's apartment. She thought she might need her witchcraft, and witchcraft required energy. She might, if the need arose, use her magic to literally lend Marek strength, but only if she had strength to lend, and for that she needed to eat.

These preparations made, she climbed the stairs and made her way to the rooms she and Marek shared. She slipped in quietly, and found him sitting at his desk, his head in his hands.

She left him there and carried her supplies back to her own dressing room—the apartment had been laid out with the assumption that the prince would have a woman sleeping with him sometimes, whether wife or mistress, so there were two dressing rooms, one equipped appropriately for a man, the other for a woman.

She settled on the stool at her vanity table and began eating, wrapping cheese and sausage in chunks of bread and washing it down with beer. When she had eaten her fill she tucked the rest away in a drawer for later; she did not want to stuff herself. Then she found a hairbrush and sat there, staring into the mirrors, as she brushed her hair.

She did not know why Marek wanted her so. She knew he *did*—that was an advantage a witch had over ordinary women, that she could see through any pretense a man might put up—but she did not understand *why*, even after spending so much time wrapped up in his emotions. She was not tall or strong, and while she could see that her face might be considered pretty in a rather ordinary way despite her long nose, Marek was a *prince*, who could have his pick of the beauties who came to the king's court looking for husbands. She was not the doting, devoted, submissive sort that many men seemed to prefer; she could not bring herself to give up that much of herself. Her current careful attention to Marek's emotional state was as far as she could go in putting another's needs ahead of her own, and even that she knew she could not keep up for long—but she also knew she would not need to; once Marek had weathered the immediate crisis and fully absorbed the shock of his brother's death, she was sure he would regain his own strength and independence.

She knew that some men wanted her because they had various lurid fantasies about what it would be like to make love to a witch—fantasies that actually had a bit of truth to them, though of course they were wildly exaggerated. Some wanted a witch because they imagined themselves exploiting her magic in other ways, as well, making themselves wealthy or powerful, avenging various slights; *that*, at least for Darissa, was even less likely than the supposed sexual ecstasies. She would never use magic like that. Vengeance was not much fun when one could feel the victim's pain, and power lost much of its appeal, as well.

Marek, though, did not seem to be interested in her witchcraft at all except as a part of her that he could learn more about. He had no more desire to exploit it for his own ends than he did to exploit his advantages as a prince. He just wanted *her*, not for her magic or her beauty, but for herself.

"Darissa?"

She put down the hairbrush. "Yes?"

"Are you all right?"

She got up and returned to the sitting room. "Of course I am," she said. "Are *you*?"

He did not answer in words, but by rising from his chair and throwing his arms around her.

She returned his embrace, and after a moment led the way to the bedchamber.

Afterward he slept through the night, emotionally exhausted; Darissa did not. She rose to eat more of her bread and cheese and finish the beer before it got too warm, and took a moment to gaze out the bedroom window at the night sky and the glow of a hundred windows scattered across the kingdom below.

It was perhaps not surprising, therefore, that when she awoke in the morning she found that Marek had already risen, dressed, and departed. The guard at the door of the apartment had a message for her.

"He's talking to the king, Mistress," the guard said. "He may be there all morning. We can have breakfast sent up, if you like."

Darissa remembered that she still had two sausages and a heel of bread left, and that she could use witchcraft to warm the sausages. "Just tea, please," she said.

After her breakfast she spent what was left of the morning practicing some of her more physical magic—heating and cooling things, moving small objects from across the room, and so on. Just because she was living in the castle did not mean she was finished with her apprenticeship; she wanted to be able to meet any test Nondel might give her, to demonstrate that she was ready to move on to journeyman. After all, Marek might send her away at any time, though so far he showed no sign of any diminution in interest.

She was beginning to wonder what she should do about lunch when the door opened and Marek stepped in. "Good morning," she said.

"Good morning," he replied. "I hope you haven't been too bored here."

"I'm fine," she said. "It gave me a chance to practice my witchcraft a little. And if I'd been *really* bored, I would have left."

He smiled. "I'm sure you would."

"How is your father, the king?"

"He is bearing up. It's hard, though—I think even harder than when he lost our mother."

"What did he want to speak to you about? Or did *you* want to speak to *him*?"

"Both," Marek replied. "We were discussing the war."

"Is there any news? Has Abran come to his senses?"

Marek shook his head. "He has not surrendered, if that's what you mean."

"I suppose it is. What did you discuss, then?"

"Well, we have…we have ways to send messages back and forth to King Abran privately. Unofficial methods. And he has been using them to threaten us, and make demands."

"*He* is making demands?"

"Honestly, I think he may have gone mad. He's certainly desperate. He's convinced he'll be assassinated if he surrenders."

"He's probably right."

"He might be. We offered to give him asylum, and see him safely into exile, if he surrenders and abdicates, but he refused. Then we even offered to keep him on his throne, just to put an end to all this misery, but he refused *that*, too—said he didn't believe we would keep our word and protect him from his own people."

"Then what is *he* proposing?"

"That *we* surrender. He says he'll give us generous terms, almost anything we want so long as Eknera loses no territory and regains Northangle, and he stays on the throne. We refused, of course—we can't let them have Northangle, not after all this. People have *died* for this, dozens of them, including my brother the crown prince. And since we turned that down, all we get is incoherent threats."

"That does not sound good."

"It's not—but we're getting other reports from inside Eknera Castle, as well, and apparently many Eknerans are not happy with their king. It does not sound as if Abran will *ever* surrender, no matter what, but there are others who might remove him for us if they have assurances of an acceptable peace."

"That would probably be best for everyone," Darissa said. "Even Abran, if he's sent into exile rather than killed."

"It's just so *stupid*," Marek said. "Did Abran really think we would be caught completely off-guard, and that we wouldn't have a counter for Bhella's attack? If he did, he's not very good at this."

"He probably isn't," Darissa said. "Who are his advisors? If he's a usurper, he may not know who to listen to."

"I'm not sure he listens to *anyone*."

"Well, that would explain it, wouldn't it?"

Marek sighed. "I just wish it was all over, so we could go back to normal. Or as normal as it can be with Terren gone, anyway."

Darissa stepped over and hugged him. "It will be better some-day," she said. "Prince Evreth will come home, and maybe he'll bring a princess who will put more heirs between you and the throne, and you can go back to being yourself."

"I hope so," Marek said, as he hugged her back. "I really hope so."

CHAPTER SIXTEEN

MORVASH OF THE SHADOWS

28ᵀᴴ OF GREENGROWTH, YS 5238

The theurgist several people had recommended, Corinal by name, had been much less helpful than Morvash had hoped. Apparently the gods had a very peculiar way of looking at enchantments, and would not, or perhaps could not, advise wizards on what spells would be appropriate for a given purpose, or how a spell had been cast. The goddess Unniel could see no connection between anything a wizard might have done and how or why a person transformed from flesh to stone, and knew nothing at all about what wizardry might be useful in restoring those people. She had no advice on finding any glass vessels used in Fendel's Superior Petrifaction. Even learning where and when each of his statues had gone from being a normal human being to suddenly remaining motionless would require the victim's name or other specifics Morvash did not have.

As for Blukros, the god of healing, he did not see being turned to stone as an injury or disease and would not or could not turn anyone back.

By the end of those two summonings Corinal appeared somewhat dazed and was suffering from a severe nosebleed, so Morvash did not pursue any further inquiries.

Morvash had also been reminded by more than one person that it was technically a violation of Wizards' Guild rules to use any other sort of magic to assist in working wizardry. It was not one of the offenses that normally carried really severe penalties such as death or exile, but it was definitely not approved procedure—and of course, if the Guild decided it was serious enough, *any* offense could result in death or exile. Some of the wizards he approached had therefore refused to discuss anything about witchcraft or theurgy with him, and it had taken some prodding to get Corinal's name, or any recommendations regarding witches who might help.

Even Corinal himself had made some mild protests at being approached, but had gone ahead and asked Unniel and Blukros some of the questions Morvash wanted answered. Not that their answers had been useful.

Advice on wizardry, on the other hand, had been plentiful; while some wizards were overly fond of secrecy, others were only too glad to have an excuse to talk shop. Vorzeth the Mage had explained why trying Lirrim's Rectification might prove a disastrous mistake—the spell transformed things into what they *should* be, not necessarily what they had been, and there was a significant chance that whatever force determined that effect might decide that rather than turning the subject back into a person, a statue *should* be just a statue, without any lingering trace of humanity.

Such a mistake could be undone with the Spell of Reversal, but that was at least a ninth- or tenth-order spell with the unfortunate feature that performing the necessary ritual generally took a little over two hours, and it would only reverse things that had had happened within perhaps half an hour of its completion. This rendered it almost completely useless except as a prepared and suspended spell—stored in a powder or elixir, perhaps. Putting a tenth-order spell into a potion would be a challenge for even the most powerful wizards in Ethshar, and a mere journeyman like Morvash had no hope of doing it.

And even the Spell of Reversal would simply restore the preexisting situation; it would not return the statue to life.

Lirrim's Rectification *might* work, but no one was optimistic about it.

The consensus was that Javan's Restorative was the only practical way to save all those poor people in his rented gallery.

None of the wizards he spoke to ventured an opinion on whether there might be some witchcraft that could be useful, but he did get the names of three witches who were reported to be good at hearing thoughts and seeing things other people did not see; he intended to find out whether he could learn anything about who the petrified people were, to determine whether Ithinia and Gror were right that some of them might be dangerous and better left as statues. After his disappointing visit to Corinal, Morvash was not optimistic as he set out to find the first of the three, a woman by the name of Ariella the Perceptive who was generally acknowledged as the best in all Ethshar at hearing thoughts, but who was said to be difficult to work with. Morvash had been told her shop was at the southwest end of Witch Alley; the sun was low in the west and hidden by gathering clouds as he left Corinal's establishment and headed in that direction.

It was raining by the time he reached the corner of Mana Street and Witch Alley, and he had not brought an umbrella or appropriate protective spell. He ducked under an overhanging upper story, took off his hat to shake off the worst of the rain, and looked for a sign-board.

"There's no signboard," a voice said behind him; he whirled, startled, to find a small dark woman leaning out a window. Before he could speak, she added, "I'm Ariella. What's this about...a talking statue? No, that's not it. Why don't you come inside and tell me about it?" She pointed to a nearby door painted with pink and white flowers on a red background.

She opened the door from inside just as he reached it—she must have moved very quickly, he thought. She beckoned him in, and he entered; he had to remove his hat and stoop to fit through the doorway, and inside the ceiling was too low for him to return his hat to its customary place, so it remained in his hand.

The room was small, with varnished wooden walls and ceiling; the single window beside the door that Ariella had leaned out let in very little light, but a roaring blaze on a hearth opposite the door provided additional illumination, as well as keeping the room uncomfortably hot.

"I like it like this," Ariella said. "Have a seat." She gestured toward a tall stool.

Morvash settled warily onto the indicated object. Ariella did not sit, but stood before him, looking him in the eye. For a moment she stared at him, saying nothing. He hesitated, unsure whether he should break the silence.

"I can hear you," she answered. "You don't need to speak aloud unless you want to."

"Then you...well, yes," Morvash said. "Obviously, you *can* hear my thoughts."

"That's what you wanted," she said. "False modesty aside, I think I do it better than any other witch in the city."

"That's perfect!" Morvash said, smiling.

"Maybe," Ariella replied. "I don't know whether I can hear a statue's thoughts or not—that isn't something I've ever tried before." She considered him thoughtfully, then nodded. "Let me get my coat."

"What? Now? But…"

"Why wait?" she called back over her shoulder as she stepped through a door to another room. "And I know it's still warm, but it's *raining*—that's why I want a coat. Yes, I know that's not important, but it's what you were thinking. As for payment, you're doing a good thing—well, trying to—and I'm happy to help for no charge, though I'll be glad to accept a share if this does turn out to be profitable for you." While Morvash was still gathering his wits to respond, she reappeared with a battered oilskin jacket over her shoulders. "Come on," she said. "Lead the way; for some reason I don't do well taking directions from people's thoughts. Maybe because I'm short, so everything looks different than it does from up there."

Morvash exited first, and waited under an overhang while Ariella locked the door. When it was secure she beckoned to him, and they began walking. Morvash glanced up at the clouds and tried to think of some spell that would keep him—or preferably both of them—dry, but could not come up with one that he could do with the ingredients he had with him.

Ariella's witchcraft did not seem to be doing any better; her hair was already soaked. Morvash wondered why she had not worn a hat; surely she must own one!

She muttered something, but Morvash did not catch it. He did notice that the water dripping from her hair somehow never went near her eyes or mouth; perhaps her witchcraft was doing some good after all.

They rounded the corner onto Mana Street and headed north. The dirt of the street was packed hard enough that it was still solid, and not turning to mud, which was a relief.

They had not covered even the single block to Games Street before Ariella said, "I think this will be an interesting experience for me, listening to statues."

They turned left onto Games Street, and then right onto Arena;

the rain briefly lessened to a drizzle. After another block or so Ariella said, "I'm not always so generous; usually I want to be paid, but you're already short of funds and it's such an intriguing project. If you think about it, you'll realize I can make money easily enough any time I want to—just walking down a crowded street I'll find a hundred secrets, dozens of things people will pay to learn, or to be sure someone *doesn't* learn. It's not why I specialized in this sort of witchcraft, but it's a nice byproduct. I devoted myself to mind-listening because it interested me, and I had a knack for it. Yes, sometimes people do get annoyed when I answer questions they haven't asked, but it's so *boring* waiting for them to speak!"

Morvash grimaced.

"I've been doing it so long I can't help myself anymore," she said. "Sometimes it takes a conscious effort to *not* hear the thoughts of whoever is within a few feet, especially once I've already made contact, and when I say 'effort' I mean it; it's hard work to shut it out. And yes, there are plenty of things I wish I didn't hear; some folks are downright nasty. *Your* mind is relatively pleasant. Yes, I can see the things you didn't mean to think about just then, but honestly, Morvash, that's nothing compared to some people. It's not as if you would ever actually *do* those things."

They walked on, past the Arena itself—if a show had been scheduled for this particular evening it had been rained out, as the gates beneath the arches were closed. The notice board was still there, of course, but no one was looking at it. It had a little cap to keep rain off, like a miniature porch roof, but Morvash could see that the papers at the bottom were getting soaked anyway as the breeze swept in the rain. He glanced at his companion, and saw that her hair was still dripping—but not into her eyes.

As they left the Arena behind the rain was coming down more heavily again, discouraging any conversation, and they picked up the pace as they continued along Arena Street.

"No," Ariella said after a silence, startling him. "I don't really know much other witchcraft. A few of the basics, like guiding small objects already in motion—that's what I'm doing to keep the rain out of my eyes—but that's about all. I put so much time and effort into hearing thoughts that I never learned much else." Morvash had not yet put the question into words even for himself, and would probably never have asked it aloud, but he *had* been wondering about that. "My master was disappointed in me; she thought every witch should know a variety of magic, not just one particular effect. She had to grant me my freedom as a journeyman, though, because I could correctly answer any question anyone asked me, even if I couldn't necessarily perform the spell they asked about—well, any question *almost* anyone asked me. There are a few witches who can block me or even lie to me. As for not needing to know any other magic, witches don't have set rules—as long as an apprentice can demonstrate mastery of some branch of witchcraft, she can make journeyman. It's not as if *wizards* have a set of specific spells they need to know, is it? Oh, besides that one. Yes, I know it's a Guild secret, but did you really think I wouldn't have found it in someone's thoughts by now?" She sighed. "I'm sorry you find it disturbing, but look at it this way—I'm letting you know everything I hear. I'm not spying on you and keeping secrets to use against you later. You're right, I can't prove I'm not digging deep down into your memory; you'll just have to take my word for it that that's not how it works. Normally I only hear what's near the surface. Why would I risk angering a wizard? There are protective spells that can shut me out, at least temporarily, and you can do things I can't possibly defend against, even if I know they're coming. How could I stop something like the Rune of the Implacable Stalker? So I won't intentionally go prying into your secrets, and I'll keep my mouth shut about any I stumble across."

Over the course of the half-mile or so they had walked Morvash's reaction to the weirdly one-sided conversation had gone from wonderment to annoyance to concern, and finally to amusement. He had not said a word since they left Ariella's house, but she had answered every question he had thought of asking.

"Not very many," she said. "You're right, most people don't like it. I could keep quiet, but what sort of a friend is someone you can't speak freely with? I do have a *few* friends, though—I'd trust my neighbor Liria with my life, and my older sister Gazi is genuinely fond of me even though she thinks I'm a pest."

Morvash glanced at her, then up at the sky; the rain was coming down steadily.

"You're right, I *am* treating you like a friend," she said. "Because I know you don't mind. You were worried about my snooping earlier, but you got over it quickly. You're a nice man, Morvash—you think well of everyone, whether they deserve it or not. Devoting yourself to saving a bunch of petrified strangers is really rather noble; there aren't many wizards who would bother to do it. You don't see Ithinia offering to help you, do you? Well, beyond that, I mean—she's not doing anything that costs her any more than a few minutes' conversation."

The sun was down and the skies dark by the time they turned left on Through Street; the rain had become a downpour. Morvash glanced at his companion's short legs, and wished she walked faster.

"You aren't the only one," she muttered.

Finally they turned left again, onto Old East Avenue, and Morvash broke into a trot, Ariella into an all-out run, to cover the last two blocks to the tall, dark house of Erdrik the Grim.

The streetlights had not yet been lit, and there were no lights in his house or the nearest neighbors, so finding the keyhole and getting the key into it was a challenge, but at last Morvash swung the heavy wooden door open and let Ariella in.

She stepped past him, and he followed her into the front hall. The darkness was very thick; he could hear furniture moving around, but could see almost nothing. He drew his athame and summoned a blue glow, fed by the ferocious level of ambient magic in the house. "This way," he said, leading his guest into the parlor.

As always, the fire on the hearth lit itself, providing some illumination. Morvash pricked his finger with his glowing blade and murmured a few words; a flame bloomed from the drop of blood on his fingertip, and he used this to light three or four candles before curling his finger to douse the flame and returning the knife to its sheath on his belt.

"Oh," Ariella said, looking around at the chairs that were walking slowly toward her.

"Don't pay them any attention," Morvash said, speaking aloud for the first time since they had left Witch Alley. Then a notion struck him. "Do *they* have any thoughts you can hear?"

Ariella stared at the chairs, at a big armchair in particular, then shook her head. "Not really," she said.

That did not bode well, Morvash thought—but then, the chairs had never been human.

At least, he didn't *think* they had; the possibility that Erdrik had turned people into furniture, rather than animating a carpenter's products, had not occurred to him until just now, but he was not sure he could rule it out.

"So where are the statues?" Ariella asked. "In the front hall?" She nodded toward the clutter they had passed.

"No, they're..." Morvash began. Then he stopped. He had not yet taken the time to check whether any of the statuary Erdrik had left behind might be petrified people. "Those aren't mine," he said. "I don't know..." There were no life-sized depictions of human beings—but they didn't really need to be life-sized, and from everything Morvash had heard about Erdrik, he seemed like the sort of wizard who wouldn't mind working multiple spells on his enemies. Morvash knew of a third-order spell called Riyal's Transformation that would reduce people to a tiny fraction of their normal size, and someone of Erdrik's abilities would undoubtedly have known either that spell or one like it. He picked up one of the candles he had just lit. "Come on," he said. "Let's see."

Ariella followed him back out to the front hall, where they carefully went through the various sculptures.

Most were, so far as either Ariella's witchcraft or Morvash's athame could determine, exactly what they appeared to be, mere carvings. A full-sized soapstone cat, however, reacted as magical, and three miniatures of soldiers also registered. Ariella picked one of them up.

"Who are you?" she asked.

Morvash heard nothing, but he saw Ariella nod. "Go on," she said. "When did this happen?"

He stepped up beside her.

"That was over a hundred years ago," she told the figurine. "I'm so sorry. Morvash, the wizard here, will try to turn you back, but it may take quite awhile—it's not easy magic."

"Is it just the one, or all three?" Morvash asked.

"All three," Ariella said, setting the figure back on its shelf. "They were sent by Azrad the Fourth to investigate a complaint about Erdrik's experiments. He shrank them and took them prisoner, and sent a message to the overlord, and when he didn't get the answer he wanted he turned them to stone. They've been here ever since."

"Oh," Morvash said. As he had suspected, Erdrik, it seemed, had not been a good person. He pushed past Ariella and picked up all three statuettes. "We'll bring these upstairs, to make sure I don't forget about them."

Looking down at them, Morvash wondered whether he had missed others in Lord Landessin's collection. There might be dozens more petrified people in Uncle Gror's rented estate that had been shrunk or otherwise disguised. He would need to check that at some point...

"What about the cat?" Ariella asked, interrupting his thoughts.

"Can you hear any thoughts?"

"No. But I can't from live cats, either."

"You can bring it along if you like, then," Morvash said. With the three miniature soldiers in one hand and the candlestick in the other, he said, "This way," and led the witch toward the grand staircase.

CHAPTER SEVENTEEN

HAKIN OF THE HUNDRED-FOOT FIELD

8TH OF LONGDAYS, YS 5231

There was no other bookmark, the green earthenware jar was un-labeled, and unless the magical powder was indistinguishable from ordinary house-dust, there was no other left-over powder to be found. Tarker refused to help beyond a quick once-over, and simply stood and watched as Hakin went over the workbench and the floor around the body half a dozen times, looking for smears of powder or scraps of notepaper or other clues. The youth did not give up until a pair of guardsmen appeared in the workroom door.

"*Hai!*" one of them said, and Hakin, who had been on his knees inspecting the gaps between floorboards, looked up to see both men staring warily at the demon.

Hakin gave Tarker a quick glance, then said, "You can come in; it won't hurt you unless you get in its way."

Tarker growled.

"We heard a demon killed a wizard," one of the soldiers said, taking one cautious step into the room, his hand on his cudgel.

"That's right," Hakin said, getting to his feet. He gestured at the corpse, then at Tarker. "There's the wizard, and there's the demon."

"They're both still here?"

"Well, the wizard is still here," Hakin said. "I brought the demon back."

"Would you care to explain that?" the soldier asked, still eyeing Tarker.

"A demonologist by the name of Karitha summoned this demon, Tarker, and ordered it to kill a wizard named Wosten of the Red Robe, which I assume was this poor fellow," Hakin explained. "But when it went back to say the job was done and ask to be released, it couldn't find Karitha anywhere, and it's stuck in the World until she either dismisses it or dies. So we're looking for her. We came here because we thought we might find something here that would give us a clue. Which we did." He waved a hand toward the open blood-stained book. "Apparently the wizard cast a spell on the demonologist. But we can't tell what *kind* of spell."

"Who are *you*, then?" the second guardsman asked.

"Hakin of…of Wall Street," he replied. "I met Tarker when it was rampaging about my neighborhood looking for Karitha, and offered to help it find her, so it can go home. I thought the sooner it's out of the city the better—it doesn't have orders to kill anyone else, and it doesn't particularly want to, but it's got a temper and accidents happen."

"So are you a demonologist?"

"Me? No, I'm…I'm a courier."

"More like a kid from the Hundred-Foot Field, by the look of your clothes," the first soldier remarked.

"I admit I do not have a permanent residence at the moment," Hakin said, drawing himself up to his full, if modest, height.

"A courier—you carry messages for a bit or two?"

"And do other odd jobs," Hakin admitted. "I'm not a beggar or a thief, if that's what you were thinking."

"An orphan?"

"Tarker, here, says my father's still alive, but I've never met him. My mother's long dead."

The soldier nodded. "So were you thinking you might make a piece or two by helping this demon?"

"The possibility had occurred to me," Hakin admitted.

The soldier glanced at Tarker again, then back at Hakin. "You didn't think it'd just kill you?"

"That possibility had occurred to me, too, but I decided to risk it."

"That's pretty brave for a street kid."

"Thanks."

"I'm not sure it was a compliment."

"I'll take it as one anyway."

"I don't know how you wound up talking to it in the first place."

"It was tearing up the Field, looking for the demonologist, and I knew it couldn't be looking for *me*, so I called to it. I half-expected it to ignore me, and I was ready to run if it came for me, but it was willing to talk to me, so we talked, and we made a deal—I'd help it if it stopped smashing things and hurting people."

"He has assisted me," Tarker growled. "Though we have not yet found Karitha. We know the wizard enchanted her before I tore his throat out."

"So now we want to know what the enchantment was," Hakin agreed.

"So you came back here," the first guardsman said.

"Right."

"Is everything he told us true?" the soldier asked Tarker.

"Yes," the demon replied.

"You trust a demon?" the second soldier asked.

"It just admitted to tearing out the wizard's throat," the first soldier said. "If it doesn't mind telling us that, why would it lie about the rest of it?" He turned back to Hakin. "You weren't involved in the killing itself?"

"Ask Tarker," Hakin said, gesturing at his demonic companion.

"He was not," the demon answered. "Karitha the Demonologist sent me, and she alone."

"Do we arrest the demon for murder, then?" the second soldier asked. "Take it to the magistrate?"

The first shook his head. "Don't you know the law? Demons aren't criminals, they're weapons. We send them away if we can, we don't arrest them." He grimaced. "Or rather, we don't waste our time *trying* to arrest them. Seriously, Orzin, how would we arrest it?" He gestured at Tarker.

Tarker growled obligingly.

"I take your point," Orzin replied. "What about the kid?"

"He and the demon both say he wasn't involved, that it was all this Karitha." He looked around thoughtfully. "On the other hand, I guess he's a witness, and he's trespassing here."

"He is *useful* to me," Tarker rumbled.

"It's all right," Hakin said hastily, gesturing for Tarker to remain calm. "Sir, what are you planning to do?"

"Well, if your demon doesn't object, I'd like to take you both to the magistrate and see what *he* thinks of all this. He'll probably want to have someone cast a few spells to figure out just what happened, and he'll want to talk to both of you."

"We want to know what happened, too, so we'll be happy to come—won't we, Tarker?"

"Willing," the demon replied. "Not happy."

"Good enough." Hakin smiled. "Come on, let's go see the magistrate—maybe he'll have a magician in court who can find Karitha for you." He glanced back at the green jar, but decided to leave it where it was, at least for now; taking it while the guardsmen were right there watching did not seem like a good idea. He had told them he was not a thief, and proving himself wrong would be stupid.

The magistrate's office turned out to be on Games Street, a few blocks away, and the foursome made the trip without incident, though Tarker continued to draw stares from everyone on the street. Hakin noticed that the spriggans that infested the Wizards' Quarter fled in terror at the sight of the demon.

Hakin had visited magistrates before, as a witness to various petty crimes or even once or twice as a suspect, but he had never encountered this particular individual. Lord Borlan administered the central Wizards' Quarter and the southern portion of Arena, neither of which lay very near to Hakin's usual home in the portion of the Hundred-Foot Field that ran through Southwark.

They had a brief wait in the antechamber, during which Hakin took the opportunity to sit and rest his feet, while Tarker and both guardsmen remained standing. The magistrate's two assistants crowded themselves as far away from the demon as their duties allowed, and Hakin suspected that the wait would have been significantly longer had Tarker not been there.

The magistrate's chamber itself was not particularly large or elegant. There were two windows on one side, a row of simple chairs along the other, and the magistrate himself seated behind a desk at the far end. The floor shook slightly as Tarker stamped into the room.

"All right," Lord Borlan said, leaning back in his chair and folding his hands over his chest. "What's the story? Why is a demon in my chamber?"

The senior soldier, whose name Hakin still had not caught, explained the situation, and Hakin was happy to let him do so; he was tired of telling people about it. He was, in fact, getting simply *tired*—he was not in the habit of running around the city like this. It had already been a very long day, and the sun was not even down.

But then the magistrate swung his gaze from the soldier to Hakin, leaned forward, set his elbows on his desk, clasped his hands, and began to ask questions—where had Hakin met the demon? Why had he agreed to help it? What had he seen in Wosten's workshop?

Hakin answered as quickly and honestly as he could, startled and somewhat impressed by how thoroughly Lord Borlan was exploring the situation. He found himself stammering once or twice, but each time Lord Borlan simply waited until he had collected himself and could give a straight answer.

Then the magistrate began questioning Tarker, but the demon quickly ran out of patience. "These two spoke the truth," he said, gesturing at Hakin and the soldier. "You are no demonologist, and I am not constrained to obey you."

"True enough, I am no demonologist," Lord Borlan replied, "but you are in my jurisdiction, so you are my concern."

"You are not *my* concern," Tarker said.

The magistrate nodded, then turned to Orzin. "Do you have anything to add? Is there anything you see differently?"

Orzin looked at the other three—his companion, the youth, and the demon—then said, "No, my lord."

Lord Borland leaned back in his chair again, considering the foursome. After several seconds of silence, he said, "Karitha the Demonologist stands accused of murder by magical means, but cannot be found. This demon wants to find her for reasons of its own, and may prove useful to this court in bringing this fugitive to justice, but may also prove a public hazard if permitted to roam freely. We have at our disposal several magicians, and I would be surprised if we cannot, given time and money, determine what has become of Karitha. We also have this young man who has involved himself in the matter, and who appears to have the demon's trust. What I propose as a resolution, at least temporarily, is that the demon shall agree to act as the city's employee—I'm sure the guard can find a use for such a creature, no?" He glanced at the two soldiers, who seemed nonplused. The magistrate did not wait for a response; as Tarker started to growl, he continued, loudly and firmly, "Naturally, we will pay it for its services, in the only way that we can—by finding Karitha, and informing it of her whereabouts and circumstances, as quickly as we can. Should the demon harm any innocent citizens of Ethshar, this agreement would be void, and our magicians, rather than aiding it in its quest, will instead do everything they can to keep Karitha out of its reach." He fixed his gaze directly on the demon. "And given the skills of our wizards, I think that everything they can do will be more than enough to frustrate you, Tarker the Unrelenting."

Tarker roared, and took a step toward Lord Borlan; Hakin shouted, "No! If you hurt him you'll *never* find her!"

"Indeed," the magistrate said, apparently unshaken. The demon stopped, glaring at him. "And that brings us to this Hakin of the Hundred-Foot Field."

"I haven't done anything," Hakin protested.

"On the contrary," Lord Borlan said. "It seems to me that you have given this demon considerable assistance, and have provided my magicians with several hints of how to start their search."

Hakin looked worried. "That's not a crime, is it?"

"No, it certainly is not. You may well have saved lives and prevented considerable destruction by heading off a demonic rampage through the streets. You aren't in trouble, lad; in fact, I'm offering you a job."

Hakin blinked. "A…what?"

"A job," Lord Borlan repeated. "As the demon's companion and advisor."

"I…" Hakin glanced at Tarker, who was still glaring at the magistrate. Then his instincts kicked in. "What does it pay?"

The magistrate turned to Orzin. "What does a new recruit in the city guard receive?"

Caught off-guard, Orzin coughed and struggled to get words out before eventually replying, "Three bits a day and free lodging, less a share of his meals when he's living in the barracks. He gets his armor, weapons, and uniforms, too, but no more than once a year—anything over that he has to pay for himself."

"There you are, then."

"What, I'd be joining the guard? But I'm not old enough!" Hakin was not absolutely certain of his own age, but his best estimate put it at fifteen, or possibly fourteen and several months, and therefore short of the guard's minimum sixteen.

"You would not be a guardsman, as such, but a civilian employee. *Tarker* would be..." The magistrate stopped in mid-sentence and looked at the demon. "How old are *you*?" he asked.

Tarker snorted derisively. "Older than your entire world, human."

Lord Borlan looked rather intrigued by that, Hakin thought, but he did not let it distract him. "Old enough, then. And it doesn't really matter—you won't be a guardsman, either. You will both be working with the guard, and will be housed with them, but you won't be guardsmen."

"I will be nothing but what I am," Tarker said.

"I'm sure," Lord Borlan said. "But for the present, one thing you are is trapped in our world, is it not?"

Tarker growled.

"You cannot go home until you find Karitha. Well, this is our offer—harm no one unless asked to do so by an officer of the city guard, carry out the tasks assigned you, and we will do everything we can to find the demonologist for you. Disobey, harm an innocent, recklessly damage property, and we will instead do everything we can to keep her from you. Simple enough. With any luck we will have her for you in a day or two and this will all be over, perhaps before the guard asks anything of you; if not, well, how is serving us any worse than the alternatives?"

Tarker still glared, but no longer growled. Hakin could feel the heat from its body, though, and saw wisps of smoke rising from its back and between its clenched teeth.

"What if *I* don't want the job?" Hakin asked.

The magistrate turned up an empty palm. "Then you are free to go."

"Three bits a day? And my meals, and a bed?"

"Three bits *or* your meals, and a bed either way," Lord Borlan corrected him.

"And my duties—I can't make Tarker do anything it doesn't want to."

"I understand that. Your duties would be to attend to the demon, to talk to it, to be its companion and advisor. You will bring it instructions and requests from the guard's officers and from city officials, and explain anything it finds unclear. You will serve as an intermediary between the demon and the rest of the city."

Hakin looked at Tarker, then at the two soldiers, then back to the magistrate.

"I'll do it," he said. "If Tarker agrees."

"I must," Tarker rumbled. "I do not want to stay here any longer than I must, and I cannot find Karitha without human assistance. If I must be your slave to earn that assistance, I will be your slave—but do not expect me to humble myself. I am a demon of the First Circle."

"Then it's settled," Lord Borlan said. "Guardsmen, escort these two to the barracks and make the appropriate arrangements."

The soldiers stepped forward to obey; Orzin reached for one of Tarker's arms, then thought better of it and simply gestured toward the door.

Hakin did not quite understand how someone could acquiesce to enslavement without humbling himself, but he did not want to argue; he and Tarker were obviously going to be seeing a great deal of each other for some time to come. But he was going to be paid for it! He would be paid, and fed, and permitted to sleep under a roof.

He turned and walked out of the magistrate's chamber with his head held high.

CHAPTER EIGHTEEN

DARISSA THE WITCH'S APPRENTICE

3RD OF LEAFCOLOR, YS 5199

The days dragged on, and the siege of Eknera continued. Prince Evreth came home briefly, but spent only a single night in his own bed before heading out again. Darissa was not invited to the private family dinner where Evreth described his travels, but Marek gave her a full report afterward, when he came up to bed.

"He visited *twenty-two* different kingdoms!" Marek explained, as they undressed. "Twenty-two! I've only ever been to nine."

"I've only seen two," Darissa interjected.

"He met every eligible princess in the region," Marek said. "It's his duty to marry soon, especially with Terren gone, and he's been hoping to find someone he could truly love, but it hasn't happened."

"I thought he was acting as your father's envoy, helping with the war!"

"Oh, he *was*—he very much was. He was essential to winning the war, assuming we ever finally do. Everything you heard about what he did in Kanthoa and Yolder and Mezgalon, it's all true, and we're all unspeakably proud of him. But he'd be an idiot not to look at the potential brides while he was there, and whatever else you might say about him, Evreth is not an idiot. So he spoke with dozens of princesses. He said none of them captured his heart, but there were a few he could imagine living with. He's going back to Kanthoa and Zedmor, officially to affirm their agreements with Melitha and each other, but unofficially he wants to see Artalda of Zedmor again—he said she's smart and pretty, and he thinks she could be good company. She's two years older than he is, and she seemed to see that as a problem, but *he* doesn't, and now that he's next in line for the throne he's hoping she might reconsider."

"Do we know for certain that Indamara isn't pregnant?" Darissa asked.

"Well…no, not for certain, not yet. She says she doesn't think so, but can't be sure. But even if she *is* expecting, she might miscarry, or it could be a girl. The chances are that Evreth will be the heir."

"You know, if I could meet Indamara, I could *tell* you whether she's pregnant. And maybe even whether it's a boy or a girl."

Marek paused with his undertunic over his head. "I hadn't thought of that," he said. "We were all just waiting to see—she says another sixnight should make it clear."

"I could tell you."

"We should do that. It's past time you met her, in any case. I'll introduce you tomorrow."

"Good," Darissa said. "So will *you* be traveling around to meet princesses soon?"

"I don't *want* to," Marek said. "I want to stay here with you, and I'd happily marry you, if you'd let me."

"You can't. I'm a witch."

"I could give up my place in the succession."

"I'm not sure that would be enough. You'd still be making me part of the royal family."

"I know." He sighed as he folded his undertunic. "But I'm not going to go looking for a marriageable princess unless my father insists."

"Do you think he will?"

"When Terren was alive, I would have said no, but now I'm not sure. I'm still not first in line, but losing Terren reminded him that bad things can happen." He turned and pulled Darissa to him. "But I know I've already found what *I* want, right here!"

Darissa giggled.

The next morning Marek left early, to eat breakfast with the royal family before seeing Prince Evreth off, and Darissa had expected to spend some time on her own. Instead, a few minutes after Marek left, someone knocked on the door.

"Yes?" she asked.

"The king commands your presence," an unfamiliar voice called.

Startled, Darissa opened the door. "What?"

"The king commands your presence," the footman in the corridor repeated. "Immediately."

"Of course," Darissa said—because what else could one say? She could see in the footman's thoughts that this was a genuine royal command, not a trick or misunderstanding. She straightened her gray robe, brushed her hair back, and followed the footman, closing the door behind her.

A moment later she was shown into the family dining room, where King Terren, Prince Evreth, Princess Hinda, Princess Indamara, and Prince Marek were eating breakfast.

Prince Evreth rose at the sight of her, took her hand, and bowed. "So *you* are the woman who has captured my brother's heart! At last we meet."

Darissa curtsied awkwardly in return, but could not think of anything to say.

Evreth was about Marek's height, but leaner, with piercing green eyes and a pointed beard. Darissa felt an intense curiosity in him, and a strong reserve—he was keeping his emotions in check.

When he released her hand King Terren beckoned to her. "Come here," he said.

"Yes, your Majesty," she replied, hurrying to his side. As the king, *he* did not rise to greet her.

He stared up at her face as she stood by his chair, studying her features, and she could feel a deep sadness and weariness. Then he gestured toward the young woman on his right. "This is Indamara, my daughter-in-law."

Darissa curtsied again.

Indamara did not say anything, so Darissa did not speak, either. She could feel a sort of wild despair from the princess, confusion and grief and anger.

And she could sense Indamara's body. She knew there was no child in her womb. Prince Terren would have no heir.

"I had wanted to meet you before I left," Evreth said. "I had heard so much about you!"

"I'm flattered, your Highness," Darissa said.

"Thank you for coming, Darissa," the king said. "But I'm afraid you must go now. We are grateful that you have provided comfort to Prince Marek, and Evreth did want to meet you, but it is not suitable for you to break bread with us. I hope you understand."

"Of course, your Majesty." She curtsied a final time, looked around the room, and headed for the door.

Evreth watched her go with sincere interest, Marek with love, the king with polite kindness, Indamara with confusion—and Hinda with hatred, which Darissa did not understand. Why would Hinda hate her?

But then she was back in the corridor, and the footman escorted her back to Marek's apartments.

About an hour later Marek returned, and asked her, "Well?" He did not need to be more specific.

"She isn't pregnant," Darissa replied. "I'm sorry."

"So am I—though I'm not surprised. It was a long shot, at best. At least you got to meet her, and Evreth, and my father."

"And Princess Hinda," Darissa said.

"You met her before, though."

"Yes, I did, but I wanted to ask you if you know why she hates me."

Marek hesitated, then sighed.

"Because she thinks you're distracting me," he said. "She wants me to marry a princess and start siring princes, and you're obviously making that more difficult. And she assumes you deliberately seduced me so you could live in luxury here in the castle, and that you're more interested in money and power than you are in me. If there's more to it than that, which I think there may be, I don't know what it is."

"Why isn't she angry at Evreth for not being married?"

"Oh, she is! And at least he's been looking, while I've been here with you. She's angry with me about *many* things, not just you. She doesn't think I take my position seriously, and she's angry that I've gotten involved in the war effort when I don't know anything about governing or fighting. She's angry about a *lot* of things."

"*She* isn't married," Darissa pointed out.

"She hasn't had any offers yet."

"Why not?"

"*I* don't know. Because there is a surplus of princesses? Because she isn't very appealing? Maybe that's another reason she's angry. Sometimes I wonder what would happen if a commoner took an interest in her—but she'd probably be more offended than pleased."

"Does she even *know* any commoners?"

"A few. She likes talking to magicians."

"She doesn't seem to want to talk to *me*."

"I… You're only an apprentice, and you… That's different."

Darissa realized she was upsetting Marek, and changed the subject. "Prince Evreth seems very pleasant."

"Oh, he's definitely the charmer in the family," Marek agreed. "That's why he's the one conducting most of our diplomacy."

"They're all grieving the loss of your brother."

"Of course. So am…"

"…So are you. I know that, Marek, and I apologize if I haven't made it clear how sorry I am for your loss. I know you loved him."

"I did," Marek agreed.

A thought struck Darissa. "Could *you* marry Indamara now?"

Marek started back, blinking. "No!" he said.

"Why not? It's not unheard of, marrying a brother's widow, and it would reinforce the alliance with her family in Pethmor."

"I don't want her, she doesn't want me, her family in Pethmor might find her more useful elsewhere, and in four years of marriage she had one miscarriage and no live births. No."

"All right; it was just an idle speculation. If you *must* marry a princess, I thought she might be a candidate."

"No."

Darissa knew better than to pursue the subject. She gave Marek a quick embrace, and there was no further discussion of dynastic marriages or Marek's family that morning.

Two days later, as Darissa was making herself useful treating burns in the kitchen after a mishap at lunch, the news came. She was not sure just how it first arrived, but in mere moments it seemed to be everywhere.

King Abran III of Eknera had been assassinated by his own guards, a man by the name of Lord Pallinus had been named as regent for the new king, whoever he was, and Eknera Castle had been surrendered to the besieging forces.

Celebrations broke out on all sides; kitchen maids who had been bickering a moment before were hugging one another and dancing. Darissa heard shouting and singing in the corridors and courtyard.

She finished soothing the burned forearm she was holding, then rose from her stool and hurried up to Marek's apartment.

She met him in the corridor just outside their door.

"I was just looking for you!" he said, striding toward her. "You've heard?"

"Of course I've heard!"

"I think my father will want me to go oversee the treaty talks—we aren't sure exactly where Evreth is right now, and one of the royal family should be there, though of course most of the actual negotiating will be done by General Tobul and Lord Kather."

Darissa's only answer was to fling herself into his arms and kiss him vigorously.

When at last they paused for breath, he said, "I shouldn't be gone for very long. You can go back to your master's place if you want, once the war is officially over, and finish your apprenticeship."

"I should probably do that," Darissa agreed, though at the moment she really did not care at all whether she ever made journeyman.

That evening, when the celebrations had subsided somewhat and those that continued had become more organized, Marek and Darissa met again in their sitting room.

"The king is sending me to Eknera first thing in the morning," Marek said. "The terms should mostly be settled by then, and I'll just give them the royal nod of approval."

Darissa nodded. She actually wanted to go along, and see something more of the world outside Melitha, and watch history being made, but she knew that it wasn't going to happen. She was Marek's mistress, with no official standing, and her presence at any sort of formal event, such as signing a treaty, would be horribly inappropriate.

"Right now, though," Marek said, "my father and Hinda are holding a victory ball downstairs. Would you like to come?"

So much for not being welcome at formal events—but there was another problem. "I don't have a ball gown," she said.

"Oh, I wouldn't worry about that! On short notice, for an occasion like this, no one expects all the niceties to be observed. We'll probably see laundresses in mobcaps dancing with courtiers in velvet and silk. Come along and dance with me!"

She looked down at her apprentice's robe. "Well, let me change into something a *little* nicer!"

"If you must, then—I'll wait."

Fifteen minutes later Prince Marek walked into the ballroom unannounced, with a girl most of the guests did not recognize on his arm, and the pair joined into the festivities with unbridled enthusiasm.

Darissa did not see anyone in a mobcap, but Marek had been correct in saying the event would not be formal. There were soldiers in uniform, courtiers in velvet, and women in skirts and dresses of every sort. There was even that tall woman Darissa had seen on her way to the castle when the war first began, the one she thought was probably a wizard, though she did not join in the dancing, but simply watched, unsmiling, from the side of the room.

To Darissa's surprise the king left early; when she mentioned it to Marek he said he had seen a messenger speaking to his father, and the king had then hurried out. He guessed it was something to do with the surrender terms.

Perhaps half an hour later Princess Hinda left as well, beckoning for the supposed wizard to follow her, but most of the other celebrants danced and drank well into the night. It was after midnight when Darissa and Marek finally stumbled back to the prince's apartments. Once they were inside, with the door locked behind them, Marek said, "And now one last celebration before we sleep, and for this one you don't need a gown. In fact, I don't want to see a single stitch of clothing!"

Darissa giggled; she had drunk more wine than ever before in her life, and was feeling its effects. "And I will be happy to oblige you, your Highness, if you will do me the same favor!"

A few minutes later they were in the prince's bed, and just beginning that final celebration, when everything went dark.

Darissa, lying on her back with her knees drawn up to her chest, thought at first that the lamp had gone out, but almost instantly she realized it was more than that. She could not see anything at all, nor could she *feel* anything, where a moment before she could feel a very great deal. She could not move. She could not hear Marek's breath, which had been loud in her ear a moment before. She could not smell anything, and did not feel her *own* breath.

This was not a spilled lamp, nor anything else simple and natural. She tried to use her witchcraft to sense what had happened, where she was, whether Marek was still with her, but even that was deadened. She could just barely detect Marek's thoughts—he, too, was baffled, uncomprehending, trying to understand what had happened. She could make out nothing of the room around them.

But she knew what had happened. Someone had cast a spell on them.

It took hours before she was able to establish exactly what sort of spell. She had hoped it was temporary, that the enchantment would wear off, but it did not, and at last, when she heard muffled voices, grunts, and the sound of something heavy being moved, she understood.

They had been turned to stone. She did not know who had done it, or how, or why, but they had been turned to stone.

CHAPTER NINETEEN

MORVASH OF THE SHADOWS

28TH OF GREENGROWTH, YS 5238

The first statue Morvash chose for Ariella's perusal appeared to be a soldier of some sort, though Morvash did not recognize the uniform, and the figure did not appear to be carrying any weapons. There was no spear or sword, but his marble tunic looked like light armor. Morvash set the candle beside the stony foot, then stepped back and gestured to the witch. "What do you hear?" he asked.

Ariella stepped forward and stared into the statue's blank white eyes. "He's not thinking in Ethsharitic," she said. "It's not Trader's Tongue, either, or anything else I recognize."

"Can you understand *anything*?" Morvash asked.

"Give me a minute. Not all thoughts are in words, and…and I think he does know some Ethsharitic, and he can hear us…" She frowned. "*Do* you hear me? Can you tell me who you are?" Then she blinked and stepped back.

"Oh, blood," she said. "By all the varied gods!"

"What is it?" Morvash demanded. Perhaps this man was exactly the sort of threat he had been warned about.

"He's…he's a Northerner. His native language—he calls it Shaslan. He was a Northern spy during the Great War. He's been petrified for…well, at least three hundred years, maybe more; I'm not sure how closely the Northern calendar matches ours."

Morvash stared. "A Northerner spy?" *That* was not anything he had anticipated.

Ariella nodded. "He was caught by a patrol and taken to a General Korzad, and Korzad's magicians questioned him, and then they turned him to stone to keep him out of the way and make certain he wouldn't escape or be rescued. They didn't just kill him because they weren't sure whether he might have more information they could use, but then they never turned him back, either, and he's been handed down from one owner to the next ever since. They long ago forgot he had ever been alive."

"A *Northern spy?*"

"Well, *he* certainly believes it, and he does mostly think in the strangest language I've ever heard."

"The war's been over for more than two hundred years; there *aren't* any more Northerners."

"I know that," Ariella said. "So does he."

"What's his name?"

"Idmyethri? Something like that. I can't be sure of the pronunciation just from his thoughts."

For a moment Morvash stared silently at the statue, while Ariella stared at the wizard and the statue stared blindly at the witch. A Northerner—but despite their status as traditional villains in old stories, Northerners were just people, and Morvash could not see how one could be a threat any more. He shook himself out of his daze and asked, "Does he know what happened to the wizard who enchanted him? Was it Fendel's Superior Petrifaction?"

"Oh, really, Morvash, how could he know? And even if he did, it's been three hundred years."

"I know," Morvash said. "I just..." He sighed. "Maybe we'll do better with some of the others." He picked up the candle. "What about this one?" he said, moving on to the next statue. This one was yellow alabaster, a tall, thin, middle-aged man in an elegant robe that swirled around his legs as he turned to glare at someone.

Ariella followed. After a moment's concentration, she said, "Oh, this one's a wizard—Halder Kelder's son, from Sardiron of the Waters." She looked at the statue's stone face and asked, "What happened?"

Morvash waited, and after a moment Ariella said, "His apprentice betrayed him, turned him to stone, and stole his book of spells and all his other magic. She hid the statue so no one would realize what had happened, but it was found eventually and sold at auction."

"An *apprentice* was able to petrify someone?"

"She was very talented, and she thought he was holding her

back—which he admits he was, because he liked having her around. He really regrets that now."

"When…?"

"In the year 5155."

"More than eighty years ago."

"Yes."

A wizard who lost an argument with an apprentice, an apprentice who was probably dead of old age by now, did not seem particularly dangerous. "Next?"

They moved on down the row of statues. Ariella stopped at the next, one of the women that had stood in the corners of Lord Landessin's foyer, and asked, "Who are you?"

Morvash heard nothing, of course, but Ariella answered her own question. "She's a dancing girl named Thetta. A slave. Her master wanted to keep her beautiful forever."

"Well, she's certainly beautiful," Morvash acknowledged, looking at the gleaming white figure. She wore only a skimpy clinging thing that did nothing to hide her lush curves, and her face was strikingly lovely.

"She has been for more than two hundred years. She's from somewhere in what are now the Small Kingdoms. She's…she hasn't taken it well. She's not *completely* mad, but she's obsessed with maiming or killing herself if she's ever restored to life."

Morvash felt ill at that, and stepped away. "Harming *herself?*"

"Yes."

"Not others?"

"Not unless her old master is still alive, which seems very unlikely—he was a merchant, not a magician, and hired the wizard who transformed her."

That did not sound dangerous, either, though she would need to be watched. "Next?"

Ariella looked at the next, a middle-aged man in good clothing, and asked him several questions. After a moment she stepped back, shaking her head. "Nothing," she said. "Might be asleep, or maybe the spell on this one didn't leave him conscious."

"All right," Morvash said. "What about that one?" He pointed to the black granite one that had been in his bedroom in Uncle Gror's house. "Who is she?"

Ariella called, "Who are you?" to the statue, then considered it silently for a long moment. At last she said, "She's pretty confused, but I think she's a demonologist named Karitha. She was feuding with a wizard named Wosten. She sent a demon after him, but then something turned her to stone, so she thinks he stopped her demon somehow and retaliated. That was only about seven years ago, here in Ethshar."

"I might be able to do something about that one. Wosten might still have the vessel he used."

"Maybe," Arietta agreed. "Wosten—that name sounds familiar."

"Do you know him, perhaps? He might still be living in the Wizards' Quarter, if it was only seven years ago."

"Seven years…oh. Now I remember."

"Remember what?"

"Wosten was killed by a demon seven years ago," she said. "It smashed its way in through the roof of his house, to get past the protective spells on the doors and windows and walls."

"So—the demon she sent got to him after all?"

"Unless he angered *another* demonologist, I guess it did."

"Then how could he turn her to stone?"

Ariella turned up an empty palm. "How should I know? And no, I don't know what happened to the vessel he used in the spell. I don't remember any details, just that he was killed by a demon smashing through his roof."

"*Someone* might know, though. His heirs, or his neighbors, or the magistrate who investigated the case. If anyone did."

"I suppose." Ariella did not sound very convinced.

"I should write all this down," Morvash said.

Ariella turned to glare at him. "*Now* you think of that?"

"Now I think of it," Morvash agreed, annoyed. "Hold on." He took the candle and lit one of the lamps on the wall, then told the witch, "Wait here." He hurried downstairs to his workroom, collected his journal and a writing desk to hold his quill and ink, then trotted back up to the gallery.

It occurred to him on the stairs that this demonologist *might* be dangerous; after all, if Ariella was right, she had killed a wizard. He might not want to free her immediately.

Ariella had not waited for him before moving on. "Nothing from either of those," she said, indicating two statues, a woman and a boy. Then she pointed at a plump, elderly man. "That one's a merchant named Kelder Sammel's son. No idea who petrified him, or why. Happened about a hundred years ago."

Morvash hurried to set up his writing desk; by the time he dipped his quill the witch had moved on and asked the next, a beautiful lavender-blue chalcedony statue of a woman, its identity. "She calls herself Sharra the Charming, though I get the impression not everyone called her that," she reported. "Disputed a bill with a wizard named Poldrian. He warned her, but she didn't think he'd really do it. From what she heard, he did offer to turn her back for a fee, but her family declined. That was in Ethshar of the Sands about thirty years ago."

Morvash scribbled, trying to keep up and get down the earlier reports. He hoped this would be legible once the ink dried.

"Abaran of Fishertown; became a warlock on the Night of Madness and was transformed by a frightened neighbor. Apparently forgotten by the time the excitement died down."

That was interesting, Morvash thought. Abran had been very young, perhaps fourteen. "Does he know there isn't any more warlockry?" he asked.

"He was never very clear on what it was in the first place—he was only a warlock for a few hours."

And if he had only been dangerous because of his warlockry, then he was harmless now; there were no more warlocks. Morvash nodded, and Ariella moved on to the next statue.

"Alder the Strong. From Lamum. A sculptor there seems to have decided to augment the income from his actual carving by petrifying his models and selling them."

They continued down the gallery; in all they found four Lamumite victims of Varrek the Sculptor scattered in the collection, ranging from a young girl to a long-bearded old man. Two other people had argued with wizards, one over unpaid bills and the other over a dispute neither Ariella nor Morvash could follow. As Morvash had guessed, one woman of twenty or so had been a burglar who made the mistake of breaking into a wizard's home. Three assorted others were petrified on the Night of Madness. One wizard had one of his own spells backfire. Out of all those who Arietta could hear, there were four wizards, four who had briefly been warlocks, the single demonologist, and a ritual dancer. Most did not know who had petrified them, or why. For eleven, she could detect no sign of consciousness.

None of them except the demonologist seemed remotely dangerous. Even the wizards would not have their spell books or ingredients, though all four still had their athames. Warlocks were no longer warlocks and could do no magic, while the magic of ritual dancers was so weak that it generally took at least half a dozen of them to accomplish anything significant. Morvash had literally never once heard of anyone being *harmed* by ritual dance; it was, if anything, even more benign than theurgy, which was explicitly incapable of evil.

And finally the pair of magicians came to the young couple, which Morvash had hidden in the windowless paneled alcove at the north end of the gallery. Ariella looked them over, then called, "Sorry to disturb you at such an intimate moment, but who are you? Who did this to you?" She listened for a moment, then stepped back.

"Oh, death," she said. "He's a prince. A real one. Marek, Prince of Melitha. Transformed about forty years ago. And she's Darissa, an apprentice witch. They don't know who did it, or why; she thinks it might be because magicians in the Small Kingdom are forbidden to marry royalty, though they were not married and she didn't expect to be. *He* thought they might get married, and was willing to give up his place in the line of succession for her. He suspects agents from one of the neighboring kingdoms might have been responsible, because Melitha had been at war with Eknera, but using magic in a war is a huge violation of law and custom in the Small Kingdoms."

"A prince? Really?"

"He and his woman both think so."

"Where was he in the line of succession?"

"Well, he had two older brothers, but one of them had just died in the war, so I suppose he was second in line."

"You said it was forty years ago?"

"Almost. It was 5199, Leafcolor of 5199."

"I wonder who's ruling Melitha now?"

"I have no idea."

A burst of rain rattled against the windows, and Morvash turned to look the length of the gallery. "None of them remembered a wizard with a glass goblet?"

"Not particularly. But we didn't specifically ask." Before Morvash could say anything, she added, "No, we didn't ask any of the wizards if they knew how they could be turned back. I didn't ask them anything you didn't hear, Morvash—they can't hear *my* thoughts, only what's said aloud."

"Then we should ask them," Morvash said, leaving the prince and his witch alone in their alcove as he strode up the gallery to the nearest of the four wizards.

A few minutes later Morvash had his answer; one of the wizards had no idea how they might be saved, and the other three all agreed that Javan's Restorative was the best counter-spell. Two of the three had no idea how to find the glass vessels used in their petrification; the third suggested Fendel's Divination.

None of them knew any lost secrets that might help.

After that, Morvash settled himself on the floor, his back to the wall, as he went over his notes and discussed the situation with Ariella. He never needed to say much; she generally heard his thoughts and responded before he could put his questions into words.

There were thirty-six petrified people, counting the three shrunken guardsmen. The oldest was the Northern spy; the most recently enchanted was the demonologist from 5228. There were eleven with no thoughts Ariella could hear, but they might just be asleep.

Some seemed surprisingly calm despite years of immobility; others, such as the slave-girl dancer, were very close to madness. At least two were convinced they were in the midst of a very persistent nightmare. Most had no idea how long they had been petrified until Ariella told them that it was the twenty-eighth of Greengrowth in the year 5238.

"They can all hear us," Ariella told him. "At least, all the ones *I* can hear. It would probably be a good thing to talk to them sometimes, and keep them up to date on your progress toward freeing them. Even the ones who don't understand Ethsharitic would probably find the sound of a human voice soothing."

"Of course," Morvash said, adding a note to his journal. "It's the least I can do for them."

Ariella snorted. "The *least* you could do would be nothing, which is what everyone else has done for them for years, or decades, or centuries."

"I *can't* do that," Morvash answered, lowering his pen.

"Because you're a nice man, as I told you before. That's why I came—and I'm glad I did; even if I can't bring them back to life, I think it's a comfort for them to know someone's trying to help them."

Morvash shook his head. "I need to learn Javan's Restorative. That's far beyond any magic I can do now; this is going to take me months, maybe years."

"It may not be as difficult as you think."

"Maybe not. But I was told it's an eighth-order spell, and I've never attempted anything *near* that level."

Ariella stared at him for a moment, then said, "I live in the Wizards' Quarter."

Morvash did not look up from his notebook. "I know that."

"I hear thoughts."

Puzzled, Morvash lifted his gaze and said, "Yes."

"That means I hear wizards' thoughts fairly often. I know a great many things I should not."

Morvash was not sure where Ariella was going with this, but she had his interest. "Yes?"

"I've heard of Javan's Restorative before—it's a very useful spell, so knowledge of it is fairly common. Whoever rated it as eighth order probably misclassified it. I'm not saying it's *easy*, but I've overheard wizards who were pleasantly surprised that it wasn't as difficult as they had expected. In fact—you're from Ethshar of the Rocks, aren't you?"

"You know I am."

"Do you know a wizard named Kilisha of Eastgate?"

"I don't..." he began. Then the name registered. "She was the one who saved the overlord's life from an animated couch, wasn't she? About the same time as Tabaea's Rebellion in Ethshar of the Sands, though I don't know whether the Empress had anything to do with the attack."

"That's right. Twelve years ago."

"I was just a child then—I hadn't even started my apprenticeship yet."

"*She* was an apprentice at the time. But her master declared her apprenticeship complete when she performed Javan's Restorative to undo a spell of his that went wrong."

"I hadn't heard that!"

"Well, *I* heard it, from a wizard's thoughts a few years back. And if an *apprentice* could do it…"

"Then *I* can," Morvash finished. "You know, I think I met her once, and she never mentioned that."

"Why would she?"

He did not bother to answer, since he knew Ariella could hear what he was thinking.

It was still going to take some time, he was sure; Kilisha had probably learned the Restorative from her master's book of spells, and he had no such advantage. He would have to find a way to trade for the spell—but if it was that common, and that easy, that might not be as big a challenge as he had feared.

"Thank you," he said. He looked along the gallery, then back at the witch. She had done all he had hoped, really, and it was past time they both got some supper.

"Yes," Ariella replied. "I know a tavern on Games Street that serves fine roast beef."

He glanced out the nearest window at the weather, which had built itself up into a serious storm—but he was a wizard, and now that he was back here where he kept his supplies, he knew a few spells that would keep them dry. "Then that's where we'll go," he said.

CHAPTER TWENTY

MORVASH OF THE SHADOWS

29TH OF GREENGROWTH, YS 5238

The morning after Ariella's visit Morvash returned to the Wizards' Quarter to ask what had become of Wosten's belongings, and to inquire what it would take to obtain the instructions for Javan's Restorative. While several people remembered Wosten and the demon that had killed him—apparently it had continued to wander around the neighborhood after the murder with a human companion until the city guard took it into custody—no one recalled what had become of Wosten's belongings. His former home and shop now housed an herbalist, who knew almost nothing about her predecessor. Cleaning out the wreckage had been an expensive undertaking; the entire house had been gutted and rebuilt. The hole the demon had smashed in the roof had become a generous skylight, allowing the herbalist to raise some of her products right on the premises.

The quest for Javan's Restorative was rather more successful; several wizards were willing to trade it if Morvash could come up with suitable spells in exchange. Morvash had expected this, and had brought a list of every entry in his book of spells.

The first wizard went through the list, then shook her head. "I'm sorry, but there's nothing there I want."

The second was willing to discuss trading the Restorative for everything on the list; Morvash was able to talk him down to a mere half-dozen of those forty-some spells, but no further. Morvash said he needed time to think it over, and moved on.

And finally Kardig of Southgate, a specialist in curses, agreed to trade Javan's Restorative for three easy spells—Hult's Visceral Pang, the Curse of Irrationality, and Lugwiler's Dismal Itch. Part of the agreement was that Morvash would never tell anyone that Kardig had not already known all three—especially the Dismal Itch, which many wizards learned fairly early in their apprenticeships.

"My master skipped it," Kardig explained. "As for Hult's, that's more a northern thing, it's not common here in Ethshar of the Sands. And I just never happened across the Curse of Irrationality before. How do you come to know it?"

"My master liked curses," Morvash replied. "That was one reason my family chose him for me."

Kardig seemed slightly taken aback by that, and Morvash went on, "I come from a family of merchants; I'm the first magician we've ever had. My father deals in weapons, supplying both sides in the Tintallionese civil war. He thought curses might be valuable merchandise. I disagreed, which is why I'm here instead of back home in Ethshar of the Rocks—you know the Guild rules about using magic as a weapon of war."

"Ah, I see," Kardig said, nodding. "Well, bring your book of spells when you're ready, and we'll each learn from the other." He leaned forward. "You know, Javan's Restorative is officially considered eighth-order," he whispered, "but I'd rate it as more like fifth or sixth. I think it may have been simplified over the years since it was first ranked. It still works just fine, though." Then he lifted his own book of spells, an impressive iron-bound volume, onto the counter, and opened the three locks keeping it closed. No longer whispering, he said, "Let me give you the list of ingredients now, so you'll know what to bring when we go over it."

"Thank you," Morvash said. Thinking over his own offerings, he said, "You'll need tannis root. And a fragment of a human skull—the younger the better."

Kardig riffled through pages, then stopped. "Younger, how? You mean more recently dead?"

"No, no," Morvash said. "I mean, the younger the person was when he or she died. An old man's skull would be very hard to use; a stillborn baby's is excellent. That's what I have. My master said a toddler, perhaps two years old, would be perfect."

Kardig looked across the counter at him. "Where am I supposed to get *that*?" he said.

"Any decent ingredients shop should have it," Morvash said,

startled. "I got mine from Gresh the Supplier, back home. You don't need the *whole* skull, just a little piece; as long as it's bigger than your thumbnail it should do."

"Which spell is that for?"

"The Curse of Irrationality."

"No wonder it's rare."

"You'll also need a drop of dragon's blood, but I assume you have that on hand."

"Of course I do. Anything else?"

"No. Tannis root for Lugwiler's, skull and blood for Irrationality, and for the Pang you'll need the target's name and a half-ounce of blood, but any kind of blood will do, including your own. It doesn't need to be human or dragon or anything; pig's blood from a butcher shop will work fine."

"All right," Kardig said with a nod. Then he turned his own book around so Morvash could read it, and set out a quill and ink.

"Feathers," Morvash said, writing notes on the back of his list. "I don't have the white one. What's jewelweed?"

"An herb. It's also called touch-me-not. Shouldn't be hard to find."

Morvash decided he would go back to the herbalist who had rebuilt Wosten's house for that, let her earn a little something for her trouble. "Where can I get the white plume and the incense?"

"Any decent... Oh, you're new in town. Try the intersection of Games Street and Wizard Street; there are four or five shops right around there."

"Thank you."

With that settled, he headed back to Erdrik's house for lunch. He double-checked his supplies to be sure he had most of what he would need, spent a few minutes talking to the statuary to assure everyone that he was making progress on their rescue, then gathered up his book of spells and his writing desk. Thus equipped, he returned to the Wizards' Quarter to continue his work.

The following day he once again headed to the Quarter, returning to his rented home around mid-afternoon.

This time he found someone waiting for him on the front steps— two men. One of them wore his uncle's livery, and Morvash recognized him as one of Gror's footmen. His name was something boring, probably Kelder, but Morvash did not remember for certain.

The other was a complete stranger, a young man in drab homespun with an iron collar around his neck. Morvash felt his belly tense.

"Who are you?" he demanded, as he neared the house.

"Your uncle sent us," the footman said. "This is your new slave."

"I never said I wanted a slave."

"Gror bought you one, nonetheless."

Morvash stopped a few feet away and turned his attention to the slave. "Who are you? What's your name?"

The young man appeared to be roughly the same age as Morvash. He hesitated, frowning, and said nothing.

"Is he an idiot?" Morvash asked the footman. "Or a mute?"

"I don't think so," the servant replied, "but his Ethsharitic isn't very good. I think your accent may be giving him trouble."

"My *accent*?"

"You have a Rocks accent, sir. You must know that."

Morvash glared at the footman, then turned back to the slave and asked, speaking slowly and with as much of a Spices accent as he could manage without sounding stupid, "What is your name?"

"Pender," the slave said, pointing at his own chest. "I am Pender *Shemarkir*."

"What does *that* mean? What *language* is it?"

"It's Sardironese," the footman replied. "I don't know what the name means exactly, but apparently it's his former occupation, not a home or parent."

"I make…things with stones," Pender said, pointing at the fingers of his left hand, then at his throat. "Stones and…gold?"

"Stones?"

"Bright stones."

"Jewels? You're a jeweler?"

Pender looked at him helplessly, and turned up an empty palm.

"How in the World did a Sardironese jeweler wind up as a slave here in Ethshar?" Morvash demanded.

"I have no idea," the footman said. "Sir, we have been waiting for you for hours. Could you please accept your uncle's gift, and let me return to my duties elsewhere?"

"Fine, fine," Morvash said with a wave. "You can go." Then he fished his ring of keys from his purse and stepped past the slave to unlock the door. "Come on," he said, opening it and gesturing to Pender.

Pender's reaction when he stepped into the cluttered front hall and saw the animated chairs startled Morvash; he broke into a broad grin and exclaimed, "Wizard!"

"Yes," Morvash said warily. "I'm a wizard."

Pender pointed at his new master. "Wizard?"

"Yes. That's right."

"You go to Tazmor?"

"What?" Morvash was vaguely aware that Tazmor was a region somewhere in the north, but that was all he knew about it.

"You," Pender repeated, pointing at Morvash again. "Go to." He made walking motions with two fingers. "Tazmor?"

"No," Morvash said. "I've never been to Tazmor."

Pender looked baffled.

"We have *got* to teach you more Ethsharitic," Morvash said. "Or maybe I can learn Sardironese.

Pender looked at him blankly.

"Are you hungry?" Morvash asked. "That footman said you were waiting for hours. Hungry? Food?"

"Food?" *That* got the slave's attention.

"This way," Morvash said, and he led the way to the kitchen.

Pender seemed familiar with kitchens, and helped Morvash put together a late lunch. He was understandably wary of the animated utensils, but did not seem shocked by them, or particularly frightened of them. The wizard explained everything in clear, simple words as he heated up some broth, served out cold salt pork, and poured beer, and Pender seemed to be following.

As they sat across the table from one another and ate, Morvash stared at Pender and wondered what Uncle Gror had been thinking. How much use could he get out of a slave who didn't speak Ethsharitic? Did his uncle think he had some translation spell that would take care of the language barrier?

Such spells did exist; Morvash had heard of something called the Spell of All Tongues, but he did not know much about it. It was probably expensive.

But then he remembered Ariella listening to the thoughts of a Northern spy and making sense of them. When they had finished eating and had tidied up, he beckoned to his new slave. "Come on," he said. "We're going to visit a witch."

Pender did not necessarily to understand the words, but the gestures were clear enough, and he seemed to have no objection; the two of them headed out to Witch Alley.

As they approached the witch's house, Ariella leaned out the window. "I'm not working for free this time," she said.

"Fair enough," Morvash said. "And I'm not sure how much you can do, anyway. My uncle…"

"I know," she interrupted. "Come on in, and we'll talk."

Morvash obeyed, ducking inside as soon as the door opened. Pender, he noticed, did not need to duck. He motioned for the slave to take the stool, while he leaned against the wall.

"Here's the thing," Ariella said, as soon Pender was seated. "He already knows a little Ethsharitic, and I can help him learn more, much more quickly than he ordinarily would. I can't magically teach him how to speak like a native—that's more in wizardry's line. If we can agree on payment, though, I'll be happy to serve as your translator for now; you can ask him anything you like, instruct him in his new duties, whatever. If I do this right, he should learn how to say any words we use in this conversation in Ethsharitic—I won't just be listening to his thoughts, I'll be guiding him to *think* them in Ethsharitic. Unless you'd prefer I teach you Sardironese? That would be slower, since I don't know it myself."

Morvash had not had time to reply aloud when she nodded. "Ethsharitic it is, then. Now, about payment…"

Morvash frowned. "Payment," he said, uncomfortably aware that he had virtually exhausted his funds on rent, ingredients, and so on. He was unsure where to start a negotiation; he had never hired a witch before. "Yes. Payment. Well."

"Payment?" Pender said.

The two magicians turned to look at the slave. He held up a hand signaling for patience, then reached into the waistband of his shabby breeches. After fumbling around for a moment, he pulled out a small blue silk pouch that looked completely incongruous on his brown woolen garments. He tugged at the drawstring, then poured the contents of the pouch into his palm and held it out.

"Oh," Morvash said, while Ariella stared silently.

Pender was holding a small fortune in diamonds—twenty or more flawless white stones.

"Pender the Jeweler," Morvash said. "That's his name, Pender the Jeweler." He turned to Ariella. "Will one of those cover your fee?"

"Oh, yes," the witch said. Hesitantly, she reached out and chose a single gem.

When she had made her selection, Morvash told Pender, "Put the rest away." He gestured, closing his own hand and pressing it against the waist of his robe.

Pender nodded, returned the other diamonds to the silk pouch, and tucked them away.

Ariella said, "So, Morvash—you want to know how he wound up as a slave in Ethshar when he was carrying around all those diamonds, right?"

She did not wait for Morvash to answer before turning to Pender and asking, "Where are you from?"

"Tazmor," Pender replied. "In...Back Foot Village."

Morvash blinked at the peculiar name, but then nodded.

Pender was reconsidering, though, and corrected himself. "Hindfoot Village," he said.

"He's learning," Ariella said.

"Why are you here?" Morvash asked. "Why aren't you home in Tazmor?"

The slave gathered his wits for a moment, then said, "I come... I *came* to find the wizard."

"Which wizard?"

Pender shook his head. "I can't say that."

"Why not?"

"I..." He looked around helplessly. "I can't say that."

Before Morvash could ask anything more, Ariella said, "He really can't. It's not because of the language problem. He can't say it in Sardironese, either; he can't even *think* it clearly when he knows I'm listening. I think there's a spell on him."

Frowning, Morvash drew his athame. Pender flinched at the sight of the gleaming dagger, and Ariella hastened to reassure him.

Ordinarily Morvash would have used the knife's point to test for magic, but to avoid upsetting his captive he flipped it around and touched the pommel to Pender's forehead. A ripple of blue-green light flashed up the blade, so quick and faint anyone not expecting it might have missed it entirely.

"He's enchanted," Morvash agreed. "Probably Javan's Geas. He can't tell us anything forbidden any more than he can turn his hair purple." He sheathed his dagger with a sigh. "What *can* you tell us?" he asked.

"We—my people—we work for the wizard," Pender said. "For many years, we all work for him. He…" He struggled for a word.

"Brought," Ariella suggested. "He brought your ancestors to Tazmor."

"Yes. After the fighting."

"After the Great War," Ariella explained. "Tazmor was part of the Northern Empire, and after the war, when the Northerners had been wiped out, his ancestors were brought there."

"Why?" Morvash asked.

"Can't tell you," Pender said. "The wizard brought them to…" He grimaced. "To do a thing."

"Something he didn't want anyone to know about, so he used Javan's Geas on you all, to make sure you wouldn't tell anyone," Morvash said.

"Yes!"

"Over two hundred years ago."

"Yes."

This did not sound like a good thing. Using Javan's Geas on an entire population to keep something secret was not the sort of thing that someone would do unless he was sure that other people were not going to be happy about his project, whatever it was.

And this wizard had apparently enchanted not only the original population, but their children and grandchildren, for the past two centuries. Whatever the project was, it had been going for a long, long time.

But Pender had come to Ethshar looking for him, which meant that he was not in Tazmor anymore. Had he lived there until recently?

"Did the wizard live in Tazmor?" Ariella asked, before Morvash could.

Pender shook his head. "No. He came every ten years to see us, and pay us."

"And to enchant all the new children to keep the secret," Morvash said.

"Yes," Pender acknowledged. "But he did not come last time."

"How long has it been, then?" Morvash asked.

"Thirteen years. Three years more…three years too long."

"And you came looking for him, to ask why he's late? You want your pay?"

Pender hesitated. "Yes. And…and to tell him."

"Tell him what?" Morvash asked.

Ariella and Pender replied in unison, "It's ready."

"This mysterious project you people have been working on for more than two hundred years—it's finished?" Morvash asked.

Pender nodded.

"But you can't tell me anything about it."

Pender shook his head.

"You came to Ethshar to tell the wizard that it was complete, though?"

Pender nodded.

"Did you find him?"

Pender shook his head.

"Then what happened? How did you wind up on my doorstep?"

Pender looked at Ariella, then began, "I brought money. Hindfoot Village gave me money to pay for…for food and sleep."

"Food and lodging," Ariella corrected. "Travel expenses."

"Yes. Coins. Iron and copper. I had stones—diamonds—too."

"For emergencies," Ariella explained.

Pender nodded. "Emergencies, yes. But things cost too much. We did not know in Tazmor what food cost in Sardiron."

"He didn't know how to dicker, either," Ariella added. "He still doesn't. Apparently that's not how it's done in Hindfoot Village."

"The money was all gone when I got to…to not Sardironese…"

"To places where he couldn't speak the local language—which is to say, Ethsharitic," Ariella explained. "To the Hegemony, he means."

"And…I did not want to use stones in Ethsharitic."

"He thought he would be robbed if anyone saw the diamonds," Ariella said. "There were some incidents along the way, some of his belongings were stolen, and he thought if his fellow Sardironese could treat him so badly, then Ethsharites would probably be even worse. He's decided to trust the two of us, but only the gods know why—a fat old witch and a journeyman wizard."

"So you ran out of money, and came to lands where you couldn't speak the language," Morvash said. "Then what?"

"I walked by the river," Pender explained. "By the river to the sea. I took food when I could. Some people gave me food, some I took…"

"Stole," Ariella said. "When no one took him in, he stole from the farmers along the Great River."

"Sometimes I saw people who spoke Sardironese, who helped me and told me where to go. For two months I walked on the road by the river. At the big bridge I went away from the river and came to the city, and the guards let me in, but I did not know where to go, and I slept on the street. Men with sticks and chains found me and took me and made me work."

"Why didn't you sleep in the Hundred-Foot Field?" Morvash asked. "The slavers don't go there! Everyone knows not to sleep on the streets!"

Pender just looked at him, not answering.

"How would *he* know that?" Ariella asked. "He didn't know the language, so no one could warn him."

"But didn't he see all the people in the Field, and didn't he notice no one else was sleeping on the streets?"

Ariella looked at Pender for a moment; he gazed calmly back.

"He was afraid of the people in the Field," she told Morvash. "He thought the streets would be safer."

"Well, he got *that* wrong!"

"Yes, he did. He didn't know any better."

"So now he's a slave."

"For the moment. I would think those diamonds ought to be more than enough to buy his freedom."

"Oh," Morvash said. "Yes, they should be." He turned back to Pender. "So when did you arrive? A few days ago?"

"Leafcolor," Pender replied.

"What?" Morvash stared. "Last year? That's six…no, seven months ago!"

"Yes."

"But then why was my uncle able to buy you now? Why weren't

you sold long ago?"

Pender looked baffled.

"He doesn't understand slavery," Ariella explained. "Not really. He knows he had to do what he was told, but he didn't really understand what was going on. From what he remembers, I think that when the slavers realized he didn't speak Ethsharitic they decided not to put him up for auction. Instead they made him part of a work gang where he was doing simple labor, where gestures were good enough to give him orders. He spent most of the winter dredging out the canals, and that was where he picked up what Ethsharitic he knows, listening to the other workers. Then a couple of days ago the slavers held an auction, and apparently they decided he had learned enough they could maybe sell him, so he was included. He still wasn't really sure what was going on, but he heard the slavers talking with your uncle, and he heard them talking about wizards, and he thought this was his chance to talk to a wizard and maybe find out what happened to *the* wizard, the one he's looking for, so he *asked* to be sold to your uncle."

"You did?" Morvash asked, looking at Pender.

Pender nodded, but did not say anything; he seemed to prefer letting Ariella speak for him.

"He did," Ariella said. "None of the other slaves wanted to be sold to a wizard for fear they'd be turned into toads or something, and none of the other bidders wanted someone whose Ethsharitic was so poor. Even when Pender volunteered, your uncle had his doubts—would *you* want a slave who couldn't speak Ethsharitic? So he wasn't interested at first, but the slavers offered him a real bargain, and Pender was practically begging to see a wizard, and here we are."

"So you wanted a wizard," Morvash said.

"Yes," Pender replied. "In the house I saw magic, so you are a wizard."

"And you want to know if I know what happened to *your* wizard."

"Yes," Pender said again.

"What's his name?"

Pender sighed. "I can't tell you."

"Of course not." Morvash gave a sigh of his own. "You said that earlier." Then he looked at Ariella. "Thank you," he said. "At least now I know how he got here."

"You're welcome." She held up the diamond she had chosen. "I've been well paid, I'd say."

"I suppose you have, at that," Morvash replied. He looked at Pender. "What am I going to do with you? I don't really need a slave. I thought I might, but it looks as if I'll be able to learn the spell I need without one."

"Find the wizard?" Pender asked.

"That's going to be challenging, when you can't tell me his name—*his*, right? Not her?"

Pender nodded.

"And you haven't seen him for thirteen years, but you know he lived in Ethshar of the Spices? *Do* you know that?"

Pender nodded again.

A wizard missing for years…a thought struck Morvash. He frowned. That would be quite a coincidence, he thought. There were almost certainly other missing wizards. Still, he had to ask.

"Was his name Erdrik the Grim?"

Pender's eyes widened, and his mouth fell open. "How…?"

"Oh, blood and death," Morvash said. "Oh, the twisted sense of humor of the gods! Erdrik the Grim was your patron?"

Pender nodded. "How did you know?"

"I'm living in his house. He disappeared eleven years ago, and no one has seen him since."

"Eleven years? Where did he go?"

"I don't know. *No one* knows. He's just gone."

"But…but how…"

Morvash looked at Ariella, who exclaimed, "*I* don't know where he is!"

"*My* guess," Morvash said, "is that a spell he was attempting went wrong. Maybe it killed him, or transformed him somehow, or transported him somewhere he can't come back from—another world, perhaps. But no one knows."

"Well," Ariella said, "was there anything else?"

Morvash considered, but could think of nothing specific. He still had plenty of questions, but it seemed likely that Javan's Geas, or whatever the enchantment was, would keep Pender from answering any of them. "I suppose not," he said. "Thank you." He looked at

Pender. "I don't really want to keep him enslaved, but he's not really in any shape to fend for himself, is he?"

"Not yet," Ariella said. "But he's learning quickly."

"And I'm living in Erdrik's house—I can't think of anywhere he'd be more likely to learn more about his village's fate."

"Neither can I."

"All right," Morvash said, getting to his feet. "Let's go home." He was not entirely happy to be leaving his translator, but he could not stay with her forever; if Pender was going to live with him, the two of them would need to get on without Ariella's assistance. He looked down at Pender's waistband, where the silk purse was concealed. "I know this isn't fair," he said, "but those diamonds would be very useful in paying my expenses. That would cover your food and lodging."

"Help find the wizard?" Pender asked.

"I don't know," Morvash admitted. "The Guild said they couldn't find him, so I don't know how *I* could, but if we find any clues in his house I'll be happy to follow them."

Pender fumbled with the drawstring of his breeches, then pulled out the little purse, fished a single diamond, and handed it to Morvash. The wizard accepted it. "Thank you," he said. He looked down at the stone, then slipped it into his own purse. "It's getting late; I'll sell this tomorrow. Let's go."

Pender nodded, and the two young men left the witch's shop.

They reached the house on Old East Avenue as the sun reached the western rooftops, and once inside Morvash lit the lamps with a simple spell. Pender smiled at this evidence that his new master really was a wizard.

Marvash wondered if the poor fool knew just what it meant to be a slave. Yes, he had spent a few months dredging canals, but did he realize he had been brought here so Morvash could test spells on him?

The wizard considered that, and resolved to do nothing to keep the Tazmorite from escaping. If he wanted to stay, that was fine, but if he wanted to leave and make his own way, Morvash would not stop him. As far as the wizard was concerned, the diamond in his purse had bought Pender's freedom.

But since Pender had come to Ethshar to find Erdrik, and they were living in Erdrik's house, Morvash doubted Pender would leave.

"Let me show you around," Morvash said. "We'll find somewhere for you to sleep, and I'll show you the other guests."

Pender looked startled. "There are others?"

"In a manner of speaking," Morvash said. "You'll see when we get to the gallery." With that, he began a tour of the house, pointing out magical items, telling the new arrival which ones were known to be dangerous, and warning him which ones were still unidentified.

When they came to the gallery he tried to explain that these statues were all people who had been turned to stone, but Pender seemed surprisingly slow to grasp the concept. Morvash wondered about that; he knew that Erdrik had petrified those miniature soldiers, but apparently he had not displayed this particular spell in Hindfoot Village.

Eventually, though, Pender understood, and nodded as Morvash explained that he intended to turn everyone back. "Good," he said. "You come to Tazmor?"

"What? No. Or at least I wasn't planning on it."

"But..." Pender frowned.

"Is there someone there who was turned to stone?"

"No, no."

"Then I don't see why I should."

Pender was clearly struggling to say something.

"Does this have something to do with Erdrik's secret project?" Morvash asked.

Pender managed a jerky, obviously painful nod; even a yes or no answer was apparently more than the geas wanted to allow.

"But...no one was turned to stone?"

Pender shook his head.

"I don't understand," Morvash said, "but maybe I *will* come, to see what Erdrik was up to, once I'm done with these poor people." He waved at the statuary.

"Not...not sooner?"

"No," Morvash said. "These come first."

Pender sighed, but did not argue.

From the gallery Morvash led Pender to his workshop. "We'll probably be spending most of our time here," he said. "I'm trying to learn a spell that can restore those people. Uncle Gror sent you here

to help me, so I can learn it faster, and maybe try out a few things…"
He trailed off as he realized that it would be neither kind nor wise to
say that Pender was there to be experimented on, and to serve as a
test subject for various enchantments.

He showed Pender where he would be sleeping—there were several small rooms available on the second floor, and Morvash had
chosen one within easy shouting distance of his own bedchamber. It
had a decent mattress, but little else; since Pender had not come with
any possessions beyond the clothes on his back and his hidden purse
Morvash did not see a need for a wardrobe.

And that completed the tour.

"I think it's time for supper," he said, and led the way down to
the kitchens.

CHAPTER TWENTY-ONE

HAKIN OF THE HUNDRED-FOOT FIELD

15TH OF LONGDAYS, YS 5231

Hakin found it slightly surprising how many things the city guard wanted torn down or smashed, but he was pleased by the discovery. It gave Tarker something to do, and the demon was always happier when it was busy. Sitting around doing nothing drove it into a fury of frustration. Far better, Hakin though, for it to knock down the remains of buildings too damaged by fire or neglect to be worth restoration, or to clear out temporary structures that had been put up in places where they shouldn't have been.

The knowledge that in theory every single structure in the Hundred-Foot Field was illegal and subject to this sort of demolition troubled him; Hakin did not want to see all his friends and former neighbors rendered homeless. No one had cleared the field in two hundred years or so, but everyone knew that it might happen; the overlord's men regularly issued warnings to keep the field's inhabitants aware that their crude shelters existed by the city's sufferance, and could be wiped away at any time.

Generally, though, the only time the overlord or the guard had anything removed from the Field was when some idiot broke the rules and tried to build something permanent. A tent or a shack was ignored, but lay a single foundation stone and you could expect to be dragged away and cast out the nearest city gate, the stone (or stones) flung after you.

But Tarker was not assigned to work in the Field, to Hakin's relief. There were enough abandoned houses and shops, or illegal stages and stalls set up in the streets and squares, to keep it busy elsewhere.

Hakin's job, when Tarker was knocking down walls with its fists or grinding bricks to powder, was simply to watch, and make sure no one wandered too close to the demon. Sometimes he called encouragement or suggestions to his charge, but usually he just watched. Tarker needed no advice in destruction.

The latest assignment, the last of the day, was a simple one; someone had put a merchant's stall in Southgate Market so that it blocked one of the gates and kept it from closing. Tarker's job was to clear the gate's path by any means necessary, which meant demolishing the wood and cloth structure. The stall's owner was nowhere to be seen; the other merchants said she had brought two wagon-loads of shellfish from somewhere out on the peninsula, set up the stall, sold her wares, and then departed again, leaving the booth where it was.

Tarker ripped one of the posts from the ground and flung it out into the square; the attached awning tore in half, but not before pulling down the other three posts. A single step brought him to the next post, which followed the first.

"Can it break them up for firewood?" the lieutenant commanding the gate guards asked.

"Certainly," Hakin replied. "But this time of year, what do you need firewood for?"

"We don't," the lieutenant replied. "But we will in a few months, so why waste this?"

Hakin nodded. "As you please, then."

Tarker had removed the other posts while they spoke, so Hakin walked over to tell him about the request for firewood. Snapping the posts into suitable chunks with nothing but its four hands took no more than another five minutes; the demon then tucked the wood under its arms and delivered it to the corner the lieutenant indicated. That done, Hakin and Tarker turned their steps to the northeast and headed back toward Camptown.

"This is not what I was meant for," Tarker growled as they turned left onto Oystershell Street.

"I know," Hakin said. "But the magicians are trying, I'm certain."

"It has been six days."

"I know," Hakin repeated. "I'm sure we'll hear something soon."

Indeed, when the pair turned right onto Camp Street, within sight of the camp's gates, Hakin saw a woman in a green robe and pointed hat waiting for them. Upon seeing the demon she waved vigorously, and Hakin waved back, albeit less energetically. Tarker snorted, and Hakin smelled smoke, offal, and hot metal.

As they approached, the woman called, "Hakin?"

"Who else walks around with a seven-foot demon beside him?" Hakin replied, annoyed.

"I am Shenna of the White Dagger. Lord Borlan sent me."

Hakin glanced up at Tarker, but could not read the demon's expression. "Has Karitha been found?" he asked, still walking toward the woman.

"No, I'm sorry," Shenna replied. "Not yet. But I can tell you a little more about what happened."

Hakin stopped about six feet away, still out of reach, for fear Tarker might harm her should its temper get the better of it. He ignored the various people on the street who were staring at them, some of them clearly trying to hear what was being said. "Go on," he told her.

"Lord Borlan has hired several magicians of different schools to determine what happened to Karitha, and whether there is some way to send Tarker home. Several of them were unable to provide any information at all—warlocks simply don't have any relevant skills, and demonologists couldn't see anything more than Tarker itself could. A theurgist managed to speak with the goddess Unniel about it, but her answers were useless or incomprehensible—apparently the gods don't understand wizardry and either can't or won't say anything about demonologists, including Karitha."

"I knew that," Tarker interrupted.

Shenna seemed startled by the sound of the demon's voice; she flinched visibly before continuing, "Yes, well. A band of ritual dancers performed a summoning to bring Karitha back, but so far it hasn't worked."

Tarker snorted again, and Hakin coughed.

"Wizardry seemed like the best chance, since Wosten's magic seems to be responsible for her disappearance, so Lord Borlan hired four of us…"

"You're a wizard?" Hakin interrupted.

"She is," Tarker rumbled. "I can smell it. She stinks of magic."

"Yes," Shenna said. "I'm a wizard. Only a journeyman, though."

"Go on."

"The problem is that both Wosten and Karitha had several wards and protections around them, far more than most magicians maintain," she replied. "Mostly to protect themselves from each other, according to the neighbors. I don't know what started their feud, but it's apparently been gradually escalating for the last two or three years, and they had both built up a lot of magic directed at one another. It's actually rather amazing that they both managed to get through the other's defenses; Tarker coming in through the roof used the only opening in Wosten's primary wards, the opening he had left for his sylph to use, and even then, the demon still had to get through four different protective spells. As for Karitha, she was guarded against not just spells, as we'd expect, but against anything solid and anything visible, so not much could get at her, but the sylph, being made of air and invisible, could—we think it came down her chimney in order to carry the powder. She couldn't block the chimney against fine powder if she wanted it to let smoke out. However it got in, the sylph used Wosten's powders once it was inside, past her protections."

"All right, it was difficult, but they *did* get through. So what happened?"

"We don't know," Shenna said. "All those barriers have kept our own spells from seeing what happened. The Spell of Omniscient Vision is our usual method for looking at things like this, but it can't get a clear image through the wards. We tried Fendel's Divination several times—that magically answers any question, spelling the answer out in letters of smoke, but we never got a useful response. We tried several different questions, and the answers were either unhelpful or the spell simply didn't work. One of us was convinced that Karitha must be dead, despite what Tarker thought, so we tried Bizen's Necromancy, and Fendel's Necromancy, and the Spell of the Necromantic Mirror, but they all agreed that wherever Karitha is, she isn't dead."

"Why are you bothering us, then?" Tarker demanded.

"Well, we've learned a *little*," Shenna said. "We analyzed Wosten's powders, and we had a couple of witches look at the two workrooms, and we did manage some quick glimpses, one way or another. We know that Wosten didn't want anyone to know what he had done—he wanted Karitha to simply disappear. Which worked. And he didn't want to kill her, though I'm not sure why."

"If you have all that necromancy, can't you ask him?" Hakin asked.

Shenna shook her head. "We're trying, but we haven't been able to contact him yet. Not everyone who dies can be reached, you know."

"I didn't. But go on."

"Anyway, he gave the sylph powders for *two* spells—a transformation of some kind, and then…something else. The first one turned Karitha from a human being to something else, and the second one made whatever that was vanish. We couldn't see the transformation clearly, but whatever he turned her into was dark, and hard to see. It wasn't a bug or a mouse, it was much bigger than that, and it was only there for an instant before the second spell made it disappear."

Tarker growled. Still, Hakin had to admit that this was progress. "All right," he said, "so she's alive but not human anymore?"

"Apparently, yes."

"So where is she?"

"We don't know. We haven't yet been able to determine *anything* about the second spell. She may still be right there in her workroom, but invisible and intangible. Or if it was a teleportation spell, she could be anywhere in the World, anywhere at all. If it was a portal, she could even be in *another* world entirely. We don't know. We're still working on it. And we're still trying to talk to Wosten's spirit."

"I killed him. He cannot be reached," Tarker said.

Shenna blinked. "You're sure of that?"

Tarker hesitated. "No," it admitted. "There may be ways his essence could still exist."

"Then we'll keep trying."

"So you haven't found her," Hakin said, "and you know she's still alive, but not human anymore."

"That's right."

Hakin looked at Tarker.

He had never intended to become a demon's keeper, but it wasn't really so bad; he had food and shelter, and companionship from the soldiers, even if he didn't see any of his old friends from the Hundred-Foot Field. He had clean clothes, even if he could not yet afford new ones; the barracks laundry had seen to that. But how long would Tarker put up with its situation?

"You'll keep looking?" he asked Shenna.

"As long as the demon does as it's told, we'll keep looking," she replied.

Tarker growled, a deep, angry growl, but it did not reach for the wizard. Hakin told it, "They're *trying*!"

"We are!" Shenna said hastily. "We've sent messages, asking if any other wizards can help. I said she might be in another world, so people are checking all the other worlds we know of—but there are many of them, hundreds, maybe thousands, and we don't know how to get to all of them. And Wosten may have created a new one."

Hakin's mouth fell open. "Wizards can *create worlds*?"

"Well, maybe. Or maybe they just find new ones that already existed but no one knew about; we really aren't sure. At least, *I'm* not sure. And I don't know any of the spells that do anything like that; that's *far* beyond my abilities!"

"But she may still be in *this* world," Tarker said.

"Yes, and we're looking here, too! But we don't know what her form is; you could have passed her in the street just now."

Tarker started to speak, then stopped.

"It might be able to smell her," Hakin said. "That's what it was going to say, that it would have recognized her scent. But it can't be sure. Her smell may have been transformed, along with her appearance."

Tarker grunted agreement.

Shenna looked at the demon. "Maybe it can tell us something useful. Would it be all right if some wizards asked it questions?"

"Ask it," Hakin said.

She turned to the demon, swallowed hard, then asked, "Would you answer questions for us?"

"I will do anything that will help me find Karitha the Demonologist," Tarker replied.

The wizard nodded. "I'll tell the others."

For a moment, no one spoke. Then Hakin asked, "Was there anything else?"

"No, I think that's everything, at least for now," Shenna said. "If there's any news, I'll tell you as soon as I can; if it's after curfew I'll send a dream."

"Demons do not dream," Tarker rumbled.

"But *I* do," Hakin said. "Thank you."

"I'll stop by once a sixnight to let you know how it's going," Shenna added, "even if there isn't any real news."

"I'd appreciate that," Hakin said.

She hesitated, then nodded. "I'll see you again, then."

Hakin bowed. He was not sure that bowing to a wizard was the correct etiquette, but he thought it would demonstrate respect. By the time he had straightened again, she was marching westward at a good pace.

For a moment Hakin watched her go; then he looked up at Tarker. "Come on," he said. "Let's go get supper."

He knew by now that demons did not eat, at least not in the material plane, that Tarker's fangs were purely weapons, but *he* was hungry, even if Tarker wasn't. He led the way into camp, the demon at his heels.

CHAPTER TWENTY-TWO

MORVASH OF THE SHADOWS

24ᵀᴴ OF LEAFCOLOR, YS 5238

Pender proved very useful. His Ethsharitic seemed to continue to improve rapidly; apparently Ariella's witchcraft had triggered an ongoing development, not merely a temporary boost, drawing on everything he had heard since he first set foot in the Hegemony.

Morvash discovered that the Tazmorite was a decent cook, and a quick and obedient assistant in the workshop. He was untroubled by the presence of magic; many people were nervous around wizardry, worried about what might go wrong, but Pender seemed completely comfortable with it. Morvash supposed that growing up in a village that existed entirely to serve a wizard's whims would do that.

The diamond Pender had given his new master was sold; the proceeds paid off all Morvash's bills, and stocked both the pantry and the workshop cupboards. Morvash laid in plentiful stocks of all the ingredients needed for Javan's Restorative—a dozen each of two kinds of peacock plumes, a large jar of touch-me-not, three pounds of incense that the supplier attested had been properly prepared on a black stone concealed in fog, a gallon of thrice-purified water, a brass tripod supporting an engraved crystal bowl, and ten pounds of charcoal. The recipe did not actually require that the water be pure, or that it be boiled in a specific vessel, but Morvash had been taught as an apprentice that higher quality ingredients improved the chances that a spell would succeed. He had never heard this from anyone except his master Avizar, so he had some doubts, but better ingredients couldn't *hurt*, and at least for the moment he could afford them.

He spent much of his time practicing spells, concentrating on some of the most difficult he knew, to build his puissance—but there were a few he did not attempt, some because they could be seriously dangerous if they went wrong, and some because they were dangerous even if they went right. He did not feel any need to cast curses on Pender merely to increase his own expertise in magic.

He also tried to stop into the gallery at least once a day to talk to the statues, reassuring them that he was working toward their salvation, and he was pleased to discover that Pender also talked to them on occasion. After being told which ones had spoken Sardironese as their native tongue, the slave even made a point of addressing each in the appropriate tongue—though of course, he did not know the Northerner's language or any of the Small Kingdoms dialects.

Morvash brought Ariella in for further consultation a few times, and noted down everything he could learn about the wizards who had transformed the various statues. Several of the transformed had no idea who was responsible, while others knew exactly who to blame, and the rest fell somewhere in between, with partial information or perhaps just a suspicion. Prince Marek, for example, could offer not even the vaguest guess, but Darissa had seen a tall woman in a blue robe around Melitha Castle who she thought might have been the wizard who enchanted them.

Morvash consulted Ithinia and the Guild records regarding the names he was able to obtain. Of the few wizards who could be identified with any certainty, at least half appeared to be dead—after all, most of the victims had been petrified for decades or centuries. There was no reason to think any of the survivors still cared what became of their victims—for example, Morvash contacted Poldrian of Morningside, who had enchanted Sharra the Charming some thirty years ago, and was told that Poldrian had no interest one way or the other. He had long ago returned the statue to Sharra's family and thought no more about it.

That left the question of how Sharra had wound up in Lord Landessin's collection, but Morvash decided there was no need to get obsessive in his research. He was content that he found no evidence that either the victims or perpetrators, with the possible exception of Karitha the Demonologist, posed a real threat to anyone once he succeeded in breaking the enchantments.

Morvash began to run through the basic motions of Javan's Restorative, though without his athame or any other source of actual magic. He wanted to be as prepared as possible when he attempted it for real. He practiced several other harmless spells as well, to advance his general facility with magic, and saw a gradual but significant improvement.

Finally, on a rainy afternoon some five months after his arrival in Ethshar of the Spices he felt himself to be ready. After getting everything in place and lighting the charcoal, he handed Pender a jar from the kitchen and a wooden mallet.

"Smash it," he said.

Pender's Ethsharitic vocabulary still had a few gaps. "I don't know 'smash,'" he said.

"Break it," Morvash said. "Hit it with the mallet as hard as you can."

Pender looked at him uncertainly. "As hard as I can? I can hit hard. I got strong dredging the canals."

"All right, not *that* hard, but I want it broken into many pieces."

Pender still looked doubtful, but he raised the mallet above his head and brought it crashing down onto the jar, which shattered in a thoroughly satisfactory manner.

"Good!" Morvash said. "Now, stand back!"

"What should I do with the hammer?"

"Just hold onto it," Morvash said, a trifle annoyed. The question had disrupted his concentration, and it took a moment to get his mind focused again. When he felt ready, he drew his athame and began the incantation.

He was not sure exactly where it went wrong, but fifteen minutes later, when the magical energies should have been building, they suddenly drained away, leaving him sitting cross-legged in a cloud of charcoal smoke and incense, coughing uncontrollably. The crystal bowl of boiling water cracked and began dripping onto the charcoal fire, adding steam to the mess, and Morvash tried to call to Pender, but could not stop coughing long enough to get out both syllables.

Fortunately, Pender had been waiting just outside the workroom door and thrust his head in when he heard the coughing.

"Should I put it out?" he called.

Morvash nodded, sheathing his dagger and staggering to his feet as he looked around for a way to clear the smoke.

In the end, once the fires were out, he and Pender had to leave the workshop until the fumes dissipated. As they sat by an open window in the gallery, gulping fresh air from the street outside, Morvash finally managed to clear his throat enough to say, "Well, *that* didn't work."

"No, it did not," Pender agreed. "What next?"

"I'll try it again tomorrow," Morvash said. "By the time the room airs out it will be too late to try again tonight."

"I should clean up the broken glass, and then find another empty jar?"

"No, no. I can use the same one."

Pender paused, then asked, "There is no magic on it now? It will not change the spell?"

"It shouldn't," Morvash said. He hesitated, wondering whether Pender might have a point, but then he remembered that his entire purpose here was to use the spell on enchanted things. "I'll use the same jar."

"You are the wizard and I am not," Pender said, turning up an empty palm.

Morvash did not reply, but sat and stared at the workroom door.

He had had spells go wrong before, back when he was an apprentice and even once or twice since, but none had been so complex or powerful. They were lucky that the magic had merely dissipated, rather than doing something unpredictable and bizarre. When a spell went wrong, *anything* could happen; the famous Tower of Flame in the Small Kingdoms was said to have resulted when a simple first-order spell, Thrindle's Combustion, misfired.

But he could not stop now. He had committed himself to saving these poor petrified people. He would just have to keep practicing until he got it right.

The next morning the workshop had a lingering sharp salty smell to it that Morvash guessed was from the incense. He hoped that would not affect anything.

His first attempt that day was aborted almost before it began, when his tongue tripped over the words of the opening incantation and he had to stop less than a minute into the proceedings. He tidied up a little, and then tried again, with the same pot of boiling water— an ordinary copper pot from the kitchen this time, rather than expensive, fragile, and now cracked crystal—over the same charcoal fire.

This time he had also opened the flue and built the fire just in front of the fireplace, in hopes of keeping the smoke under better control.

He took a deep breath, raised his knife, and began the chant, and this time it went smoothly; he lit the incense, and had a sudden sensation of magic surging up around him.

He had felt magic before, of course; he wouldn't be much of a wizard if he hadn't. On this particular occasion, though, the sensation was stronger than he had ever experienced before, almost overwhelming in its intensity.

So *this* was what high-order magic felt like! He just hoped it was the *right* high-order magic. He moved on to the next step, taking jewelweed leaves into both hands and rolling them on his palms, then crushing them.

Step by step, he worked his way through the spell. Once again the room filled with smoke, but this time his throat remained completely untroubled; he felt in control. When the time came, perhaps three-quarters of an hour into the operation, he used his athame to shape the smoke, turning it into a sort of helical form that settled over the broken glass on the floor.

His control began to slip, but at that point the spell was almost complete. Morvash's eyes began to water, forcing him to blink repeatedly, and the instant he finished the final incantation he began coughing again and almost dropped his knife.

But then the smoke abruptly cleared, and Morvash was sitting cross-legged on the floor, trembling from exertion, coughing, half-blind with tears, and staring at a perfectly restored glass jar.

It had worked. He had performed Javan's Restorative.

At lunch that day Morvash celebrated by drinking almost half a bottle of *oushka*. He was not ordinarily much of a drinker, but on this occasion he felt something stronger than beer was called for. He was still shaking, and thought the liquor might steady him.

It steadied him to the point he fell asleep in his chair. Pender made sure he was positioned securely, leaning against a wall next to the chair where he was unlikely to fall, and then left the wizard there to sleep it off.

When he finally came to the sun was setting and his head ached, but he did not really care. "I did it!" he said, as he had several times that morning.

"Yes," Pender agreed. He did not seem impressed—but then, he had undoubtedly seen plenty of magic before, and putting a shattered jar back together was not particularly showy. Morvash thought Pender did not realize just how difficult that spell was, even if the test run had not accomplished anything spectacular.

"Tomorrow we'll see if it can remove an enchantment," the wizard said, straightening in his chair.

"You will try one of the statues?"

"No, not quite yet. I want to try it on something easier first. I'll put a spell on *you*, and then see if I can take it off."

Pender froze. "What did you say?"

"I'm going to cast a spell on you, an easy one—maybe Lugwiler's Dismal Itch—and then see if the Restorative will take it off."

"But...what if it does *not*?"

"Oh, don't worry. There's a simple counterspell. It has to be spoken by the wizard who cast the spell in the first place, which will be me, but so long as I don't get killed or turn myself into a teapot or something, I'll do that if the Restorative doesn't work."

It occurred to Morvash that it might not have been wise to give Pender that much detail; the man looked seriously concerned. Perhaps the effects of the *oushka* had not entirely worn off. It would *definitely* be unwise to attempt any more magic just now—not that he had intended to.

"I think I'll take a walk," he said. "Clear my head a little."

Pender made no objection, so Morvash got to his feet and wobbled up out of the kitchens—just as someone knocked at the front door.

Startled, Morvash looked back at Pender. "Are we expecting someone?"

"No."

Morvash looked down at his rumpled working robe and said, "Go see who it is."

Pender went, and Morvash tried to straighten his clothes and smooth out the worst wrinkles. If this was someone important he could not keep whoever it was waiting while he changed into something better, but he preferred not to look totally unconcerned with his appearance.

Pender reappeared. "It is your uncle," he said. "The man who paid for me."

"Uncle Gror?" Morvash said, astonished. "What's *he* doing here?"

"I don't know."

"Well, bring him in, sit him in the parlor! I'll be right there!" Morvash gave his robes another quick brushing, then hurried to the parlor, arriving there just as Pender led Uncle Gror in.

"Uncle!" Morvash said. "What an unexpected pleasure! Sit down, please. What brings you here? And so late in the day?"

"It's not going to be a pleasure, Morvash," Gror said. "At least, I don't think so." He settled onto a chair Pender held for him, and Morvash took a seat nearby.

"Why?" Morvash asked. "What's happened? Has something gone wrong back home? Is anyone sick?"

"No, no," Gror said quickly, dismissing the notion with a wave. "It's nothing like that. But I've had a visitor."

"What sort of a visitor?"

"One with a pretty thick Small Kingdoms accent—somewhere in the northern kingdoms, and inland, from the sound of him."

"And…"

"And he's looking for one of those statues you took."

Morvash blinked. Of all the things he might have imagined this mysterious visitor wanting, that would have been very, very low on the list. "Which one? Did he say?"

"Oh, yes," Gror said. "He was very specific. It's the one of the young couple."

"You mean the prince and the witch?"

It was Gror's turn to be surprised. "Is that who they are? How can you tell, when they're stark naked?"

"I'm a wizard, Uncle, remember?"

"Oh. Yes. But you know the one I mean, don't you?"

"Yes, of course I do. What does this person want with it?"

"He won't say. Believe me, I asked."

"Tell me what happened."

"Well, he came to the door, and asked to see Lord Landessin, and Karn—my footman, you remember—said that Landessin had been dead for years. That seemed to upset him, but then he asked to see whoever was the master of the house, so I met with him, and he explained that he was there on behalf of his employer, who had once seen that statue and was now determined to own it and would pay five rounds of gold for it."

"I don't know the art market, Uncle; is that a fair price, if it were just a statue?"

"Fair, maybe, but not especially generous for a piece like *that* one."

"It might have just been an opening bid."

"Oh, of course it was! He got up to eight rounds before I convinced him that I really didn't have it anymore."

"Did he say who his employer was? Or why they wanted the statue?"

"He rather carefully did not. Made a point of it, in fact, dodging every question I asked."

Morvash considered for a moment, then said, "I haven't made a secret of what I'm doing. I didn't think I needed to."

"Which means he can probably find you. He wouldn't even need magic; he could talk to the neighbors, and the workmen we hired to move the statues, and *someone* will talk."

"Are we sure that would be a bad thing, if he found me?"

"Morvash, he wouldn't say who hired him, or why. That's never a good sign."

"I know, but…what does he want with the statue? Do you think he knows who it really is? What's he going to *do* with it?

"I have no idea."

"I mean, if he's going to turn them back, that would be fine—it would save me the trouble."

"Unless he's doing that so he can kill one or both of them."

"Um."

"You said he's a prince, right? I mean the young man who is… on top?"

"Prince Marek of Melitha," Morvash said thoughtfully. "Petrified about forty years ago by person or persons unknown, for reasons unknown."

"Well, that could be it right there! Maybe he has a better claim to the throne than whoever has it now, and the usurper has decided to remove a threat by smashing a statue."

"That could be," Morvash admitted.

"And the girl—she's a witch?"

"An apprentice witch. Almost a journeyman."

"Maybe she angered someone who's been nursing a grudge all these years and finally found out what happened to her."

"Witches don't usually do anything that's going anger anyone that much," Morvash objected. "Most of them can sense people's emotions, so they don't like hurting people."

"Maybe it was an accident."

"Hmm."

"You said you don't know who transformed them—maybe whoever it was has decided it's time to finish the job."

"He could have done that forty years ago! Or she—Darissa thinks she saw a female wizard who may have cast the spell. But whoever it was, it's much harder to turn people to stone than to kill them."

"Well, you would know better than I," Gror admitted. "Maybe she wanted to keep them as prisoners in case she ever needed them alive again, and now she's decided she never will."

"Or maybe she *does* need them alive now!" Morvash suggested. "We don't *know* her intentions are bad. Or his, or whoever's."

Gror grimaced. "Honestly, Morvash, if someone offered you a wager on that, which way would you bet it?"

"All right, fine, Uncle—I admit there's probably ill intent here somewhere." He sighed.

"Well, I guess I know who I'll try to restore first. Though I'd have been happier doing a *single person* as my first. I know the spell I need, and I've done it successfully, but I'm not very comfortable with it yet."

"Do you have time? Because it probably won't take him more than a day or two to find you."

"I don't…well, it depends. This house has some powerful protective spells on it, but I don't know how they all work. If he just comes here by himself, I'm pretty sure I can keep him out as long as I need to. If he comes here with a good wizard, though, or some other powerful magician, I can't be certain."

"Can I do anything to help?"

Morvash considered that for a moment, then said, "I don't think so. But thank you for the warning, Uncle; I really appreciate it."

"You're family, Morvash; it's the least I could do." He rose, and

Morvash followed suit.

A moment later he closed the front door behind Gror, and immediately turned to Pender. "Do you know how to find Ariella's place?" he asked. "Because I think we need to talk to Prince Marek again."

CHAPTER TWENTY-THREE

MORVASH OF THE SHADOWS

25TH OF LEAFCOLOR, YS 5238

Ariella joined Morvash and Pender for an informal late supper in Erdrik's kitchen, where the situation was explained to her—as much as anything needed to be, given her abilities. When the three had eaten their fill they climbed the stairs to the gallery, and made their way to the alcove at the north end.

"Prince Marek?" Morvash said. "Someone is looking for you."

"He wasn't listening," Ariella said. "Say it again."

Morvash repeated, "Someone is looking for you. Someone who knows you were turned to stone. My uncle had a visitor who wanted to buy this statue—the two of you."

"He's confused," Ariella said. "It's been years, hasn't it? Many years?"

"Almost forty years," Morvash agreed. "It's very odd."

"Are you sure that he's the one they were looking for?"

"Well, no," Morvash said, "but a prince seems more likely than an apprentice witch, especially after so long, and he was *definitely* looking for the pair of you. We thought it might have something to do with the line of succession."

"He's still confused. He wants to know who's on the throne now. Is his father still alive?"

Morvash and Pender exchanged glances. "I have no idea," Morvash admitted. "I thought *you* might know." It occurred to him that this was something he should have researched during the last few months, but he had never gotten around to it. Magical matters had always seemed more important.

"He thinks you're being stupid," Ariella said. "He wouldn't

phrase it so bluntly if he could speak for himself, but that's what it boils down to. How would *he* know? Until you started talking to him, no one had told him *anything* since he was petrified. He doesn't know who enchanted him and Darissa, or why, or how they wound up in Ethshar of the Spices, or anything that's happened in Melitha since. They're blind, they can't feel or taste or smell, the only sense they have is hearing, and no one has said anything interesting near them since the spell was cast."

"Does Darissa know anything?" Morvash asked.

"No more than Marek. She's been listening, of course, but she doesn't have any more idea of what's going on than he does. She lost almost all her magic when she was turned to stone—wizardry blocks witchcraft sometimes, and apparently this was one of those times—so she's almost as blind and helpless as the prince. She can generally tell when someone is near them, but not who it is or what they want. It took her hours just to figure out they had been turned to stone."

"So they don't have any suggestions."

"No, they don't."

"What do they want me to do?"

"Turn them back to people, of course. Prince Marek is trying not to think you're an idiot, but right now you're making it more difficult by asking that."

Morvash addressed the statue. "You don't think you might be safer like this?"

"No, they do *not*," Ariella said, very emphatically. "Stone can't defend itself against a sledgehammer."

"I'm not really ready," Morvash said. "I know the spell that should turn you back, and I've tried it a few times, but it only worked properly once so far. I was planning to practice it for another few sixnights, work my way up, maybe start with some of the smaller statues—you two are the biggest in Lord Landessin's entire collection, mostly because there *are* two of you. I can't do you one at a time."

"Marek thinks you should go ahead anyway, but Darissa isn't as sure. What's another sixnight or two after forty years?"

"Well, that's the part I haven't told you," Morvash said. "The man looking for you will probably find out where you are in a day or two, at most. I haven't been keeping my plans secret, and there are the workmen who brought all the statues here, and that doesn't even consider using magic. He should have no trouble finding out where you are. The house has some protective spells, so just knowing you're here won't mean he can get at you, but for all I know he's a wizard himself and can walk right through them."

"Then do it. Turn them back. Marek is very insistent now, and Darissa thinks it's more dangerous to wait than to try it."

"She's never seen a wizard's spell go wrong, has she?"

"Not unless that was what turned them to stone in the first place."

"Huh," Morvash said. "I wonder if it was? It's possible."

"Marek wants to know what could happen if the spell goes wrong."

"Oh, just about anything. I could be turned to stone, or we could all become weightless and bump on the ceiling, or monsters could come out of the walls."

For a moment no one spoke; then Ariella asked, "What's the most *likely* way it could go wrong? You said you had tried it before and it didn't always work; what happened when it didn't?"

"Nothing," Morvash said. "Nothing at all. That's the most common way spells fail."

"Darissa is still uncertain. Marek thinks you should try the spell, but he admits that may be selfish of him, since there are plenty of things that could happen that could hurt *you*, but not a statue. The decision, he says, has to be yours."

Morvash looked at Pender. "It seems I won't bother casting Lugwiler's Dismal Itch on you after all," he said. "I'll be going straight to attempting depetrifaction."

"Now?" Pender asked.

"Oh, no," Morvash said. "My head still hurts, and attempting wizardry when I'm not sure I'm completely sober is never a good idea. In the morning is soon enough, when I've had a good night's rest—when we've *all* had a good night's rest."

Pender nodded.

"Will you need me?" Ariella asked.

"I don't think so," Morvash said. "In fact, it might be safer if you weren't here—as Darissa told you, and I'm sure you already knew, different kinds of magic can interfere with each other. The less witchcraft we have around, the better."

"You won't need to talk to them? To make sure they're ready?"

Morvash almost laughed. "Believe me, Ariella," he said, "the spell doesn't care whether *they're* ready. Do they look as if they were ready when they were turned to stone in the first place?"

Ariella glanced at the pair, at Darissa's arched back and raised legs, and Marek's straining limbs. "I suppose not," she said.

"I know witchcraft works better when everyone involved is calm and cooperative," Morvash said, "but wizardry isn't like that. Only the wizard casting the spell has to be ready."

"As you say," she replied. "Then perhaps I should go on home now."

"Well, actually, as long as you're here, perhaps you could spare a moment to listen to the others one more time? I've spoken to them often, but of course they couldn't answer when you weren't here."

"Oh, of course! How thoughtless of me." She turned to the statue. "Best of luck to you two tomorrow," she said. "I hope everything goes well, and this stranger, whoever he is, doesn't find you until you're ready." Then she turned back to the main gallery. "Where shall we begin?"

Opting for simplicity, Morvash pointed to the first statue outside the alcove and said, "There."

It was about an hour later that Ariella finally departed, having checked on every statue. There were no significant changes from her previous visits. Morvash saw her out the door, then turned to Pender.

"I'll have to perform the spell in that alcove," he said. "It's much easier to move all the magical paraphernalia than it would be to move that statue."

"Yes, wizard," Pender agreed. He had never acquired the habit of calling Morvash "master."

"Give me a hand; we'll get it all ready up there, and I can start right after breakfast."

Pender nodded, and the two of them headed for the workroom.

Morvash debated whether to bring a table or workbench to the gallery, or to leave everything on the floor; he eventually decided to use the floor. There was no chimney to vent the charcoal, but he thought that opening the big gallery windows just beyond the archway should do; he would set the brazier right there, in the entrance to the alcove. He glanced around, to see if there was anything else he would want to attend to.

The gallery itself was straightforward—windows on one side, painted walls and white pilasters on the other, statues arranged along its entire length. The three miniature soldiers and the soapstone cat were gathered in the corner where the west wall met the alcove's entrance. The alcove itself was about twelve feet square, behind a white-painted arch; its ceiling was lower than the rest of the gallery, and all three sides were paneled in some rich-looking wood he could not identify, with ornate moulding on every seam and a small empty niche in the center of the back wall. The statue that was Marek and Darissa took up almost half the floor space.

Morvash had not thought much about it until now, but as he looked around, trying to decide how to arrange the ingredients of his spell, he wondered what the alcove had been *for*. What was meant to go in the niche? Why was the ceiling lowered?

Then he decided it was just one more of the mysteries surrounding Erdrik's house. He would probably never know. He set the big jar of touch-me-not in the niche, where he would not accidentally kick it over; everything else, even his book of spells, was arranged on the floor along the walls, against the carved and polished baseboards.

When everything was in place he looked it over, looked at the statue of Marek and Darissa, sighed, then turned and went to bed.

He felt better in the morning, but he was still not entirely confident he could perform the spell successfully. His first attempt had failed completely. Arguably, his second had, as well, if he chose to count that abortive start when he fumbled the incantation. Yes, the third had gone well, but that did not exactly make him an expert. He generally did not consider himself to have mastered a spell until he had performed it successfully three times running.

But this mystery man from the Small Kingdoms could arrive at any minute.

Morvash ate a hearty breakfast that Pender had prepared—ham, cheese, small beer, and fried cauliflower—then walked slowly up to the gallery, mentally reviewing the procedure for Javan's Restorative.

When he got to the alcove he opened his book and read through the instructions he had gotten from Kardig, checking to see if he had remembered everything correctly; once he started the spell he wouldn't be able to safely do anything that would divert his attention, such as looking at the directions.

He fetched the container of touch-me-not from the niche and set out generous handfuls at the base of the alcove's arched entry, much more than he had used before—the statue was so much larger than the broken jar! He filled the brazier with charcoal, along with a little oil and kindling to help light it, just as Pender arrived with a pot of clean water. Morvash set the pot on the tripod. Then he placed a porcelain bowl nearby, broke off a generous chunk of incense, and set it in the bowl. He arranged the peacock plumes as the spell initially required—later on they would be moved and would help shape the smoke around whatever the spell was being cast upon, but initially they needed to be set on either side of the incense, curling so that they touched at the tip but nowhere else.

He laid his book nearby, then opened the nearest casement a crack so that fresh air could get in and charcoal fumes could get out. If he felt ill or light-headed it would be easy enough to shove or kick the window further open.

"Here we go," he said aloud, so that Darissa and Marek could hear him. Then he drew his athame and jabbed his right index finger, drawing a drop of blood. A quick incantation turned the blood into a flame, which he used to light the incense and the kindling for the charcoal.

Ordinarily one dowsed the Finger of Flame by curling the finger, but instead Morvash thrust it into the pan of water, to add a little more heat and make it boil more quickly. Then he sat and waited.

It took longer than he had expected to bring the water to a rolling boil, and his concentration wandered slightly, but at last there was sufficient steaming and bubbling; he flexed his shoulders, focused his mind, and began the chant.

This time the magic seemed to gather quickly, and the slow curls of smoke from the incense began to weave themselves together almost immediately. Morvash quickly grabbed up a handful of jewelweed and crushed it between his palms, rolling it, then tearing at it with his fingertips before tossing it into the boiling water.

A cloud of scented steam billowed up, and the streamer of smoke from the incense wrapped around it, like a coil of rope around a windlass. Morvash dropped leaves onto the incense, where they flared up into ash and smoke, and the entangled smokes merged into a single growing cloud.

The magic felt stronger, wilder, this time; Morvash was not sure whether this was because he had been more generous with the ingredients, or because he was more experienced with the spell, or both, or neither, but whatever the reason he felt simultaneously more powerful but less in control. The cloud of smoke seemed to be growing more than it should, and more quickly, but he attributed it to that additional magical power.

The entire alcove around him seemed to shimmer with magic, and the possibility that his spell was interacting with some lingering remnant of one of Erdrik's spells occurred to him, but it might already be too late to stop safely. He kept on.

At some point, perhaps half an hour into the ritual, Morvash realized that he was no longer breathing, but that the lack of air did not bother him, and the words of the spell were still audible even though nothing was actually coming from his throat. This was both exhilarating and frightening; he had never experienced this effect before. He definitely could not stop now, though, even had he wanted to—he was firmly in the grip of the magic, and in any case, disrupting the spell at this point, when so much magical potential had built up, would be an invitation to disaster.

The time came to shape the cloud of smoke around its intended target, and Morvash tried to begin, lifting his athame in both hands, but the cloud resisted; it spilled out around his knife, as if it had a will of its own. It swiftly filled the entire alcove, and as far along the gallery as Morvash could see. It definitely covered the cat and soldiers, and at least two of the other statues.

He knew, with a sinking heart, that he should not have increased the ingredients he used. There would have been enough for the statue; wizardry did not concern itself with physical mass in the same way everyday life did. Perhaps he should not have attempted the spell in the mysterious alcove, either.

He struggled to pull the magic back, to force the smoke into the alcove and over the two stone figures there. He could feel himself sweating, and steam condensing into his hair and beard, as he dragged the cloud downward onto Marek and Darissa.

He could not look out at the rest of the gallery without losing what little control he had, but he knew that the smoke there had not dissipated as it should have.

This, he told himself, was what came of attempting a spell when insufficiently prepared. He just hoped the results would not be *too* horrible.

Everything was covered in smoke, so that he could not actually see anything but gray, but at the same time he could see the statue—and he could see living flesh, as well, superimposed upon the stone.

And behind the statue, in the niche in the wall, something else was moving. Morvash did not know what it was, or why it was there, but he could simultaneously see the carved wood of the niche's frame and a wooden door, and he was suddenly aware that the ceiling was at two different heights, the familiar lowered level perhaps seven or eight feet above the floor, and the full ten feet of the rest of the gallery.

This was *not right at all*—unless the spell was somehow restoring the alcove itself to its original condition, before something had damaged it.

But it had never *looked* damaged.

There were runes on the higher ceiling, runes Morvash did not recognize. There was clearly some other magic at work here, something beyond his faulty casting of Javan's Restorative.

Although he knew the spell called for him to keep his attention on his target, a panicky Morvash glanced back over his shoulder to see if Pender was near—not that the Tazmorite could have done much of anything to help, in any case. He did not see Pender, but instead he saw the nearest dozen statues, and *all* of them were simultaneously flesh and blood and clothing, and lifeless stone.

Then all at once the spell was over, the smoke vanished in a swirling vortex, and Morvash said, "Gods!" as at least a dozen living people staggered in the gallery, staring around in astonishment. A cat hissed as it dodged between the legs of three full-sized soldiers who were stumbling against one another; they had been placed too close together to allow for their restored dimensions.

Morvash turned quickly back to the alcove to see a naked couple sprawled awkwardly on the floor, the girl saying, "Get off me!"

Behind them was that unfamiliar door, above them the rune-adorned ceiling; the alcove was completely transformed.

And as Morvash watched, a latch clicked and the mysterious

door at the back swung open.

CHAPTER TWENTY-FOUR

HAKIN OF THE HUNDRED-FOOT FIELD

26ᵀᴴ OF LEAFCOLOR, YS 5238

Hakin leaned against a wall, watching Tarker lift the keel into position. It was a job that would have ordinarily taken a dozen men with ropes and pulleys. A couple of years ago a warlock could have handled it; now there were no more warlocks, but the city of Ethshar of the Spices still had a demon available. Tarker was more efficient than a dozen men, and much cheaper than a warlock would have been. The demon had heaved the massive wooden beam onto its back and carried it, single-handed, to the waiting framework.

It had taken Hakin's bosses three or four months to realize that the demon could lift and carry, as well as smash things. It made Tarker's work far more interesting to watch; raw destruction got boring after awhile, but heaving boats off sandbars, shoving huge stones into place on the city walls, and other such tasks provided welcome variety. The city's shipyards were particularly eager to make use of Tarker's immense strength, and the two companions were out here, just outside the city's northwestern corner, fairly often. Hakin had gotten to know several of the people who worked here—shipwrights and laborers and chandlers.

He had met various other people, as well, over the last few years. In the effort to find Karitha he had located and interviewed Wosten's mother Reska of the Curly Hair, and Wosten's former apprentice, the journeyman wizard Inza of the Bright Smile—or really, Tarker had located them, and Hakin, Shenna, and Orzin had interviewed them.

Neither woman had known what had become of Karitha. The interview with Reska had been difficult—after all, she had lost her only son. She had been aware that Wosten was feuding with the demonologist, but had no idea what Wosten might have planned, or what had become of Karitha. She had given Hakin the names of a few of Wosten's friends who she thought might know something.

Inza had seen the earliest signs of the feud first-hand but had had nothing to do with her former master since completing her apprenticeship. She had stayed away from him specifically to avoid any involvement in his disputes with Karitha. While he had not been an unpleasant master, she claimed to have seen that he was on a path to destruction, and had deliberately tried to erase any emotional connection.

Neither woman had any idea what Wosten might have done to his foe.

Hakin and Shenna had gone on to find and talk to the friends Reska suggested, but none were able to offer any help.

Hakin had also tracked down his father, Chend the Navigator, even though that had nothing to do with finding Karitha. They had hardly developed a close relationship. Chend barely remembered Nerra—it had been a single night, and he had been very drunk. He was perfectly willing to admit that Hakin might be his son, but he did not see that as very significant; he had a wife and four young children, and did not feel any responsibility for an accidental impregnation so long ago.

Over the past seven years Hakin had gotten to know Shenna, the journeyman wizard, well—though she was a journeyman no more, but a master magician, ready to take on her first apprentice should a likely candidate apply. They spoke regularly, though she was no longer the junior magician on the magistrate's list and could have sent someone else with the regular updates.

After seven years, despite everything, they had still not found Karitha. They knew more than they had, though; a few months after Wosten's death a combination of the Spell of Omniscient Vision and the Spell of the Slow Hour had finally allowed a wizard named Korun the Clever to see that Wosten's spell had turned Karitha to stone, black stone.

"But she isn't dead?" Hakin had asked. "How is a stone statue not dead?"

"It depends which spell Wosten used," Shenna had explained. Apparently there were at least four different ways a wizard could petrify a person, and two of them weren't fatal and could, under the right circumstances, be reversed.

So they knew they were looking for a black stone statue, but that was not really very helpful.

Over the years they had also conducted a series of tests that Hakin did not understand at all, and suspected Shenna didn't, either, and concluded that Karitha was *not* invisible or intangible, had not been shrunk down too small to see, and had almost certainly not been sent into another world. The most popular theory—though at least one senior wizard dismissed it as nonsense—was that Wosten had used something called Pallum's Returning Crystal to transport the Karitha statue from her workshop to somewhere else. If this was true, then the statue had been sent to the spot where Wosten had performed part of the spell that created the crystal, that being the nature of the magic in question.

But that spot could be anywhere the wizard had set foot since learning the spell. He might have made the crystal years before he ever met Karitha.

A few wizards were gradually trying to retrace Wosten's steps from the start of his apprenticeship to the day of his death, looking everywhere for a black statue of a demonologist, but as yet they had not found it. Other spells had also been used in various attempts to locate it, but without success; apparently some combination of Karitha's own demonological magic, Wosten's lingering wizardry, and the statue's neither dead nor alive status blocked the divinations.

If a score of wizards had devoted themselves to the task, Shenna said, the statue would probably have been found by now, but after the first few sixnights the whole matter had been given a low priority; the demon was in check, not rampaging through the streets, and Karitha had no friends or family pressing to find her. Lord Borlan still wanted her found and Tarker released, but the overlord was not willing to provide unlimited funding for the search, so it had become something that a few wizards worked on in their spare time, rather than a matter of any real urgency.

There had been other distractions, as well, such as the departure of the Warlock Source and the Great Vond's attempt to take over the city. There had been much discussion of whether to involve Tarker in that, but matters were settled before Hakin and the magistrates reached a decision.

The keel thumped into place, and Tarker stood beside it, panting.

The demon did not seem as big and strong as it used to be, Hakin thought, and he was not sure whether it had genuinely shrunk, or whether familiarity, or his own growth, made it seem smaller. He had reached his own full height and was at least an inch or two taller than he had been on that long-ago day when he had stood up in the Hundred-Foot Field and asked the demon what it was doing there.

But it might be that spending so long in the mortal world was wearing on poor Tarker, weakening it. The demon would not give a straight answer when asked. It had generally been cooperative when various magicians—not just Shenna's wizards, but also a couple of witches in Lord Borlan's employ, and at least one demonologist hoping to improve his mastery of his craft—had questioned it, but there were certain subjects it avoided, or addressed only in vague and ambiguous fashion.

Hakin didn't think it would have been panting like that when Wosten's blood was fresh on its claws.

He pushed off the wall and ambled toward his waiting charge. "That's all for now, Tarker," he called.

The demon turned toward him, started to nod—and then froze, eyes wide and alert, its whole body tensed.

"I smell her," it said.

Hakin blinked. "What?"

"I smell her! *I have her scent!*" Tarker the Unrelenting seemed to swell as it spoke, and smoke rose from its mouth, its nostrils, and its back—a phenomenon Hakin realized he had not seen in years. Its yellow eyes gleamed, and almost seemed to glow.

"What are you talking about?" Hakin asked.

"I have her scent! Karitha the Demonologist!"

"But she's a *statue*," Hakin said, baffled. "Why can you suddenly smell her after all these years?"

"I do not know. I do not care. I have her scent." It turned and began marching, not toward the workmen's entrance they normally used, but in a straight line toward a spot on the city wall.

Hakin hurried after the demon, which was taking longer, faster steps than it had in years, so that he had to run to keep up. It ignored him as it strode forward.

While there were a few possible reasons for this behavior, Hakin thought only one explanation was likely—someone had found the statue of Karitha and brought the demonologist back to life.

When it reached the wall Tarker did not hesitate, but began punching handholds in the stone blocks and climbing straight up. Hakin stared at it for a moment, then turned and dashed for the nearest gate, running as fast as he could.

CHAPTER TWENTY-FIVE

MORVASH OF THE SHADOWS

26TH OF LEAFCOLOR, YS 5238

A dozen or more voices were clamoring for his attention, talking over one another, and at least one person was laughing hysterically, but Morvash ignored them as he watched this mysterious door swing open.

Beyond it stood a room with bare gray stone walls, and the door was being opened by a tall, slender man in an ankle-length velvet robe of a blue so dark it was almost black; his face was lined, but his hair and beard were still black, unmarred by any gray.

"Finally!" he said, as he stepped out into the alcove and pulled the door shut behind him. Then he looked down at Marek and Darissa, who had managed to sit up but were still stark naked, at the assorted ingredients and paraphernalia scattered on the floor, at Morvash, and finally past him at the others. "What is going *on* here?" he demanded. "Who are all you people, and what are you doing in my house?"

My house? "Erdrik the Grim, I presume?" Morvash said.

The clamor of other voices faded as the newly-liberated former statues turned to watch the two wizards.

"Yes," Erdrik said. "And who might you be?"

"Morvash of the Shadows," Morvash replied. He decided against offering a hand; someone called "the Grim" was not likely to accept the gesture. "The Wizards' Guild allowed me the use of your house for certain experiments. They believed you to be dead."

"*Did* they? How convenient for them!"

"In their defense, you vanished without a trace eleven years ago. They *did* search for you, without success."

"I dare…" He stopped in mid-word. "Eleven years, did you say?"

"Yes."

"I knew it was a long time, but I had hoped my mind was playing tricks on me, making it seem longer than it really was. Apparently not." He looked past Morvash at the motley assortment of people in the gallery, then down at Marek and Darissa. "And who are all these people?"

"They were the subjects of my experiments," Morvash said. "They had all been turned to stone, and I took it upon myself to turn them back."

"I see. How noble of you. I want them out of my house."

"And I am sure that that can be arranged, but there may be a few delays. Those two need clothing, for one thing, and someone, possibly an assassin, is looking for them. I would prefer to keep them here, behind your protective spells, for the present."

"This is not my problem."

Irritated, Morvash replied, "And it is not entirely your house at the moment. You have not paid the overlord's taxes in more than a decade; the Guild has. There is no need for hostility, sir; I have, after all, just freed you from some sort of imprisonment, have I not?"

Erdrik frowned. "Have you?"

"I believe so. I cast Javan's Restorative on this alcove and its contents."

Erdrik turned and looked at the wall, and the door, and the ceiling. Then he scanned the remnants of Morvash's spell-making that were still scattered on the floor. "Indeed," he said. "I take it you had no particular intention of freeing me, though."

"Not particularly, no. I had no idea you were in there. *No one* knew where you were."

Erdrik gestured toward the door. "I was in my vault. It would seem something out here triggered the transformation spell that normally hides it, trapping me inside. I did not have with me the ingredients I would need to free myself."

"I am somewhat surprised that the Guild did not find you."

"Don't be," Erdrik replied. "After all, I did everything I could to make the vault difficult to find. The entire house tests as magical, so that this alcove would not stand out, and none of the usual spells would show anything here. I admit it had not occurred to me that I might someday *want* someone to find it." He stepped past Darissa and Marek and looked out at the gallery.

A crowd of strangers stared back.

Erdrik turned to Morvash. "Who are all these people?"

Morvash turned around, and began walking along the gallery. "This is Alder the Strong," he said, pointing to an exceptionally large and well-muscled young man wearing only a kilt. "I don't know these next two. This is a wizard who had a spell backfire—I'm not sure of his name."

The unidentified wizard started to speak, but Erdrik held up a hand for silence. "Yes, I see," Erdrik said. "Just people who had been turned to stone. Wherever did you *find* them all?"

"The late Lord Landessin's gallery," Morvash replied. "He collected statuary, and wasn't very careful about his sources." He looked down the gallery, trying to see how many of the statues had been restored to life.

It appeared *all* of them had. He had not expected that; he had been unable to see just how far the cloud of magical smoke had extended.

That, it seemed, put a successful end to his experimentation with Javan's Restorative. He smiled at the thought.

"What happens now?" a woman asked. She had been one of the statues Ariella had not been able to hear.

That, Morvash thought, was an excellent question, and one it was his responsibility to answer. He raised his arms and shouted, "May I have your attention, please? Everyone?"

The room, already relatively quiet, fell silent.

"Forgive me if I repeat things you already know," Morvash called, "but not all of you responded to attempts to communicate, so I can't be certain who knows what. Bear with me. I am Morvash of the Shadows, a wizard, originally from Ethshar of the Rocks but sent several months ago to live with my uncle in Ethshar of the Spices. Some of you may know the city by its older name, Azrad's Ethshar; some of you may not know it at all. Some of you may not understand a word I'm saying; we'll arrange for translations later.

"All of you were turned to stone, by one spell or another, and wound up in the collection of a wealthy nobleman named Lord Landessin, who was obsessed with sculpture and statuary. When Lord Landessin died his heirs rented his estate to my uncle, which was where I found you and realized you had been transformed, rather than carved. I took it upon myself to learn enough magic to turn you back. My uncle, understandably, did not want me conducting dangerous magical experiments in his home, so I rented this house and brought you all here.

"And now, much more quickly and thoroughly than I expected, here you are—a spell I intended to rescue just two of you has misfired, and instead brought *all* of you back to life at once.

"Today is the 26th day of the month of Leafcolor in the Year of Human Speech 5238. You are in Ethshar of the Spices, in the upstairs gallery of a wizard's house on Old East Avenue, near the southern boundary of the district known as the New City, not far from Southmarket and Arena.

"For the most part, I know nothing of what has become of your homes or families or possessions; I had not yet taken the time to do any research about these matters, since I had not intended to release you quite so soon.

"You are not prisoners. If you feel you are ready to deal with the World of the present day, you are free to go; my assistant Pender will show you to the door."

He paused, looking for Pender, but did not see him anywhere. "Just a moment," Morvash said, hurrying through the crowd and out to the stairway. "Pender!" he called. "Where are you?"

"Here," Pender replied from somewhere downstairs.

"Well, get up here! I need help!"

"You were doing magic. I did not want to be in the way. I heard voices, and did not want to interrupt. Were you talking to gods?"

"No! I'm not a theurgist, I'm a wizard. Get up here!"

Pender appeared on the stairs, trotting up.

"The spell worked," Morvash said, as he led the way back to the gallery. "They're all alive again."

Then they stepped through the door, and despite what Morvash had told him Pender stopped dead at the sight of all the former statues. His mouth fell open, and he stared.

Then his gaze fell on Erdrik, and his mouth and eyes opened even wider. He fell to his knees, flung out his arms, and shouted something in a language Morvash did not immediately recognize.

Erdrik stepped forward and answered in the same language.

All other discussion ceased as everyone turned to watch the wizard and his kneeling supplicant converse. They spoke loudly, obviously unconcerned who might listen. Then Erdrik turned to Morvash.

"It seems I have important matters to attend to elsewhere," he said. "There is no rush about removing these people after all. I trust, though, that they will all be gone before I return."

"When will that be?" Morvash asked.

"At least a sixnight. Perhaps a few months."

"I think that should be possible."

"Good! Thank you, Morvash, for releasing me, however inadvertently. I will deal with the fools who gave you access to my home later, but I will consider us to be even. See to it, though, that *you* are out of here as well when I return." With that, Erdrik swept out of the gallery door, and Pender hurried to follow him.

Pender paused just long enough to call back over his shoulder, "I'm sorry, Morvash." And then they were gone, Pender's feet clattering down the stairs, Erdrik's unnaturally silent. The footsteps reached the bottom and faded away as the two men kept moving.

The cat that had once been soapstone, which turned out to have gray fur, appeared from concealment behind a door and followed the pair down the stairs.

Morvash stared after them for a moment, then crossed to the windows and looked out at the street in time to see Erdrik marching away to the south, Pender hurrying along behind his master. He did not see the cat.

When they had rounded the corner out of sight, Morvash turned to the others and said, "It would appear I have lost my assistant. Did anyone here recognize the language they were speaking, and understand what was said?"

A man raised his hand, and Morvash recognized him as the wizard Halder Kelder's son—his yellow robe was almost the same color as the alabaster he had been for the last several years. Morvash beckoned the man forward, and the crowd parted to let him through.

"What did they say?" Morvash asked.

"They were speaking Sardironese," Halder replied. He had a noticeable Sardironese accent himself, but Morvash could understand him well enough. "The servant spoke a mountain dialect, so I didn't follow every word, but when he saw the tall man he shouted, 'Master! You're here!' Then the tall man asked him who he was and what he was doing here, and the servant said he had come to find his master because the master had not come to the servant's village on schedule, but everyone here had said the master was gone, so he had been working for Morvash—that's you, isn't it?"

Morvash nodded. "I am Morvash of the Shadows," he said.

"Yes. The servant said he had been working for you because you were in the master's house and he didn't know what else to do, but now the master was back, and he needed to tell the master that the project was complete and everything was ready."

"Did he say what the project was?"

"No. The tall man seemed to know what he meant. He asked whether the servant was sure, and then said they would need certain things before they could return to Tazmor. He asked whether his supplies were still here, and the servant said no, but he had brought... I don't know the exact Ethsharitic equivalent. Not precisely money, but close. Wealth, maybe. Anyway, the tall man ordered the servant to come with him. Then he spoke to you in Ethsharitic, and they left."

"Thank you," Morvash said. It seemed that Pender's original loyalties were intact, and had overruled his supposed position as a slave, which was not really a surprise. And the wealth he had mentioned clearly meant his hidden cache of diamonds.

At least he had apologized for his desertion.

"Well," Morvash said, straightening up, "if anyone would like to leave now, and fend for himself, I will show you to the door. Those who would prefer to take a little more time, and receive what assistance I can provide in adapting to your new surroundings, please wait here; I'll be right back. Now, who's ready to go?"

Three men in the uniform of the city guard stepped forward, along with a middle-aged woman Morvash recognized as one of the unidentified statues, as well as Thetta, the suicidal dancing girl from the Small Kingdoms, and Sharra the Charming, the beauty who had refused to pay a wizard's bill thirty years ago.

Morvash hesitated. Thetta was wearing nothing but a bit of flimsy drapery, and would not be safe on the streets, not even when accompanied by three guardsmen—she might well not be safe *from* the three guardsmen. Furthermore, she had been enchanted for *two hundred years*—it was amazing she even understood modern Ethsharitic, and Morvash could only guess that for most of that time she had stood somewhere she could often hear people talking. Reluctantly, he caught her arm. "Not you," he said. "I need to talk to you before you go."

She said something that sounded as if he *ought* to understand it, and he recognized the words "you" and "not," but he could not make it out.

"No," he said. "Stay here." He gestured to Alder the Strong. "Hold her, please. Don't hurt her, she hasn't done anything wrong, but don't let her leave."

"I don't know," Alder said, with a thick Lamumese accent. "Why should I do what you want?"

"Because I just brought you back to life after that unspeakable Varrek turned you to stone for almost sixty years!"

Alder still hesitated.

"I'm not going to hurt her," Morvash said, "but she won't be safe going out dressed like that, she's speaking a dead language, everyone she ever knew is gone, and I want to talk to her before I let her go out and get herself killed!"

"All right," Alder said, taking Thetta's arm. "But just for a little while."

"Thank you!" Morvash said. Then he beckoned to the others. As they followed him toward the stairs, he asked, "Are you sure about this? It's not too late to reconsider."

"We need to report in," one of the soldiers said.

"It's been… I forget how long. A hundred years, maybe?"

"Is the guard still barracked in Camptown?"

"Well, yes," Morvash admitted. "Right at the end of Camp Street. But everyone you knew must be gone."

The soldiers exchanged glances.

"We need to let them know Erdrik is back," one of them said.

"And they'll take care of us, no matter how long it's been," said another. "We're members of the guard!"

"Maybe one of us should stay, at least for now," said the third.

"Fine, you stay."

That drew general agreement, and one of the soldiers turned back, while the others continued on.

"What about you?" Morvash asked Sharra.

"I'm going home," she said. "I'm not like these others; it's only been thirty years. Even if my husband is gone, my nephew will still be there."

"How will you get back, though? It's a long way to Ethshar of the Sands."

"I'll find a way. Come on!"

"All right," Morvash said. He turned to the other woman, the one whose name he had never learned.

"I'll be fine," she said.

"You're sure?"

She nodded.

"As you wish, then."

Erdrik and Pender, he discovered, had left the front door wide open; animated furniture was crowded around it, as if looking out at the street despite not having eyes. Morvash herded the chairs and tables aside, and watched as Sharra, and the unknown woman, and the two guardsmen walked carefully down the steps, looking up and down the street.

Then he closed the door and marched back upstairs to the gallery.

CHAPTER TWENTY-SIX

MORVASH OF THE SHADOWS

26TH OF LEAFCOLOR, YS 5238

Darissa had wrapped herself in a bedsheet, and Marek had managed to squeeze himself into a purple velvet robe from Erdrik's wardrobe, which was about the right length, but so tight across the shoulders that Morvash expected a seam to split. Several people were sitting on the floor, while a few were leaning against walls; Morvash supposed they thought they had been upright for long enough, since almost all the statues had been standing. They looked up when he stepped back into the gallery.

"Now what?" someone called.

"Now," Morvash said, "we'll see about finding places for all of you. We can send messages, and see whether you have any family or friends who could help." He spotted the Northerner, Iddamethi or whatever the name was, standing apart from the others, looking bewildered. "Does anyone here speak…whatever language the Northern Empire spoke?"

There was a chorus of variations on "no."

Morvash pushed his way through the crowd and went up to the Northerner, his hands open to show his friendly intentions. "Iddamethi?" he said.

The Northerner looked puzzled for a moment, then pointed to himself and said, "*Dmyethriy.*"

"D'methri," Morvash tried.

The Northerner nodded.

Morvash pointed to his own chest and said, "Morvash."

"Morfyash," the Northerner said.

"Close enough. We'll help you. We'll find someone to translate.

Hold on." Then Morvash looked around, wishing he still had Pender, or someone else, to run errands for him.

"What about her?" Alder called, holding up Thetta's wrist. "She tried to bite me."

Morvash looked around and spotted the guardsman who had decided to stay. "Can you take charge of her for now?"

The soldier did not look pleased, but he took Thetta's arm from Alder.

"All right," Morvash called, "I know who some of you are, but not all of you. Most of you understand Ethsharitic, but not all of you, which is going to complicate matters. I had not actually intended to bring all of you back to life at once; my original plan was to rescue you one or two at a time, but I accidentally made my spell more powerful than it should have been, and here we are. I don't have room for all of you here. I don't have *food* for all of you here. I had intended to send my assistant out to bring help, but he deserted me because his former master showed up, so there's just me, and about thirty of you. For anyone who missed it before, we are in Ethshar of the Spices, in the district called the New City, and the year is 5238. For most of you that must seem like the far future, but if you look out the windows you'll see it isn't all *that* strange. The Hegemony of the Three Ethshars has been fairly stable for about two hundred years now, and most of you aren't *that* old." His eye happened to catch one particular face, and he continued, "I know there are at least four of you who were warlocks, though you may not all be familiar with the word. You aren't warlocks anymore; that magic stopped working a little over a year ago, when the thing that appeared in Aldagmor on the Night of Madness went away again. Whether that's good news or bad for you, I don't know."

Another face caught his attention. "Some of you are wizards. I don't know what spell-making supplies you have with you—probably not much. I don't have any to spare. However, the Wizards' Guild knows about what I was doing here, and will probably be able to help you. Once I have matters a little more sorted out I will arrange for you to see a Guildmaster, Ithinia of the Isle, who will decide what to do with you."

"Ithinia is still alive?" someone called.

"Oh, yes," Morvash replied. "Very much so." He tried to think what other magicians there were. "Virzia of Freshwater," he asked, "are you here?"

"Where else would I be?" she replied, from her seat against the far wall. She looked miserable, which seemed odd, given that she had just been freed from imprisonment.

"You're a ritual dancer, aren't you?"

"Yes. Or I was seventeen years ago, anyway."

"In Freshwater? Or is that just where you grew up?"

"In Freshwater."

"As soon as I have a chance, I'll see if your old troupe is still in business. Do you have any family?"

"Seventeen years ago I did."

"Do you want to go see if they're still there? Freshwater isn't very far, after all."

"I'm thinking about it."

"Well, if I can help—"

"Just *shut up*, will you, wizard?" she burst out. "I've just lost *seventeen years*. I spent seventeen years as a stupid *statue*, blind and mute, unable to move; I thought it was a blasted nightmare, I *hoped* it was, and now I'm awake and alive and it's all real! Give me a little time to take that in, will you? Let me think about how my parents are going to react if I show up—if they're still alive! And my sisters, the three of them were all younger than me, but they aren't anymore, are they? So leave me alone and let me decide how I feel about it and what I want to do!"

"I'm sorry," Morvash said. "Of course. Take your time."

The dancer curled up, arms wrapped around her knees, and buried her face in her arms.

"For those of you with nowhere to go, and no family or guild or brotherhood to help you," Morvash announced, "I'll see if you can stay with my Uncle Gror; his home is much larger and more comfortable than this house. Not permanently, but until you can find a place for yourself."

"What about us?" Darissa called. "Didn't you say there was an assassin looking for us?"

"I don't know if he's an assassin," Morvash said. "Uncle Gror did say someone was looking for you, but we don't know why. He *might* be an assassin."

"It's been what, forty years? Then the war with Eknera is long over," Marek said. "We were celebrating the victory when we were enchanted. Why would anyone be looking for us *now*?"

"I don't know," Morvash said. "If you'll recall, I asked *you* that last night."

"Would we be safe at your uncle's place?" Darissa asked.

"I don't know," Morvash said. He looked around thoughtfully. "Maybe you two should stay here; this house has protective spells on it. A *lot* of protective spells. Powerful ones."

"Why can't we *all* stay?" someone called. "Why should we go live with this uncle of yours?"

"Because…well, two reasons," Morvash said. "First, this house isn't big enough; it was never meant for so many guests. But second, and more importantly, this is a wizard's house, it's been home to that same wizard for two hundred years, and there is dangerous magic scattered all over it. Nobody knows how many odd spells and artifacts have accumulated here. You were all just rescued from petrifaction; do you really want to risk being turned into a rat or a squid if you pick up the wrong thing, or sit on the wrong chair?"

There was a murmur at that, but no one spoke up.

"Then Uncle Gror's place it is. You'll like it; it's much nicer than here. I'd have done my experimenting there if my uncle hadn't been afraid I'd blow something up."

As if summoned by the mention of explosions, there was a sudden loud crash. The windows rattled, and the entire house seemed to shake slightly.

"What was *that*?" several voices asked.

Darissa, still only wearing a sheet, stepped to the window Morvash had opened for ventilation, to be greeted by a loud, inhuman roar. She leaned out and looked down.

"What is it?" Morvash called.

"A demon," Darissa said. "There is a demon on your front steps, trying to smash in the front door."

The house shook again.

"It just hit the door with all its fists," Darissa reported. "It has four."

"Did it come for us?" Marek asked.

"Karitha!" a hoarse voice bellowed.

A few confused voices asked, "Who's Karitha?" or something similar, but one woman let out a frightened yelp and abruptly sat down. Morvash recognized her—the only known magician he had not yet spoken to.

"Karitha?" he said. "The demonologist?"

Another roar sounded.

Morvash hurried to her side and knelt beside her. "Do you know who that is, and why it's looking for you?"

Marek leaned out the window and called, "What do you want with this Karitha?"

"She must free me, give me a name, or die!" the demon roared.

"I don't...I don't remember," Karitha said, taking Morvash's hand.

"I know she is in there!" the demon called. "I have her scent!"

"I don't..." Karitha said again. Then she took a deep breath. "I summoned it. To kill Wosten."

"It did kill him," Morvash told her. "Seven years ago."

"I don't remember," Karitha said again. "Did it? But it didn't come back. There was a wind, and a powder that blew in my face, and then everything disappeared, and I thought I was dead, but I didn't go anywhere."

"It's come back to you now," Morvash said. "Why? Why is it so angry?"

"I don't know!"

Another wordless roar came from outside.

"Well, what *do* you remember about it? You summoned it, yes?"

Karitha nodded. "Wosten cheated me," she said. "And he stole herbs from my garden, and mocked me, and he wouldn't apologize or pay me back, and finally I had enough, and I gave him a final warning, but he still wouldn't give in, so I summoned Tarker the Unrelenting to kill him, and then...then there was the wind and the powder and I thought I was dead. I thought my summoning had gone wrong."

"Wizard!" the demon bellowed. "Come speak with me!"

Morvash looked up, and saw that everyone was staring at him, even the other wizards. He gave Karitha one more quick glance, to make sure she was not about to faint or scream, then got to his feet and made his way through the crowd to the window.

Everyone, even Prince Marek, stepped aside to make way for him, and in a moment he was leaning out the window, staring down at the demon on the front steps.

It was as big as a large man, or perhaps slightly larger than a mere man, with black hide and four heavily-muscled arms. It was staring up at him with two blank yellow eyes that almost seemed to be smoking.

"You are the…no. You are not the wizard who made these spells."

"No, I'm not," Morvash said. "He's not here right now. I'm renting the place. What did you want?"

"I want Karitha the Demonologist! Either allow me to enter, or send her out to me."

"Why? What do you want with her?"

"She summoned me! She must release me!"

"When did she summon you? She's been right here ever since she was brought back to life, and we didn't see her summon anyone."

"*Seven years ago!*" The roar was loud enough to rattle the windows, and Morvash could smell what he took to be the demon's breath, reeking of smoke and hot metal. "I have been trapped in your miserable world for *seven years!*"

"Oh," Morvash said. "Hold on." He pulled his head back into the gallery and called to Karitha, "It says it's been waiting seven years for you to release it."

"I think she could hear that," Marek remarked from beside Morvash's shoulder.

"That's right," Karitha said, so quietly Morvash almost did not catch the words. "I summoned Tarker the Unrelenting, but I never released it."

"How does that work?" someone asked. Morvash did not see who had spoken.

"The summoning—when you summon Tarker, you must immediately tell it the name of the person you want it to kill," Karitha explained. "If you don't, it kills *you*, instead. Then it pursues its target, smashing through any defense, until it catches and kills him—that's why it's called 'the Unrelenting,' because it won't stop until its target is dead. It *can't*, no matter what it needs to do or how long it takes. But when it's done, it comes back to the summoner, and you must either speak a secret name to release it, or name a new target, and if you take too long it kills you."

"A little like the Rune of the Implacable Stalker," remarked a wizard who Morvash now remembered had given his name as Lorgol the Mighty; Lorgol was the one who had turned *himself* to stone when one of his spells went wrong.

"So release it," a merchant, Kelder Sammel's son, said.

"Yes," Morvash said. "Wosten is long dead, I promise you."

"I don't know *how*," Karitha said.

"But you *summoned* it!" Darissa exclaimed.

"I know," Karitha said, "but I don't remember how! I've forgotten all my spells—I didn't think I would ever need them again. I thought I was dead!"

"You can't just say, 'I release you,' then?" Morvash asked.

She shook her head. "No, there's a ritual."

Another thump came from below as the demon pounded on the door again.

"Can't we find another demonologist who knows the right summoning?" Kelder asked.

"You'd need to go past the demon to get to him," Morvash pointed out. He looked out the window again, and saw that Tarker had descended the steps to the street and was looking up at the window in a calculating way that made the wizard suddenly nervous.

"It wouldn't work," Karitha said. "When you summon Tarker, you give him a secret name to bind him, and you need the secret name to release him, and it has to be a *different* secret name each time—in fact, that's why it's a dangerous spell, because if you try to use one that's bound him before it doesn't work, and he'll kill you, even if the demonologist who used it before has been dead for a thousand years."

"So what secret name did you use?" Morvash asked, watching the demon. It was backing away and looking up.

"I don't know! I don't remember! It was about fifty syllables long, so that I could be sure no one had used it before; I had it written down, but I don't have the paper anymore, it was hidden in my workroom, and I don't remember it! It's been seven years!"

"Darissa," Marek called, "do you think you could help her remember?"

"*Send her out to me!*" came a roar from the street.

"I don't know," Darissa said. "A memory like that from seven years ago? What happens if she gets a syllable or two wrong?"

"Then it kills me," Karitha said. "No one ever said demonology was safe."

"Then give it the name of someone else to kill," Kelder suggested. "You don't need the secret name for that, do you?"

"That would be murder!" Darissa protested.

"So was killing this Wosten character, wasn't it?"

"I don't want to kill anyone else!" Karitha wailed. "If being dead is like the last seven years—and besides, after it killed whoever I sent it after, it would come right back to me again, and anyway, except for you people right here, I don't know who's still alive and who's died since I was turned to stone, and if I tell it to kill someone who's already dead, that doesn't work, it kills me instead."

"I always thought demonology sounded like a stupid occupation," someone muttered.

"It's what I could get, all right?" Karitha snapped. "Not everyone has a dozen masters clamoring for her as an apprentice."

"It sounds to me," said one of the former warlocks—Abaran of something, Morvash thought, maybe Fishertown, "as if we will not be going to your uncle's place any time soon. *I* am certainly not going to try to slip past an angry demon."

"I'm just glad the protective spells on this place are strong!" Lorgol said.

"So am I," Morvash said, closing and latching the window as he saw Tarker prepare to leap. He knew it was magic and not wood and glass that guarded the house, but he was not sure the spell would work properly if there was an actual physical opening. "So am I," he repeated.

CHAPTER TWENTY-SEVEN

HAKIN OF THE HUNDRED-FOOT FIELD

26TH OF LEAFCOLOR, YS 5238

Hakin had lost Tarker's trail briefly at the Cut Street Market in the Old Merchants' Quarter, but of the six streets leaving the market only two ran in approximately the direction Tarker had been heading, and after a few seconds' hesitation he chose the left-hand one, running west up the hill into the highest part of the New City. That seemed as if it would be a shorter route to the Wizards' Quarter, and he thought that was the part of the city where the long-lost demonologist was most likely to have turned up.

He did not know the street's name; he was not familiar with this part of the city. It was a well-to-do area, certainly; there were more gates than doors along the sides. He guessed that Tarker was just cutting through, and would probably come out on Arena Street and turn south.

But then he heard the demon roar, and it seemed to be coming from one of the cross-streets. He picked up his pace.

He followed the bellowing, turning right at the next corner, and spotted Tarker standing on the steps of a strange dark stone house, pounding on the front door with all four of its fists clasped into one massive hammer of demonic flesh and bone.

The door did not yield an inch. Hakin's eyes widened. That, he knew, must be magic; there was no natural substance that could withstand such a blow without cracking.

That made sense, though. If Karitha really had been turned to stone by Wosten's sylph, and someone had turned her back, it would have to have been a wizard. Not all wizards lived in the Wizards' Quarter, or even in Arena; almost every part of the city had a few magicians scattered about. That ghastly stone monstrosity certainly *looked* like it should belong to a magician of some sort, though Hakin might have thought a demonologist would be a better fit than a wizard.

He hurried up the street, and began calling Tarker's name.

The demon ignored him as it stepped back and bellowed, "*Send her out to me!*"

There was a moment of silence as Tarker looked up, waiting.

Hakin saw a hand appear, and realized an upstairs window was open—and then it wasn't, as the hand pulled it shut.

Tarker roared again, gauged the distance, crouched, and jumped. It punched at the upstairs window as it passed, but caught the stonework a story above, and scrambled up to the roof. It was obviously looking for a weak spot in the house's magical defenses.

Two gargoyles Hakin had not noticed at first sidled quickly away from the demon. It was *definitely* standing on a wizard's house. Interesting that the gargoyles made no move to defend their home from attack; presumably their creator had not thought their help would be needed.

Indeed, whatever wizard had placed the protective spells on *this* house had not made the same mistake Wosten had; Hakin could see Tarker's blows bounce harmlessly from roof tiles, chimneys, and stone walls.

Hakin slowed to a trot, and then a walk, as he drew up to the house. He could not see Tarker now, as it had crested the rooftop and was somewhere toward the back of the house. Hakin formed a trumpet of his hands and called, "*Hai*, in the house!"

That same upstairs window opened a crack, the hand ready to slam it shut again at the first glimpse of the demon. "Who are you?" someone called.

"My name's Hakin. I've been looking after the demon for the last few years, keeping it out of trouble. Is Karitha the Demonologist really in there?"

There was a pause before a different voice called down, "Yes, she is!"

"Then let the demon in, and have her release it! It'll go back to the Nethervoid and no one will be hurt."

The first voice spoke again. "First off, we *can't* let it in—the wizard who placed the protections isn't here. Second, she doesn't remember how to release it!"

Hakin could hear thumping and banging as Tarker tried to smash a hole into the house, but it did not sound as if it was meeting with any success. "What do you mean, she doesn't remember?"

"She spent seven years thinking she was dead; she doesn't remember her magic! Releasing it requires a secret name, and she doesn't know what name she used."

"That's…really unfortunate," Hakin called. "*Really* unfortunate. Because for the seven years since I first met Tarker, all it has ever wanted was to find Karitha and be released." Then he heard monstrous footsteps and looked up.

He did not need to say anything; whoever had been looking out the window must have seen him look up, because the casement slammed shut and Hakin thought he could hear the click of a latch from thirty feet away.

"Hakin!" Tarker bellowed from the edge of the roof. "Talk to them! Make them give me Karitha!"

"I'm trying!" Hakin called back. "But there's a problem!"

"I do not care about problems! Give me Karitha!"

"I'm working on it!"

Tarker swung down over the edge, hanging from two of his hands, while his other two and both feet slammed against walls and windows, trying to break through whatever magic guarded the house.

Hakin watched the demon pound ineffectually for a few seconds, then sighed, crossed the street, and settled onto the front steps of a far more ordinary home. He was not sure whether Tarker would ever tire of its futile task; he knew he had never seen the demon sleep, or show any sign of fatigue, and its very *name* was 'the Unrelenting.' It might be able to beat uselessly on that place for the rest of time.

That might be interesting, Hakin thought. Maybe he could charge admission, or sell souvenirs. The famous whomping demon! Watch it try unsuccessfully to smash its way into a wizard's house!

But what would become of Karitha? She couldn't stay in there forever; wouldn't she starve to death?

Of course, if she died, *that* would release Tarker. That would be unfortunate for her, but would put a peaceful end to the matter for everyone else, and she *had* sent a demon to murder Wosten, so she wasn't exactly an innocent.

But there were other people in there with her—or at least one other person, because he had heard two voices from that window. *He* shouldn't need to starve, whoever he was.

Of course, whoever that was, wizard or someone else, he could leave any time he wanted to; Tarker wouldn't bother anyone except Karitha.

But maybe he didn't *know* that. He had said the wizard who placed the protections wasn't there, so maybe this poor unfortunate wasn't a magician at all, and didn't know how any of this works.

Even if he *was* a wizard, it might not be obvious that Tarker wouldn't hurt him. With a sigh, Hakin got to his feet, trying to ignore the soreness in his calves and feet that had resulted from running halfway across the city. He ambled across the street and up the front steps of the strange gray house and knocked on the blue-painted door.

He waited, and after awhile he knocked again. Perhaps whoever was inside had not heard his knock, or had thought it was more of Tarker's bashing.

Eventually, a voice that he thought was the same one who had done most of the talking through the window called through the heavy wood, "What is it?"

"I just wanted to point out," Hakin said, "that anyone in there who wants to leave can do so—the demon won't bother anyone but Karitha. The rest of you, whoever you are and however many, can come and go safely."

There was a momentary silence; then the door swung open a few inches and a tired-looking young man said, "Are you sure of that?"

"Pretty much," Hakin said. "The one exception is if it decides you're in its way. It's under various restrictions—you know how magic is—and it can't intentionally harm anyone other than its target unless that person is keeping it from its objective. If you block its path to Karitha it'll rip you to pieces, but if you step aside it won't touch you. I've lived around it for seven years, and it's never so much as scratched me."

"*Aaaaarh!*" Tarker had dropped to the ground behind Hakin, and now it was charging up the steps. Hakin quickly stepped out of its path, and watched as the demon slammed into…*something*. Not the door; whoever was behind it had not reacted quickly enough, and the door was still unlatched and open a crack.

It had not budged under Tarker's assault, though, and now Hakin could see that the demon had not actually touched the door at all. It had been stopped short at the front edge of the threshold, silently pounding its four fists on thin air.

For a moment the two men froze where they were as the demon thrashed and shoved; then the man inside swung the door wide and stared, fascinated, as Tarker failed to force its way in.

"That's a pretty good protective spell you have there," Hakin remarked, shouting over Tarker's shoulder.

"It's not mine," the other man replied. "It came with the house. I think it was cast by a wizard called Erdrik the Grim."

"Whoever did it, I'm impressed." Curious, Hakin reached past the raging demon, to see what the invisible barrier felt like.

It did not feel like anything at all; his hand passed through it as if it was not there at all.

"Oh, now *that's* interesting," he said, as he wiggled his fingers.

The other man thrust his own hand out, and also found it unimpeded. He and Hakin clasped hands briefly, then released.

Tarker bellowed deafeningly. Hakin cringed.

"Would you like…" the other began, and then stopped, with a glance at the demon.

"Yeah, I wouldn't issue any invitations to *anyone* just now," Hakin said. On an impulse he squeezed past Tarker and slipped through the doorway, then turned to look at his long-time companion thrashing against empty air.

"I'm Morvash of the Shadows," the other man said, holding out a hand. "I'm renting this place from the Wizards' Guild—or I *was*; I suspect that whole arrangement has been ruined by today's events."

Hakin took his hand. "Hakin the Demon's Master," he said. "Or at least, that's what I've been called lately."

"What were you before?"

Hakin hesitated before admitting, "Hakin of the Hundred-Foot Field."

"Ah, I see." Morvash looked at the demon. "How did that happen?"

"I don't mind telling you, but first, how did Karitha the Demonologist wind up in here with you?"

Tarker let out a howl of rage and frustration; Morvash winced, then closed the door. "Come on upstairs and meet the others," he said, "and we can tell one another all about it."

CHAPTER TWENTY-EIGHT

MORVASH OF THE SHADOWS

26TH OF LEAFCOLOR, YS 5238

By the time Morvash, Karitha, and Hakin had exchanged stories, and the newcomer had been introduced to the former statues, the western sky was streaked with orange and the sun was brushing the rooftops across the street, leaving Old East Avenue mostly in shadow. A dozen or more people were standing in the street in front of the house, watching as Tarker flailed away fruitlessly at doors, walls, and windows. They had apparently concluded that they were safe, that the demon's attention was directed elsewhere.

Several of the former statues had been shown the kitchen, and the household's meager supply of food had been distributed; now a few sat around the kitchen table, while most of the group, including Morvash and the other wizards, idled in the gallery.

"You know, those are really excellent wards," Halder Kelder's son said, "but the demon may wear them down eventually."

"*Could* it?" Morvash asked.

"It depends how they were done," Lorgol the Mighty said. "Some protections wear down, some don't."

The guardsman, who had given his name as Bern Bern's son, was watching out the gallery window; he interrupted the wizards with an exclamation.

"The guard's here!"

Morvash turned and looked. "So they are," he said.

Indeed, half a dozen men in the familiar yellow and red uniforms were standing in the street, arranged in two rows of three; all of them wore breastplates and had truncheons hung on their belts, but five were carrying spears, while the center man in the front row wore a sword on his belt.

"I'd better go talk to them," Morvash said.

"Shall I come along?" Hakin asked. "I work with the guard."

"I think that might be helpful, yes." He turned and gestured to Bern. "You, too. Alder, can you keep an eye on Thetta?"

Alder reluctantly agreed to watch the dancer again, and Bern joined Morvash and Hakin. Together, the three men made their way down to the foyer, where Morvash opened the door. He glanced out to see where Tarker was, and heard roars coming from above. With that in mind he kept his head inside the door, so the demon could not drop down on him, while he cupped his hands to his mouth and called, "Can I help you?"

The swordsman, presumably the squad commander, turned to look at Morvash. Then he glanced up at the demon. "That depends," the soldier called back. "Is that thing safe?"

"The demon? No, of course not; it's a demon."

"Tarker the Unrelenting," Hakin helpfully called over the wizard's shoulder.

"What it is, officer, is completely uninterested in *you*," Morvash called. "Or me, for that matter. Unless you give it some reason to think you might aid it, or you get in its way, it will ignore you. Now, would you prefer I came out there, or you came inside, to speak? Because I really do want to talk to you."

"I think you had better come out."

Morvash turned to Hakin and Bern. "We'll all go."

Bern looked as if he was about to protest, then nodded.

Morvash paused, gathered himself, then dashed down the steps. When he was out on the street, clear of the house, he turned and looked back.

Tarker was working its way along the cornice between the second and third floors, systematically bashing it every foot or so, striking the stone a few times in each spot before moving on, obviously looking for some weak spot in Erdrik's magical defenses—and, thank the gods, not yet finding one.

Morvash beckoned, and first Hakin, then Bern, came running out. Morvash was mildly irked that they had left the door standing open, but he supposed it did not really matter. He turned and led the threesome over to greet the guardsmen.

"I am Morvash of the Shadows," he said. "I have been renting that house to provide a space for certain magical experiments. This is Hakin, and that's Bern. Bern has spent the last century or so as a piece of bric-a-brac; I restored him to his natural form this morning."

"Were you the one that enchanted him in the first place?"

"Oh, no! I wasn't even born a hundred years ago. My *grandfather* wasn't born. No, it was Erdrik the Grim, the former owner of the house, who enchanted him."

"I see." He glanced at Bern. "As it happens, I have spoken with two of his supposed companions, and their story matches yours."

Morvash nodded.

"Now, what is that demon doing there?"

Morvash started to turn to Hakin, but the soldier stopped him. "I want to hear it from you first," he said.

"Oh. Well, I don't know the whole story, but the demon is looking for the demonologist who originally summoned it, seven years ago."

"Her name is Karitha," Hakin offered.

"Yes," Morvash said. "Her name is Karitha, and as I understand it, she sent the demon to kill a wizard named Wosten of the Red Robe—and while she was doing that, Wosten conjured a sylph..."

"A what?" one of the other five soldiers asked.

"A sylph. An air elemental. A living wind."

"Go on," the commander said.

"Yes, well, Wosten sent a sylph armed with a spell to turn Karitha to stone, so when the demon returned to say its task was done, Karitha wasn't there. In fact, the statue she had become had been spirited away—we don't know exactly how or where, but it eventually wound up in the sculpture collection of the late Lord Landessin, where I found it and resolved to restore her to life."

"You did."

"Yes."

"Why?"

Morvash opened his mouth, closed it again, and then said, "It seemed like the right thing to do. I took *all* the statues from Lord Landessin's gallery that I knew were really enchanted people, and brought them here to restore them."

"All right, go on."

"Yes, well, when the demon returned, expecting to be released and sent back to its infernal home, it could not find Karitha, so it was stuck in our world. Hakin, here, befriended it, and has guided it ever since, keeping it busy with heavy labor in the overlord's employ—until today, when it sensed that Karitha had been restored to life, and it came to find her, so she could release it."

"I'd heard there was a demon working in the shipyards; that's this one?"

Morvash turned to Hakin, who said, "Yes, sir. Its name is Tarker the Unrelenting."

"Fine. So why is it roaring and pounding on walls? Why hasn't this Karitha sent it back home?"

"Because she doesn't remember how," Morvash explained. "She spent seven years as a statue, and she thought she was dead, so she made no special effort to remember anything. She needs a particular magic word that she had written down, rather than memorizing it. And there are two ways the demon can be released—if she says the magic word, or if it kills her. She doesn't want to be killed, so she's staying in Erdrik's house, behind the most powerful wards I've ever seen, where the demon can't get at her."

Hakin hesitated, and then said, "There are actually *three* ways. And there might be a way it can get at her."

"What's the third?" the officer asked.

"If she orders it to kill someone else."

"No," Morvash said, "that wouldn't *release* it; that would just postpone matters until it kills the new victim."

"Oh, but..." Hakin stopped and said, "Oh. You're right. I'm sorry."

Morvash turned and peered at him. "And what's this about there might be a way it can get at her?"

Hakin glanced back at the house, where Tarker was approaching the corner, still hitting the stone cornice. "I don't want to say," he said. "Tarker has very good ears. I'm not *sure* it would work, but it might. If we were somewhere there was no chance Tarker could overhear, I would like to discuss it with you, but not here. But I will say that Tarker may eventually figure it out for itself, just as I did. You might not want to let this present situation go on indefinitely."

This made Morvash very curious, but he knew Hakin was probably right. He almost certainly knew better than anyone how good Tarker's hearing was, after spending seven years with the demon.

"All right," the officer said. "That explains the demon, and your well-intentioned experiments explain why I had two men I never heard of reporting back to the barracks a hundred years late. Now, what about Erdrik the Grim? Where does he fit into all this?"

"Well, it's his house," Morvash said. "Or it was, anyway."

"But he's been missing and presumed dead for the last eleven years. I read up on the case before we came here."

"Yes, well, he wasn't dead. He had accidentally trapped himself in a hidden room, and when I cast my spell to restore things to their natural forms, it restored that room to its normal existence, and Erdrik walked right out."

"So he's in there now?"

"No, he left, hours ago. Before the demon got here. There was a messenger who had come looking for him, and wound up working for me so he could stay in Erdrik's house; he's from somewhere far away in the north, and he came to tell Erdrik that his secret project was ready."

"What secret project?"

"I don't know; Erdrik had put a spell on the messenger so that he couldn't tell me. But whatever it is, as soon as Erdrik heard it was ready, he took the messenger and left, and I haven't seen them since."

"So he's loose somewhere in the city? The north part of the city?"

"Oh, he may well be outside the city by now. The messenger was from somewhere north of Sardiron."

"Ah."

"I take it, officer, that you were sent to learn what the situation is, and do whatever might be necessary to keep the people of Ethshar safe?"

"More or less," the soldier said. "You do know that Erdrik is a wanted criminal, don't you?"

Morvash blinked. "Ah...no," he said. "Ithinia and her agent did not see fit to mention this to me."

"Of course they didn't." The soldier sighed. "So who else is in the house, besides this demonologist? Is there anyone else who might be dangerous?"

"Not particularly," Morvash said.

"There are more wizards," Bern announced, speaking for the first time since they left the house.

"There *are* more wizards," Morvash agreed, "but they don't have their supplies, and aren't wanted criminals—just a handful of unfortunates. One turned himself to stone accidentally, one was petrified by a rebellious apprentice…that sort of thing. And there are four people who used to be warlocks, but they're obviously harmless now. Listen, I don't want to keep them here—there isn't really room. I said I'd see that the wizards were taken to Ithinia, so *she* can figure out what to do with them—could you arrange that, maybe? And I was going to send the rest to my uncle's place on Canal Avenue until we could figure out what to do with them—they're from all over the World, and from different times in the past. The oldest one was a captured Northern spy from the Great War; there are probably historians at the Palace who would love to talk to him. Assuming they know his language, which no one here does; we only found out who he is by hiring a witch to hear his thoughts."

"So you just want to get rid of them?" the soldier asked.

"Mostly, yes," Morvash said. "I just wanted to save them from being petrified, I don't have anything in mind for them now they're alive again."

"It's like the warlocks all over again," one of the soldiers said.

"More or less," the commander agreed. "But none of *them* went back more than thirty-five years."

"Will you help?" Morvash asked.

The commander looked past him, at the demon hanging from the cornice by one hand and pounding on the wall below it with its other three. "How long can your magic keep that thing out?"

Morvash said, "It's not *my* magic, it's Erdrik's. And I don't know."

"All right, let's get everyone out of there, and find safe places for them," the commander said. He turned to one of his men. "Thorun, go back to camp, report to Captain Vengar, and ask him to send more men—maybe a dozen. Istram, run down to Ithinia's house on Lower Street—the one with the gargoyles, you'll recognize it—and tell whoever answers the door that we have a situation here that requires the Guild's attention."

"And could you ask her whether Zerra is available?" Morvash asked. "Her flying carpet could be very handy for transporting people."

The soldier looked at his commander, who nodded. "Do that," he said.

"Zerra? Was that the name?" Istram asked.

"Yes," Morvash said. "Zerra the Ageless."

"Got it." With that, he turned and trotted down Old East Avenue, headed north. Thorun set out in the opposite direction, then turned left and vanished around the next corner.

"Sir," Morvash said, "there are three people I think should stay in the house, behind protective spells."

"I assume one of them is the demonologist?"

Morvash nodded.

"Who are the others?"

"A young couple from the Small Kingdoms. He's a prince of Melitha, and someone's after them, possibly an assassin. It might be a dynastic thing. I don't know if it's safe for them to come out."

"I'm staying until I see what happens to Tarker," Hakin said.

"Please yourself," Morvash said, turning up an empty palm.

"Fine," the commander said. "So the wizards go to Lower Street, you keep those three and this man, and the rest go to…where?"

"My uncle's house on Canal Avenue," Morvash said. "Unless you have somewhere better."

"No, that sounds fine. How many people are we talking about?"

Morvash had lost track of the exact numbers. "About two dozen," he said.

"I'll wait until we have more men, then, but…Dabran! Get directions to this house on Canal Street, and go see that they're ready for two dozen guests. If you can bring back people to help, do it."

Morvash beckoned to Dabran, and explained exactly how to find and recognize Uncle Gror's place. The soldier nodded, and set out at a trot.

The commander waited until Morvash had finished with Dabran, then said, "You mentioned something about a magic word the demonologist wrote down. Where is it?"

"Ah…it was in her workroom somewhere. But that was seven years ago! I doubt it's still there."

"What's happened to her workroom?" the officer demanded.

"*I* don't know." Morvash looked at Hakin.

"I'm not sure," Hakin admitted. "Shenna of the White Dagger was in charge of the investigation of Karitha's disappearance, and for a long time she kept me up to date on what they had and hadn't found there, but that all sort of faded away. I haven't heard anything for a few years now."

"So the workroom was searched?"

"Very thoroughly, as I understand it."

"Was a note found?"

"I...I don't know. Shenna might. Or Lord Borlan."

"Lord Borlan? The magistrate?" the commander asked.

"Yes," Hakin said. "He was in charge of handling Wosten's murder and Karitha's disappearance."

The commander turned and looked at his two remaining men. "Neran, have you been following all this?"

"Yes, sir," one of the spearmen said, straightening up.

"Do you know where Lord Borlan's office is?"

"Yes, sir. I've made arrests in the Wizards' Quarter."

"Good. Go find him, tell him Karitha the Demonologist has turned up and the overlord's pet demon is trying to get at her, and we need a note that was in her workroom when she vanished. He'll ask you a lot of questions; he always does. Answer them, and do what he tells you, and if you get back here with that note before dawn you'll get first pick at the barracks' next pig roast."

"Yes, sir!" Neran hefted his spear, then set out up Old East Avenue at an easy, loping run.

That left two soldiers—or three, counting Bern. The commander looked at his companion and said, "You're staying here with me." Then he turned back to Morvash. "I hope you don't have any more errands for me, because I'm not sending any more men. We're going to keep an eye on the demon."

"Yes, sir," Morvash said.

"Is there anything else I need to know?"

Morvash glanced at Hakin, who turned up a hand.

"I don't think so," the wizard said.

"Good," the soldier said. "Then you can go back inside and keep an eye on your people, including the demonologist." He pointed at Hakin. "You go with him."

"What about me?" Bern asked.

"You stay here. I may need you to carry messages into the house for me."

"Thank you, sir," Morvash said. He took a look at the crowd before heading back to the house—and froze. "Pender!" he called. "What are *you* doing here?"

CHAPTER TWENTY-NINE

MORVASH OF THE SHADOWS

26TH OF LEAFCOLOR, YS 5238

Pender stepped out of the crowd. "I did not have another place to go," he said.

"But you were with Erdrik!" Morvash exclaimed. "I thought you'd be on your way back to Tazmor by now!"

"He did not want to carry me."

"But…carry you?"

The commander interrupted. "Who is this man?"

"This is Pender the Jeweler," Morvash explained. "He worked for Erdrik the Grim. He was working as my assistant while Erdrik was missing, but when Erdrik reappeared he left with him, and I didn't expect to see him again." He glanced at Pender. "He's from Tazmor, and his native language is Sardironese; his Ethsharitic isn't very good."

"You were with Erdrik?" the soldier asked Pender.

"Yes."

"Where did he go?"

"Tazmor."

"He's on the way to Tazmor?"

Pender looked confused for a second, then said, "He is *in* Tazmor now. By magic."

"What?" Morvash demanded. "What magic?"

"The…" Pender frowned. "The orange stone that he broke."

For a moment Morvash could make no sense of this, but then he understood. "You mean Pallum's Returning Crystal?"

Pender looked completely baffled. The soldier asked Morvash, "You know what he's talking about?"

"It's a spell," he said. "I can't do it, but I've heard about it. The ritual creates an orange crystal about the size of a child's fist, and when someone crushes it in his hand, he's instantly transported to wherever the crystal was made, no matter how far that is."

"Shenna thought that was probably how Karitha was hidden away after she was petrified," Hakin offered. "Someone used a crystal to transport her."

"That is it," Pender said. "That is how the wizard goes to Tazmor, and to Ethshar. But he could not carry me, so I am still here."

"That would explain why no one here knew about his trips to Tazmor," Morvash said. "No one ever saw him on the way between them because he *wasn't* between them—he was moved instantly from one to the other."

"So Erdrik is in Tazmor now?" the commander demanded.

"Yes," Pender said.

"That's in northern Sardiron?"

Pender looked uncertain. "It is very north," he said. "Farther than Sardiron of the Waters."

"Good enough." He turned to look at his remaining underling, and for the first time Morvash saw him hesitate.

"Blood," he said. "I need more men, and they probably won't be here for half an hour or more. Captain Vengar will want to know where Erdrik is, and probably Ithinia, too."

"She may be able to locate him magically," Morvash said.

"And she may not," the soldier said. "She didn't find him during those eleven years he was missing."

Morvash started to protest that that was different, Erdrik had been behind a concealment spell, no mere illusion but the kind that actually physically changed a hiding place, but then he caught himself. Erdrik could well have used the same spell somewhere in Tazmor, or might have some other, equally effective way to avoid discovery.

While the wizard was trying to decide what to say, the soldier turned to the crowd that had gathered to watch the demon and shouted, "Will anyone here volunteer to run an errand, or are you all determined to waste your time here?"

A boy of about ten called, "Does it pay?"

"Half a round," Morvash offered, reaching for his purse. "Two bits now, two bits when you bring back the answer."

"I'll do it," the boy said.

"Thank you," the officer said to Morvash. Then he turned to the youth. "The message is very simple—Erdrik the Grim is in Tazmor. The tricky part is making sure it gets to the right person."

"Erdrik the Grim is in Tazmor. Got it. Who do I tell?"

"Captain Vengar, at the guard camp. They'll try to stop you at the gate; tell them Lieutenant Fullan sent you and said it was urgent."

"Lieutenant Fullan says it's urgent. Erdrik is in Tazmor." The boy held out a hand, and Morvash dropped two wedge-shaped coins into it. Closing his fist, the boy turned and ran.

Morvash handed the lieutenant, whose name and rank he finally knew, two more bits. He turned toward the house, and was startled when Hakin grabbed his elbow.

"We need to get inside," Hakin said. "Now!"

Puzzled, Morvash let himself be hustled back across the street. He beckoned for Pender to come, and Bern and the Tazmorite followed. Tarker had made its way around to the north side of the house for the moment, so there was nothing to keep the foursome from hurrying into the house.

As soon as they were inside, Hakin said, "Do you have magic that can keep us from being overheard?"

"Ah… Fendel's Rune of Privacy," Morvash replied.

"Cast it. I need to tell you something without any chance at all that Tarker will hear it."

"All right. This way." He gestured to Pender and Bern. "You two go up to the gallery; we'll be up soon."

They went, and Morvash led Hakin to the stone-floored workroom. The daylight had faded enough that it was difficult to see; the wizard pricked a finger with his dagger, and a flame blazed up. Morvash ignored the oil lamps and instead lit a thick candle that stood on his workbench, then curled his finger, extinguishing the flame. He went to a cabinet where he found a box of ingredients he had brought with him from his home in Ethshar of the Rocks; then he took a little velvet pouch from the box, tugged open the drawstring, and fished out a small pearl.

"I need something to draw with," he said, looking around.

"There's ink over there," Hakin said, pointing.

"I'd rather use something less permanent."

"We need to hurry!"

"Fine!" Morvash said. He set the candle in the middle of the floor. Then he took the ink bottle and placed it a foot or two away. "Sit down," he ordered.

Hakin seated himself, cross-legged, on the floor.

"Closer to the candle," Morvash ordered, as he dipped his athame in the ink. Hakin scooted forward, and Morvash went down on one knee next to him, drawing an elaborate rune that surrounded the base of the candle and extended out to one side, where it ended in a small circle.

"Hold still," he said, as he set the pearl in the circle.

The ink of the rune seemed to glow faintly purple for a second, and then subsided, and the world was suddenly silent. The pounding of Tarker's fists was gone, as were the normal faint sounds of the city going about its business. All the two could hear was their own breath.

"Is it working?" Hakin asked, looking around.

"It should be," Morvash said. "Everything felt right and did what it was supposed to. If you hear a pop, though, that means the spell's been broken."

"So no one can hear us?"

Annoyed, Morvash said, "There's a barrier around us, ten feet from the pearl in every direction. Absolutely no sound can get through it, but it's very fragile, so we may not have much time. Now, what is this about?"

"The protective spells on this house—Tarker is testing them systematically. It started on the roof, and now it's working its way down, trying every bit of the walls and windows."

"Yes, I noticed."

"Do you know how extensive the protective spells are?"

"No. They're Erdrik's doing, and he's apparently not especially eager to share his secrets."

"They cover all the sides of the house, and the top. Do they cover the bottom?"

"What?"

"Wosten's house had protective spells on all the walls and doors and windows, so Tarker smashed its way in through the roof. That didn't work here, but what if it tunnels down and comes at the house from below? Are there safeguards to prevent that?"

"I have no idea," Morvash admitted, worried for the first time since he saw the demon unable to pass through the open front door. "The cellar floors appear to be bedrock. I didn't notice any magic."

"It's working its way down, and I don't think it's going to stop when it reaches the ground."

"Oh, death. I have *no idea* what will happen then," Morvash said. "Erdrik *might* have thought of it, but we can't be sure."

"Maybe we should get Karitha out of here."

"But where can she go? Where could she go that Tarker can't follow her?"

"*I* have no idea," Hakin admitted. "I hoped you might. He claims he can smell her and follow her scent anywhere in the World."

"Well, I can't get her *out* of the World," Morvash said. "There are wizards who can, but I'm just a journeyman. I don't even know what spells might work, let alone how to perform them."

"Could you turn her back to stone until we find somewhere safe?"

"No. I didn't bother learning any petrifaction spells, only how to undo them."

For a moment they were both silent; then Hakin said, "Maybe you should just let it kill her."

"Maybe I should," Morvash said, "but I don't *want* to. Yes, she killed Wosten of the Red Robe, but then she spent seven years as a statue, which must be absolutely horrible." He stood up.

"It's your house," Hakin said, also getting to his feet. "She's your guest."

"That's a big part of it, you know," Morvash said. "It's Erdrik's house, not mine, but for the last few sixnights it's been my home, and I've been telling all these people I was going to save them, and mostly I *did*, and I don't want to think I doomed her instead of rescuing her."

"Well, unless you can think of something, you may not be *able* to save her."

"There's that note she wrote, if Lord Borlan's people found it."

"If they found it and *kept* it," Hakin corrected him.

"Maybe Erdrik *did* defend against underground attacks."

"Maybe. I wouldn't want to bet on it."

Morvash knew he would not want to make that bet, either. "Perhaps we should talk to Karitha," he said.

"All right." Hakin looked around. "How do we get out of this enchantment?"

"Just walk through it," Morvash said. "I told you, it's fragile. Or I can destroy it by blowing out the candle, or taking the pearl out of the circle, or scuffing the rune. Are we done with it?"

"I think so," Hakin said.

"Fine." Morvash bent down and picked up the little pearl, and just as he had said, there was a faint "pop!" and the sounds of the outside world burst in on them.

One of those sounds was Tarker roaring from just outside the workroom's one window, "Hakin! What did you tell him? Do you know a way in?"

"No!" Hakin shouted. "I was wrong!"

"I don't believe you! Hakin, I have served you for seven years even though you did not summon me—do not lie to me!"

"Come on, let's go upstairs," Hakin said.

Morvash took a moment to put away the pearl and scrape as much of the ink off the floor as he easily could, then sheathed his knife, set the candle back on the workbench, blew it out, and followed, closing the workroom door behind him.

By the time they reached the gallery Tarker was perched outside one of the windows, bellowing with rage. "Hakin! One of you! *Let me in*!"

"It can't get in, can it?" Alder asked as Morvash stepped into the room.

"I don't think so," Morvash said.

"I was worried when these people said Hakin had a secret to tell you."

"He was worried about something, but it's not a problem after all." Morvash hoped no one could tell he was lying. He crossed the room to look out the window.

Lieutenant Fullan and his subordinate were still keeping watch in the street; the sun was down and the street lamps had been lit. The crowd had thinned; Morvash supposed it was harder to see what the demon was up to than it had been earlier.

Or maybe people had just wanted to get home to their supper. Morvash wished *he* could eat supper, but the earlier foraging had wiped out his food supplies.

But then the crowd on the street parted, and a maroon and silver coach appeared, with a guardsman squeezed onto the driver's bench beside the driver. The soldier was waving to Lieutenant Fullan.

"That must be Dabran," Hakin said.

It did look like Dabran, Morvash had to agree, and he recognized the coach, as well. "That's my uncle's carriage," he said. "I had better go see what's happening." He turned and hurried down the stairs.

By the time Morvash got out the front door, a stout figure had emerged from the coach and was speaking to Lieutenant Fullan. Dabran had climbed down and was next to Fullan, listening.

"Uncle Gror!" Morvash called. "I didn't expect you to come in person!"

"I wanted to see for myself what all the fuss was about," his uncle replied. He looked past Morvash at Tarker, who was now standing on a ground-floor windowsill, pounding at the wall. "What's going on?"

Morvash quickly explained the situation as best he could.

"So your experiments worked?" Gror asked. "You turned all those statues back into people?"

"Yes, I did."

"Then will you be coming back home?"

Morvash opened his mouth, then closed it again. "I don't know," he said. "I need to clean up the mess first."

Gror nodded. "I understand we are to have guests in Lord Landessin's mansion?"

"Several of them," Morvash admitted.

"How long will they be staying?"

"Until they can find places. For some of them that shouldn't take more than a day or two, but for some it could be awhile."

"I see."

"There's a witch named Ariella the Perceptive who lives at the corner of Witch Alley and Mana Street who can help sort them out," Morvash said. "Some of them don't speak Ethsharitic, but she can hear their thoughts and translate for you."

"All right. Have they had supper?"

"No. We ate all the food I had in the house for lunch."

"Then I'll feed the ones I take back to the house, and I'll send someone over with some groceries."

"*Thank* you, Uncle! That's very kind."

"Don't be silly. You're family. Even if you don't always act like it."

"I'll try to be a better nephew now that this is all done, Uncle."

"I hope so." He glanced at the coach. "So where are these people? I can fit four or five right away, and I'll send the coach back for more without me, which will mean room for one or two more."

"They're inside. Come on in and meet them."

Gror hesitated. "What about the demon?"

"It won't hurt you. You don't have anything it wants."

"You're sure?"

"Quite sure."

Gror nodded, then turned to Fullan. "Is there anything else I can do for you, Lieutenant?"

"I think we're fine," Fullan replied. "Go get those people out of there."

Gror pounded a fist on his chest in a rough approximation of a salute, and then followed his nephew into the old gray house.

CHAPTER THIRTY

DARISSA THE WITCH'S APPRENTICE

26TH OF LEAFCOLOR, YS 5238

Darissa sat on the polished wood floor of the gallery, watching the others milling about and listening to their moods.

She was in a wizard's house in Ethshar of the Spices. She was still trying to comprehend that. She had looked out the gallery windows at the street and had seen a place like nothing she had ever imagined—so many houses, crowded together so closely! Such strange architecture!

And the house itself, with its wooden floors and walking chairs— she had heard of animated furniture, but she had never seen any before, had not really believed the stories.

These people around her were all so strange and varied—people from all over the World and four different centuries, all as confused as she was.

How had she wound up *here*?

"This doesn't make any sense," she said.

Marek, who was standing beside her, looked down at her and said, "What doesn't?"

"All of this. Everything."

"I'm not sure I know what you mean."

"*Everything*. Who turned us to stone? Who would do that? Why? We weren't bothering anyone."

"Maybe King Abran arranged it. Maybe he had some idea he could use us as a hostage to force Dad to surrender—offer the counterspell in exchange for victory. After all, he wanted to capture Terren to use that way, and threw away any chance at a legitimate victory to do it."

Darissa could hear a note of bitterness in Marek's thoughts at that—that failed gambit had wound up killing his brother.

"But Abran was assassinated," she said.

"Maybe the wizard he hired didn't know that."

"Using magic in a war like that is forbidden."

"I don't think Abran cared very much about rules by that point."

That was true, but it still didn't make sense. "But why didn't anyone turn us back?" Darissa protested. "Abran was dead, Eknera surrendered—why didn't someone find us and do something about it? Your father could have hired a wizard; he wouldn't have left us as a statue for forty years!"

"Someone must have hidden us."

"But who would do that, and why?"

"I don't know," Marek admitted. "Any wizard Abran hired— well, maybe the plan was for us to disappear, and then Abran would offer us back, but when he was killed the wizard decided it would be better to just get away and leave us."

"But how did this Lord Landessin get us?"

"I don't know."

"You see? It doesn't make any sense. Why didn't anyone find us sooner? Why didn't your father hire a magician to find us? It obviously wasn't impossible, or whoever it is that's looking for us now wouldn't have come to Morvash's uncle."

Marek had no answer.

"There was a woman hanging around the castle I thought was a wizard," Darissa said. "I wonder whether she might have been involved. Tall, usually wore a blue robe. Do you know who I mean?"

"I saw her," Marek said. "I don't know who she is. Was."

"Did your father invite her? Maybe he knew Abran was crazy enough to use magic, and wanted to have someone in reserve to counter him."

"I don't know," Marek said again. "It seemed as if I saw her talking to Hinda more than to Dad, though. No one ever introduced her to *me*."

"Maybe they wanted to keep you out of trouble if they did something to antagonize the Wizards' Guild."

"I don't think the Guild would worry about such details."

"Maybe not. But you did see her talking to the king and your sister?"

"I saw her in the room with Dad, I'm not sure I ever saw them speak to one another. I did see her talk to Hinda."

"Do you think she's involved?"

"I have no idea, Darissa. It's all a mystery. Maybe when we get back to Melitha it will all be explained."

Darissa looked across the gallery at the broad casement windows. "I wonder what's happened in Melitha."

"So do I," Marek said. "Is my father still alive? Is Evreth king? Did he ever find a wife? Did Hinda ever marry? Do I have a dozen nieces and nephews I've never met?"

"Have there been any more wars?" Darissa suggested.

She could feel Marek's annoyance at her pessimism. "I'm just being realistic," she said. "You told me they came along every twenty years or so."

"Historically, they do," Marek admitted. "But if Evreth is king, he's smart enough he might have avoided them."

"Evreth would be what, sixty-two?"

"Almost sixty-three."

"And if he's still alive your father would be…eighty-five? Ninety?"

"Ninety-two. He married late. He's probably gone." Marek swallowed hard at the thought.

"He could have remarried," Darissa mused. "You might have half a dozen half-siblings back home."

"Maybe, but I doubt it. He always said my mother was the only woman he wanted."

Darissa had enough knowledge of male appetites and children's fond delusions to doubt that, but kings who already had a few heirs often avoided remarriage just to keep lines of inheritance simple. A second marriage really might be unlikely.

It was hard to believe that forty years had passed. Yes, she had spent most of that time conscious, but consciousness as a statue was *different*. There was no pain, no sensation, no heartbeat, no flow of blood, no experiences to remember, no way to judge time; it did not feel entirely real. She had never felt tired, or hungry, or hot, or cold, or much of anything. Thinking back, she could not really remember anything about all those years, because she had not *done* anything.

When she was herself she was constantly experiencing little things without noticing them—sights and sounds and smells, warmth and cold, the feel of air on her skin, of her hair on her neck. If she was angry she felt her skin grow warm and her pulse quicken; if she was sad she would feel her mouth turn down. As a statue she had felt none of that; she had existed in a timeless void. For most of the time the only thing she could sense was Marek's presence, and he, too, had been in that dreamy half-alive state.

She had heard Morvash wondering how people had stayed sane after centuries of isolation, and that was the explanation—it didn't *feel* like centuries. It didn't feel real.

Now the world was real again, but she was in a bizarre foreign land and had missed forty years. She heard the people around her talking about warlocks, which were apparently a new variety of magician that had been around for more than three decades and then vanished again, and she had missed the entire phenomenon. When she had looked out the window earlier she had spotted little green creatures that someone said were called spriggans, which were now a common nuisance, and she had never heard of anything like them. Someone had referred to the Empress Tabaea, who had tried to use strange magic to conquer the Hegemony of the Three Ethshars—she and Marek had missed that, too.

Others here had it much worse, of course; some of them had lost *centuries*. That poor dancer, Thetta—she had spent two hundred years as a statue, and all of it out in public, where she could hear people talking. They had mostly ignored her, and the ones who did say anything about her had only discussed her beauty, and the amazing talent of the nonexistent sculptor who was supposed to have created her. The discussions had often been unspeakably vulgar. No wonder she was half mad. Darissa had been sensing her thoughts, and trying to use witchcraft to calm and soothe her, but she did not think she had been having much of an effect yet.

The Northerner—Darissa could not make sense of his thoughts at all. She was unsure whether it was the language difference or something more.

And Karitha. She had only lost seven years, but she had never understood that she had been turned to stone. She had thought she was dead, and doomed to an eternity in emptiness, and then had been flung back into life only to find herself hunted by her own Tarker the Unrelenting. Every time the demon pounded on the house, Karitha flinched. She was confused and guilt-ridden and terrified. She was *trying* to be hopeful, but not succeeding very well. Morvash appeared to mean her no harm, and was even trying to protect her, but Karitha did not understand why—shouldn't he want her dead for killing one of his fellow wizards? Even he really did want to help her, how long could he protect her from the demon?

For most of these people, at least no one was actively trying to kill them. Karitha did not have that comfort—and neither did Marek or Darissa, if Morvash was to be trusted.

Morvash was out in the street talking to the soldiers and whoever was in that coach, so Darissa could not sense his feelings, but earlier she had not found any indication that he was lying. Since he was a wizard she could not hear his thoughts the way she might with ordinary people, but he had seemed honest. Darissa did not think she would trust anything that other wizard, Erdrik, might say, but she gave Morvash the benefit of the doubt. If he said someone was looking for her and Marek, someone probably was.

But who? And why?

"Why would someone be looking for us *now*?" she asked.

"I don't know," Marek said. "I really don't know."

CHAPTER THIRTY-ONE

MORVASH OF THE SHADOWS

26ᵀᴴ OF LEAFCOLOR, YS 5238

Lamps had been lit and introductions had been made all around, insofar as was possible. Gror had chosen his first batch of guests—Thetta the dancing girl, Alder the Strong, the merchant Kelder Sammel's son, and a woman who Ariella had never been able to reach while she was petrified, but who gave her name as Inririan the Hairdresser. Morvash guessed his uncle wanted Thetta and Inririan because Gror had always enjoyed looking at pretty women, and was taking Alder to keep an eye on Thetta, and Kelder so that they could talk shop. Morvash escorted the five of them to the front door and watched as they crossed the street and boarded the coach.

Then he returned to the gallery, where Karitha was staring out the window, watching Tarker work his way along the front of the house.

"Did anyone find my note?" she asked.

"Not that I know of," Morvash said. "I wonder whether a witch might be able to enhance your memory, to help you remember the secret name." He glanced at Darissa, who had used a cord from one of the drapes to tie her bedsheet in place. Morvash reminded himself he would want to find her and Marek some real clothes once daylight returned; Erdrik's robe was definitely overstretched on the prince's frame. Perhaps Gror could spare some, or Pender could do some shopping. Some of the others were not suitably attired, either.

Morvash assumed his uncle would find a better garment for Thetta than what she had been wearing; perhaps he would look after most of the others, as well.

"I don't think that can be done," the witch replied. "I tried to look into Karitha's memory a little while you were out talking to the guards, and couldn't find anything at all. Ariella might do better—she hears thoughts more clearly than I do. I still don't think she could safely get all fifty syllables, though."

Prince Marek interjected, "Have you heard anything more about the person who was looking for us?"

"I'm afraid not," Morvash replied. "For all I know, he's out there right now, watching Tarker."

Marek glanced toward the windows. "I wish I knew what he wanted. Maybe it's *good* news of some kind, and not an assassin at all."

"Maybe," Morvash said, obviously unconvinced.

"It's going to get me, isn't it?" Karitha asked, still peering out the window.

"I hope not," Morvash said.

"Everyone else will go to your uncle's palace as honored guests, but I'll stay trapped here until Tarker finds a way in, and then I'll die."

"Not everyone!" Darissa said, taking the demonologist's hand. "We'll stay with you!"

"That's because there's someone after you, too!"

Darissa did not deny it, and Morvash decided a small distraction would be in order. "The wizards aren't going to my uncle's house," he said. "Lorgol, Halder, Artalda, and Quirris are going to Guildmaster Ithinia's house."

"But they're *going*," Karitha said. "And I'm not."

"*I'm* staying," Morvash said. "So is Pender. So is Hakin. At least until we figure out what to do about your demon."

"Thank you," Karitha said. "But you won't be able to stop Tarker."

Once again, Morvash looked for a distraction. "Pender," he said, "do you think you could get Ariella and bring her here?"

"You told your uncle of her, to help with his guests."

"Oh. So I did." Morvash had honestly forgotten that. A footman was probably already on the way to Witch Alley, or would be as soon as Gror had his guests inside. "Well, my uncle's coach will be back in a few minutes—who will go in the next group?"

That kept everyone reasonably occupied for a few minutes, and when the coach did, in fact, return, it only took a moment to herd six more former statues out to the street.

More soldiers had arrived, with torches; they had formed lines blocking Old East Avenue in both directions, and were keeping a close watch on Tarker. Morvash was horrified to see that the demon was now working its way along the foundation, crouching down to pound at the stone footings; its inch-by-inch examination of the wards was almost complete. He hoped that when it finished it would start over, but feared that it would instead do as Hakin had suggested.

Or perhaps it would come up with something else to attempt.

As he stood on the steps, watching the coach roll away, Tarker spotted him. It stood upright.

"You! Wizard!" it demanded. "Let me in!"

"I couldn't even if I wanted to!" Morvash replied. "I didn't set up these protections, and I don't know how they work. I'm not sure there *is* a way to let a demon through."

Tarker let out a deep growl at that. "Let us see if you can pull me inside," it said, whereupon Morvash turned and ran up the steps and across the threshold, slamming the door behind him.

He caught his breath on the stairs, then trudged up to the gallery. This had become a very long and exhausting day.

As he approached the gallery door he saw that Darissa had opened a window and was leaning out. "Officer!" she called. "Has anyone found the note the demonologist wrote?"

Morvash suddenly found the energy to run the last few feet. "Keep your head inside!" he shouted. "We don't know how far the wards extend!"

Startled, Darissa pulled her head back inside, and a fraction of a second later a leaping demon struck the window-frame, slashing at the air where that head had been.

Morvash pushed Darissa aside and slammed the casement shut. "What were you thinking?" he asked.

"I was thinking the demon has no reason to harm me," Darissa replied angrily. "You said it wouldn't hurt anyone but Karitha!"

"Or someone who gets in its way," Marek said, putting his arms around Darissa's shoulders. "It thinks that if it can grab a human who is partly in the house, he or she might be able to pull it through the wards. It might even be right—I don't really know."

"Oh," Darissa said, her anger fading. "No one told me."

"You're a witch," Morvash said. "Couldn't you sense that it was a threat?"

"No, I couldn't," Darissa replied, visibly annoyed. "It doesn't work like that. I can sense people's intentions, but that thing isn't 'people.' I can't sense its spirit at all, any more than you can."

Morvash thought that was interesting, and filed the information away, even as he struggled to find a response and failed. Instead he walked down the gallery, past most of his remaining guests, and opened a different window, where he carefully did *not* lean out.

"Lieutenant Fullan!" he called. "*Is* there any word on that note from the demonologist's workshop?"

"All the demonologist's papers were burned, years ago," the soldier called back. "No one's sure, but it probably went with the rest!"

Karitha had come up behind Morvash; now she let out a low moan. "I'm doomed," she said.

"Not yet," Morvash said, as he closed the window. "The wards might hold for years." He glanced at Hakin.

"Or they might shatter any minute," Lorgol said. "We don't know. If I had all my supplies and equipment I might be able to learn more, but I don't." Morvash noticed his hand falling to the hilt of the knife on his belt, and guessed that was Lorgol reassuring himself that at least he still had his athame. He was still a wizard; everything else could be replaced.

Morvash looked around the room. There were still about two dozen people, and they all looked tired and hungry—Gror's promise of groceries had not yet been fulfilled. Many of them were wearing skimpy or outlandish clothes, with hair in styles decades obsolete. He wished he could do more for them, could find them refuge more quickly. So far as he knew they were all innocents, none of them guilty of anything worse than failing to pay a wizard's bill…

Except Karitha, of course. She was, by her own admission, a murderer, whatever the provocation might have been. Was it really wise to risk all these others for her sake? What if the demon were somehow able to bring the entire house down? What if it undermined the foundations, and the whole structure collapsed?

And as he thought that, Morvash realized that he did not hear Tarker pounding on anything. The volume and frequency of the demon's blows had varied, but it had thrashed away at the wards for hours, stopping only to climb or leap to a new position, or to shout at Hakin or others.

But now it was silent. Worried, he looked back out the windows, just as someone whose name Morvash did not remember called, "Look!"

A light was approaching the house—not down on the street, amid the streetlamps and the soldiers' torches, but above the rooftops to the north. The gallery windows faced the wrong direction to look at it clearly. Ignoring his own warning, Morvash opened the window and prepared to stick his head out, but then the light came swooping over the street, where he could see what it was.

Zerra was sitting cross-legged on her flying carpet, one hand steadying an unnaturally-bright lantern that stood on the fabric beside her.

Morvash caught himself with his head still inside, and called, "Zerra! Over here!"

Zerra waved, and a moment later the carpet was hanging motionless outside the open window.

"*Hai*!" Morvash called. "Do you see the demon?"

"I saw him as I approached," the older wizard replied. "He's digging a hole in the alley beside the house."

Morvash felt sick. Tarker *was* going to try to go underneath the wards.

"All right, listen," he said. "I have four wizards here to take to Ithinia." He beckoned to Lorgol, Halder, Artalda, and Quirris "But we have a demonologist we need to get out of here, too—that demon is trying to kill her."

Zerra cocked her head. "Why does that concern *us*?" she asked.

"Because I say it does!" Morvash snapped. He was in no mood for argument.

"Fine. Do you want me to take her to Ithinia along with the others?"

Morvash hesitated. If they did that, Tarker would just follow the carpet. "I don't think the Guildmaster would appreciate that," he said.

"Ah," Zerra said. "Listen, Morvash, I'm not sure you understand the situation. I'm not sure *I* understand the situation. Some guardsman showed up at Ithinia's door saying that there was something going on here that needed the Guild's attention, and that you had asked that I be sent. Ithinia spoke to him and asked a few questions, and then she sent me here to ask *you* a few questions. No one said anything about taking anyone to see her."

"But…" Morvash had forgotten how much had happened since Lieutenant Fullan had sent a man to see Ithinia. "All right," he said. "Ask your questions."

"They aren't *my* questions, they're Ithinia's."

"Fine. Ask them."

"You turned *all* those statues back to people?"

"Yes. The spell got away from me; I had only intended to rescue two of them this time."

"Do you know who they all are?"

"Most of them. Some of them don't speak Ethsharitic, so I'm not as sure about them."

"Are you planning to send *all* of them to see Ithinia?"

"What? Of course not! There's no reason for the Guild to be involved with most of them. I'm sending most of them to my uncle's house, to be sorted out later. But there are four wizards here, and I thought *they* should see the Guildmaster."

Zerra nodded. "I can see that." She gestured toward the foursome clustered behind Morvash. "These four?"

"Yes."

"And what about Erdrik? The soldier said you had set him free from some sort of magical imprisonment."

Morvash nodded. "He had accidentally locked himself in his vault. I disrupted the spell hiding it, and he was able to escape."

"Do you know where he is now? Is he here?"

"Oh, he left hours ago!"

"Do you know where he went?"

Morvash glanced at Pender. "More or less."

"Where?"

"Tazmor, in the far north. He had some sort of secret project there, and he seems to have used Pallum's Returning Crystal, so he's probably already there."

"Secret project? What kind of secret project?"

"I don't know; Erdrik cast Javan's Geas on the man who told me about it, so he couldn't give me any details."

"So what do you want from the Guild?"

"I want someone to help these four wizards find their place in the World, and I would appreciate some help protecting Karitha the Demonologist from the demon she summoned—she's lost control of it, and it's trying to kill her."

"Is that demon Tarker the Unrelenting?"

Startled, Morvash admitted, "Yes."

"So this demonologist is the one who killed Wosten of the Red Robe?"

"Ah…" Morvash could see where this was heading.

"Morvash, why would the Guild help a woman who murdered a wizard?"

"Because she spent seven years as a statue!"

"She *killed* a *wizard*."

"I know, but…"

"I'm not going to do anything to help her without a direct order from Ithinia."

Morvash threw up his hands. "Fine! Then take these four back to Ithinia and tell her I want to save the demonologist from the demon, and ask what she wants to do about it."

"I'll do that," Zerra said.

"Thank you for that, anyway." He stepped aside. "You four, onto the carpet, quickly!"

Lorgol scrambled up onto the windowsill, then dived out onto the carpet. Quirris came right behind him, and then Artalda, with Halder making a more cautious and dignified exit behind them.

When all four were seated in a square surrounding Zerra the carpet swooped a few away, and hung over the street for a moment. "Good luck," Zerra called back. She glanced in the direction of the alley. "Whatever you're going to do, you might want to do it quickly."

Then the carpet swung around and swooped away over the rooftops.

Morvash watched it go, then closed the window and looked along the gallery at his remaining company.

"We need to get you people out of here," he said. "Not Karitha, or Prince Marek, or Darissa, but the rest of you, there's no reason to stay in here. There are plenty of guards in the street who can take care of you until my uncle's coach collects you. Come on." He started toward the stairs.

"What was that about the demon digging a hole?" someone asked.

"Don't worry about it," Morvash said, as he beckoned to the others. "It's nothing that concerns you."

"It concerns *me*," Karitha said loudly, her voice unsteady.

"Shut up," Morvash replied, as he got a line of people moving out of the gallery. "We'll talk about it later."

If, he thought but did not say, the demon doesn't burst up through the floorboards and kill you first.

CHAPTER THIRTY-TWO

MORVASH OF THE SHADOWS

26ᵀᴴ OF LEAFCOLOR, YS 5238

Morvash looked out a gallery window, and watched with relief as the next group of passengers was loaded into Gror's coach. The rest were surrounded by guards, many of them newly arrived, and there was some sort of discussion going on with the guard officers, but that was no longer his problem.

He had taken a moment to look into the alley before he reentered the house, and Tarker had excavated a good-sized pit. The wards apparently extended well down the foundation, because the demon had not been able to smash its way into the cellars, but Morvash doubted they extended *under* the house. Once Tarker was deep enough to tunnel sideways through the stone on which the house was built, he would probably be able to get in. No ordinary creature could burrow through solid stone, but Morvash had little doubt that the demon would manage it.

The wizard turned to look at the room's other occupants.

Karitha was still here, of course, crouching against a wall; Hakin stood beside her, though Morvash was not entirely sure why he had chosen not to leave. Prince Marek and Darissa were in one corner, arms around one another, talking quietly. And Pender was standing in the middle of the room, looking uncertain.

Just the six of them remained; everyone else had left.

Morvash wondered whether they might be safer downstairs, where they would not have as far to fall if the demon broke the floor out from under them. Or maybe being higher up would mean they would have a little longer to react, and less stone above them to crush them if the house collapsed.

Maybe it would be worth the risk to get the prince and his witch out of the house. There had been no sign of their mysterious seeker yet; perhaps he had not yet located them.

Or he might be among the handful of gawkers still milling around on the street, beyond the guardsmen's lines. Morvash wished he had thought to ask Uncle Gror for a description of the man.

One of the small bedrooms had a window overlooking the alley. Morvash decided he wanted a look, to see how long they had before Tarker got below the foundation. "Wait here," he told the others. "I'll be right back."

He crossed the hall, crossed the little bedroom, climbed onto the unused bed, and opened the casement. He could hear the demon digging. Cautiously, he leaned out and looked down.

The alley was dark, and Morvash could not see much more than vague shapes, but Tarker's pit seemed to be deep enough that the demon's entire body was below street level now. Dirt and small stones were fountaining out; the demon's four clawed hands appeared to be scooping the ground away at a prodigious rate. Morvash could hear talons scraping down the foundation every so often, presumably to test the wards.

And then the demon let out a roar of triumph. Morvash leaned out dangerously far, peering down into the gloom.

One of Tarker's hands had thrust past the foundation wall, below the wards.

"Blood and death!" Morvash muttered, pulling his head back inside. He closed the casement and knelt silently on the bed for a few seconds, trying to think what he should do.

Pender and Hakin could leave safely at any time—as he could himself, for that matter. Marek and Darissa were an unknown.

But if Karitha were to set foot outside the demon would smell her and be upon her almost instantly.

If she stayed in the house, the demon would almost certainly break in soon. Tunneling through the stone beneath the house might slow it somewhat, but not enough. Morvash could not be sure just how solid the ground was; the cellar floors had *looked* like solid bedrock, but that appearance might be deceiving.

Still, she would have a little longer to live if she stayed in the house, and perhaps someone would think of a way to save her. The rest of them should leave, though.

It might mean that Erdrik's house would be destroyed, and his animated belongings scattered or killed. Morvash frowned. The house itself was just a house, and could be rebuilt, but the chairs and teapots and so on gave every appearance of being alive. If they had been animated with Ellran's Immortal Animation they would survive, but if other animations had been employed, those creatures could die.

Maybe they could be persuaded to leave, or could simply be dragged out—but there were so many! Morvash had never done an inventory, let alone attempted to determine which had been made with Ellran's and which were mortal.

But they were just objects, not people. Karitha was more important.

It was time to tell the others what was happening. He clambered off the bed.

He had barely gotten to his feet when the entire house shook with a sudden impact. Morvash hurried back to the window, opened it, and looked down.

Tarker was halfway under the house. Apparently the stone down there was not as solid as it looked.

"Gods," Morvash said. He did not bother closing the window as he stumbled off the bed and ran to the gallery.

The others were waiting; they had felt the impact, just as he had. All five were now standing, staring at him as he burst in.

"It's under the house!" he called. "The demon's under the house!"

"Do the protective spells extend under the house?" Darissa asked.

"I don't know!" He gestured to Hakin and Pender. "You two should get out of here; the demon doesn't care about you. Prince Marek, Darissa, I'm not sure where you'd be safer…"

Then he stopped in mid-sentence as a light appeared outside the gallery windows. He started across the room, but Marek was there first, opening the casement.

It was Zerra, once again alone upon her carpet. This time, in addition to the lantern, she had a large bundle with her. "Morvash of the Shadows!" she called. "The Wizards' Guild requires your obedience!"

Marek stepped aside, and Morvash came to the window just as the house shook again from another mighty blow. "What are you talking about?" he demanded.

"I'm talking about orders from the Guildmaster," Zerra replied.

"Since when does the Guild give me *orders*?"

"Since you unleashed the criminal Erdrik the Grim on the World."

"What? Listen, Zerra, we have a more immediate problem..."

"No, you don't," Zerra said. "You know what happens to a wizard who breaks the Guild's rules."

Morvash opened his mouth, then closed it again. He *did* know. Minor infractions might result in exile or various unpleasant enchantments, but there were only two possible punishments for any *serious* offense. The lesser, only offered in cases where there were perceived to be mitigating circumstances, was to have one's athame destroyed, destroying part of the wizard's soul with it and rendering him or her forever incapable of performing wizardry.

The other, far more common, penalty was death.

A Guildmaster was entitled to give orders to rectify a problem of a wizard's own creation. Disobeying such orders could be a serious infraction.

"What are the orders?" Morvash asked. "And make it quick, please—the demon is under the house, trying to smash its way up."

"You are to find Erdrik, observe his actions, learn the nature of his secret project in Tazmor, destroy it if you deem it a threat, and then report back to the Guildmaster, Ithinia of the Isle."

"But he's in Tazmor! It would take me months to get there! Whatever he's doing will probably be long since done by then!"

"It won't take you months," Zerra said. "I'm to fly you there. The guild offered me three times my usual rate."

Morvash stared at her, then lowered his gaze to the carpet. It was perhaps ten feet wide and fifteen or sixteen feet long, patterned in green and gold, and it rippled gently in the evening breeze. Even though he had seen it carry massive statues, or half a dozen people, it did not look at all safe. He had never ridden a flying carpet, nor had he particularly wanted to.

"Get on," Zerra ordered.

"Wait," Morvash said, as another impact shook the house. "Give me a moment. Shouldn't I bring some supplies? If I'm going to do any magic, I'll need them."

"All right, get them. I'll give you two minutes."

"Another thing," Morvash said, as inspiration struck. "We're taking my assistants."

"What?"

"Pender, there, is the only one who knows *exactly* where Erdrik's secret project is," Morvash said, pointing. "And Karitha has agreed to help me—haven't you, Karitha? A demonologist might be useful."

"What?" Karitha had been staring at the floor, Following her gaze, Morvash could see that some of the seams in the fine hardwood planking, which had been virtually invisible before, had opened slightly.

"You're coming with us," Morvash told her. "The demon can't get you when you're on a flying carpet, can it?"

"It can jump *really well*," Hakin said. "You'll want to fly high." He glanced down. "May I come, too? I don't think Tarker is going to be very pleased with me right now."

"Fine," Morvash said. "Get on the carpet while I fetch some supplies."

"Wait a minute…" Zerra began, but Hakin was already climbing out the window. Morvash turned and sprinted for the stairs.

When Morvash returned with his box of valuables—the pearl, a bloodstone, and dozens of other small, reusable items—and a large bag of miscellaneous supplies he had thrown together quickly, including his book of spells, he found the carpet was relatively crowded. Pender, Marek, and Darissa had followed Hakin onto it. Karitha still hesitated.

"Come on," Morvash said. He threw his burdens onto the carpet, where Marek and Hakin grabbed them; then he dived through the window, grabbing Karitha around the waist and pulling her out after him. The two of them tumbled onto the carpet. For a moment Morvash feared it would give beneath them and let them plummet to the street in front of the house, but it did not; it yielded slightly, like a soft mattress, and held.

"Get us out of here!" Hakin called. Zerra made a gesture; the carpet suddenly soared upward.

There was a sudden bellow of rage, and Erdrik's house shook visibly; Morvash could hear furniture crashing as they sailed up past the gables and chimney-tops into empty air.

It was a cool night, as was to be expected in mid-autumn, and combined with the sudden wind and poorly-suppressed terror that was enough to send Morvash into a brief fit of uncontrollable shuddering. He struggled to control himself as the others exclaimed around him.

"It's beautiful!" Marek said, gazing at the city below them.

Karitha let out a wordless moan.

"Go! Go!" Hakin called. "Higher!"

"Which way?" Zerra demanded.

"North!" Pender replied.

The carpet wheeled, and once again Morvash thought he was going to fall off. His stomach lurched.

When he was a child, he remembered, he had dreamed about flying. One reason he had asked to be apprenticed to a wizard was in hopes he might someday learn to fly.

Now, though, the idea had lost its appeal. It was not that he was particularly afraid of heights, though they were already astonishingly, terrifyingly high up, far above even the tallest towers; it was that the carpet seemed so *flimsy*. There was nothing to hold on to, no railing to keep him safe. He wondered why he had never heard about anyone falling off a flying carpet; surely, it must have happened!

The city below was like a maze dotted with the orange glow of streetlights; he realized that the dark tangle to one side ahead was the Old City, and the big block surrounded by a black ribbon reflecting the light of the newly-risen lesser moon was the Palace in its ring of canals. The black reflective stripe that connected the Palace to the sea was the Grand Canal, where his ship from Ethshar of the Rocks had docked, and the cluster of torchlit little squares on the right must be Fishertown Market, and the subtly moving shapes ahead on the left must be ships moored at the Spicetown wharves.

And then they were out of the city, over open water—the Gulf of the East.

"Go to the river," Pender said, pointing ahead.

"*Hai*," Hakin said, obviously over his initial fear that Tarker might be able to catch them. "This is *amazing*!"

"Are we high enough to escape the demon?" Zerra asked sardonically.

"Oh, yes!" Hakin said. "This is wonderful! But where are we going?"

"Tazmor," Morvash said.

"Where's that?" Hakin asked.

"North of Sardiron of the Waters."

"That far? Won't it be cold?"

Morvash shivered; he was already chilled, and they were still over the warm waters of the Gulf. "Yes, it will," he said.

"It may be," Pender corrected him. "We will see."

"But I didn't bring a coat!" Karitha moaned.

"None of us did," Morvash said.

Hakin, who was at least wearing a workman's vest, looked at Zerra, and Morvash followed his gaze, noticing for the first time that Zerra *was* wearing a coat, a brocade-trimmed one with fur at the cuffs and collar. She smirked, and pointed to the bundle behind her.

"I came prepared," she said. Then she turned to Pender. "You said go to the river. What river?"

"The big river," he said. "From the north."

"Oh, *that* one." Zerra leaned, and the carpet suddenly veered to the left. Far below, a dark shoreline appeared alongside them.

"How long will it take us to get there?" Morvash asked.

"I don't know," Zerra said. "I don't know how far it is."

"I went for almost three months, at all," Pender said. His Ethsharitic seemed to have gotten worse again, Morvash thought. Perhaps it was from all the excitement of this very long day, or perhaps he was simply exhausted.

"Well, we're flying at least ten times as fast as a man can walk," Zerra said, "so it shouldn't be more than a sixnight and a half." The carpet turned again; Morvash looked down and saw that they were leaving the Gulf, turning over a narrower body of water, where both shores were visible. He saw few buildings, but the land seemed to be divided up into roughly square patches—farmers' fields, perhaps? It was hard to see in the dark; the lesser moon's pink glow was not bright enough to illuminate much.

"Ten times as fast as a man can walk," Hakin said. "Karitha, how fast can Tarker run?"

"I don't know," she said.

"He's going to follow us."

"I know."

"I think we can stay ahead of him," Zerra said. "At least for awhile." She did not sound particularly concerned.

"I hope so," Morvash said. The water below had narrowed, and was clearly a river now, presumably the Great River. He had to strain to see any details. He decided to close his eyes for a moment, to rest them.

And the next thing he knew the sun was bursting up over the eastern horizon and the carpet was descending toward a small village.

"I want some breakfast and some rest," Zerra explained, when she saw him raise his head. "I think all of you got at least a nap, but I couldn't—I was flying the carpet. So we'll stop here for awhile, and continue when I'm more awake."

"Oh," Morvash said. That made sense. Then he frowned. "How will we pay for the food? I don't think I brought any money."

"We have two wizards, a witch, a demonologist, and a prince," Zerra said. "I think we can manage something." Then she patted her bundle. "And *I* brought money, in any case."

And then the carpet settled to the ground, surrounded by staring villagers.

CHAPTER THIRTY-THREE

DARISSA THE WITCH'S APPRENTICE

27TH OF LEAFCOLOR, YS 5238

Darissa was shivering with cold as she looked around at the villagers. The bedsheet she wore was not meant for this sort of use; she had it wrapped around her so that one shoulder was bare, and the improvised skirt flapped open in the breeze.

She could have used witchcraft to keep her warm, but that would use up energy and then she would need food and rest. She decided that at least for the moment, she preferred being cold to being tired and hungry.

Not that she *wasn't* tired and hungry, but she did not want to make it worse.

"Can we get me some clothes?" she asked. She glanced at Marek. "And him, too?"

"Of course," Morvash said. He looked at Zerra, who had been moving her baggage off the carpet to one side.

"Hello!" Zerra said to the villagers, ignoring her fellow wizard. "Is there an inn here, or someone who takes in lodgers?"

"We don't have an inn," a woman replied.

"Do you have a witch?" Darissa asked, hoping to appeal to sisterhood—the generic sisterhood of a fellow practitioner, not the organization called the Sisterhood, which she had not yet joined.

"No," the woman said.

"Do you have food, and somewhere we could sleep?" Zerra asked. "We have money."

Darissa noticed a man on a crutch. "Or we may have other ways to pay," she said. She could feel his pain from a dozen feet away; one of his feet was distorted and wrapped in fraying once-white rags.

Zerra threw her an annoyed look, but Darissa paid no attention as she shuffled, shivering, to the injured man. She put a hand down toward his bandaged foot. "What happened?" she asked.

"Cow stepped on it," the man replied. "It's broken."

Darissa forgot the cold and her indecent dress as she squatted down and put her hands on the bandages. He was right; the bone *was* broken, and it was healing incorrectly because no one had positioned the broken pieces properly. She could feel it, through cloth and skin, and she honestly wasn't sure how much of that was coming through her fingertips and how much was witchcraft.

"Hold on," she said, "this is going to hurt." She did try to block the pain, but she knew she would not stop it completely. She placed both hands on the foot, and twisted, using magic more than muscle.

The partially-healed bone snapped, and then the pieces slid into place, aligning as they ought to, and Darissa poured warmth and healing magic into them. She could feel the hard tissues melt and flow together.

She was only very vaguely aware that the man had let out a yelp of agony, and that other people were shouting, and moving around near her. Her entire attention was focused on the healing.

Her vision began to dim, and she realized she had overextended herself. She looked up and saw Marek struggling to hold back two women who were trying to get at her; she saw the man's expression shift from pain to astonishment; and then she fell over, exhausted.

She was vaguely aware of more shouting, and arguing, and then she was picked up in strong arms and carried somewhere, and the next thing she knew she was sprawled on a small couch and someone was feeding her a wonderfully rich beef broth.

"How did you do that?" someone asked, and she looked up from the wooden spoon to see the man with the broken foot sitting across from her on a sturdy chair.

"I'm a witch," she answered. Then she corrected herself, "Well, a witch's apprentice."

"It feels better—is it healed?"

"Only partly," Darissa replied. "It will need a few sixnights, but it should be fine by Festival, at the latest. The way it was before it would never have healed properly; the bones were out of line."

"Keep eating," Marek said, and Darissa realized that he was the one feeding her the bowl of broth. She obeyed.

"You've earned us a meal and a place to rest for today," he told her as the bowl emptied.

"How are the others doing?"

"I don't know," Marek said. "Zerra really *does* have money, and Morvash can do some magic tricks, so they should be fine."

Darissa glanced at their hosts and switched from Ethsharitic to Melithan to ask, "Is the demon still chasing us?"

Marek spread his hands, the bowl in one and the spoon in the other. "Who knows?" he replied, also in Melithan. "Probably. Hakin said it could follow Karitha anywhere in the World."

"Then we don't want to stay here very long; we'll need to keep moving."

Marek frowned. "*Karitha* will need to keep moving; *we* don't."

Darissa was too weary to think about that right away; instead she let her gaze wander around the room. Marek was perched on one end of the couch where she lay; the man with the broken foot was sitting opposite; and two women were standing off to one side. Darissa thought they were probably the two Marek had held off, but she was not certain.

"I'm Arl Tagger's son," the injured man said, speaking Ethsharitic with a slightly peculiar accent. "This is my house. Thank you."

"Healing is part of my job," Darissa said.

"Still, thank you."

"I'm sorry I tried to stop you," one of the women said. "I thought you meant to harm him."

Darissa shook her head. "Why would I do that?"

The woman took a step back in confusion and did not reply.

"I'm Bela," the other woman said. "I'm Arl's sister."

"Darissa." She looked up. "This is Marek." She had deliberately not given his title; she thought it was more likely to complicate matters than to improve the situation.

"If you don't mind my asking," Bela said, "is that garment something you wear because you're a healer?"

"Or a witch?" the other woman added.

"No," Darissa said, with a wry grimace. "This is something I wear because my clothes were lost and the only things I could find to replace them were a bedsheet and a drapery cord."

"Oh. It...it doesn't cover you well. Would you like something warmer?"

"I would *love* something warmer!"

"I don't know how well it would fit, but I still have some clothes I outgrew when I was...well, I don't know how old you are, but you're smaller than I am and you *look* young."

"I'm seventeen..." Darissa began. She stopped and frowned. "Or maybe I'm not. My age is something of a complicated question right now."

"Let me get the clothes," Bela said; then she scurried into a back room.

"My name is Peretta," the other woman said.

"She's my wife," Arl explained.

"Is there anything else you need?" Peretta asked.

"Is there anything else you need healed?"

Arl and Peretta exchanged glances. "Well, not *us*..."

An hour later Darissa had treated a cow's cracked hoof, healed several chickens of bumblefoot, assured a neighbor that she was healthy and her failure to produce children as yet was just bad luck and not barrenness, and cleaned out an old man's excess of earwax. She was now wearing a sturdy old blue-and-white cotton tunic over a blue wool skirt, and over that a wonderfully warm sheepskin coat—Bela had outgrown the tunic, which fit Darissa surprisingly well, and the skirt, which was too long but could be taken up. The coat had belonged to someone named Rulura who had died recently, whose heirs had not yet divvied up her belongings. It was too big, but as far as Darissa was concerned that was just fine, given the chilly weather. The extra material could be wrapped around her for added warmth, and the stains and stretched-out seams didn't matter.

There were no boots to spare, but someone had found a battered pair of slippers that were better than nothing.

Marek had been outfitted with Arl's second-best leather work tunic, which fit him far better than Erdrik's robe had, and a pair of badly-sewn doeskin breeches that Bela had made long ago for practice; Peretta had assured him that the fancy fabric of Erdrik's robe would more than cover the cost of these garments. Alas, no slippers were found for him, let alone boots, but an old pair of sandals turned up, and strips of wool he could use to wrap his legs.

With winter coming there was little food to spare—the cupboards and attics were almost full, but no one knew how much of that would be needed. Arl and Peretta were happy to provide a meal or two, and a stale loaf of bread for the journey, but no more than that.

Marek and Darissa understood, and expressed their gratitude for that much, and for the clothing.

During this time they had not seen any of the others—Morvash, Zerra, Hakin, Pender, or Karitha—beyond brief glimpses; it seemed that Zerra had bought the others a meal and somewhere to sleep.

And now, with the witchcraft done and clothing acquired, Darissa and Marek settled onto Arl's couch, near a warm hearth, while Peretta and Bela began preparations for a proper breakfast.

"How long do you think we'll be staying?" Darissa asked Marek in Melithan.

"However long you need to regain your strength," he replied.

"No, I mean…" She hesitated. "Aren't we going to Tazmor with the others?"

"We don't have to. We could go home."

Darissa could not reply to that immediately. There was too much to consider.

Except for a brief trip to Trafoa, she had spent her entire life in Melitha and had been content to do so, up until she had suddenly found herself naked on the floor of a wizard's house in Ethshar. She had been in *Ethshar of the Spices*, the largest, grandest city in the World, and she had spent the entire time locked up in a wizard's house; she had only gotten a glimpse of the rest of the city when she flew away on a magic carpet.

She had been traveling on a flying carpet! That was amazing. Those few hours felt more real than her forty years as a statue because she had been able to *feel*—feel the wind, the cold, the farbic beneath her. She had heard the wind and seen the stars and moons overhead, had smelled the night air and Marek's flesh beside her.

And now she was in some village somewhere along the Great River in the Hegemony of the Three Ethshars, one that so far as she knew didn't even have a name, trading healing for clothes and food.

Her whole reality had transformed in an instant, without any warning, that night the siege of Eknera ended, and the idea of returning to her old life was tempting, but she knew it wasn't possible.

They had been gone for forty years; they could never really go home. Everything in Melitha must have changed by now.

Besides, this was an *adventure*. Going home now meant giving up whatever Zerra and Morvash were doing. She knew they were looking for Erdrik, that the Wizards' Guild had ordered them to find him and see what he was up to, and she was curious herself. Erdrik had not been turned to stone, but he had been trapped in a vault for eleven years, and when he was returned to his own home the first thing he had done was leave; what could be so important that he would go off to Tazmor immediately without even looking over what had become of his own house and city during his absence?

And there was the man who had been looking for them. Who was he, and what did he want? What if he had gone back to Melitha and was waiting for them when they got there?

"It's been forty years," she said at last. "We don't know what we'd find there."

"But it's still our home."

"Is it? We don't know that! And besides, how would we get there?"

"Walk." Marek said. "Or take passage on a boat—the closest port to Melitha is Lumeth of the Coast, but from here we might do better with Perelia or Kushin. We won't get lost; we can follow the river."

"We don't have any money, Marek. We don't have anything but these clothes we were just given. How could we pay for passage? Or if we walk, how could we feed ourselves?"

He turned up a palm. "You have your magic. I have my arms and a strong back. We won't starve."

Darissa answered, "And if we meet assassins on the way?"

"You have your magic," Marek repeated with a smile. "I have my arms and a strong back."

Darissa shook her head. "I think we should talk to the wizards first, at the very least. Maybe one of them can tell us what's become of Melitha."

"Morvash said he didn't know."

"But we didn't ask Zerra, and maybe one of them has magic that can find out."

Marek sighed. "All right," he said.

They ate breakfast, then napped, to be awakened in mid-afternoon by Morvash's arrival.

"We're getting ready to go on north," he said. "Do you two want to come with us, or stay here?" He hesitated, then added, "I'd like it if you joined us; a witch may be useful."

Marek looked at Darissa.

"We're coming," she said. "What about the others?"

Morvash glanced over his shoulder. "Well, Zerra and I are following orders, so *we* need to go on. Pender lives in Tazmor and is acting as our guide, so *he's* coming—we're taking him home. Karitha wants to stay with Zerra so the flying carpet can keep her out of the demon's reach, and Hakin is worried that Tarker will be angry with him for helping Karitha, so they're both coming. You two are the only ones we weren't sure about—the assassin, or whoever it is looking for you, is probably still back in Ethshar, so you should be safe."

"It's a long walk," Darissa said. "If we come with you, can we get a ride to Melitha eventually?"

Morvash frowned. "You'll have to talk to Zerra about that."

"We'll do that."

"Then join us at the carpet as soon as you can."

Darissa nodded.

A few minutes later they were in the village square, such as it was, taking their places on the carpet. Zerra was already seated in the center, with Pender at her right hand; Darissa and Marek settled behind her, where they could lean against her bundle of belongings. Morvash and the others were talking about something; Darissa reached out with her witchcraft and sensed that Karitha wanted reassurance that they were not going to hand her over to the demon, which the others were trying to provide. They were hindered by the fact that they had no long-term solution to her situation; all they could do was promise to keep her away from it for as long as they could.

Rather than intervene, Darissa leaned forward and tapped Zerra on the shoulder. Startled, the wizard, who had been trying to listen to Karitha and Morvash, turned.

"What is it?" she asked.

"Do you have any idea what's happened in Melitha over the last forty years? Who the king is, or anything?"

"No," Zerra said. "I don't keep track of every silly little country in the Small Kingdoms."

"Is there any way you could find out?"

"I'm not much on divinations, but I might know a spell or two that could be useful. If you can give me the true name of someone in Melitha, I can probably find out a few things."

Darissa and Marek exchanged glances.

"We don't know who's still there and still alive," Darissa said. "That's what we were hoping *you* could tell *us*."

"I'll keep it in mind."

"And could you fly us there, when you're done in Tazmor?"

"Can you pay me? I thought you didn't have any money."

Darissa gestured at Marek. "He *is* a Melithan prince."

"Well, he *was*—can we be sure his family wasn't overthrown?"

Marek grimaced at that, and Darissa admitted, "No, we can't be sure."

"Well, maybe we can work something out." She turned as they heard Morvash, Hakin, and Karitha approaching. "Right now, it's time to get airborne, and put more distance between us and that demon." She raised a hand, and said a word.

The others hastened to seat themselves as the carpet rose a few inches, and a moment later, when everyone was secure, they zoomed off to the north.

Darissa looked behind to see Arl and Bela and other villagers waving farewell. She waved back, then turned forward, pulled the sheepskin coat around herself, and watched as they soared along the river.

CHAPTER THIRTY-FOUR

MORVASH OF THE SHADOWS

1ˢᵀ OF NEWFROST, YS 5238

They spent the afternoon of the fifth day, the first day of New-frost, in Sardiron of the Waters. Except for the first village they had slept on the carpet, ready to flee at a moment's notice, if they slept at all—Karitha and Hakin had become concerned that they were not traveling fast enough and not gaining enough ground on Karitha's demonic pursuer, and they had now accumulated enough warm clothing that they were no longer in danger of freezing if they slept in the open. For that matter, the autumn weather was not that cold at ground level by day, even this far north, and they were still doing most of their traveling at night, their resting by day.

Hakin and Morvash had taken turns standing watch, ready to wake Zerra should Tarker appear, so that they could get airborne again.

In Sardiron they did not bother with such precautions, on the theory that the dense population and the city walls would create enough noise and delay to warn them, should the demon approach. Tarker was, as they all knew, not given to stealth or subtlety. Instead they roamed the city a little.

Of the seven of them only Pender and Zerra had ever been in Sardiron before, so they served as guides. Many of the locals spoke some Ethsharitic, while Pender was able to translate for those who did not, and Darissa could sense some of what people wanted, so they were able to negotiate for food and better clothing. Zerra's funds were holding out, even after she had been convinced to make loans to the others, and she suggested they might find lodging at an inn, rather than spending another night huddled on the carpet, but Hakin and Karitha objected, pointing out that Tarker was undoubtedly still on their trail, and any delay gave it time to gain on them.

Morvash was also firmly on the side of a quick departure, and in the end they were airborne again an hour before sunset.

"No more river after this," Pender announced, as the carpet sailed over the city walls.

"What?" Zerra asked.

"The river goes that way." Pender pointed northeast. "We go that way." He pointed north. "To mountains."

"How are we supposed to find our way in the dark?" Zerra demanded.

"Follow the road," Pender said, pointing down. "After ten leagues it breaks, and we go to *right* road."

"I think he means to take the right-hand fork when the road splits," Darissa offered. "I can sort of feel the image in his thoughts."

Zerra frowned. "I'll try," she said, "but a road is harder to see in the dark than a river. If I lose sight of it, I'm landing, no matter where we are."

No one argued, and they flew on.

They reached the first fork in the road while the sun was still above the horizon, and took the right branch, as Pender instructed. Almost immediately after, though, they left the plowed fields behind and soared over increasingly hilly pastures.

And then, as the light began to fade, and Zerra lit her lantern, they came to the end of the pastureland, where the road vanished into the forest.

Morvash had never seen an actual forest before, let alone from above, and marveled at it—so *many* trees! It was like a vast green blanket covering the hills ahead.

Zerra was not so enthusiastic. "I can't see the road through the trees," she said, slowing the carpet to a standstill. "Especially not in the dark." She turned to Pender. "Is there some way I can find the route without following the road?"

"I don't know," Pender said. "I know only the road. Go to the right at every branch."

Zerra sighed. "This will slow us down," she said, as she spiraled the carpet downward until it hung only four or five feet above the hard-packed dirt of the road. Then she started it moving forward again, following the road into the woods.

Their speed here was only a fraction of what it had been above the trees, but it was easy to see where to go. They did not need to actually see the road below them at all, but merely to stay on the only open path through the trees.

Morvash stared at the dark trunks sliding past on either side, then looked up at the interweaving leafy branches above. They really did block out the sky completely, just as the songs and pictures described.

Hakin looked more and more uneasy as they left open land behind, and finally said, "Tarker can reach us at this height."

"I'm sure it can," Zerra said, focused on guiding the carpet.

"If we go this slowly, it might catch up."

"We'll worry about that if and when it happens. You and the others might want to keep a good watch on the road behind us. The more warning you give me, the more likely I can get through the treetops and out of range in time."

"The whole reason we're *here* is to get away from Tarker!"

"That may be why *you* came along, you and Karitha," Zerra said, "but Morvash and I are looking for Erdrik, Pender's on his way home, and these Melithans are just along for the ride."

"Does anyone live around here?" Prince Marek asked, looking around at the unbroken lines of trees on either side.

"No," Pender said. "People come to cut wood sometimes, or hunt, but they do not *live* here."

"Where *are* we?" Karitha asked.

Pender thought for a moment to find the right Ethsharitic word, then said, "The Passes."

"I thought the Passes were in the mountains," Hakin said, without taking his eyes off the road behind them.

"Yes. Mountains," Pender said, pointing ahead.

Morvash had noticed that the road was rising—as were they. Riding the carpet meant that going up the slope did not require any extra effort, and the darkness made it a little less visually obvious, but they were definitely going higher. He turned and looked back, and pointed. "Look how steep that road is," he said to Hakin.

"Oh," Hakin said, finally registering the slope.

"I thought there were people who lived in the Passes," Darissa said.

"Not on *this* road," Pender said. "There are two others on this side of the…the…"

"Ridge?" Darissa suggested.

"I think that is the right word." Pender nodded. "Three roads west of the *zir*, and on the east side there are many. We stay on this road. When there are choices, we always go right."

"What if we go left?" Morvash asked.

"Then we do not go to Hindfoot Village. We go to mines, or farms, or…or sheep."

"Is there anywhere to stop?" Zerra asked. "Flying through these woods in the dark is tiring."

Pender turned up an empty palm. "There is no village."

"Does anything dangerous live in these woods? Could we make camp somewhere?"

Pender hesitated. "It is said there are dragons. It is even said there are mizagars. But I have never seen those here."

"Mizagars?" Darissa asked.

"Legendary monsters that were said to fight on the side of the Northern Empire in the Great War," Zerra explained. "If there are any left, this is as likely a place as any to find them. So maybe I'll keep flying after all."

"Why are they more likely here than anywhere else?" Hakin asked.

"Because this land was part of the Northern Empire, of course," Zerra told him.

"It *was*?"

"Certainly! We crossed the old boundary yesterday morning."

Hakin stared around. "So are these *trees* evil, too?"

Zerra sighed. "No, of course not. They're just trees. The Empire is gone. There's no lingering taint; anyone who tells you that there is, is just trying to scare you."

Hakin looked at Pender. "So he's a Northerner?"

"No, Hakin," Morvash explained. "There aren't any more Northerners—well, except that spy I turned back. Pender's people are descended from the soldiers General Anaran and General Gor sent in to make certain the Empire was really gone."

"You're sure?"

"Hakin, you've spent years living with a demon, and now you're worried about one man who *might* be a Northerner?"

Hakin started to say something, then stopped. "You're right," he said. "I'll just watch for Tarker. Though it's getting too dark to see very far."

"Maybe it was a mistake traveling by night," Marek said.

"Maybe," Zerra said. "But it worked fine along the river, and we're here now."

They flew on in silence for some time after that, some of the passengers dozing. Morvash had not intended to sleep, but he was startled awake when Darissa asked, "Is it my imagination, or are the trees getting smaller?"

"It's definitely getting colder," Karitha said. "I'm freezing!" She had never managed to acquire more than a light jacket.

Morvash looked around. The forest did seem less dense, and the cold wind was more penetrating.

And then the woods seemed to part before them like a curtain, and the carpet sailed up out of the forest onto bare stone, lit dimly orange by the greater moon that was just now rising.

"Mountains," Pender said, with a sweeping gesture.

They were indeed in the mountains; the ground beneath the carpet was so steep that climbing it might be a challenge, but Morvash could see a smooth path zigzagging up the slope. Zerra was not bothering to follow the road's switchbacks, but was going directly up the slope.

Then they crested the ridge, and before them was a much longer slope stretching down into a broad, grassy valley. There was no forest on this side, but only a few scattered trees, casting long black shadows in the orange moonlight. Far off to the left there was a faint glow, as if from a village.

"Tazmor," Pender said, with a sweep of his arm.

The road forked just ahead, one branch turning diagonally to the left, toward those distant lights, while the other proceeded straight down the slope toward the valley. Both forks were clearly visible in the moonlight, and Zerra aimed for the right-hand branch, going straight down into the Valley of Tazmor.

She did not, however, let the carpet descend as the road did; the ground fell away beneath them until they were once again well above the tallest trees and safely out of Tarker's reach, should the demon turn up on their trail. She also increased speed, so that they were soaring along as swiftly as any hawk—or even faster.

The road was plainly visible below them now in the moonlight, either stone or bare dirt; once they were clear of the ridge grass grew on either side, but not a single blade could be seen on the road itself. Morvash guessed that meant that the road saw plenty of use.

They passed another fork, bearing right once again, taking them further out into the valley. Morvash could see tall mountains curving around them to the left, much taller than the ones behind them, and each of the left-hand roads seemed to be heading directly toward those mountains.

Then lights appeared ahead of them. "Village," Pender said, pointing. "Food. Beds."

"Tempting," Morvash said. "It's too cold to sleep out in the open here, I'd say. What do you think, Zerra?"

"How much farther to *your* village, Pender?" she asked.

Pender considered that. "Four days walk," he said. "Fly in one, maybe."

"Four days' walk?" Morvash asked. "Twenty-five leagues, maybe?"

Pender nodded.

"I'm not going that far without a break," Zerra said. "Food and bed it is." She aimed the carpet directly at the village lights.

The innkeeper had not expected guests in the middle of the night, but Zerra promised enough coin to overcome his misgivings, and the party was given two rooms and a warmed-over meal. As their food was being set out, Zerra tried to offer a gold bit to have him post a guard and wake them if a demon came after them, but the innkeeper had never seen gold before and would not take it.

"Could you pay him with a diamond?" Morvash whispered to Pender.

Pender looked startled. "Of course not. Erdrik took all of them."

The innkeeper, it turned out, understood silver, and four bits were enough to buy a promise that someone would stand watch for a demon.

As the negotiation concluded, Darissa leaned over and whispered something to Marek in Melithan. Morvash overheard, but could not understand the language; he looked at her inquiringly. She glanced around, then whispered, "He's not going to worry about falling asleep. He doesn't believe in any demon pursuing us."

"Maybe one of us should stand guard, then," Marek whispered.

"Or I could place a warning spell," Morvash said. "Kandif's Spell of Warning, maybe. It would wake me if anyone enters the room it's placed on."

"If the demon is already in the room, it's a little late," Darissa said.

"That's true. Besides, it takes about an hour and I'd need a live chicken. It would be much simpler to post a guard. Were you volunteering, your Highness?"

Marek smiled wryly. "I suppose I was. Though if the demon *does* turn up, I'm not sure what I can do about it."

"You can wake up Zerra and Karitha, and they can fly up out of reach," Darissa said.

"Oh. Well, yes, if there's enough time."

"I know no one wants to sleep outdoors again, but maybe they should spread the carpet on the floor of their room and sleep on it."

"It won't fit out the window, though," Morvash said. "I suppose we can risk it for one night. We've come a long way very quickly; it will probably be a few days before Tarker catches up with us."

"I hope so," Darissa said, with a glance at Karitha.

"What are you three mumbling about?" Hakin called. "Come and eat!"

Still worried, Morvash came.

In the end Marek stood guard, and their stay passed without incident. The sun was well up by the time Zerra awoke; the others had all awakened earlier. Morvash had taken over the watch, letting Marek get some rest, but the prince still dozed off within a few minutes of the carpet becoming airborne once again.

By daylight the Valley of Tazmor was mostly green and gold. There were farms below, on both sides of the road, but they were scattered; most of the countryside was meadowland. Morvash looked out across it, marveling at this completely unfamiliar realm. He could see mountains in the far distance to north and west, and to the south the misty horizon seemed to be broken by peaks as well, but to the east the farms stopped after a mile or so and the meadows seemed to stretch out forever.

"What's out there?" he asked Pender.

"Nothing," Pender said.

"What do you mean, nothing?"

"The flat…the land with grass…"

"Meadows," Morvash offered.

"Yes. The flat meadows go on for twenty leagues or more, but Tazmor goes only five leagues. I have never been so far as five leagues. Stories say that when the meadows end you find the Wilderland forest, hundreds of miles of forest. They say the Wilderland is home to dragons and mizagars and many other beasts. No people live there, not since the Northern Empire was destroyed. No one after Tazmor."

"Huh." Morvash was not sure how much faith to put in such stories.

They flew over another fork in the road, and followed the right-hand branch again. Morvash thought the left-hand road looked more heavily traveled.

Less than an hour later they came to another fork, but at this one the right-hand branch looked almost abandoned, the edges uneven, the weeds along the sides crowding in. Zerra turned to the right anyway, following the formula Pender had given her.

"No, no, no!" Pender called. "This is not a road! The other way!"

Annoyed, Zerra swung the carpet back toward the other route. "You're sure?" she said. "You said to always take the right fork."

"Not *that* one!" Pender said. "That is not a road."

"What *is* it, then?" Morvash demanded.

"It was a road long ago," Pender said. "It is not now."

"Then what *is* it? Where does it go?"

"It is nothing. It goes…" He hesitated. "It goes to the Northern Deserts, where the heart of the Northern Empire was. It was a big highway once, in the Great War. Now it is nothing."

"Northern Deserts?" Morvash asked, staring off to the northeast.

"They were not deserts in the war. The gods made them deserts when the Northern Empire was destroyed."

"Oh," Morvash said—still intrigued, but no longer considering any further investigation.

"You see how there are spaces between farms, below us?" Pender asked.

"Yes, of course."

"Some of those are the places where there were things left from the Northern Empire. Buckles, and shoes, and coins, and building stones, and things I do not know names for. The magicians say they are harmless now, but people like to be cautious. In the deserts, they are everywhere."

"Oh," Morvash said again. They were actually *inside the Northern Empire*, he thought—or at least, where it had once been. That was an odd feeling.

"We are getting close now," Pender said, looking north. "One more fork, and then to the mountains, and I will be home."

"And I'll finally get to see Erdrik's secret project."

Pender smiled. "Oh, yes," he said. "You will see it."

Morvash did not like that smile.

CHAPTER THIRTY-FIVE

MORVASH OF THE SHADOWS

2ND OF NEWFROST, YS 5238

When they were over the foothills Zerra asked Pender, "Which village is yours?"

"Not one of these," Pender replied. "Over the ridge." He pointed ahead, where a high stone crest blocked their view

Morvash looked down.

The road they had been following had disintegrated into dozens of small paths, connecting a network of farms, villages, and mines; Pender had continued to direct them always to the right, to the east, as they made their way north into the snow-capped mountains rimming Tazmor.

All the villages and farms and mines were now to the west of them, and none of them extended more than halfway up the stony line of mountains that formed the ridge Pender indicated. *Nothing* extended up that ridge—except one winding trail, at the easternmost limit of the settlements. A heavy gate blocked this path well below the peak, a stone barrier extending to either side.

That trail was apparently the route to Pender's home, and to Erdrik's mysterious project.

"How much farther *is* it?" Zerra asked, as they passed over the barred gate—barred on the *north* side, Morvash noticed. It was not meant to keep whoever lived beyond the ridge out of the countryside below, but to keep the rest of the world from intruding on Erdrik's mysterious project.

What's more, Morvash realized that the gate was enchanted—he could sense powerful wizardry. He guessed that Erdrik had put some sort of wards or other spells on it to keep visitors out. The magic only extended up a few feet, though, so the carpet passed over it unhindered.

"Over the ridge," Pender said. "You will see." He hesitated, then added, "There are two villages. My village is to the west of the road. The other is to the east. I don't know where Erdrik will be."

"Hmph." The ridge was high enough that Zerra had to send the carpet higher, then still higher, and by the time they reached the snow-dusted crest they were at least a thousand feet above the highest of the villages on the southern slopes, yet skimming no more than fifteen feet above the gap in the rocks that was all that remained of the road.

And then they were through the gap, giving Morvash and the carpet's other passengers their first sight of what lay beyond. It rose before them, and for a moment Morvash thought he was dreaming, or seeing some sort of magical vision.

The ground below them dropped off abruptly into a steep, deep valley, perhaps three miles across, much of which seemed to be full of boulders, though there were cleared areas on the far slope that appeared to be farms. The year's crops had been harvested, leaving stubble and exposed black earth. The valley was somewhat strange, but none of them paid much attention as they stared instead of what stood on the far side.

At first they could not grasp what they were seeing, but finally it sank in.

"It's a *dragon*!" Darissa gasped.

It was indeed a dragon—or rather, a statue of a dragon, carved from the same gray stone as the mountains around them. In fact, it had clearly *been* a mountain before it was carved. It was the largest man-made thing Morvash had ever seen, and that was counting the city walls and towers of Ethshar of the Spices; in fact, he thought it might well be larger than the entire city.

Its head was at the eastern end of the carved ridge, its hundred-foot stone eyes staring at the eastern horizon, the mouth below open and displaying gigantic stone fangs; the slit nostrils in its immense muzzle were the mouths of caves that could hold entire houses—or mansions, or possibly whole villages. Its monstrous gray chin rested on a vast framework of massive timbers, gigantic beams that must have come from trees larger than any Morvash had ever seen.

Behind the base of the mountainous skull the neck stretched a thousand feet back to shoulders like cliffs, that long throat resting on a dozen pillars each as big as the watchtowers at Westgate, each stone pillar capped with a wooden bed between the stone throat and its supports.

A village—a town, really—stood beneath the base of the throat, beside a foreclaw the size of a palace. It did not look even the size of a toy, but rather as if the dragon's foot rested beside a patch of moss.

Behind the shoulders wings sprouted from its mountainous back, but they were not raised; they were folded back and wrapped around that long, reptilian body. Morvash guessed that there had been no natural stone formation that could have served to create them in any other position. He glimpsed more wooden frameworks, barely visible, in the gaps between wings and body. An entire forest must have been obliterated to supply so much lumber.

The hips must once have been the top of a mountain, but now joined two tremendous legs and a long, long tail to the stone body. The tail was supported by a thin layer of timbers, as were the feet—it appeared that no part of the tremendous creature was still attached to the ground beneath.

Morvash stared, taking in the whole thing, then began focusing on little details.

He could see now why Pender's home was called Hindfoot Village. It was built up beside the outermost right rear claw.

He could see why Erdrik had needed such an isolated location, and two hundred years, for his project; he could never have kept something like this hidden anywhere nearer civilization, and carving an *entire mountain*—really, an entire *ridge*—would obviously require centuries.

He estimated the thing's length and concluded it was at least two miles long, probably much more; the tip of the tail was hidden, and the only things he had to judge the scale against were the two villages, so he could not be sure.

"I don't understand," Karitha said. "Where did it come from?"

"They carved it," Morvash said. "Pender's people. They carved an *entire mountain* into the shape of a dragon."

"What *for*?" Hakin asked. "No one can *see* it way out here!"

"Look at the wings," Morvash said. "See those wooden beams

that hold the wings out from the body? If it was just to look at, no one would bother—they'd have just left the wings attached."

"It was scary, climbing under there," Pender said, nodding. "It's dark and narrow, and if the stone broke…" He shuddered.

"But it didn't," Morvash said.

"No, it didn't," Pender agreed. "I brought the carvers food when I was a boy, climbing up the wood. And when the wings were finished, and I was old enough to cut stone, I worked on the tail, polishing scales to shape."

"I still don't understand," Hakin said. "What's it *for*?"

"Erdrik is going to bring it to life, isn't he?" Morvash said, looking at Pender. "He's an expert on animation spells—his house was full of animated furniture and nicknacks. That was all practice for *this*. I'm sure of it."

"*Animate* it?" Hakin exclaimed. "*That* thing?"

"Of course," Pender said.

Hakin stared at the immense carving. "*Why?*"

"Probably just to prove he can," Morvash said. "Old wizards get strange sometimes."

Zerra had let the carpet slow almost to a stop as they topped the ridge, so that they could all look at the gigantic sculpture; now she turned to Pender. "Where would I find him?" she asked.

"I don't know," Pender said. "But someone in my village might." He pointed at the buildings clustered around the monstrosity's right rear claw.

The carpet hesitated for another few seconds, then swooped down toward Hindfoot Village.

They made no attempt at stealth, and by the time they reached the town dozens of people were shouting and pointing. Pender leaned over the edge of the carpet and called out in Sardironese as Zerra guided their craft lower.

Morvash could hear several people shouting Pender's name as they cruised up the central street about a dozen feet off the ground, and Pender called back, but since everything else was in Sardironese he had no idea what they were talking about.

Pender had always called his home a village, but what Morvash saw around them was more than that. This was no simple cluster of homes with a smithy and perhaps a few shops at the center; this was a good-sized town, with solid houses of stone and wood standing in tidy rows, and collections of shops that would not have been out of place in Ethshar's New Merchants' Quarter. And there were hundreds of people out in the streets, watching as the carpet swooped into the town square at the tip of one of the dragon's huge claws.

The surrounding houses stood three stories high, with a few peaked roofs thrusting even higher—but that gigantic talon was taller than them all, and the foot behind it, resting on a shallow bed of ancient timbers, rose like a great stone hill until it curved up to become the monster's leg. To the north the vast stone belly was like a huge roof, hundreds, perhaps thousands, of feet above them, shadowing everything north of the town.

Zerra brought the carpet to a halt two or three feet off the stone pavement of the town square—a pavement not of rough cobbles, but of smooth stone, cut and fitted in an elaborate pattern of squares and diamonds. "Talk to them," she told Pender. "Find out what's going on, and where Erdrik is."

"I'll try," Pender said, dropping from the carpet to the ground.

He was promptly grabbed and vigorously embraced by several of the locals, and a babble of Sardironese surrounded the travelers.

A man with a dark blue sash over one shoulder, apparently marking him as an official of some sort, stepped up to the front of the carpet and asked a question.

"I don't understand Sardironese," Zerra said. "None of us do."

Prince Merek asked a question back in another tongue—it did not sound quite like the Melithan Morvash had heard before, and he thought it might be Trader'sTongue. He had learned a few words of Trader's Tongue when working for his father, before he had been sent into exile at his uncle's place, but he was far from fluent. He thought he caught the word for "we," but could not make out the rest.

The official looked from Zerra to Marek, then to each of the others on the carpet—Morvash, Hakin, Darissa, and Karitha—then turned up his hands in defeat and walked away.

"Doesn't *anyone* here speak Ethsharitic?" Hakin asked.

"Probably not," Morvash said. "I don't think they have much contact with the outside world."

"No?" Zerra asked. "Then how do they have all this?" She waved a hand to take in the surrounding town.

That, Morvash thought, was a good question. From Pender's descriptions he had pictured Hindfoot Village as a rural, poverty-stricken place, eking out a meager existence in the cold and barren north, where the people devoted their spare time to laboring on whatever Erdrik's mysterious centuries-old project might be.

That did not match the reality around them.

He saw the man with the blue sash talking to Pender, and a moment later their companion came over to talk to them.

"Welcome to Hindfoot Village!" he said.

"Where's Erdrik?" Zerra demanded, obviously not interested in pleasantries.

"Our master, Erdrik the Grim, is up on the…the head," Pender replied. "He appeared in Forefoot Village a sixnight ago, and talked to the village elders. He took the spells off them! And everyone! But I wasn't here, so I still can't talk about…" He waved at the belly far above.

"What's he doing?" Morvash asked.

"What has he *been* doing?" Zerra asked.

"He looked at…he…" Pender looked helplessly at the others.

"He inspected the creature," Darissa offered. "I can sense the image."

"Yes!" Pender agreed. "He inspected everything. It had to be perfect. And it is! My people have worked on it for two hundred years, and we made it *perfect*—every scale, every joint."

"So is he still inspecting it?" Morvash asked. "Is that why he's up on the dragon's head?"

"No, no," Pender said. "He finished inspecting last night. This morning he started his spell."

"What spell?" Zerra asked.

After living in Erdrik's house for so long, Morvash did not need to ask. "You mean…he's bringing it to life? Right now?"

"Yes," Pender said happily. "He told my friends the spell needs two days. He must not be interrupted."

"Two days?" Morvash felt his belly tighten. He had studied up on animation spells when he was trying to find the best way to restore all those statues to life, and he only knew of one that took two days, neither more nor less. "He's using Ellran's Immortal Animation? On *that*?"

"Ellran's?" Zerra said. Her face went pale.

"Wait a minute," Darissa said. "He's really bringing the entire *mountain* to life?"

Pender nodded.

"He's trying, anyway," Morvash said. "No one's ever animated anything close to that size before; I don't know if it will work."

"That's insane!" Darissa said. "A dragon *that* size?"

"An *immortal* dragon that size," Morvash said. "The spell's name is not an exaggeration."

"But there must be some way to stop him!" Marek said. "What if we interrupt the spell before it's finished?"

"I don't know," Morvash admitted. "But interrupting a spell is always dangerous. And if he started this one this morning, then it's already been building up magical potential for hours."

"We can't interrupt it," Zerra said. "That could be even worse than letting him finish."

"Worse than unleashing a dragon *three miles long*?" Marek demanded. "What could possibly be worse?"

"You don't want to know," Morvash said. "I mean that literally."

Darissa looked genuinely frightened by that, but she asked, "What will a dragon that size *eat*?"

"Nothing," Morvash said. "That's the good news, such as it is—creatures brought to life with Ellran's Immortal Animation don't need to eat. They live on pure magic. Most of them *can't* eat anything; they don't have throats." He glanced at Pender. "Your people didn't give this thing a throat and stomach, did you?"

Pender shook his head. "The mouth goes back just a hundred yards. To look real."

"That's more than enough to chew things up and spit them out," Zerra said, "even if it can't swallow."

"Why would it do that?" Pender asked.

"Because its master told it to, perhaps?" Darissa suggested.

"That's another thing," Morvash said. "I'm sure Erdrik *intends* to be its master, but it may not work. Its personality will be determined by its natural composition, and the precise proportions of the ingredients Erdrik uses in his spell, and the texts I've read on the subject say that it's extremely difficult to predict just how those will interact. The wizard performing the spell can adjust the ingredients, but he can't do anything about the mountain's elements, and the larger the spell's subject, the more its own materials matter, and the less important the spell's ingredients. With something *that* size, I don't think there's any way Erdrik can ensure obedience."

"Does *he* know that?" Darissa asked.

"He *ought* to," Zerra said, "but from what I've heard about him, he was always prone to rejecting news he didn't want to hear."

"Like those poor tax collectors he enchanted," Morvash said.

"There were other things, too," Zerra said. "There were several reasons the Guild wasn't happy with him before he disappeared."

"The Guild," Morvash said. "Maybe we should go tell them what's happening. I mean, what can *we* do?"

"By the time we could get back to Ethshar, that dragon would be alive and stomping all over Tazmor."

"Couldn't they send someone with a spell to kill it?" Darissa asked.

Morvash sighed. "You don't understand," he said. "Once it's alive, *nothing* can kill it. Ever. Everything that's ever had Ellran's spell used on it is still alive, and the spell has been known for centuries. People have been trying to find a counter-spell since the Great War, and have never succeeded."

"I'll contact Ithinia," Zerra said. "Tonight, with the Spell of Invaded Dreams. She may have some ideas."

"Good," Morvash said. He looked up at the towering stone carving. "I hope you get through. We only have until the day after tomorrow."

"I know," Zerra said, her gaze following his. "Believe me, I know."

CHAPTER THIRTY-SIX

HAKIN OF THE HUNDRED-FOOT FIELD

2ND OF NEWFROST, YS 5238

The entire party was welcomed into Pender's family home for supper, but the language barrier made that somewhat awkward. Hakin watched as Morvash and Marek and Darissa tried to communicate with their hosts, and were introduced to various people with odd Sardironese names that he did not bother to remember—after all, when would he need them, since none of them could understand a word he said? For his own part, he made the usual polite gestures and spoke the polite words, but did not really pay much attention to the locals.

Karitha just sat there, dazed and miserable, not talking to anyone, and Hakin felt a wave of sympathy for her—but on the other hand, she was a murderer, and her current ghastly situation was at least partly her own doing. He decided that if she wanted to continue wallowing in her own gloom, he would not try to stop her.

Instead he found himself speaking to Zerra as they dined. He and the wizard had wound up seated at the foot of the table, far from Pender and Morvash struggling to keep up a polite conversation with Pender's parents. Three teenaged girls separated them from the others, so if they did not want to eat in complete silence they had only each other.

They discussed the journey from Ethshar over the soup, and then Hakin told Zerra the entire story of how he had become Tarker's companion—she had heard the rough outline before, but now he filled in the details. By the time the hosts cleared away the chicken bones and brought out a platter of fruits both fresh and dried that subject had been largely exhausted, and Hakin began asking questions about this animation spell that Erdrik was trying to perform.

"Ellran's Immortal Animation," Zerra explained. "It will bring anything at all to life, and once that's done, nothing can kill it. Oh, it can be smashed, or imprisoned, but not killed—if you break it into pieces, each individual piece will be alive. Which is really pretty horrible, when you think about it. Fortunately, its creations can't feel any physical pain, and not much emotional pain, so they don't seem to suffer much."

"But how can they not be killed? What if you ground one to powder?"

"Then you have living powder. Ithinia of the Isle has a jar of the stuff, in fact; it's weird."

"But…" Hakin tried to imagine how this could work. "What if you brought a piece of wood to life?"

"You'd have an immortal piece of wood."

"But would it still burn?"

"Of course. And then you'd have a pile of immortal ash, and living smoke."

"That's just…hard to grasp."

"Wizardry often is. It's based in chaos."

"All right, suppose you brought something to life, and then cut it in half?"

Zerra took a drink of wine—Pender's parents apparently kept an excellent cellar. "You'd have two living halves."

"Would they be two separate beings, or would they still be parts of one?"

Zerra emptied her glass. "I'm not actually sure about that," she said. "But if you put them back together, however many pieces it is, and attached them by sewing or gluing or something, I know they'd merge back into a single creature."

"What if you brought two things to life separately, then put them together?"

"Oh, that one I know. They'd still be separate, and probably not happy about being stuck together. It's whatever was included in the original transformation, nothing more, nothing less. You can't add or subtract any substance. Something that's been brought to life with Ellran's can't ever digest food, for example. It may be able to go through the motions of eating, if it's been constructed for it, but the food will just sit there in its belly."

"That's…wait, so they don't eat?"

"No, they live on magic. Didn't you hear Morvash telling Darissa that? They can't eat, they don't need to breathe…"

"But if they don't breathe, are they really alive?"

"Well, we *say* they are, because we don't have any other word for it. They can move. If one has a mouth, it can talk, even though it doesn't have any lungs or breath—it's not the way people talk, it's like a speaking rune, with the voice coming out of nowhere."

"But if it doesn't have a mouth, it *can't* talk? That doesn't make sense."

Zerra turned up an empty palm, then reached for the wine decanter. "Wizardry often doesn't."

"But *any* kind of mouth can talk?"

"Well…" Zerra paused to pour. "Not necessarily. I don't know the details of the spell, but apparently it's possible to make creatures that don't talk. But they all *understand* human speech, and I think they can all talk unless the wizard actively prevents it."

"You've never done the spell?"

"*Me*? Oh, gods, no! It's not my sort of magic at all. I've never tried it, never even read the formula. But I've seen it done, and Ithinia used it a few times, and I've talked to her about it."

"So it can't be reversed? I know there are spells to undo things, like the one Morvash used to turn all the statues back into people."

"It can't be reversed. I don't know why. *Nothing* can undo Ellran's. Something brought to life with Ellran's won't age, won't die, is never ill even in the middle of a plague, is immune to death spells, is immune to *most* magic, really. Gods don't see them as alive in the first place, so theurgists can't do anything to them. Warlocks, back when there *were* warlocks, could smash them, but not kill them; the usual way a warlock killed anything was by stopping its heart, and most animated creatures don't *have* hearts. Witchcraft can't do *anything* to them—I don't know why not."

"So why isn't the World *full* of these immortal creatures? I mean, spriggans got into everything in just a few years, and they're a real nuisance; why aren't these Ellran things all over the place, getting in everyone's way?"

"Because it's a really, really difficult spell, and not many people know it, and most of the ones who do are bright enough to only use it very rarely. Nobody left a magical mirror lying around popping these out every few minutes. And there *are* ways to get rid of them in an emergency—break them up small enough that they aren't very strong, seal them in a box, and drop them in the ocean, for example. Though why you'd bother once they're broken up small enough to be harmless I'm not sure; as I said, Ithinia has one she ground to powder and keeps in a jar." She took another gulp of wine. "Or you could send one through a portal to another world, I suppose. I don't know whether anyone's ever done that."

Hakin glanced at the window, where he could just barely see a little of one of the gigantic dragon's legs. "Nobody is going to keep *that* thing in a jar," he said.

"No," Zerra agreed. "You'd need *millions* of jars, and that's after you broke it up. How do you break up a *mountain*? And it's too big to fit through any portal I ever heard of."

"So if Erdrik brings it to life, it's going to be around *forever*?"

"Probably. We might be able to talk it into living out in the wilderness, where no one will bother it and it won't hurt anyone, but we can't kill it."

"You said it won't need to breathe, so we couldn't drown it."

"No. It won't need air, or food, or anything but magic."

"And there's magic everywhere."

"That's…" Zerra stopped, with her glass halfway to her mouth. She blinked, then set it down again and stared at Hakin.

He stared back, realizing for the first time that Zerra had been drinking a *lot* of wine, and was feeling its effects.

"You know," she said, almost whispering, "there *are* places where there *isn't* any magic."

"There are?" Hakin asked, startled.

Zerra looked around at the others, then leaned close to Hakin. He could smell the wine on her breath. "It's a secret," she said. "Or at least, it was until they killed Empress Tabaea."

Hakin blinked. He knew that Tabaea the Thief had been an ordinary criminal who had somehow gotten hold of some incredibly powerful magic a decade or so back; she had used it to conquer Ethshar of the Sands and declare herself Empress of Ethshar. The Wizards' Guild had killed her, almost destroying the overlord's palace in the process, but Hakin had never heard any of the details. "What are you talking about?" he asked.

Zerra glanced again at the other diners, who were paying them no attention as they focused on Pender, who was translating multiple conversations back and forth. "It's not something the Guild is proud of," she said. "They try to keep it quiet, but when it's *in the middle of a city*, you can't really keep it secret."

"Keep *what* secret?"

"You know they killed Tabaea, right?"

"Right."

"They tried a lot of different magic, but she could counter everything that *had* a counter, so finally they resorted to something that *doesn't*. Which was really stupid."

"What did they do?"

"There's a spell—I forget what it's called, maybe it's just called Death. Anyway, you know wizardry works by tapping into the chaos underneath reality?"

"I've heard that," Hakin agreed. He did not mention that he had only heard it twice, once from Shenna, and then in Zerra's own remarks a few minutes earlier.

"Well, this spell, the Ultimate Death or whatever it's called, *turns that chaos loose*. It just lets everything dissolve into unreality. And it spreads, and there's almost no way to stop it. The spell has only ever been used maybe twice, because it could *destroy the entire World*. We don't even know how they stopped it the first time, when the spell was originally discovered, but the *second* time was when they used it to kill Tabaea, and they thought they had a way to stop it, but they were wrong. It didn't work, and this thing was spreading, eating the overlord's palace from the inside, and that's when they used this *other* spell, one that was so secret only a few wizards had ever heard of it, that makes magic stop working completely. Well, wizardry, anyway; I think *other* magic may still work, but I don't know for certain. *Wizardry* doesn't. And it's permanent—once it's used in a place, wizardry will never, ever work there again. Never. It was discovered during the Great War, and it was immediately banned—anyone who even mentioned that it existed would be executed, because Old Ethshar used wizardry and the Northern Empire mostly didn't, so it would only really be useful against our own side. They really, *really* didn't want the Northerners to know about it. But it got written down anyway, because we wizards are obsessive about this stuff, and a couple of wizards knew it, and years later one of them used it, maybe in a feud with another wizard, and ever since there's been a dead area in the mountains in the Small Kingdoms, out in the wilderness where nobody knew about it. I've heard that was about five hundred years ago. Nobody knows where the *first* dead area is, from when the spell was originally discovered, but the second one is still there, up in the mountains, somewhere. I don't know where; they keep it secret."

"Wow," Hakin said, leaning close.

"Yes. So anyway, the Guild tried to trick Tabaea into going to that dead area, but it didn't work, and they had to use that death spell on her instead, but then they used the magic-absorbing spell to stop the death spell, so the *third* dead area, the one that made it imposs…impossible to keep the secret, is in the middle of Ethshar of the Sands, inside the overlord's palace. Wizardry doesn't work there anymore. Lots of people know about it, but the Guild doesn't like that."

"I see."

"*Anyway*," Zerra said, her speech now noticeably slurred, "I don't think anyone's ever tried it, if they did I never heard about it, but I bet that if you took a creature that had been brought to life with Ellran's Immortal Animation to the dead area in the palace there, it would die. It would starve to death without magic to keep it alive."

"That's fascinating." Hakin was not merely humoring the wizard; this *was* fascinating, if not particularly useful. They could not expect to lure a mountain-sized dragon into the overlord's palace.

"Yes." Zerra looked over her shoulder. "I wonder if Ithinia ever thought of that? I'll have to ask her when we get back to Ethshar."

"You should do that," Hakin said. "Or tonight—weren't you going to try to contact her tonight?"

"Was I?" She looked confused.

"Yes, you said you were," he replied, carefully moving the wine decanter out of Zerra's reach. "Something about dreams." He looked up the table. "Pender, do you have any tea? I think Zerra's had too much wine."

"I'm fine," Zerra said, but she pushed her wineglass away. "What's for dessert?"

CHAPTER THIRTY-SEVEN

MORVASH OF THE SHADOWS

2ND OF NEWFROST, YS 5238

The entire party from Ethshar had dined with Pender's family, and they all had been introduced to Pender's parents and his three younger sisters, though Morvash had not gotten the names straight. After the meal, though, they had been scattered to several places for the night, since Pender's father did not consider the house big enough for everyone—or at least, that was the excuse he gave, by way of his son, but Morvash suspected he thought it might be unhealthy to have so many foreigners under the same roof as his teenage daughters. The house, while not a palace by any means, seemed large enough to Morvash to accommodate half a dozen guests, but he did not argue.

He himself was assigned the one guest bed, in a pleasant little sitting room/workshop on the upper floor. Hakin stayed at the home of the man with the blue sash—the mayor, Morvash decided, from Pender's stumbling attempt to find an Ethsharitic equivalent for his Sardironese title. A smiling, elderly woman whose exact position Morvash did not quite understand took in Darissa and Prince Marek, while after much discussion Karitha and Zerra were allowed to sleep in the town's immense workshop, where centuries of accumulated tools and papers lined the walls, while stone fragments, unused timbers, and iron brackets were stacked on all sides, providing some idea of how long and carefully the townspeople had worked on their gigantic task.

Zerra had clearly drunk more than her share of the family's wine at supper, but she assured everyone that she would still be able to perform the Spell of Invaded Dreams; the cool air on the walk to the workshop had cleared her head. Just to be sure, she used an amethyst enchantment to dispel the last of the liquor.

The workshop was clearly not meant for guests, but they chose it anyway. This rather unusual accommodation was not because the village had nowhere better, but because Zerra wanted space to perform her magic, and because she wanted room to keep the carpet ready in case she had to whisk Karitha skyward to keep her away from Tarker, should the demon arrive in the middle of the night. The big double doors that had once allowed workers to move slabs of stone, support timbers, and other large objects in and out were easily large enough for the carpet.

Morvash was reasonably pleased with these arrangements, since they left him with the only man in town who spoke Ethsharitic; he thought Hakin came out the worst, but the lad did not seem to mind.

Before the group split up, Darissa suggested that when Zerra talked to Ithinia that night, if the Spell of Invaded Dreams worked, that she might also ask Ithinia if someone could find out who ruled Melitha now. Dealing with Erdrik's monster was obviously the more urgent concern, but if she was going to be talking to Ithinia anyway…

Zerra nodded. "I'll try to remember," she said.

Once everyone had been distributed Morvash and Pender returned to Pender's home, where the expectation was obviously that everyone would be going to bed, but Morvash held Pender back for a moment.

"I wanted to ask you a few things," he said.

Pender glanced at his bedroom door, but then followed Morvash to the sitting room. "What do you want?" he asked, sitting on a chair as Morvash settled onto the edge of his bed.

"Tell me about this place," he said. "When we spoke back in Ethshar and you talked about your home I had pictured a miserable little village, dirt-floored huts and muddy streets, enslaved to Erdrik, but instead I find a flourishing town with fine houses and fancy pavements. Why is your home wealthy?"

Pender took a moment to compose his reply, clearly searching for unfamiliar words. At last he said, "The wizard is not stupid. People work better when they have full bellies and strong arms and calm heads, and when they are allowed to rest. He did not want a tired or hungry stone-carver to ruin his work when a chisel slips. He did not want us to run away to find better places when he was not here to watch us. So yes, we must do as he commands, but he pays us well, and we do not work on the mountain when the weather is not safe. The stone we cut away was ours to use for walls and pavements. When the snow came or ice made the mountain too dangerous, our carvers would work in town, on our homes and streets. There was much more than we needed, so we threw the rest down in the valley, but we had all we wanted for the town. When we cut down trees for bracing, the part that was not needed was ours to use as we pleased. When our carvers dug gold or gems from the mountain, we could keep them, and sell them to people in other towns—that was how I became a jeweler and how I had the diamonds. Children or women or old men who were not strong enough to work on the mountain could do other work instead. So we had money and workers, and hunters and gardeners, and money to buy from the farmers on the other side of the ridge what we could not grow or make for ourselves, and if there was not enough food the wizard brought us more. We have lived this way for two hundred years. Why would we not do well?"

Morvash could hardly argue with that. He was honestly surprised, though; most people did not treat their slaves as people, but as cattle, and however comfortable Pender's people might be, they were still effectively Erdrik's slaves.

He understood now, though, why Pender had come to Ethshar seeking his master, and why he had gone with Erdrik when Javan's Restorative freed him—Pender's people did not want to lose their comfortable lives. If Erdrik had died, or had decided to abandon them, their entire economy would have been ruined.

And it meant, he realized, that these people would probably side with Erdrik in any dispute.

"What did you tell everyone about why we came here?" he asked.

"I told them you had come to see Erdrik perform his great magic," Pender replied. "And to get away from the demon."

"Oh," Morvash said. A thought struck him. "Do you have any magicians here?"

Pender shook his head. "The wizard does not allow other magicians."

That did not surprise Morvash at all; he would not expect Erdrik to risk any sort of magical interference.

"Why does no one else speak Ethsharitic?"

"Why would we? None of us ever left Tazmor before I did. All the people we trade with speak Sardironese."

"But speaking Ethsharitic is not actually forbidden?"

Pender hesitated. "I don't *think* so," he said. He frowned. "I hope not. The wizard heard me talk in Ethshar and did not say anything about it."

"You should be fine, then."

"I hope so."

"Thank you," Morvash said. "I think that's everything, and I'm sure you want to get some sleep."

"Yes. Good night, Morvash."

"Good night, Pender."

With that, Pender rose and left the room, closing the door gently behind him.

Morvash sat thinking for several minutes—not about anything in specific, but reviewing everything that had happened to him in the last couple of sixnights. Almost forty people rescued, a demon chasing one, a mysterious someone from the Small Kingdoms after one or two of the rest, Erdrik freed and come to bring his masterpiece to life, a journey by flying carpet to the far north of Tazmor, deep inside the old Northern Empire and on the very edge of civilization, where an entire mountain had been carved into the shape of a dragon...

It was a lot to take in, but he did eventually get to sleep.

His sleep was uninterrupted. Morvash was not included in Zerra's dream message. He did not know the Spell of Invaded Dreams himself, nor any of its variants, so he could not have contacted anyone directly; he could only wait until Zerra's report in the morning.

When he awoke he found Pender waiting to take him down to breakfast with the family, and as they ate he realized they had not made any arrangements for meeting up with the others. He mentioned this to Pender.

"We will go to the workhouse," he said. "After we eat."

That seemed as good an approach as any, so Morvash returned his attention to the ham and barley cakes.

A moment later there was a knock at the door; Pender's mother answered it, and then called, "Pender!"

Startled, Pender rose and left the kitchen. Morvash heard voices, and a loud thump, like something heavy hitting the floor; then Pender reappeared, leading Zerra and Karitha and talking to his mother in Sardironese.

"They had nothing to eat," he told Morvash in Ethsharitic.

"Oh!" Morvash exclaimed, feeling stupid. He quickly rose and offered Zerra his seat, while Karitha settled where Pender had been. He had not given it any thought, but of course the workshop had no kitchen and no pantry, and no one had been looking after the two women.

He thought Hakin, Marek, and Darissa should be all right, though—they had hosts attending to them, despite the language barrier.

After allowing Zerra time to down a barley cake and half a mug of small beer, Morvash asked, "Did the spell work?"

Zerra nodded as she took a bite of ham. "I spoke to Ithinia," she said. "She says we should observe, but not interrupt the spell—it's too dangerous."

"Isn't a *three-mile dragon* dangerous? Especially one that can't be killed?"

"Of course it is, but Ithinia thinks there are ways to handle it."

"I don't know what they are," Morvash replied.

Zerra swallowed, then said, "*You*, Morvash of the Shadows, are a mere journeyman. Ithinia of the Isle is a senior Guildmaster."

"I know that, but…" Morvash stopped. He glanced at Karitha. "Is there any news of the demon?"

"Not yet," Zerra replied, reaching for another barley cake. "But I brought the carpet with us."

"What do you plan to do?"

"Today? I plan to fly up and see how Erdrik's spell is going. If it fails on its own, then we don't need to worry about any giant dragon. I can talk to him between incantations about what he thinks he's doing. He can't use any other magic while he's in the middle of Ellran's Animation, so I'll be safe."

Morvash had never actually seen the spell performed, but he had read about it during his months of research; he knew it required the wizard to stay awake for the entire two days, and that for most of that time he had to be stirring at least one of the three cauldrons the magic required, but there were times when he could talk safely, or use one hand to eat or drink. Morvash did not remember any specifics of when they might occur in the proceedings, or how long these breaks might last. "May I come along?" he asked.

"Of course. And I'll bring Karitha—I don't want to leave her unprotected down here if the demon shows up."

"I don't see any reason to bring the others, though," Morvash said. "Let them rest with their hosts. Pender can stay and translate for them."

Pender looked suddenly worried. "We can't leave Darissa and Prince Marek where they are!" he said.

"Why not?" Zerra asked, startled.

"They are in the wizard's house! If he finds them there it could be bad."

"They're…what?"

"That is the wizard's house! Pancha is his housekeeper! When he is busy with his spell we thought it would be all right, but if he comes back and finds them there…" He shook his head.

"Well, then go get them and take them somewhere else," Morvash said.

"Besides," Zerra added, "Erdrik won't be coming down today unless his spell goes wrong."

"If it goes wrong he will be angry," Pender pointed out.

"So go move them!" Morvash answered.

"I will," Pender said. "I will go now." He started toward the door.

His mother stopped him, and they spoke briefly in Sardironese; then he called back, "Finish eating, and go!"

"Right," Morvash said.

Then Pender was gone, and the other three hurriedly finished their meal.

A quarter of an hour later they were in the street, where Zerra unrolled the carpet on the stone pavement and the three of them sat down, cross-legged, near the center. A word and a gesture sent them rising gently into the damp morning air.

Several villagers watched this, and stood staring as the carpet spiraled upward and then vanished above the gigantic dragon they and their ancestors had devoted their lives to carving.

Morvash marveled at the detail as they soared up the dragon's flank; each individual scale was perfect, from its smooth forward edge to the thicker, rougher rear side. Then they came to the trailing edge of the monster's wing, and he was freshly astonished by the veining, the ribs, and the massive, intricate wooden framework that held the wing out from the body. When he had first heard that Pender's people had spent two hundred years working on Erdrik's secret project he had wondered what could possibly take so long; now he wondered how they had ever accomplished so much in so short a time.

He also wondered what would become of them now; their task was finished, and Erdrik no longer needed them. Would they find some other employment, or were their two beautiful towns doomed?

Looking down at Hindfoot Village, he thought it was entirely possible that the town was doomed because when the dragon came to life it might shuffle its feet and stamp the entire community flat without even noticing it was there. Had Pender's people ever considered that? They had known Erdrik intended to animate the monster; surely someone must have realized what that might mean.

Between the dragon's hind legs he could see a huge stack of ladders and wooden frames that he guessed had been used as scaffolding during the carving, but which were no longer needed. They had probably been attached to the legs, giving the carvers access to the beast's haunches; from there they could have climbed up onto the monster's back.

Then the carpet rose high enough for them to see the dragon's back spread out below them, a huge stone surface at least a quarter mile wide, probably more, far above the valleys on either side. The outline of bone and muscle where the wings joined in just behind the shoulders; despite the slopes curving down from the ridged spine there would be no danger of falling off, because the wings, and further up the shoulder blades, would stop any slide.

The surface was empty, though; Erdrik was nowhere to be seen.

"Pender said he was on the head," Morvash remarked.

"I know," Zerra said, aiming the carpet in that direction.

They soared on, past the wings, across the shoulders, up the neck as it narrowed, and then over the hump that was the back of the monster's head. Ahead they could see the end of the creature's snout, and the flared stone rim above each nostril, but there was no sign of Erdrik.

Then they passed between the huge pointed ears, and Morvash

called, "Over there!" He could feel magical energy simply *seething* all around them, and that had directed his attention to a particular spot.

Zerra turned to see where he was pointing, then swung the carpet around.

Erdrik was seated inside the left ear, cross-legged on a round rug perhaps ten feet across, surrounded by his supplies and apparatus. He had a small cauldron on either side, and a third in front of him, each hanging from a tripod over a small fire. A pungent scent of powerful herbs reached Morvash's nose.

Erdrik wore the same dark blue robe he had worn when Morvash freed him from his vault, but oddly, his feet were now bare. He had been wearing sturdy slippers when last Morvash had seen him. Morvash wondered why his feet weren't cold—or perhaps they were, but he had some reason to leave them uncovered. At least he was out of the wind, there inside the dragon's ear—and that was probably *why* he was there, so that his three fires would be sheltered from the weather.

He was stirring the front cauldron with one hand, and holding a book with the other, but as the flying carpet blocked the early morning light he looked up from the page. Still stirring vigorously, he called, "You're trespassing. Who are you, and what do you want?"

Zerra brought the carpet to a stop just outside the ear, hovering about a foot above the stone.

"The Wizards' Guild is not pleased with you, Erdrik," she said.

CHAPTER THIRTY-EIGHT

MORVASH OF THE SHADOWS

3ʳᵈ OF NEWFROST, YS 5238

Erdrik laughed, then caught himself before he let the rhythm of his stirring slip. "And why should I care what the Guild thinks of me?" he demanded.

"Because you are not omnipotent," Zerra retorted.

"I do not fear the Guild. I ask again, who are you?"

"I am Zerra the Ageless—as you ought to know. We've met before. I am here as the Guild's representative, at the direction of Ithinia of the Isle."

"Ah, I believe your face *is* familiar. And that young man with you—Morvash of the Shadows, was it?"

"That's right," Morvash said.

"And this other person?"

"Karitha the Demonologist," Morvash said. "She has nothing to do with you; she just needed to get away from Ethshar, so we brought her along."

"And do any of you intend to interrupt my spell?"

"Probably not," Zerra admitted.

"Then why bother to come all this way?"

"We came to see what you were up to," Zerra replied. "And now that we have seen, allow me to ask, one wizard to another, what in the World do you think you're doing?"

"I am animating the largest dragon that has ever existed."

"I can see that. *Why* are you doing this?"

Erdrik smiled, then set the book down on the rug, glanced around at his other possessions, all while continuing to stir the cauldron. He said, "I have at most perhaps a quarter of an hour before the next stage of the spell requires my full attention, so I will keep this very brief: I am doing this because I want to. I have been planning this since the end of the Great War. I had proposed using gigantic creations like this to destroy the Northern Empire, but those fools, Azrad and Gor and Anaran, would not agree, and before I could put my scheme into practice the gods intervened and ended the war."

"Then why do it *now*, when there's no Northern Empire to fight?" Morvash asked.

"To show how effective it would have been! To exterminate anyone who opposes me!"

"Azrad and the others are long dead," Zerra said. "Who do you want to prove yourself to?"

"Myself, if no one else!"

Morvash bit his lip and said nothing, but remembered his remark to Hakin that old wizards got strange sometimes.

Strange, but not stupid; casting the spell from inside the monster's ear meant that not only was Erdrik sheltered from the weather, but when the spell was complete he would be in position to give his creation orders. It might well not be able to hear normal human voices, but it could scarcely ignore someone inside its ear.

"If you think I should fear the Guild, Zerra, consider rather that they should fear *me*," Erdrik said. "Me, and my creation! An immortal dragon big enough to flatten Azrad's Ethshar in half a day—what can they do to oppose me, when harming me will unleash its wrath upon them?"

Zerra pursed her lips. "I see," she said.

"Now, are you going to try to interrupt this spell, knowing that to do so will loose vast uncontrolled and unpredictable magical energies, or are you going to leave me in peace to complete my magnificent achievement?"

Zerra looked around, obviously sensing the wizardry that surrounded them; the dagger on her belt was glowing a brilliant purple. "I'm not even sure we *could* interrupt you at this point," Zerra said. "*You* could stop, but you may be beyond the point where outside influences can affect you."

"I assure you, I have no intention of stopping."

"I thought as much." She sighed. "Then I will leave you to it, and hope that the spell fails harmlessly." She gestured, and the carpet rose.

Morvash glanced down and noticed that his own athame was glowing dark blue, but the light was fading as they moved further away from Erdrik. "So what do we do?" he asked Zerra.

"I don't know," the elder wizard replied. "I'll have to ask Ithinia tonight. Or maybe I can catch her during an afternoon nap."

Morvash nodded, then looked at Karitha.

She had not said a word the entire time; in fact, he was not sure when he had last heard her speak. "Are you all right?" he asked.

"No," she said. "I don't know what to do."

The carpet had swooped across the dragon's head, and was now starting down toward the valley below.

"What do you mean?" Morvash asked.

"I mean *I don't know what to do*," Karitha exclaimed. "I thought I was dead, but now I'm back, but my old life…is my house still there? Is someone else living there? And how can I ever go back, when Tarker is after me? It'll catch me eventually. Even if I somehow manage to dismiss it, then what? I barely remember any of my own magic! My friends have probably forgotten me, if they're even still alive."

Morvash suppressed the urge to say, "What friends?" He and Hakin had discussed some of Tarker's history during the trip from Ethshar to Tazmor, and Morvash had the definite impression that Karitha had never been popular.

"You can start over," he said. "You can go on as a demonologist, or you can learn a new trade. You must have something you're interested in."

"But Tarker is after me! I can't stay in one place for long enough to do anything. And I can only move fast enough to stay ahead of it by using magic—*other people*'s magic, because I don't know any demon that can help me."

"Could you summon another demon to fight Tarker, perhaps?"

"No! Demonology doesn't work like that. I can't… Demons don't fight each other. It's not in their nature. They'll fight and kill and destroy anything else, but not other demons. None of them will do *anything* to protect me from Tarker."

That was not something Morvash had ever heard before, and he was fascinated. "Really?"

Karitha did not answer, but just stared at him, her eyes wild.

"What about a god?" Zerra asked.

"I can't summon a god! I'm not a theurgist."

"Doesn't sound as if you're much of a demonologist anymore, either," Zerra said. "You can't hire someone to summon a god on your behalf? The god of protection, whoever that is?"

Karitha shook her head. "Gods and demons don't interact," she said. "Not since the war. It's part of the agreement they made."

"Well, I can't fly you around forever," Zerra said. "Once Erdrik and his ridiculous pet are dealt with, however that may happen, I'm going home to Ethshar and you'll be on your own."

Karitha burst into tears. "I wish you'd left me a statue!" she said to Morvash, slapping him on the arm.

"Maybe I could turn you back," he said, not mentioning that he had never attempted any sort of petrifaction spell and did not have the necessary instructions.

"That won't...no!" She turned away, sobbing.

For the remainder of the descent to Hindfoot Village neither Zerra nor Morvash said a word; the only sounds were the wind rushing past the carpet and Karitha crying.

As they approached the town Zerra spotted someone waving to them, swinging both arms above his head; she directed the carpet toward him, and as they drew nearer Morvash recognized him as Pender. Hakin, Darissa, and Marek were standing behind him, the four of them in the street near the workshop, and the official with the blue sash was beside him.

Zerra brought the carpet to a halt a few feet away, and Pender trotted up to the edge of the fabric. "What's happening up there?" he asked. Behind him, the other three were staring at Karitha, who was still weeping.

"Erdrik's performing his spell," Zerra said. "It should be complete tomorrow morning."

"Is it working?"

Zerra and Morvash exchanged glances. "It's doing *something*," Morvash said. "We could feel powerful magic, and it felt..." He groped for a word before finally settling on, "It felt right. As if it's doing what it's supposed to."

"We can't know for certain until the spell is complete," Zerra said.

"Will it bring the *entire* dragon to life, or just the head?" Pender asked.

Morvash blinked in surprise.

"That's a very interesting question," Zerra said. "We don't actually know. He's certainly *trying* to bring the whole thing to life."

"He would never tell us," Pender said. "The spell will happen tomorrow morning?"

"Yes."

Pender turned and spoke to the mayor in Sardironese. The mayor frowned, then turned and hurried away, calling something.

"What's going on?" Morvash asked.

"We need to leave," Pender said. He pointed at the gigantic foot that rose up from one side of the town. "If that moves, everything will be broken, even if the dragon does not try to."

"We had wondered about that," Morvash said.

"We have a place," Pender said. "A narrow place, a crack in the stone. We have stored things we need there, food and other things. We can hide there until the dragon is gone."

"That would be wise," Zerra replied.

"We have been making the place for years, while we waited for the wizard to return."

"Good."

"Excuse me. I must help my family."

"Of course."

Pender turned and hurried away, leaving the six visitors. Karitha was still snuffling; Hakin leaned forward and asked Morvash, "Is she all right?"

"She's *terrified*," Darissa said, before Morvash could respond. "Wouldn't you be? There's a *demon* after her, one called 'the Unrelenting.' I'm amazed she's held up as well as she has."

"I know that!" Hakin said. "But she wasn't crying before. And don't you have an assassin after *you*?"

"We have someone who was looking for us, but we don't know if he's an assassin, and he's just human, so far as Morvash's uncle could tell; he isn't a demon. He's probably still back in Ethshar, looking for an indecent statue." She eyed Hakin, then said, "You spent so long with Tarker that you aren't afraid of it, didn't you? The rest of us haven't, you know."

"I..." Hakin frowned. "I know it's dangerous, but yes, I lived with it for years and it never hurt me."

"You probably have a better idea of how fast it is than the rest of us do; when do you think it will get here?"

Hakin looked up at the ridge to the south that separated them from the rest of Tazmor. "It's hard to say," he said. "I don't really know how far we came, or how fast we were flying."

"Maybe a hundred and twenty leagues," Zerra said. "Give or take a few miles. Maybe a little more."

"And it's been what, seven days? Eight?" Hakin frowned. "I think Tarker should be here by now—it isn't as fast as the carpet, but it doesn't need to eat or sleep the way we did. I'd estimate it should be able to cover at least twenty leagues in a day. Something must have delayed it. Or maybe it had to rest—it isn't as strong as it once was. Being in our world for so long has weakened it."

"Has it?" Marek asked. "I didn't realize that was how it worked."

"I don't think *anyone* did," Hakin said. "No one ever held a demon in our world for so long before."

"I didn't do it on *purpose*!" Karitha sobbed.

"No one suggested you did," Darissa told her. "No one is blaming you!"

Zerra and Morvash exchanged glances at that, and Darissa gave them an angry glare.

It was all very well to be polite, Morvash thought, but Karitha *had* summoned a demon to murder someone; she was hardly an innocent in all this. Some would consider it simple justice if Tarker got her.

For his own part, he thought seven years as a statue was enough of a punishment to at least win her a second chance, especially since it had been her victim who petrified her—her own attack could even be considered self-defense. But telling her no one blamed her for summoning Tarker was going a little further than Morvash considered reasonable.

"Listen," Hakin said, "if Tarker shows up, you can just tell it to kill Erdrik, can't you? You don't need the secret name for that."

"So what?" Karitha asked. "It'll kill Erdrik and ten minutes later it'll be after me again."

"It may not be that easy to kill Erdrik," Zerra said. "He's more powerful than Wosten ever was. His protective spells kept Tarker out of his house for hours."

"But Tarker did find a weakness eventually, and besides, Erdrik doesn't have all those wards in place up here," Morvash pointed out. "I didn't sense *any* protections around him except the animation spell's aura."

"*I* did, journeyman," Zerra retorted. "You're right that he doesn't have many in place, because he doesn't want anything to interfere with Ellran's Animation, but he has *some*, and he has a levitation spell in that bracelet he's wearing, so he could fly out of the demon's reach."

"He does? How do you know that?" Morvash had never heard of any spell that would have revealed that to Zerra without attracting any notice.

"Because he had the same bracelet when I met him twenty years ago, when the Guild was still trying to get him to behave himself. He made that black stone with Tolnor's Synthetic Jewel; not sure which levitation spell it is."

"That explains how he got everything up to the dragon's ear," Morvash said. "I'd thought maybe that rug of his could fly."

Zerra shook her head. "No, I'm pretty sure it's just a rug. Sitting on bare stone for two days isn't very comfortable."

"But wait," Hakin said. "If he can fly out of Tarker's reach, that's even *better*. Tarker won't be able to catch him, and it won't hurt Karitha until it catches Erdrik."

Zerra and Morvash looked at one another. "Would that work?" Morvash asked.

"Probably not forever," Zerra said. "I don't know how long he could levitate. There might be a time limit, or he might need to be awake. And he'll need to come down to eat."

"Not if he has a bloodstone with the Spell of Sustenance on it," Morvash replied. "Which I assume he does, since he survived eleven years sealed in that vault."

"But he probably has *some* limit—needing sleep, or renewing the spell, or something."

"That's probably true," Morvash agreed. "But ordering Tarker to kill him could buy Karitha some time to escape."

"*Can* you give Tarker a new target without the secret name?" Darissa asked.

Karitha nodded. "I think I remember how. It's not hard."

"But does Erdrik deserve to die?" Prince Marek asked. "Who are we, to sentence him to death?"

"He's already lived at least three hundred years," Zerra said. "And he's violated Wizards' Guild rules; that carries a death penalty, and he swore to obey Guild law when he was an apprentice."

"Did he?" Darissa asked. "Did the Guild *exist* three hundred years ago?"

Zerra started to reply, then caught herself. "I'm not completely sure," she said. "But I know there was some sort of regulation of magic in Old Ethshar's military. Erdrik isn't free to do anything he wants with his magic."

Morvash was not entirely convinced Zerra's argument really worked, since Old Ethshar' military had long ago ceased to exist, but he was not inclined to disagree with the basic conclusion. Erdrik could not be permitted to simply operate unchecked; wizardry had the power to destroy the World, and had come close to doing so on at least two occasions.

But that meant he should be stopped, not that he should be *killed*. Prince Marek had a point. This idea of setting Tarker after him was not necessarily the right thing to do, despite its obvious benefits—especially since Tarker and Erdrik might do a great deal of damage to the surrounding area in their eventual conflict.

But Morvash had no better plan.

CHAPTER THIRTY-NINE

DARISSA THE WITCH'S APPRENTICE

3RD OF NEWFROST, YS 5238

Darissa finally managed to pull Zerra aside early that afternoon. The people of Hindfoot Village were packing up and removing their more valuable possessions, carrying them away to the ravine beyond the dragon's tail where they intended to take shelter if the monster their people had spent two centuries carving were to go on a rampage, and Zerra had been providing airborne transportation for large quantities of this cargo, accepting payment in fine gemstones. Morvash and Hakin and Marek had been providing more mundane assistance, and had been talking to Karitha about what might be done to protect her from Tarker; Pender, of course, had been assisting his family in their relocation. Darissa had been using her witchcraft to learn a little Sardironese, and to heal a few minor injuries.

For the most part, the people of Hindfoot Village were a healthy lot; Darissa suspected their isolation had something to do with that, or perhaps Erdrik had cast a spell of some sort to protect them. Any time you had hundreds of people working stone, though, there would be injuries—mashed toes, bruised shins, dislocated fingers.

But even while she was healing the townspeople and consuming large quantities of food to replace the energy spent on this magic, she kept an eye out for a chance to talk to the older wizard, and at last she saw one.

"Excuse me," she said, as she intercepted Zerra on her way back from a quick break. "Did you have a chance last night to ask Ithinia about Melitha?"

"Oh, Darissa!" Zerra said, startled, her hand falling to the hilt of the knife on her belt. "Yes, I did. She said she didn't know a thing about it, that most of her interests in the Small Kingdoms concerned areas much further south than Melitha, but she would check on it and should know something in a day or two."

"She has interests in the Small Kingdoms?"

"She's been involved with the Vondish Empire, and Lumeth of the Towers. I suppose that's what she meant."

Darissa blinked. She had heard of Lumeth of the Towers, though she did not know much about it, but the other name was new. "What's the Vondish Empire?" she asked.

"Oh, that's right! You wouldn't know. Well, late in 5220 a warlock named Vond overthrew the king of Semma, then started using his magic to conquer the neighboring kingdoms as well. Eventually the Calling got him—but you don't know about that, either, do you?" Zerra sighed. "You've missed forty years of history. Let me just sum it up—Vond is gone, but the empire he built is still there, occupying what used to be more than a dozen of the southernmost of the Small Kingdoms. It's now ruled by a council of nobles. And because magic was involved in creating it, the Wizards' Guild took an interest, which means Ithinia took an interest."

"Wait, so a dozen kingdoms are *gone*, absorbed by this empire?"

"Yes, exactly."

"And they fought a war using magic?"

"It wasn't much of a war, since no one there had any magic that stood a chance against Vond, but yes."

"The Guild let that happen?"

"I'm afraid so. We weren't paying attention."

Darissa needed a moment to absorb this. She had always been taught that the Guild rules were absolute and inviolable, yet this Vond, this warlock—whatever a warlock was—had been able to break them, and even after he was gone, the empire remained and the old kingdoms had not been restored.

And if *that* was possible...

"Is Melitha even *there* anymore?" After all, her homeland had never been blessed with defensible borders, and most of its neighbors had not been particularly fond of it.

"Oh, I'm fairly sure that it is," Zerra said. "The northern Small Kingdoms weren't involved in any of Vond's adventures. Ithinia didn't say anything about it being gone, and I think she would have known about *that*."

That was not actually very comforting.

"Ithinia said she would check on it," Zerra said. "That's all I know. I understand that it's your home and that it matters to you, but that was all decades ago, and the rest of us are far more concerned with what Erdrik is doing right now."

"And with what these villagers can pay to use your magic carpet."

"Well, yes. That's how I make my living. Just as you do with your healing."

Darissa did not think the two were exactly equivalent—for one thing, she would never refuse to heal someone simply because he couldn't pay. She saw no point in arguing, though. She looked around at the rapidly-emptying town. "What do you think is going to happen to these people?" she asked.

"I expect they'll hide in their little hole until Erdrik and his dragon go away, and then they'll come out and look for a new home."

"You don't think they'll stay here?"

"Why would they? There won't be a wizard supporting them anymore—at least, not unless Erdrik has some *other* insane scheme that calls for stone carvers. And judging by what it's like now, this place must be horrible in the winter. If I were one of them, I know *I* would head south."

Darissa nodded. "But is Erdrik really going to go away? What if the dragon stays here?"

"I'd say that's all the more reason to go somewhere else."

Darissa could not argue with that.

She tried to imagine what it would be like for Pender's people. They had worked toward a single goal for two hundred years, and achieving it meant destroying their own homes—how could they *do* that? Or had they never really thought about it? She supposed that for most of the time that they had been working on the dragon statue completion had seemed so far away that it wasn't an issue, and by the time it came within reach they were so set in their ways they could not imagine stopping. They had even sent Pender to see why Erdrik had not come.

But then, Erdrik must have been the source of their prosperity. This cold, stony land would not have supported them so well without the wizard's help, and if he never came back their little society would eventually have collapsed. They really had not had much of a choice.

She looked up at the belly of the dragon, far overhead, and tried to imagine what would happen if it came to life.

She shuddered.

Maybe, she thought, she and Marek should just leave; they were not accomplishing anything significant here. They should head south.

Maybe they did not even need to go to Melitha. Maybe they should make a new life for themselves somewhere else. She had demonstrated that she could make a living as a witch...

But Marek could not make a living as a prince anywhere in the lands outside the Small Kingdoms. And even though she had been gone for half a lifetime, so that half the people she had known were probably dead and the rest might not even remember her, Melitha was *home*. Once the carved mountain and the mad wizard were dealt with, she wanted to go back there.

"You're staying here?" she asked Zerra.

"Until Erdrik completes his spell one way or the other, anyway. After that, it depends."

"What if Karitha's demon shows up?"

Zerra sighed. "We'll see."

"When it's all over, what would you charge to take Marek and me to Melitha?"

Zerra cocked her head. "You don't have any money, do you? You've just been healing people for food and lodging and clothes, haven't you?"

"So far, yes."

"In fact, I've already loaned you two a couple of rounds on the way north."

"That's true. And if you ever expect us to repay it, we'll need to get to Melitha."

"Fine. I'll take you for one round of silver."

Darissa started to protest that that was far too much, then caught herself as she remembered the day she had first met Marek, when he had dismissed *two* rounds of silver as nothing. If he was recognized as Melitha's prince, he would be able to pay Zerra's fee easily.

And if he was not, well...things would be complicated in that case, and another debt might not matter.

"All right. Though it may take us a little time."

"I'll add it to your bill, along with the two rounds of copper. Fair enough?"

"Fair enough." She looked around. "Now, shall we see if anyone else needs healing or transportation?"

CHAPTER FORTY

MORVASH OF THE SHADOWS

3ʳᴰ OF NEWFROST, YS 5238

By sunset, Hindfoot Village had been evacuated and Tarker had still not arrived. After some discussion, the Ethsharites—Hakin, Karitha, and the two wizards—had decided to stay where they were, in town, rather than risk leading the demon to the townsfolk. Darissa and Marek stayed, as well, if only to have someone to talk to; between them they could hold a conversation in Melithan, Ethsharitic, Trader's Tongue, Trafoan, or Ressamoric, but even after Darissa's witchcraft-enhanced studying neither of them knew enough Sardironese to be comfortable.

Besides, Darissa did not want to get too far from Zerra, who was to provide their ride home.

Pender's family had left their house open for the visitors, but all of them, including Pender himself, had fled. Pender had told the foreigners, before his departure, that Forefoot Village was also being abandoned, at least for the present. The general belief was that if and when the spell worked, Erdrik would send the dragon out into the wastes to the east that had once been the heart of the Northern Empire, and when it was safely gone the locals would reemerge and reclaim their homes, rebuilding anything that had been smashed.

Morvash thought that was probably over-optimistic, that the community could not survive for long without Erdrik's support, and that Erdrik would probably not continue that support now that his insane project was complete, but he did not say so. He saw Darissa's expression and guessed that she shared his doubts.

Once Pender and the rest were gone the little group settled into their borrowed home, with Zerra's carpet rolled up just inside the front door and ready to be hauled out into the street on a moment's notice. A guard rotation was arranged to warn them if Tarker showed up, though Karitha, due to her fragile emotional state, was not assigned a turn. A suitable post was found up the street from the house, near the dragon's talon, where one could see across the rubble-filled valley to the trail coming down from the crest of the far ridge, and it was agreed that if the guard saw any movement anywhere on that trail, or along the ridge-top, he would wake everyone immediately. A false alarm would be preferable to being caught sleeping when the demon arrived.

It was decided that if the dragon started to move, or if Erdrik appeared, that would also mean everyone should be roused. The spell was not due to be completed until an hour or two after the first light of dawn, but wizardry did not always operate on an exact schedule.

Prince Marek took the first shift, which passed uneventfully. Darissa had the next, and Hakin the third.

Morvash's turn followed Hakin's, and he was accordingly awakened by Hakin shaking his shoulder—and dripping on his face. Startled, Morvash sat up and wiped his cheek.

"Your turn," Hakin said. He was leaning over Morvash, holding a very dim lantern. "It's raining."

"Raining?" Morvash said, not entirely awake yet.

"Yes. It started during Darissa's watch."

"But…" Morvash blinked, then rubbed his eyes. "So it's cloudy?"

"It generally is when it's been pissing down rain for several hours, yes."

"But then there's no moonlight; how can you see anything?"

"That's a very good question," Hakin said. "You *can't* see much. But once your eyes adjust you can make out shapes, and I doubt Tarker is making any attempt at stealth, so you should *hear* it coming. I hope."

"Hear it? In the rain?"

"Yes, I know. Not very cheering, I'm afraid. Do you maybe have a spell you could use to let you see in the dark?"

"No," Morvash said, sitting up in his borrowed bed. "If I'd thought of it sooner maybe I could have set up some kind of warning, but at this point I don't know if it's worth it, or whether I could manage it in the dark."

"You'll have the lantern," Hakin said, offering it.

Morvash accepted it. "But what…"

"Whatever you like," Hakin said. "It's up to you now, and I need some sleep." He waved over a shoulder, then vanished into the gloom as he headed for his assigned bed.

Morvash sighed, and set the lantern down. He had packed hurriedly back at Erdrik's house in Ethshar, not thinking to fetch a change of clothing or a decent coat, but he had brought a hat—not because he had been clever enough to prepare for inclement weather, but because it had been sitting there with some of his spell ingredients and he had thrown it in without thinking. Now he dug it out, straightened it up, and set it on his head. He looked at the magical supplies, ran quickly through the various warnings and protections he knew, then closed the bag up; nothing he could do safely in darkness and rain would be worth the trouble. He got up and headed for the door, almost tripping over Zerra's carpet on the way.

He could hear the rain even before he opened the door, and he knew it was not going to be pleasant walking up the street to their chosen vantage point—though at least the street was paved, and he wouldn't get his feet seriously muddy. Then he lifted the latch and swung the door inward.

Cold rain blew into his face and across his chest, and he stared out into nearly total blackness. With a sigh, he lifted the lantern and stepped out.

Hakin had not mentioned the wind, which was blowing steadily from the east. It was not a full gale, by any means, but it was enough to make his hat almost useless—in fact, he needed the hand that wasn't holding the lantern simply to keep the hat on his head. Taking a few seconds to close the door behind him meant catching the hat as it tilted precariously backward and tried to fall off.

The lantern was not really all that helpful; it mostly illuminated fat, shiny raindrops, rather than anything that would tell him where he was. Still, it was better than nothing, and once he turned north, rather than looking directly into the wind, the hat's brim kept the rain out of his eyes. He trudged up the street, dodging streams that ran down every joint and seam in the pavement, and finally arrived at his designated post. There the dragon's belly, hundreds of feet above him, provided a little shelter, though plenty of rain still blew in. He set down the lantern, then turned and stared into the darkness to the south, trying to make out the ridge.

He couldn't see a thing. He couldn't hear anything but the rain. He was wasting his time out here.

But rain and darkness would not stop a demon, and Tarker was coming. It could easily have already crossed the ridge. The best Morvash could do was hope to glimpse movement as it approached.

And given that he could not even make out the ridge, let alone something not much bigger than a man moving on it, staying where he was seemed ridiculous. Tarker would be coming from the south, and would presumably come straight up the path to the village, and then up the street to Pender's home, where Karitha was asleep on a blanket by the hearth. It would make far more sense, Morvash thought, to walk down to the southern edge of town, where Tarker would have to pass; then he could turn and run and hope he got to the house before the demon did.

Hakin had said Tarker was tired from having spent so long in the human world; it had not looked tired when it was pounding on Erdrik's protective spells. Morvash frowned. He remembered that the stone fence on the south slope of the ridge had some sort of magic on it to keep out trespassers; was that why Tarker had not already appeared? But given that the demon had eventually found its way into Erdrik's house despite all the protections, Morvash had no doubt that it could get across the barrier on the ridge in time. The carpet had flown over it easily, and Tarker might be able to leap it; if not, it could probably tunnel under it.

But it might be tired. He might be able to stay ahead of it long enough.

Down at the south end of the street he would not have the modest shelter provided by the dragon's body, but perhaps he could find a porch or overhang of some sort, or a shed door someone had left open.

This was not anything he had ever expected to be doing, he thought as he picked up the lantern. Standing guard in the rain to warn people about an approaching demon while waiting for the largest statue ever created to be brought to life—how had he wound up *here*? All he had ever wanted to do was to use his magic to help people. He had apprenticed to a wizard…well, mostly because apprenticing to a wizard and learning magic was about the most marvelous thing ever, and he had desperately wanted it and had begged his father to arrange it, but he had also wanted to help his family. He had thought that he would be able to use wizardry to help the family business.

At twelve, he had not given much thought to the fact that the family business involved selling supplies to both sides in an ongoing war. He had not thought about what that meant, had not realized that his father would want to use his wizardry as a weapon, and had not immediately realized that to do so might violate Guild rules. He had learned all those stupid curses when he never wanted to hurt anyone, when he would have preferred to learn love spells and scrying spells and the like—not that love spells were exactly harmless, but at twelve he had not thought about *that*, either.

His reluctance to hurt people, even indirectly, and his refusal to break Guild rules even for the sake of his family, had gotten him exiled to his uncle's estate, and he had thought of that as a new beginning, a chance to help Uncle Gror in his business—*Gror* wasn't smuggling weapons to the Tintallionese armies. He was a respectable merchant, dealing in a variety of luxury goods, not just in weapons. Yes, he provided the arms that Morvash's father and Uncle Kargan sold to the smugglers, but that was not technically illegal.

And then Morvash had found those statues in Lord Landessin's collection, and had tried to rescue all those poor people, and how did *that* get him *here*, standing in cold rain in the middle of the night, waiting for an enraged demon and a mountain-sized monster? A monster that a deranged wizard, a wizard Morvash had accidentally freed from imprisonment, apparently intended to use to wreak vengeance and destruction on his enemies, which seemed to include pretty much everyone Erdrik had ever dealt with.

That was not how it was supposed to work. Doing good things for people might not always turn out perfectly, but *this* was a disaster. It wasn't fair.

He glanced up at the blackness above that he knew was the dragon's belly, and wondered how Erdrik was doing up there. The huge stone ear would presumably provide some shelter from the rain, but the wind was blowing from the east, almost directly into that ear. Would the animation spell's aura keep out any of the wind and rain? Would the rain get into the cauldrons, and unbalance the ingredients, and disrupt the spell? Erdrik would have been at least three-fourths of the way through the process by the time the rain arrived, but that didn't mean the rain did not interfere.

Would the spell still work?

He wanted to ask Zerra what she thought; she was a far older and more experienced wizard than he was.

But waking her before her assigned watch would not be fair. She needed her sleep. She had been flying that carpet almost constantly for more than a sixnight, trying to do the right thing for Morvash and the Guild.

Of course, she was being paid, which he was not.

Morvash sighed, shook the water off his hat, then set it back on his head and started walking down to the south end of the street, rather than continuing to pretend he had any chance of seeing the southern ridge through the darkness and rain.

He was almost tempted to just keep walking, all the way home to Ethshar. He did not really need to be here. He had done his part—Karitha and Darissa and Marek were human again, Pender was safely back home, and Zerra had found Erdrik. The rest of it was not really his problem.

But it would take a month or so to walk the whole way, and it was raining, and he still wanted to help, even if he was not sure what he could or should be doing.

He reached the end of the pavement; the street continued another fifty yards or so from here, but he hesitated. He set the lantern down on the ground, to get a better look at the surface, and as he feared, he saw a mix of rocks and mud. He straightened up, leaving the lantern where it was, and stared into the darkness.

Now that the lantern was farther from his eyes, he realized he *could* see the southern ridge from here, just barely—a darker shade of black against the overhanging clouds. Making out an approaching figure still seemed unlikely, but perhaps not completely impossible.

He picked up the lantern, opened it, and blew out the flame. He could relight it easily enough with the Finger of Flame, but for now he thought he would do better to let his eyes adjust. Maybe this standing watch idea was not completely useless. He leaned forward, peering into the gloom—and the brim of his hat tipped, sending cold water down the back of his neck.

"Blood and death!" he hissed, as he snatched the hat from his head and shook it, before clapping it back in place. He straightened up and stared into the night.

He waited, and his eyes gradually grew more accustomed to the darkness. Extinguishing the lantern had made a real difference. He could make out the shape of the ridge, the gap where the trail came through—but not much more than that.

He leaned back against the wall of the nearest building, a small stone house, and stared.

Every so often the rain would lessen, and after what he estimated to be an hour or so it thinned to little more than a faint drizzle. His eyesight had adjusted as far as humanly possible, and he could still only see the outline of the ridge, none of the details—but then something changed. In places, black turned to deep dark gray; looking up, he could see dark, dark clouds, rather than an unbroken blanket of black.

The eastern sky, beyond the end of the valley, was lightening rapidly.

None of them had had any way to tell time, not with the skies overcast; apparently the earlier watchers had stayed at their post longer than necessary, so that the first faint glimmer of dawn was beginning while he was still on duty, before he woke Zerra to take the final nighttime shift.

That was good. He had not liked the idea of possibly facing Tarker in the dark. He did not like the idea of facing it *at all*, really, but the darkness made it worse. He turned his attention back to the south—and something moved. Something on top of the ridge was *moving*, something bigger than a man.

And it was moving toward him—there was just barely enough light now to see it racing down the ridge, into the valley below, coming straight toward Hindfoot Village.

"Gods!" Morvash said. He turned, leaving the unlit lantern where it was, and sprinted up the street, shouting, "It's here! It's coming!"

He burst into the house still shouting, and grabbed one end of the rolled-up carpet. "Zerra! Karitha! You need to get airborne!"

Neither woman emerged immediately, but Hakin staggered into the room. "It's Tarker?" he asked.

Morvash nodded. "If it had come a few minutes earlier I don't think I'd have seen it in the dark, but the sun is almost up. It's on its way across the valley. Go get Zerra!"

"You get her—you're a wizard. I'll get Karitha."

That did seem to make sense, so Morvash dropped the carpet so that it held the front door open, then dashed to the upstairs room where Zerra had been sleeping.

He found her awake, sitting on the edge of the bed and pulling on her shoes in the soft gray light of early dawn. "How close is it?" she asked.

"I don't know," he said. "I lost sight of it once it was across the ridge. It was moving fast, though."

"Where's Karitha?"

"Hakin is getting her."

"What about the others?"

"Still asleep, so far as I know. They don't need to go anywhere."

Zerra nodded and got to her feet. The two wizards hurried down the stairs, and a moment later they were hauling the carpet out into the street.

"It's wet," Zerra said, trying to maneuver the carpet onto the driest possible stretch of pavement.

"It rained," Morvash replied. "You're lucky it's stopped."

"This will do. Let's unroll it."

Together the two wizards spread the carpet on the street; when it was entirely unrolled Morvash set about smoothing the edges, trying to flatten it as much as possible. Zerra didn't bother; she sat in the middle and looked down the street.

"Gods, it's coming *fast*," she said. She muttered a word that was not Ethsharitic, and quite possibly not any human language, then spread her hands. "Where's Karitha?" she asked.

"Here she comes," Morvash said, as the demonologist came stumbling out the door, obviously still half asleep.

"Good!" Zerra said, and Morvash felt the carpet move beneath him.

Karitha tripped, and fell forward onto the carpet; Morvash pulled her the rest of the way on. Zerra did not wait for them to recover; the carpet rose straight up into the damp morning air, carrying the three of them.

Morvash had not actually intended to ride it; he had thought he would stay behind. It was too late to do anything about it now, though; they were already high enough that falling off might well be fatal, especially given the stone-paved streets.

And here was Tarker charging up the street, and Morvash could see Hakin standing in the doorway of Pender's house, and then the carpet was soaring up past the dragon's right wing, headed for the monster's head.

CHAPTER FORTY-ONE

MORVASH OF THE SHADOWS

4ᵀᴴ OF NEWFROST, YS 5238

The sun was just beginning to peek over the horizon, beneath the thinning clouds, as the carpet cleared the dragon's side and sailed above its long back. Zerra slowed their flight and sent the carpet into a gentle turn as they looked back down at the town far below.

Tarker was staring up at them from the street. Hakin had stepped out of the door and appeared to be talking to the demon.

"What's he doing?" Morvash asked.

"How should I know?" Zerra said.

"What do *we* do now?" Karitha asked.

"*You* order the demon to kill Erdrik, as soon as he finishes his spell," Zerra replied. "I talked to Ithinia again last night, and she wants him dead. He's angered the Guild once too often. When he's dead he won't be able to order the dragon to do anything terrible, and maybe we can bring it under control."

"But once Erdrik is dead, Tarker will come after me again!"

"It may take a little while, though," Zerra said. "He's a powerful wizard."

"Tarker's a powerful demon. Well, not compared to other demons, but compared to humans."

"We'll take you somewhere else, once Erdrik is dead," Zerra said. "Frankly, *you* aren't my problem; the Guild sent me to deal with Erdrik, not to save you from your own magic."

"But we have to protect her!" Morvash protested.

"*I* don't," Zerra retorted. "I don't know what sort of promises *you* made."

"I didn't... I mean, someone needs to help her!"

"Why?"

"Because she's a human being!"

"There are eight million human beings in the Hegemony of the Three Ethshars; I think we can spare one."

"Shut up!" Karitha burst out. "Just shut up, and tell me what to do!"

Neither wizard bothered to point out the contradiction.

"We don't want to do anything until Erdrik finishes his spell," Zerra said. "Disrupting it is too dangerous."

"If the rain didn't already disrupt it," Morvash said.

Zerra threw him an annoyed glance, then continued, "Once the spell is finished, tell your demon that its next target is Erdrik the Grim. You can do that, right?"

"I think so, yes."

"That's it; after that I'm done."

"But we'll figure out something," Morvash quickly added. "We won't just hand you over to Tarker." He looked over the edge of the carpet, to see where the demon was.

He did not see it. He saw Hakin looking up at him, though, and pointing to the northwest. Morvash frowned. What was Hakin trying to tell him?

Then he understood. "The demon is coming up the dragon's tail," he said. "The legs are too steep to climb with the ladders and scaffolding gone, and we're too high to jump, but the tail should be easy for it."

"Take us higher!" Karitha cried.

The carpet rose. "I don't want to go too far," Zerra said. "This could all work out. I want to lead the demon right to Erdrik before he has time to invoke his levitation spell."

"I can't tell Tarker to kill anyone if it kills me first!"

"Don't worry, I'll keep you out of its reach."

"Remember, it could jump to the roof of a three-story house with no trouble at all," Morvash reminded her.

"I know that!" Zerra replied angrily, but the carpet rose another twenty feet. She had rotated it so that the three of them were looking along the dragon's back, past its tremendous wings toward its tail. Morvash crept toward the leading edge and peered into the distance. The morning sun was behind him, which worked in his favor.

For several long minutes nothing happened save that the sky grew brighter and long shadows appeared, but then Morvash spotted something moving up the dragon's distant tail.

"I see it!" he called. "The demon is coming!"

At first Tarker was little more than a dark dot, but it was running toward them at an inhuman pace. It was not long until Morvash had to poke his head over the front of the carpet to keep it in sight.

It slowed, glaring up at them. "Karitha the Demonologist!" it bellowed. "I have fulfilled your command! Release me, or die!"

Karitha shuddered, cowering back from the carpet's edge. She took a deep breath, and Morvash thought she was steeling her nerve, getting ready to speak, when Zerra said, "Not yet! Wait until Erdrik's spell is complete!"

Tarker apparently heard that; it growled, gathered itself, and leapt upward. Morvash started back, but that turned out to be unnecessary; the demon fell about fifteen feet short of the carpet and plummeted back down to the scale-carved stone of the dragon's neck.

It got quickly to its feet, though, and looked around, taking in its surroundings. It considered the ridges where the wings joined the dragon's back, and the upward curve of the neck, and the top of the dragon's head...

"Take us higher," Morvash said. "And let's get a look at Erdrik and make sure he's still there."

He did not for an instant think Erdrik was *not* still there—he could feel the roiling magic gathered around the dragon, and knew the spell was almost complete—but he wanted to keep the carpet in motion, if only to give Tarker a moving target.

Zerra nodded, and the carpet rose another ten feet or so, swinging out to the side, flying around the left side of the dragon's head rather than over the top of its skull.

Morvash approved; if Tarker took another leap at them and missed again, it would plummet down into the ravine north of the dragon, rather than landing safely on the monster's back. He did not think that would do Tarker any harm, but it would need to make its way back up the dragon's tail again, which would delay any further conflict.

They were almost over the dragon's left ear, the very spot where Erdrik was working his spell, when there was a sudden sensation of release, and the magical tension in the air was gone. Morvash sat bolt upright, startled, but before he could do or say anything else, the gigantic stone dragon stirred. It stretched its immense wings for the first time, unfolding gigantic expanses of carved stone; Morvash guessed its total wingspan at somewhere between three and four *miles*. Wooden frameworks twisted and fell as the wings rose, freed from beneath them, and seconds later Morvash heard the massive timbers crashing onto the rocks below.

The wind from the wings' movement caught the carpet like a falling leaf in an autumn gust, and the magical conveyance went spinning away, its three passengers clinging desperately to the fabric. Zerra struggled to hold on while gesturing and calling a command, and after a moment she regained control, bringing the carpet back into level flight perhaps a hundred feet above, and almost as far north of, the dragon's left eye.

The dragon blinked, vast gray stone eyelids descending over gray stone eyes, and twitched its immense head. Its jaw moved, and it spoke, in a voice so deep that it was felt more than heard, a voice so loud that it shook the carpet and made Morvash's ears ache.

"*There is something in my ear,*" it said, in flawless, if old-fashioned, Ethsharitic.

Those first words were still echoing from the surrounding mountains when it added, "*It itches me.*" And it tilted its head and shook it to dislodge the irritation.

Erdrik had time to scream, and to shriek a word that activated his levitation spell just before he and his rug and his cauldrons and the rest hit the rocky ground, but that was not enough. The animated mountain lifted its left forefoot and stamped on the annoyance, stamped so hard the land itself shook.

The shriek was cut off abruptly. Morvash, Zerra, and Karitha stared down at the stone foot that was planted firmly on the wizard.

"*That's better,*" the dragon said. Then it turned its head, looking about curiously.

For a moment none of the three people on the carpet moved or spoke; then Karitha asked, "Is he dead?"

"Erdrik? I'd guess so," Zerra said. "He just had a bleeding *mountain* step on him."

"He didn't have his usual protective spells in place," Morvash said. "They would have been in the way while he was working the animation spell, and he didn't have time to restore them after it was done."

"Karitha the Demonologist!" Tarker roared. The voice that had seemed so deep and powerful before was little more than a squeak compared to the dragon's, but it was still loud enough to be heard. "Release me or die!" Morvash turned to see the demon standing on the dragon's neck, swaying as the stone moved beneath him.

"*Did someone speak?*" the dragon asked, twisting its head around.

"Why does it know Ethsharitic?" Karitha asked. "Shouldn't it speak Sardironese?"

"Because Ethsharitic was Erdrik's native tongue," Zerra explained.

Karitha glanced down at the dragon's left forefoot again, and she shuddered. "But he's dead," she said. Then the realization struck her. "He's *dead*," she said. "What do I do *now*? I can't order Tarker to kill a wizard who's already dead!"

"Well, it can't get at you up *here*," Zerra said.

"I can't stay up here forever!"

"I know," Zerra said. "I'll need to renew the spell on the carpet next year—it doesn't last forever."

"We'll starve to death long before that!" Karitha exclaimed. "We don't have any food or water."

"I do have a bloodstone I can activate," Zerra said, "but only the one."

Morvash doubted that Karitha understood the significance of a bloodstone; she had probably never heard of the Spell of Untiring Nourishment. What's more, when he looked around the carpet he did not see anything that might hold Zerra's magical supplies. "*Do* you have a bloodstone?" he asked. "It looks as if you left everything behind."

"What?" Zerra glanced back to where she had usually kept her baggage. "Oh, death," she said. "You're right. We were in such a hurry to get the carpet in the air I forgot."

"Well, I'm sure we'll figure something out," Morvash said. "Right now I think the dragon may be a bigger issue than food."

"*By the gods I charge you, speak louder!*" the dragon rumbled.

"I can scarce hear you! 'Tis like the buzzing of an insect."

And then it spotted the carpet.

Karitha moaned.

"What is this I see? Some wizard's toy, come to plague me?" The dragon stepped forward and bent its neck to the side get a better look at the carpet and its passengers, and Morvash heard a horrendous crunch as the houses and shops of Forefoot Village were crushed.

"Karitha the Demonologist!" Tarker called again.

"Who is that?" the dragon demanded. *"Is someone perched upon my neck?"*

Morvash cupped his hands around his mouth and shouted toward the dragon's ear as loudly as he could, "Yes! A demon is on your neck!"

"A demon, say you? How can this be?"

"It was summoned!" Morvash called—which was true, but not really very informative. And then an idea struck him, an obvious idea that he had somehow not hit upon until now. "Karitha," he said, "tell Tarker to kill the dragon!"

"What?" Karitha said.

"It *can't* be killed," Zerra protested. "It's immortal."

"*I* know that," Morvash said. "And *you* know that. But does *Tarker* know that? Does it even matter? It has to kill whatever it's ordered to kill, doesn't it? Anything alive, right?"

"That's right," Karitha said. "It *is*! That's right!" She straightened up, and told Zerra, "Take us closer, where it can hear me." Then she told Morvash, "Tell me if it's getting ready to jump."

"What are you saying, you gnats, you carpet-borne mites?" the dragon asked.

"Just a moment!" Morvash shouted, as Zerra turned the carpet in Tarker's direction. "There is something we must attend to!"

The dragon turned, its claws shredding earth and stone, trying to swing its head far enough around to see the back of its own neck.

"Karitha the Demonologist!" Tarker bellowed again.

"Yes!" Karitha shouted. "Can you hear me, Tarker?"

"I hear you, demonologist!" Tarker replied. "Release me or die!"

"I will do neither, for I have a third choice!" Karitha called back. "I am she who summoned you, Tarker the Unrelenting. I am she who bound you to my will."

"And I have done as you commanded, O Summoner! Wosten of the Red Robe is dead!"

"Indeed, but I have another charge to lay upon you!"

"*What are you two talking about?*" the dragon asked querulously.

"Before I release you, Tarker the Unrelenting, I, Karitha the Demonologist, by the power of the secret name I placed upon you, do hereby set you another task!" She pointed at the dragon's immense eye. "Kill this nameless dragon!"

"*WHAT?*" The dragon's question shook the entire area. Morvash heard rocks tumbling somewhere far below.

Tarker looked down at the stone beneath its feet. They were not close enough for Morvash to read the demon's expression clearly, but he did not think it looked at all happy.

"I have summoned and bound you, Tarker the Unrelenting, and now I set you a task within your rightful domain—kill the dragon!" Karitha's voice was stronger and more confident than Morvash had ever heard it before.

"I shall obey," Tarker replied. Then it turned and began making its way back toward the dragon's left wing.

"*What are you doing?*" the dragon demanded. "*Why would you kill me?*"

"Because you don't belong here!" Morvash called back. "Look at you! You're far too large for this world, and you have no purpose here. Even when you mean no harm, you smash everything in your path."

"*For that you would sentence me to death?*"

"Yes!" Morvash called back.

"Don't worry," Zerra called. "The spell that brought you to life made you immortal! You can't be killed!"

"*But this demon...*"

"It will try, and try," Morvash called, "but how can even a demon harm something as magnificent as you?"

Tarker had reached the joint where the wing met the dragon's back; now it joined two fists into one and brought them smashing down on the stone.

Nothing happened.

Tarker growled, and struck again.

"Let's get out of here," Morvash said. "They'll keep each other busy for years!"

"*I see it strike, and feel the blow as if it were a puff of air,*" the dragon said. "*There is no pain.*"

"You can't *feel* pain," Zerra called. "It's part of your nature, the nature of the spell that made you! Even if the demon somehow finds a way to smash you to pieces, it won't hurt!"

"*Truly? Then let it strike, and I will pay it no heed.*" The dragon swung its head back around to the east, gazing off into the distance.

"I *really* think we should go," Morvash said. "I don't want to be here if those two start thrashing around."

Zerra nodded, and the carpet began picking up speed, flying west.

"*But still, it was unkind, to bid this demon strike me down. Perhaps I should strike YOU down.*"

"Go, go go!" Morvash shouted.

Zerra did not argue, and sent the carpet soaring upward, high into the western sky, but as they rose Morvash looked back and saw the dragon turning, wings raised, clearly intending to pursue them.

CHAPTER FORTY-TWO

HAKIN OF THE HUNDRED-FOOT FIELD

4ᵀᴴ OF NEWFROST, YS 5238

Once he was sure Morvash had seen him, and had understood that Tarker was on its way to climb up the dragon's tail, Hakin allowed himself to relax a little. Matters were out of his hands. He went back into the house to make breakfast.

Darissa was already in the kitchen, though from her hair and generally rumpled appearance Hakin guessed she had only just gotten out of bed. Prince Marek appeared a moment later, and the three of them prepared the meal in mostly silent cooperation.

"The dragon should be coming to life soon, shouldn't it?" Marek asked, as they ate.

"Yes," Hakin said. "We should probably get out of here, in case it smashes the house."

"You're assuming the spell will work," Darissa said. "I've heard that wizards' magic fails more often than they want to admit, and with that rain last night Erdrik may just be sitting up there cursing."

"Or the dragon may come to life any minute," Marek said.

"Or it may come to life," Darissa acknowledged.

Hakin pushed his plate aside. "I think I..."

He did not finish his sentence, as a ferocious wind suddenly slammed against the house, and a deep shadow fell over every window. A tremendous clatter sounded somewhere nearby. The three all started; Hakin dropped his spoon and ran for the door.

He was struggling with the latch when a sound like nothing they had ever heard before, a rumble so deep and loud that he felt it in his belly more than in his ears, said, "*There is something in my ear.*"

"What was *that?*" Marek exclaimed.

"*It itches me,*" that impossible sound continued.

"The dragon's alive," Darissa said. "I was wrong."

Hakin got the door open and looked out, and up.

The dragon had spread its wings. The clatter had been the supporting timber framework crumbling away. A look to the east showed him that the monster had lifted its head, raising its neck from its supports, and one of the pillars had shattered and fallen, though the others still stood.

It was shaking its head, like a dog shaking off water.

"Get out of the house!" Hakin shouted to his companions. "Get out *now!*"

Then the dragon stamped its left foreleg; Hakin could not see why, or what that distant foot had landed on, but the ground shook slightly, even though the impact must have been at least a mile away.

"*That's better,*" the dragon said. After a single glance down at whatever it had stepped on, it raised its head and looked around.

Darissa and Marek joined Hakin on the street, staring up at the gigantic creature. The tremendous wing that curved above them was strangely beautiful, gray stone a shade darker than the gray skies, catching an orange glimmer of morning light.

Hakin heard a very faint and distant sound; he was fairly sure it was a voice, but he could not make out any words.

The dragon's long neck curved, and it looked back at itself. "*Did someone speak?*" it asked.

"I don't see the carpet," Darissa said. "Do you think they landed on its back?"

"Tarker was climbing up its tail," Hakin said. "Maybe it's what the dragon heard." He stared at the monster, trying to make out details and spot either Tarker or the flying carpet.

"*By the gods I charge you, speak louder!*" the dragon said. "*I can scarce hear you! 'Tis like the buzzing of an insect.*" It turned its head forward again, and seemed to notice something. "*What is this I see? Some wizard's toy, come to plague me?*"

With that, the dragon's immense legs began to flex, and Hakin spun and ran southward, down the street, away from the towering shape that gave Hindfoot Village its name. Marek and Darissa were close on his heels.

The hind foot only moved forty or fifty yards, grinding half a dozen buildings to rubble, but from the sound and a quick glimpse to his left Hakin guessed that Forefoot Village had been almost completely destroyed. He flung himself off the end of the pavement, onto the stony mud beyond, and found himself lying in the street with his nose inches away from an unlit lantern. Even as gigantic events were playing out behind him, he wondered who had left it there; it looked like the lantern that they had been using to keep watch the night before.

"*Who is that?*" the dragon roared. "*Is someone perched upon my neck?*"

Hakin turned and sat up, his tunic covered in mud.

"*A demon, say you?*" the dragon said. "*How can this be?*"

"Tarker's up there," Hakin said.

"Obviously," Darissa said.

"What about the others?" Marek asked.

"The 'wizard's toy' must be the flying carpet," Hakin said. "They're up there, too."

"*What are you saying, you gnats, you carpet-borne mites?*"

"See?" Hakin said.

The dragon moved, its mass shaking the earth as it shifted position. Another section of Hindfoot Village was smashed flat as its feet were repositioned.

"*What are you two talking about?*"

Hakin did not like the sound of that. He took another two steps down the street, away from the ruins and the monster. Darissa and Marek exchanged worried glances.

Then came the most tremendous roar yet, a single word that seemed to shake the entire World: "*WHAT?*"

"What's going on up there?" Marek asked.

Hakin thought he knew, but he did not reply; instead he muttered to himself, "That's almost clever."

"What is?" Darissa asked.

The dragon spoke again. "*What are you doing? Why would you kill me?*"

"Kill it?" Darissa asked. "*How?*"

"Tarker," Hakin said. "Karitha's told Tarker to kill it."

"But it can't!" Darissa said. "It's immortal!"

"It's more complicated than…" Hakin began, but the dragon's

voice interrupted him.

"For that you would sentence me to death?"

"I think it's getting angry," Marek said.

"Wouldn't you?" Darissa retorted.

"Of course I…"

"But this demon…"

Then the dragon jerked its head around to look at its own back again.

"Tarker's trying something," Hakin said.

"I see it strike, and feel the blow as if it were a puff of air. There is no pain."

"According to the wizards, it doesn't feel pain," Hakin said. "That's part of the animation spell."

"Truly? Then let it strike, and I will pay it no heed."

"I'd guess someone up there just told the dragon the same thing," Marek said.

"But still, it was unkind, to bid this demon strike me down. Perhaps I should strike YOU down." The dragon snapped at something, but Hakin was too far away to see whether it was Zerra's carpet or something else. Then it turned, and he was grateful to whatever gods might be responsible that it turned to its left, to the north side, rather than toward the three humans huddled on the street to the south.

But then he saw the tail sweeping around, smashing aside rocky outcroppings and large trees, and his gratitude vanished. "Look out!" he shrieked. He fell to the ground, and the monster's stone tail whipped over his head, passing through the houses around him as if they were so many soap bubbles; stone and wood exploded around him, and he flung his arms up to protect the back of his skull.

Something bounced painfully off his back, and then a great downrushing wind pressed him into the mud, and he was unsure whether he might have lost consciousness for a moment.

When he could move again he raised his head.

Darissa was standing unscathed amid the devastation, staring at the western sky; Marek lay on the ground by her feet.

Hindfoot Village was gone; only scattered wreckage remained. The dragon, too, was gone; where it had been Hakin saw only sky, and the distant crest of the next ridge to the north. He pulled his knees under him, then got slowly to his feet.

His back ached where whatever it was had struck him. He reached around and found a tender area larger than his spread hand could cover.

Marek, too, was stirring, and Darissa turned to help him up. "Don't put too much weight on your left leg," she told him. "That ankle is sprained. And you have a mild concussion, so don't try to move quickly. The rest is nothing, just scrapes and bumps." She pulled his left arm across her shoulders. Then she looked at Hakin. "That's a bad bruise on your back," she said, "but it's just a bruise."

"Why weren't *you* hit?" Hakin asked.

"I'm a witch," Darissa replied. "I may not bring statues to life, but I do have *some* magic." She looked at Marek, who seemed dazed. "I'll do what I can to heal you both, starting with his ankle—we may need to move quickly. But I hadn't finished breakfast, so my reserves are low."

"Where's the dragon?" Hakin asked.

Darissa pointed to the west.

Hakin looked in the direction she indicated, and saw the dragon flying, somewhat awkwardly, above distant mountains.

"How can something that size *fly?*" he asked.

"Magic," Darissa said. "Stupid wizards, messing around with things like that! *Look* at it!"

Hakin did not need to be told; he was staring at the monster. "Do you see our friends?" he asked.

Darissa shook her head. "No," she said, "but I haven't felt them die."

"*Would* you, at this distance?" Marek asked, the first words he had spoken since the dragon's tail had swept over them.

"Maybe not," she admitted.

Hakin was about to say something more when he caught himself. The dragon had wheeled around and was coming back.

Obviously, they wanted to stay well away from the monster, but which way to run? It was not coming in a straight line, but seemed to be wavering back and forth.

"***Get off me, foul demon!***" it said, as it swept nearer. It banked steeply, and Hakin could see a tiny figure clinging to one of the dragon's wings. The monster flapped fiercely, clearly trying to dislodge this pest.

"Tarker," Hakin said.

Its struggles were causing the dragon to lose altitude; it flapped ferociously, clawing its way upward again, and its momentum was carrying it closer and closer to the ruined villages.

Then it flipped over, and the demon lost its grip on the creature's wing, plummeting toward the ground—but the dragon lost control, and it, too, fell, struggling to right itself.

Hakin saw it falling, and tried to judge where it would land. The outstretched wing would cover a vast amount of territory…

Heading southeast seemed like the best idea. He turned and ran, calling over his shoulder, "Come on!"

Darissa and Marek followed, and the three of them plunged down the hillside, but they had gone scarcely a hundred feet when the dragon crashed to the earth.

The ground shook with the impact, knocking all three to the ground, but at least this time no debris flew at them, and they were well clear of the dragon.

In fact, they would have been fine where they started; Hakin had misjudged the monster's size. It had come down half a mile or so west of the remains of Hindfoot Village. Now, as they watched, it squirmed and then managed to roll over and get itself upright once again. It scanned the sky, but apparently found nothing.

"*Trouble me no more, fools!*" it roared. "*Send no more demons, or I shall crush them as I have crushed this one!*"

It straightened up, shook itself off, then marched eastward, the land shaking at its every step. Hakin and the others watched as it walked past, never so much as glancing in their direction.

"Where's it going?" Marek asked.

"The open plains to the east, I think," Darissa said. "Where it won't bump into things as much."

"Where did *Tarker* go?" Hakin asked. "And the others?"

"I don't know," Darissa said, turning to look to the west.

"Didn't it…well, *squash* the demon?" Marek asked.

"You can't squash a demon," Hakin said. "I don't think you can kill them at all. I read up on this during all those years I was Tarker's keeper. Sometimes there are ways to send them back to the Nethervoid, but that doesn't kill them, they just need to be summoned again. And Tarker was on an assigned task, I think, so it *can't* be sent away until its target is dead."

"But the dragon fell on it!" Marek said.

"That wouldn't kill it," Hakin replied. "From the demonology I studied, demons simply don't die."

"Maybe we should find it," Darissa said.

"I think we should," Hakin agreed, "but we need a few things first."

"We do?" Marek asked. "What sort of things?"

"Tools," Hakin said. "Stone-carving tools. Because I'm pretty sure Karitha ordered Tarker to kill the dragon, and even a demon can't smash that much stone with its bare hands, but with the right tools maybe it can do something."

"The workshop," Darissa said. "Where Zerra and Karitha slept."

"Exactly," Hakin said. "It's smashed flat, but the tools should still be buried in the wreckage."

"Come on, then," Darissa said.

As they walked back up the slope toward what had once been the center of town, Marek said, "I thought the spell made the dragon immortal."

"It did," Darissa said.

"Then even if the demon smashes it to bits, won't all the pieces still be alive?"

"Yes," Darissa said. "But that's better than a giant dragon rampaging around the countryside."

"Actually," Hakin said, "Zerra told me something. There may be a way to kill the pieces."

"Really?" Darissa turned to look at him.

"I'll tell Tarker," Hakin said. "Now let's find our demon, and some tools for it to use."

They found that due to its simple construction the workshop had more or less folded up, rather than being smashed and scattered; the three of them joined forces to lift up a section of one of the fallen walls, and Darissa then squeezed beneath it while the two men held it up. Hakin's arms trembled as he struggled with the weight, grateful that the workshop's builders had not bothered with a more substantial structure. Prince Marek, larger and stronger than he, did not seem to be having a much better time.

Darissa emerged a moment later dragging a massive sledgehammer in one hand, and an iron digging bar in the other. The instant she was clear Hakin and Marek released the wall and let it fall; it landed with a tremendous boom, landing inches from Darissa's feet. She let the tools fall, as well.

"Good!" Hakin said, picking up the hammer as soon as he was sure his still-shaking fingers could grip it securely. It was heavy; he was impressed that Darissa had been able to move it with one hand, but he guessed she had used her witchcraft to help. Marek took the digging bar, and the three of them stood for a moment.

"Which way?" Marek asked.

The dragon was off to the east now, wandering aimlessly, taking in its surroundings; they had last seen Tarker fall somewhere to the west. "It should be…" Hakin began. Then he thought he glimpsed movement. "*Hai!* Tarker! Here!" he shouted, waving a hand above his head.

The others turned, and saw a dark shape making its way through the rubble. They, too, began waving and calling.

"It doesn't know you two," Hakin said. "Maybe I should…"

"It's coming this way," Marek said.

Indeed, that dark shape was coming nearer, and they could now see that it was definitely Tarker—but it was not headed directly toward them. If it continued on its present course it would pass a hundred yards to the north of them. "Over here!" Hakin called, waving.

"You are not my concern," Tarker roared back.

"Yes, we are!" Hakin called. "We can help you kill the dragon!"

The demon hesitated. Hakin started toward it, picking his way through the ruins.

"You are no longer my concern," Tarker said, marching eastward once again.

Hakin took the sledge in both hands, and with an effort he hoisted it above his head as he jogged closer. "Yes, we are!" he called. "We have tools!"

Tarker stopped, and turned to look at the three humans.

"Stone-smashing tools!" Marek called.

"And information!" Hakin added.

Tarker started toward them.

A moment later the four met on a pile of stone that had once been someone's home. "Here," Marek said, handing Tarker the digging bar.

The demon accepted it. "I am a demon," it said uncertainly, hefting the bar in one of its four hands. "I do not need weapons."

"Against *that* thing?" Marek said. "I think even *you* can use these without shame."

Tarker looked at the dragon.

"And there's something else—you know the dragon is said to be immortal, don't you?" Hakin asked.

"Zerra the Ageless said this," Tarker acknowledged. "I do not know it to be true."

"Well, it sort of is, and sort of isn't," Hakin said. "Once something is brought to life by that spell, Ellran's Immortal Animation, it can't die by any ordinary means. Zerra explained it all to me. It's not indestructible, but even if you chop it into a million pieces, each piece will still be alive, and if you reassemble it they'll work together as if it were still a single creature."

"Then I will not allow it to be reassembled," Tarker growled.

"Yes! That's a good start," Hakin said, "but there's more. It's almost like a demon in some ways. You can't kill it with weapons, or magic, or any natural force, it doesn't need to eat or breathe, and it will never age or sicken, but there *is* a way it can die."

"There is?" Darissa said, startled. "I never heard of one."

"Well, Zerra *thinks* there is," Hakin admitted, "but no one has ever tried it."

"What is this method?" Tarker demanded.

"It's supposed to be a Wizards' Guild secret," Hakin explained, "but other people discovered it after the Empress Tabaea's reign, more than ten years ago, so Zerra didn't mind telling me when we were talking at dinner last night." He did not mention that she had been tipsy at the time. "There are three places in the World where wizardry *does not work*, and if you took the broken pieces of something brought to life with Ellran's Animation into one of those places, they would die, because the spell on them would stop working."

"I never heard anything about this," Darissa said.

"Well, one of the three didn't even exist when you were petrified," Hakin said.

"I don't understand," Marek said.

"There is a spell—I don't know what it's called or how it works, or who knows it, or much of anything about it—that makes a place dead to wizards' magic. Permanently. It sucks up all the magic in that place, forever."

"How can it do that?" Darissa asked.

"How should I know? But it does. I don't know whether it affects other magic, or just wizardry. It's completely forbidden; the Guild will kill anyone who attempts it. But it's been used three times. Once was when it was first discovered, early in the Great War, and I don't know who did it, or how, or why, or where; if anyone knows where that dead area is, I never heard about it, and Zerra swore she never had, either.

"The second place is a Guild secret, Zerra says. Some of them *do* know where it is, but Zerra isn't one of them. She's pretty sure it's a long way away, and hidden, and it's been there for centuries, but that's all she knows—or at least, that's what she told me. She's heard rumors it resulted from a feud between wizards, but she doesn't really know.

"But the *third* one, the newest one, is in the overlord's palace in Ethshar of the Sands. The magic they used to defeat Empress Tabaea went wrong, and they used this *other* spell to stop it, so now wizardry doesn't work in the middle of the Palace.

"If you drag pieces of the dragon there, they'll die."

"The middle of the overlord's palace in Ethshar of the Sands?" Darissa asked. "Are you mad?"

"That's what I heard," Hakin said. "We worked together for years, Tarker—we trusted each other. If you don't find a way to kill that thing you'll be trapped in the World for eternity, and I don't think that's right, so I'm telling you the only way I know that you can kill it. Chip it apart, and haul each piece to the palace in Ethshar of the Sands."

"That will still probably take a hundred years," Marek said. "Think of the size of that thing!"

"And Karitha will probably die of old age before it's finished," Darissa said.

"That does not concern me," Tarker said. "My task now is to kill the dragon. If this is how it must be done, then this is what I will do." It held out a hand. "Give me the hammer."

Hakin obliged.

"If you carve handholds, it won't be able to throw you off so easily," Marek suggested, stepping forward and offering the demon the iron bar.

"And if you break its wings, it won't be able to fly," Darissa added, as Tarker accepted this second implement.

"I understand," Tarker said. It turned and started eastward, but then it stopped again. It turned back, hesitating, as if struggling to say something.

The three humans waited, and at last the words came.

"Thank you, Hakin of the Hundred-Foot Field," Tarker said. "You have been a friend."

Then it turned, and began bounding eastward across the rubble-strewn surface that had once been the base of a mountain.

CHAPTER FORTY-THREE

MORVASH OF THE SHADOWS

4ᵀᴴ OF NEWFROST, YS 5238

"I don't know whether we can outfly it," Zerra said, as she sent the carpet into swooping curves over the forested slopes of the mountains below. The dragon was not far behind them, and gaining steadily despite her attempts to dodge.

"Don't try," Morvash said. "Go somewhere it can't—somewhere it won't fit."

"Right," Zerra said. "I should have thought of that. I'm not used to dealing with flying monsters." She sent the carpet into a dive so steep that Morvash feared he would fall forward, and a moment later they were swooping between huge pine trees, the rug's selvage rippling as it brushed against the trunks on either side. Then she veered left, tilting the carpet up on edge for an instant.

Morvash looked up through the tree branches and saw the dragon weaving back and forth, looking for them.

"I think you lost it," he said.

Zerra did not reply as she dove the carpet again, down into a narrow tree-lined ravine. She turned left again along a stream at the bottom, swerved to the right, and then brought the carpet to a halt so abrupt that the cross-legged Morvash and squatting Karitha tumbled over. Morvash caught himself against a tree limb and pushed himself back onto the carpet; Karitha slammed into a tree trunk and let out a cry of pain as she tumbled to the needle-covered ground below.

"Sorry," Zerra said, but she was looking up, not at her fallen companion. Morvash looked up as well, and realized why she had chosen this spot. They were underneath a stone overhang, behind a small waterfall, where the dragon would not easily find them, and where it could not possibly fit without smashing the ledge. It was only fifty or sixty feet between the overhang and the ground where Karitha lay; the dragon would be unable to squeeze even its immense head into such a space.

The limb that Morvash had caught was on a pine that had somehow managed to grow in this confined and shadowy space, but was stunted by the barrier above, its topmost branches twisted out of shape as they scraped against the stone; Karitha had bounced off the same tree's trunk.

Morvash slid off the carpet and made his way down to Karitha's side, moving carefully; the footing was treacherous, as the thick layer of pine needles was slippery and hid gaps in the stone beneath. When he reached her he knelt down and gave her a hand, helping her sit up.

She rubbed her head and asked, "Where are we?" Her breath was a faint puff of fog; the air around them was cool and damp.

"We're in a ravine in the mountains, somewhere west of the villages," Morvash told her.

Just then the daylight, not very bright to begin with, vanished for a moment; both of them looked up.

The dragon was flying overhead, but gave no sign it had seen them.

Then it moved on, and the light returned. Morvash thought the clouds above were thinning; the sky that had been mostly gray was now blue and white.

He turned his attention back to the demonologist. "Are you all right?" he asked.

"I think so," she said. She got slowly to her feet, discovering for herself how unstable the bed of needles could be but eventually standing upright. Together, the two of them climbed back up the stony slope toward the hovering carpet.

"I think it's giving up," Zerra said, as they drew near. "It turned back east."

"Good," Morvash replied.

"It's a good thing it doesn't breathe fire," Karitha said.

"Oh, it's not a *real* dragon," Zerra assured her. "It's just stone. A mountain brought to life."

"It's still a good thing," Karitha mumbled. She started climbing back onto the carpet, and as she did the dragon's voice echoed down the ravine.

"*Get off me, foul demon!*"

"Apparently Tarker's still holding on," Morvash remarked, as he gave Karitha a boost.

"That's impressive," Zerra said.

"I doubt it can keep it up forever," Morvash said.

"But...it has to kill the dragon!" Karitha said. "I ordered it to!"

"And it will keep trying," Morvash said, "but what can it do, really? It will chase the dragon forever, but they're both sleepless, undying creatures, and the dragon is huge and made of solid stone. I doubt Tarker will ever be able to kill it."

"But it'll keep trying," Zerra said, "which will keep them both busy."

Morvash hopped up onto the carpet, and the three of them arranged themselves near the center once again. "Now what?" he asked.

Just then there was a tremendous crash; the earth shook, and a shower of pine needles scattered across the carpet. The patter of the waterfall changed its rhythm for a moment before returning to its usual steady beat.

"What was *that*?" Karitha asked.

"I'd guess the dragon miscalculated and ran into something," Morvash said.

"Or maybe Tarker found a way to knock it out of the sky after all," Zerra suggested.

"Seems unlikely. More likely it was stamping on Tarker, trying to squash it the way it squashed Erdrik."

"Things weren't *that* loud when it squashed Erdrik," Zerra objected.

"Tarker is bigger and tougher."

Then the dragon's voice spoke again. "*Trouble me no more, fools! Send no more demons, or I shall crush them as I have crushed this one!*"

"All right, maybe it stepped on Tarker," Zerra acknowledged. "But it still seemed too loud for that."

"Do you think it really crushed Tarker?" Karitha asked.

"You're the demonologist," Zerra answered. "You tell us."

"I don't think it could have," Karitha said. "But it could have trapped it—driven it into the stone, maybe."

For a moment the three of them sat listening, but all Morvash heard was the drumming of the waterfall, and the wind whistling through the pines.

"Now what?" he asked again.

No one replied, and after a moment he said, "Really, what should we do now? We don't have any food or other supplies—we left them in Pender's house, which is probably smashed to bits by now. We can't stay here indefinitely."

"We have to go back for the others," Karitha said.

"No, we don't," Zerra said. "We can go back to Ethshar and leave them to fend for themselves. I've done what the Guild sent me to do, and I want to go home."

"You can't just leave them!" Karitha protested.

"Yes, I can," Zerra said.

"But you won't," Morvash said. "Because you're a better person than that, and besides, you want to find out what's going on with that mysterious person looking for Marek and Darissa."

"I do?"

"Yes, you do."

Zerra sighed. "*You* obviously want to find that out," she said. "Will you pay me to fly you to Melitha?"

"I don't have any money with me."

"I can wait. Shall we say, five rounds of silver within a year?"

That was more money than Morvash expected to net in half a year, even given that he had finished his statue-rescuing project and could now get serious about earning his keep; he was just a journeyman with no reputation. "Shall we say we'll negotiate a price after we talk to Prince Marek?"

"He *is* a prince, isn't he? All right, we'll go see if any of the others are still alive, and go from there. If that's all right with the demonologist."

Karitha nodded vigorously. "It's fine!" she said.

Zerra raised a hand, and the carpet moved slowly out from under the ledge; all three of its occupants eyed the sky nervously, but there was no sign of the dragon.

Cautiously, Zerra took the carpet up above the trees, then up the side of the ravine. Taking her bearings from the sun she turned east, across a mountaintop, skimming just a few feet above the pines.

Looking at the bright spot in the clouds where the sun should be, Morvash was startled to realize it was still only mid-morning; the dragon had been alive for no more than an hour or two.

It was not long before they spotted the dragon strolling eastward onto the barren plain. "I wonder where it's going?" Karitha said.

"Probably nowhere in particular," Zerra said, as she kept the carpet moving east just above the trees. "It has no purpose, no goal—at least, not if it's like most of the other Ellran's animations I've seen. If you mix the spell right you can make them obedient, but if Erdrik intended to do that it obviously didn't work. A different mix makes them playful, or loving, but I don't think that happened, either."

"I think the rain may have diluted something," Morvash suggested.

"That could be it," Zerra said. "Or maybe the size of it dispersed the magic."

"The first thing it ever experienced was someone tickling its ear," Karitha said. "And right after that, everyone else agreed it should be killed. You can't expect it to feel especially loving after that!"

"I'm just glad it hasn't decided to stamp out the entire human race," Morvash said.

"Yet," Zerra answered. "Or maybe it thinks all our cities are to the east, for some reason."

"Maybe it will keep going until it falls off the edge of the World," Karitha said.

"The poisonous air wouldn't bother it," Zerra said. "It could just fly back."

"Or maybe it went that way because there's flat ground to walk on, and when it gets bored it will come back," Morvash said.

"Maybe," Zerra acknowledged.

Then they were out of the pines, into the cleared land that had once surrounded the gigantic carving, and Zerra took them down lower, trying to stay below the dragon's line of sight. The ruins of Hindfoot Village lay ahead, and she directed the carpet toward them.

They were still perhaps half a mile away when Karitha pointed. "There!" she said.

"I see them."

A moment later they glided up beside the trio, who had seen their approach and stood waiting.

"It's good to see you!" Morvash called. "I was afraid you might have been stepped on."

"We almost got hit by its tail," Hakin said. "I have the worst bruise of my life on my back. But we're all right."

"Good," Zerra said. "Climb aboard, and we'll get out of here before it comes back."

"Wait a minute," Morvash said. "Shouldn't we see if we can find your luggage, or other things we want to keep?"

Zerra hesitated.

"Pender's house was over there," Hakin said, pointing.

"Oh, all right," Zerra said. "Some of my things might be hard to replace."

"Climb on," Morvash said, holding out a hand. "No reason to risk tripping over something."

"Thank you," Marek said, as he climbed onto the carpet. As soon as he was aboard he turned to help Darissa.

Hakin managed without assistance, his bruise notwithstanding.

A moment later five of them were picking through the wreckage of Pender's family home. Morvash found it deeply saddening to see familiar objects smashed and scattered, but at least, he told himself, everyone had gotten out safely.

As they picked through the rubble Karitha asked Hakin, "Did you see what happened to Tarker?"

"Oh, we meant to tell you about that," Hakin replied. "That's why we were up by the workshop. We gave it some tools to use against the dragon, a sledgehammer and a…a mining drill, maybe? I'm not sure what it's called. And I told it something Zerra had said that might be a way to kill the pieces after the dragon's broken up."

Morvash turned to look at Zerra. "I thought you said there *wasn't* any way."

"Well, I'm not sure whether there is or not," she replied. "And if there is, it doesn't seem very practical."

"What is it?"

"Have you heard about the Palace in Ethshar of the Sands?"

"Oh." Morvash did not need any further explanation; his master had told him about that particular fiasco midway through his apprenticeship, when once more drumming the dangerous and unpredictable nature of wizardry into his head.

"I didn't think dragging something that big into the middle of a city was practical," Zerra explained.

"Well, not all at *once*," Hakin said. "But Tarker can break pieces off and take them there. It'll take years, but eventually he should be able to kill it."

"That's pretty clever," Morvash said. "That, and the tools."

"Found it!" Zerra said, pulling her familiar bundle out from beneath the remains of a bed canopy. She tossed it onto the carpet, then said, "We can go any time, so far as I'm concerned."

Morvash had gathered some useful kitchen items, and found his own much smaller pack. "I'm all set," he said.

Karitha had never even gotten off the carpet. "Me, too," she said.

Darissa had found a sack somewhere and collected several items, though Morvash did not know what they were; now she took a look around, and said, "Was there anything in particular anyone wanted? Witchcraft is good at finding things."

Hakin shook his head. "I'm not a thief," he said, "and I have everything I brought. Not that I had much to begin with."

"I'm fine," Marek said.

With that, everyone clambered aboard. The added people and baggage made the carpet more crowded than Morvash liked, but it wasn't any worse than when they had flown up the river from Ethshar.

"Should we find Pender, and let him know we're leaving?" Hakin asked.

"I think he can figure..." Morvash began.

"*What have you done, you unbearable pest?*" The words roared down on them without warning.

"I think we should go," Hakin said. "Right now."

"Absolutely," Zerra said. "Everyone secure?"

"At least we know Tarker got to the dragon," Darissa said, as the carpet began rising.

They were halfway across the valley when Marek asked, "Where are we going? Back to Ethshar?"

"Actually," Morvash said, "we're bound for Melitha. You may need to help Zerra find it."

"Oh," Marek said.

Darissa added, "Thank you."

"Ithinia told me that someone named Hinda is queen there now," Zerra said, as the carpet picked up speed. "She didn't know much more."

Then they were topping the southern ridge, and Morvash could see the dragon taking to the air, far to the east, so distant it looked not so very much larger than an ordinary dragon.

He hoped Tarker could hold on this time.

CHAPTER FORTY-FOUR

DARISSA THE WITCH'S APPRENTICE

8ᵀᴴ OF NEWFROST, YS 5238

The journey to Melitha took four days—as Zerra had promised, they were able to make much better speed when they didn't need to follow any roads. The first day took them over the mountains to Aldagmor, where they eventually found an inn; the second brought them to a farmhouse near the River somewhere in the heartland of the Hegemony of the Three Ethshars, where they were relieved to once again have hosts who spoke Ethsharitic.

The third day took them to the famous Inn at the Bridge, where Zerra greeted the innkeeper, a man called Valder, as if he was an old friend.

And the fourth took them east into the Small Kingdoms, where Marek assisted with navigation, and they spotted the tower of Melitha Castle just as the sun was setting. It rose high above the surrounding countryside, on that odd lonely hill, catching the golden light of late afternoon.

"At least it's all still there," Marek said. "After so long I wasn't sure it would be."

"Of course it is," Darissa said. "It's been there for hundreds of years!"

"Well...over a hundred, anyway," Marek admitted. "But you know, it's been a long time, and if Hinda is queen, rather than my father or Evreth or Evreth's son, then there's probably been trouble. I thought Melitha might have been conquered at some point, and the castle torn down."

"That's the right one, then?" Zerra asked.

Marek nodded.

"But you didn't expect this Hinda to be in charge?"

"No, we didn't."

"You don't know who she is?"

"Oh, of course we do!" Marek replied. "She's my sister. But she wasn't the next in line; we had an older brother."

"You think there's been trouble?"

"I do."

"Then maybe we shouldn't just fly right into the courtyard—it will be getting dark by the time we get there."

"Maybe we shouldn't," Marek agreed. "But where else can we go?"

"Aren't there any inns?"

"I would be recognized..." Marek stopped.

"It's been forty years."

"You're right. I wouldn't be."

"He might be, if there's someone old enough," Darissa said. "But instead of going to the castle, maybe we could see if my master is still alive."

"Your master?"

"I was still an apprentice. His name was Nondel of the Oaks, and he would be... I'm not sure. Old, but not *that* old."

"I suppose it can't hurt to look," Zerra said. "Where did he live?"

"In the capital, but down the western slope, at the edge of town, not right by the castle."

"Point the way."

"Excuse me," Morvash said, "but won't we draw attention flying in? I doubt they see many flying carpets around here."

"That's true," Marek said. "In fact, take a look—even when we're all the way up here, people are pointing."

Morvash leaned over one side, Darissa over the other. "He's right," Morvash said.

Zerra sighed. "So should we land, and walk?"

"I'd say so, yes," Marek replied.

"There's a little grove over there," Darissa said, pointing.

"Someone might see us land," Hakin said. "I mean, if they see a flying carpet go into the grove, and a bunch of people walk out..."

"I don't actually see why anyone needs to stay here at all," Zerra said. "I could just drop Marek and Darissa off, and then the rest of us could head home."

Hakin and Morvash exchanged glances.

"You're right," Darissa said. "There's no reason to keep you here. We can take care of ourselves."

She could sense that Marek was perhaps not as certain as she was, but he said, "Of course. We'll be fine."

"But we haven't paid you," Darissa said.

"And is the money right on hand?"

"Well, no."

"Then I can come back for my pay later, when you've settled back in."

Darissa and Marek exchanged glances. "I would be fine with that," Marek said.

"I wouldn't feel right about it," Morvash said. "After all, someone was *looking* for you."

"And he's probably back in Ethshar," Darissa said. "Or on his way to Tazmor."

"Ithinia said he wasn't an assassin," Zerra remarked.

"She did? When? Who *is* he, then?"

"Oh, she didn't tell me that. I don't think she knew. But she used Fendel's Divination, and it said the man wasn't an assassin."

"You might have mentioned this sooner," Darissa said.

"I didn't think of it," Zerra replied.

"Still, I'd feel better if I could be sure you'll be all right," Morvash insisted. Darissa could sense that he meant it—but his main reason for arguing was that he was intensely curious about what had happened to them, who was looking for them, and what would happen next.

She did not blame him; *she* certainly wanted answers to all those questions.

"I'll check in on them with the Spell of Invaded Dreams once we're safely back home," Zerra said. "Will that satisfy you?"

Reluctantly, Morvash said, "All right." Darissa reached out to him with her witchcraft and tried to soothe his disappointment a little.

Zerra had not waited until the matter was settled; they were already dropping down toward the grove Darissa had noticed. A moment later the carpet slid between two of the trees and came to a hovering stop about two feet off the ground. Darissa hopped off, then helped Marek down—she had long since healed his ankle, but sprains could be tricky, and she did not entirely trust it yet. She was also unsure whether there might still be lingering after-effects from the blow to his head, though she had not sensed any.

They had scarcely straightened up when the carpet reversed direction. "Good luck!" Zerra called, as she turned the carpet around.

"Be careful!" Morvash added.

"Goodbye," Karitha said.

Hakin waved, but said nothing.

And then the carpet was soaring upward and westward, back toward Ethshar, and they were on their own.

"Come on," Darissa said, and led the way out of the grove toward a nearby road.

They had no possessions but the clothes on their backs, which were largely the same garments they had acquired in that first village on the way to Tazmor; anything else they had picked up, not that there had ever been much, had been lost in the ruins of Hindfoot Village. Darissa hoped they would not stand out too much; their coats and tunics were not styled like the Melithan garments she remembered, but she was unsure how much of that was because the clothes were foreign, and how much was because they were forty years in the future. They might well blend in perfectly, if the difference was due to time rather than distance.

They had no money, and no one would recognize them, but she was still a witch, which had been enough to support her in Ethshar and Sardiron and Tazmor. When they had last been in Melitha Marek would have been recognized as a prince and given whatever he asked for, but after so long an absence, and wearing these strange clothes, Darissa doubted anyone would believe him if he claimed to be royalty. That left her magic as their only resource beyond simply being human.

At least it was not difficult to find their way; the castle dominated the landscape, and even as the sky darkened Darissa could see lights in the lower levels of the central tower, so that it would be easy to see even by night.

She saw farmers working in the fields, or carrying their tools home for the night, but no one else was on the road this late. She considered the direction of the sun and the route to the castle, and concluded that they were on the road from Trafoa.

She had been to Trafoa once, when she was a girl of twelve, and her family farm was in this general area, but she did not remember any grove along that highway like the one where Zerra had dropped them off. In fact, she did not remember such a grove anywhere. It must have grown up while she was a statue.

That was a disturbing thought, reminding her how long she had been gone. Would *anyone* in Melitha remember her? Would she recognize anyone?

The next farmhouse they passed looked vaguely familiar, though the roof was sagging more than she remembered and a shed had been added to one side. That was slightly comforting—like the castle, it showed her that *some* things from her time remained.

"Do you recognize anything?" she asked Marek.

"Just the castle," he said.

They reached the outskirts of town as the dusk was fading, but candles and lanterns shone in several windows, dimly illuminating the streets. And although there were many differences, shops and houses added or removed or enlarged, this was still the town she remembered, with the streets in the same places. She turned and headed for her master's house, which had been her home for more than five years—years that seemed both recent and impossibly long ago. It was not on the Trafoa road, but on the next street to the north.

There were a few people about, but none of them so much as glanced at the travelers—a behavior Darissa subtly and magically encouraged. The clothes she saw around them were not exactly like the sort that had been commonplace when Darissa was last in Melitha, but they were not like the ones she and Marek wore, either. Her pleasantly-warm sheepskin coat was seriously out of place.

The tavern on the corner had been expanded, an upper story added, and the signboard—also an addition—said it was an inn now, called the Oaken Table. That might be convenient if any of those Ethsharites ever came to visit; she could hardly expect her master to accept guests on behalf of a wayward apprentice. Lanterns hung on either side of the front door, and on the street corner.

"It is not quite as it was, is it?" Marek asked.

"Not quite, no," Darissa said.

They rounded the corner and started back down the slope toward

Nondel's house.

The big oak was still there, but different—it had lost several limbs and did not look healthy, but was even bigger, its topmost limbs lost in the darkening sky. Its roots had pressed up out of the ground, and the front walk of Nondel's home—if it was still Nondel's home—had been re-routed to avoid them.

Darissa slowed as she approached the front door. It had been re-painted, probably more than once. The shutters on the windows had been replaced, and of course the roof had been re-thatched, but it was the same house.

Did it have the same owner? Would Nondel answer her knock, or some stranger? She hesitated.

"We'll need to know sooner or later," Marek said, guessing her thoughts.

Darissa took a deep breath, then nodded and stepped up to the door. She rapped firmly on the wood.

For a brief moment there was no response, but then she sensed life and movement on the other side. "Someone's coming," she said, but her heart sank. It did not feel like Nondel.

The door opened, and a young man looked out. "Can I help you?" he asked.

"I don't know," Darissa said, staring at him.

Marek took charge. He stepped forward, hand out. "My name is Marek Terren's son," he said. "My friend here was looking for Nondel of the Oaks—does he still live here?"

The stranger took the offered hand, then said, "Yes, he does, but I'm afraid he's too ill to come to the door. May I ask why you wanted to see him?"

Darissa felt a rush of conflicting emotions—her master was still alive, but seriously ill. She reached out with her magical perceptions, and sensed his presence in his own bedroom, where he had always slept.

"I was his apprentice," she said.

The young man frowned. "I doubt that," he said. "*I* was his last apprentice, and I remember the one before me—her name was Luralla—and you don't look old enough…"

Darissa looked him in the eye. "You're a witch? Then you can see I'm telling the truth. I was his apprentice."

"I don't…"

"We're older than we appear," Marek said. "There were wizards involved."

The young man looked at Marek, then dropped his gaze to Darissa again. "Darissa?" he asked.

She nodded.

"By the gods! I heard the stories, but I never thought… That was years before I was born! Come in! Come in!" He swung the door open. Then his eyes widened. "And…you're Marek? *Prince* Marek?"

"It would seem that we are not as forgotten as we thought we might be," Marek said.

"But your clothes—you look like Northerners!"

"We have just come from Tazmor, in the Baronies of Sardiron," Darissa said. "May I see him?" She gestured toward Nondel's room.

"Yes, of course!" He followed as Darissa headed across the main room. "I'm Lador. I'm a journeyman, but I've stayed on to take care of him."

Darissa opened the bedroom door and peered in.

The frail old man in the bed did not look like the Nondel she remembered; he was lying on his back, eyes closed, breathing loudly. His hair and beard were as white and thin as seeding dandelion heads. She approached him, and at the sound of her footsteps his eyes opened.

Behind her, she heard Marek ask Lador, "I'm told my sister Hinda is queen. Then my father is dead?"

Startled, Lador said, "Old King Terren? He's been gone for more than thirty years! You hadn't heard? He died of a fever. Queen Hinda has reigned ever since."

Darissa's mouth tightened at Lador's insensitivity. That was no way to tell a man his father was dead! How had Lador ever made journeyman with no better feeling than that?

She heard Marek start to ask what had happened to Evreth, but then the man on the bed said, "Darissa?" While the voice was thin and weak, it was Nondel's, and she forgot about Lador and Marek.

"Yes, master," she said. "I'm back."

"It's been so long. What happened?"

"We were turned to stone. We don't know who did it, or why; we've come to find that out."

"Stone?"

"That's right. A wizard named Morvash of the Shadows turned us back. But what happened to *you*?"

"I'm old, that's all."

"You aren't *that* old, are you? You were a witch, able to heal yourself!"

"I am probably older than you thought; I kept my appearance young. Vanity. And I only healed myself when I noticed that something needed healing, which was not enough." He turned his head to look at her. "*You* still look young."

"I did not age while I was made of marble, master."

"I'm glad. And I'm glad you have returned; I always wondered what happened to you. I thought you must be dead."

"I'm alive and well, master. Is there anything I can do for you?"

He managed to raise a hand and wave a gentle dismissal. "No, no. Take care of yourself."

Darissa bowed, and stepped back. She hated seeing Nondel like this, but there was nothing she could do; witchcraft could slow aging, but not reverse it. After a moment's further hesitation, she turned and left the room.

Lador and Marek had been speaking quietly; after their first exchange Darissa had not listened, though she thought she had heard that the country was at peace at the moment. She had assumed that, from the lack of visible soldiers, guards, and fortifications, but it was reassuring to have it confirmed. Now Marek said, "We'll stay here tonight, and go to the castle in the morning."

Darissa nodded. "All right," she said.

The only extra bed was the cot where sick visitors could rest while healing; Darissa remembered delivering poor Alasha's dead baby there. It was small, but so was she; she and Marek were able to squeeze onto it in reasonable comfort.

She half-expected to see Zerra in her dreams, but she did not; if she dreamt at all, she retained no memory of it.

Darissa had not realized how tired she was, but the sun was well up the sky behind the castle when she finally awoke and looked out the kitchen window. Marek had managed to arise without waking her, and together he and Lador had cooked sausages for breakfast; Darissa thought the mouth-watering smell might have been what woke her.

As they ate, she asked Marek, "Do we have a plan for how we want to approach this?"

"No," he said. "We will go to the castle, and if I am not recognized I will request an audience with the queen. Since she's my own sister, I expect *she* will recognize me even after so long an absence, and we will see what develops."

Darissa nodded, and reached for another sausage.

When they were done Darissa took the time to wash her face, brush her hair, and generally do everything she could for her appearance. Ordinarily she didn't worry about such things, since witches were expected to be a little disheveled and unconcerned with their looks, but they were going to talk to a queen, and she wanted to make the best impression she could, especially since the conversation might well cover her relationship with the queen's own brother.

She could feel Marek getting impatient, but he did not say a word; he understood her concerns. When at last she deemed herself ready to go he started for the door, but she held up a hand. "One more thing," she said.

"What?" Marek turned.

Darissa held up a hand, then went to Nondel's bedroom. She slipped quietly inside, where she found the old man asleep. She crept up, kissed him lightly on the forehead, and said, "Goodbye, Master. Thank you."

Then she followed Marek out the front door, and up the street toward the castle.

CHAPTER FORTY-FIVE

MORVASH OF THE SHADOWS

9ᵀᴴ OF NEWFROST, YS 5238

Morvash had dozed off somewhere over the western Small Kingdoms, but he awoke with a start when Zerra announced, "We're here!" He sat up.

The carpet was carrying them slowly up a street in Ethshar, at roughly the level of the second floor, and the street lamps at every corner gave enough light for Morvash to recognize it as Canal Avenue, in the New City district. In fact, even before he saw the wrought-iron dragons on the gates, he knew they were approaching his uncle's home.

Zerra did not bother with the gates, but sent the carpet over the walls into the forecourt and then let it settle to the pavement at the foot of the front steps.

"Go on," she said, gesturing to Morvash.

It took him a second to realize what she meant, but then he rose, took a moment to stretch legs stiff from sitting cross-legged for so long, picked up his bag, then walked up the steps and pulled the bell-rope.

Behind him, Hakin and Karitha also rose. "Is this where we're staying?" Karitha asked.

"Yes," Zerra said. "Off the carpet." She brushed at Hakin's calves.

Startled, Hakin stepped off the carpet onto the bricks of the front drive. Karitha, too, stumbled off.

Then, without further warning, Zerra sent the carpet upward. "Good night, and good luck!" she said, as she rose into the night sky.

The three watched as the carpet ascended to fifteen or twenty feet up, then turned and zoomed away into the night sky.

When she was gone Morvash snapped his mouth shut, yanked at the bell-rope again, and knocked loudly on the front door.

Nothing happened for a moment, and he was about to knock again and maybe start shouting, despite the lateness of the hour, when the door finally opened a crack. "Who is it?"

"Morvash," Morvash replied. "I'm back."

"At this hour? Do you want me to wake your uncle?"

"No, of course not! I just want you to let me in—I don't have my key."

The door opened a little further, enough for the man inside to peer out; Morvash recognized him as Karn, the senior footman. Morvash repositioned himself to provide a decent view of his face; there wasn't enough light for a *good* view.

Once the doorman had satisfied himself that the person outside was indeed his master's nephew he opened the door further.

Morvash promptly stepped up and held it while beckoning to Karitha and Hakin. "Get inside, you two."

"Sir, I don't—" the footman began.

"I take full responsibility," Morvash said, following them into the house and closing the door behind him. "These two are friends of mine. Find beds for them, and make sure that Uncle Gror is informed promptly, once he's awake, that he has guests." He remembered the other former statues, and added, "Or perhaps I should say *more* guests; I assume some of the last batch are still here."

"About half of them," Karn said. "But we still have enough room for this pair."

"Separate beds, please, if that's possible. And is my old room available?"

"Of course, sir! Your uncle had expected you back before this and kept it open. But it may need some attention; could you wait here for just a moment while I wake the housekeeper?"

"What time is it?"

"I'm not entirely certain, sir, but it's definitely after midnight."

"I *am* sorry to get you up like this!"

"I'll fetch the housekeeper." The footman turned and hurried away, leaving the three travelers in the foyer.

"I thought we'd be going back to that *other* house," Hakin said.

Morvash blinked. "I'm not sure why we didn't," he said. "But I don't know whether I have the key for *that* one, either, since we went out a window. Besides, there's more room here, and helpful staff, even if it's half full of other formerly petrified people."

"It's big," Karitha said, looking around at the foyer. Most of the lamps were dark, but the footman had left a single lit candle on a small table; it gave just enough light to soften the shadows on all sides. The numerous sculptures cast shifting, distorted shadows, giving the entire place an eerie feel.

"It is," Morvash agreed. "You were here before, you know, but you were made of stone at the time. You were in one of the rooms upstairs, at the foot of my bed. You were what convinced me Lord Landessin's statuary collection wasn't all just sculpture."

Karitha shuddered.

"Your uncle owns this?" Hakin asked.

"He rents it."

"What does he do for a living, to afford a place like this?"

"He's a merchant. My whole family is merchants of one sort or another, except for me. My parents thought it might be useful to have a magician in the family."

"He must be pretty good at it."

Morvash turned up a palm. "He's the family's success story, where I'm the failure."

"What does he sell?"

Morvash hesitated, then said, "Luxury goods." Then his conscience got the better of him, and he admitted, "And he deals in weapons. That's most of what he sells, really. That's what my father's side of the family sells. Uncle Gror gathers in weapons from the Small Kingdoms and Sardiron, then ships them on to my father and Uncle Kargan. But he also sells whatever the richest people in Ethshar might want—whatever they might be looking for, my uncle will find it for them. He inherited the business from my grandfather, who modeled himself on the people who supply wizards, but for people who *aren't* magicians, just rich. The weapons came along later, when my parents got married, and turned out to be a steadier income."

"Interesting," Hakin said.

A light reappeared; Karn was returning. He beckoned to Karitha and Hakin. "This way, please, and I will show you to your rooms.

Morvash, sir, I assume you remember yours?"

"I do, thank you."

"The housekeeper is on her way there right now, to make up the bed, and she'll do the same for your guests as soon as she's done with yours."

Morvash nodded. "Perfect," he said. "Please do make sure my uncle knows we're here, and that we want to speak with him when it's convenient. Feel free to wake me, should he ask you to."

"Of course, sir." The footman gave a final bow, then raised his candle and led the others into the unlit passages beyond.

Morvash took the candle from the table to light his own way to bed. As promised, he found the housekeeper just straightening the last pillow. He thanked her, and the moment the bedroom door closed behind her he fell onto the bed, still dressed, and fell asleep.

He woke gradually, vaguely aware of sunlight pouring in the windows and footsteps in the corridor. He took his time about getting up. Most of his clothes had been transferred to the late Erdrik's house, but he had left one of his better robes here in case he needed to impress one of Uncle Gror's clients; now he pulled it on, along with a pair of black slippers, and headed downstairs.

A footman, not Karn from the previous night but one whose name Morvash did not remember, met him at the foot of the steps and informed him, "Your uncle is waiting, sir."

"Lead the way," Morvash said.

Gror was just finishing his breakfast; he gestured for Morvash to join him. Morvash was glad to oblige; he took a seat at the table and was delighted to see a plate of cakes and sliced ham appear before him.

Gror dabbed his mouth with a napkin, then said, "You'll have to tell me all about it. Do you have time, or will you be rushing off again?"

"I have time," Morvash said. "I'm all done with my adventures. There are still a few loose ends, such as finding places for all your house guests, but I've finished my experiments and rescues."

"Speaking of guests, I understand you've brought me two more."

"I have," Morvash confirmed. "Karitha the Demonologist was that black granite statue in my bedroom, and Hakin of the Hundred-Foot Field was the keeper of that demon that tried to knock down the house on Old East Avenue."

"He wasn't a statue, though?"

"No."

"Does he have a home somewhere, then? Or does he still live in the field?"

"I don't really know," Morvash admitted. "We got here so late last night that I wasn't going to send him away no matter *where* he's been living."

"I see," Gror said. He set his plate aside and leaned back, but before he could say anything more Hakin appeared in the dining room door. "Ah!" Gror said. "We were just talking about you! Come in, come in, sit down, and I'll have someone fetch you breakfast."

"That would be greatly appreciated," Hakin said, crossing to the table and choosing a chair.

Gror gave him a minute to settle in and start eating before he began his questioning.

"Morvash tells me your name is Hakin of the Hundred-Foot Field," Gror said.

Hakin swallowed a bite of cake. "Well, Hakin, certainly," he said. "I haven't lived in the Field for seven years, though. I'm mostly known as Hakin the Demon's Master, though I wasn't Tarker's master so much as its companion, and I'm not even that anymore." He reached for his mug.

"Then where *do* you live?"

"I work with the city guard, so I sleep wherever they put me." He took a swig of small beer. "Most recently we were working in the shipyards, so I've been staying in the north tower at Westgate."

"You work with the guard?"

Hakin nodded. "By order of Lord Borlan, the magistrate in the Wizards' Quarter," he said. "He put me in charge of managing Tarker."

"That was the demon that tried to smash the house on Old East Avenue?"

"That's right. Tarker the Unrelenting. Karitha the Demonologist had summoned it to kill an enemy of hers, and when she was turned to stone it was stranded. But now that she's back and Tarker is busy in the far north, I suppose I'm out of a job."

"Tarker is...oh, never mind; I'll hear about that later. What are you going to do now?"

"I'm going to talk to my boss, Captain Arnen, and explain the situation to him. I'm guessing he'll send me back to Lord Borlan, and after that I don't know. I've done my job for seven years, so I hope they'll treat me fairly. I have some money put aside, so I won't starve; I can probably find another job if I need to."

Gror nodded. "So you don't need our help?"

Hakin looked from Gror to Morvash and back, then picked up another cake. "I should be fine, thank you."

"And what about this demonologist, Karitha?"

"Oh." Hakin set the cake back down. "I hadn't thought about that. That's a problem."

"Why is that?"

"Because she's wanted for murder. She summoned a demon to kill a wizard named Wosten of the Red Robe. Lord Borlan has been looking for her for seven years, to try her for that."

Gror looked at Morvash.

"It's true," he said. "Well, I hadn't specifically known Lord Borlan was looking for her, but I knew she killed Wosten. It was apparently one of these stupid feuds that got out of hand; she killed Wosten, but he turned her to stone. She spent seven years as a statue thinking she was dead. She was…well, *broken* by the experience, I would say."

"As badly as that poor slave-girl, Thetta?"

"Probably not *that* badly. But I would say that she was worse off emotionally than almost any of the other statues."

"But she was only petrified for seven years," Hakin said. "Weren't some of the others stone for *centuries*?"

Morvash turned up an empty palm. "Temperaments vary. I don't think she was ever very stable."

Gror nodded. "Actually, some of them seem to have gotten *better* after they had been frozen for a decade or two. They adjusted to their situation. I suppose she never got that far."

"Are you going to turn her over to Lord Borlan, then?" Hakin asked.

"I don't know," Gror replied. "It seems a waste to save her from petrifaction just to see her hanged."

"She *did* summon Tarker to kill Wosten," Hakin pointed out.

"And she's suffered for it," Morvash said. "For seven years. Wosten got his revenge without any magistrate's involvement."

"You know it doesn't work like that," Gror said.

"If you don't want her hanged, she can't stay in the city," Hakin said. "Lord Borlan has magicians looking for her. She hasn't been a high priority, but they probably know that Tarker is gone, so that will stir things up."

"That's another question," Gror asked. "What's happened to this Tarker?"

Morvash and Hakin exchanged glances.

"You tell him," Hakin said. "I'll eat."

With that, Morvash began explaining everything that had happened since he had received Gror's warning that someone had come looking for Prince Marek. Hakin interrupted every so often to add his own comments or correct details, and Gror occasionally asked for clarifications, but after about half an hour the tale was concluded.

"So what happens if Karitha is hanged?" Gror asked. "What would Tarker do?"

Hakin and Morvash looked at one another.

"I don't know," Morvash said.

"I *think* it would finish its assignment," Hakin said. "Then it could go home."

"Are you sure it wouldn't stop halfway through killing the dragon?" Morvash asked. "I mean, it's not like killing an ordinary person, where it only takes an instant."

"No, I'm *not* sure," Hakin said. "I did read up on it, but I'm not a demonologist, and this isn't a question I ever thought to ask anyone. Besides, I'm still not completely certain Tarker *can* kill the dragon."

"I think we need to know," Gror said. He beckoned to a footman. "Go fetch our other late-night arrival," he said. "Wake her if you need to."

The footman hurried away.

For the next few minutes the three men reviewed matters; Gror explained that he had been doing his best to get the other former statues safely settled into new lives. The various wizards had been taken under the Guild's wing, and Gror was not involved with them. The Northerner was now living in the Palace with one of the overlord's relatives who took an interest in history, and the two were learning each other's languages. Some of the others still had family and had gone home. More than a dozen were still living in the mansion, though, including poor mad Thetta. At Gror's request, Ithinia had sent a wizard to enchant Thetta so that she could not harm herself.

"Javan's Geas," Mornash said, nodding.

"Why aren't they eating breakfast with us?" Hakin asked.

"I asked that they take their meal in the courtyard," Gror explained. "It's a lovely day, warmer than usual for this time of year, and I thought we might want some privacy here."

As he was finishing his sentence the door opened, and Karitha entered, a footman at her elbow. The footman guided her to the chair at Hakin's left, then headed for the kitchen to fetch her food.

"Good morning, my dear," Gror said. "I hope you slept well."

Karitha stared blankly at him for a moment. "The bed was lovely," she said at last.

"I understand you're wanted for murder," Gror said, with a nod toward Hakin.

Morvash thought this was a very abrupt way to open the conversation, but Karitha did not seem troubled by it. She threw Hakin a glance, then nodded. "I killed a wizard," she said. "But he turned me to stone."

"So I heard. Now, I'm not a demonologist, but I had a question or two. You set Tarker the Unrelenting on Erdrik's giant stone dragon, didn't you?"

"Yes."

"So it can't go home, or kill you, until the dragon is dead? Not just smashed to pieces, but actually dead?"

She nodded.

"What happens if you die before it kills the dragon?"

Karitha blinked. "It still has to… It still has to kill its target," she said. After a second, she added, "I think."

"You're a demonologist, and you summoned Tarker in the first place—don't you *know*?"

"Well…no one ever ordered a demon to kill an immortal construct before," she said, almost apologetically. "At least, not that I ever heard of."

"If you're still alive when it's finished with the dragon, it will come after *you* again, is that right?"

"Yes." She nodded. "I'm sure of *that*."

"All right," Gror said. "What happens if we let you go, and Lord Borlan decides not to hang you? What will you do?"

"I…I don't know. My home… I'm told my home is gone, and I don't have any family… I don't know."

"Can't you just open a new shop and go back to working as a demonologist?"

She shook her head violently. "I don't know where my book of summoning rituals is, and I don't remember enough to go on without it, and I don't *want* to be a demonologist anymore. It was never a good job. I apprenticed to a demonologist when I was young and stupid because I was angry at everyone, but people…my customers were terrible people, when I *had* any. Nobody likes demonologists, nobody trusts us, not even other demonologists. I made a mistake when I was twelve and newly orphaned, and I've been stuck with it ever since. Most of the time I could barely afford my rent or food, and even that much came partly from frightening people instead of earning anything honestly. Yes, my customers had to pay me huge sums, I charged enough to live for half a year on a single summoning, but I was lucky to get *one* paying customer a year, let alone two. I'd get people offering to split the proceeds with me if I'd summon a demon to kill or rob their enemies, but they never had any money for me up front, and they never had any plans to keep the magistrates from finding out, and besides, I was a magician, not an assassin! I didn't want to hurt people—well, Wosten, because…but I didn't want to hurt anyone else. Maybe those people found other demonologists who would work for them, but I wouldn't. And maybe other demonologists did better with honest work, some of them claimed to, but they could have been lying—you can't trust demonologists. *I* don't trust demonologists. I won't go back to being one. I've had seven years to think about what I did, and I won't do it."

"What *will* you do?"

"I don't know. I hadn't thought about it yet. I had dreams when I thought I was dead, but none of them… I don't know."

Gror gazed at her silently for a moment, as the footman brought her breakfast from the kitchen and set it on the table in front of her. She stared back, not touching her food.

"Are you going to take me to the magistrate?" she asked at last.

Morvash struggled to keep quiet, not to argue against turning her in; he looked at his uncle.

"I don't think I am," Gror replied. "I don't like the uncertainty about what Tarker will do if you die before the dragon does. I don't like the idea of maybe leaving half a giant stone dragon still alive, somewhere in the Northern Deserts. I want you to live long enough for the demon to finish its job. So I'm going to offer *you* a job."

"What?" She stared blankly at him, her food still untouched.

"Morvash's old job, to be exact," Gror said. "In Ethshar of the Rocks. I don't think it would be wise for you to remain in *this* city, where you might be recognized and delivered to Lord Borlan, and my brother Morrin still needs a magician—not to actually do magic, though. That was where it went wrong for Morvash, when his father asked him to cast spells that he didn't want to cast. We won't do *that* again. But having a demonologist on the payroll, standing behind him during negotiations, looking scary, being a threat just by *being* there—I think that would be useful for a smuggler and arms dealer."

"But that..." She threw a glance at Morvash. "That..."

"It won't pay much," Gror said. "Probably not anything beyond room and board and enough to buy a few fancy black robes. And you might need to run a few actual errands, though they won't involve magic. I'll tell Morrin in no uncertain terms not to ask you to actually summon demons—not unless you feel ready, anyway."

"My father isn't a bad man, even if he is an arms smuggler," Morvash said. "*I* didn't get along with him, but I'm family."

She looked from one man to the other. "I...I still don't..."

"Lord Borlan would be happy to know where you are," Hakin said. "But if you're in Ethshar of the Rocks, and not around here, I wouldn't mind letting him think Tarker killed you."

"I'll do it," Karitha said.

The three men looked at one another, smiling.

"Then I think that's everything," Gror said. "Morvash, will you finally have time to work for *me*?"

"Oh, yes," Morvash said. "I'll need to talk to Guildmaster Ithinia, just to be sure, but I think I'm done with turning stones."

CHAPTER FORTY-SIX

DARISSA THE WITCH'S APPRENTICE

9TH OF NEWFROST, YS 5238

The town was very much as they remembered it, but none of the faces were the same, and the clothing was all a little odd—even here, fashions had changed over the intervening years. They reached Castle Square without incident, and headed up the right-hand stair toward the guard platform.

Two of the half-dozen guards met them at the top of the stair. "Who are you, and what business do you have here?" one of them asked.

Even though they had discussed it, and an instant's thought told her that these men had not even been born yet when she and Marek were turned to stone, she was somehow surprised they did not recognize their prince. Every other time she had been to the castle, everyone had known him immediately.

"I am hoping for an audience with Queen Hinda," Marek said. "It's a family matter."

"What sort of family matter?"

"I need her permission to marry my beloved," Marek said, gesturing at Darissa. "I'm of royal blood, and she's a witch, and...it's complicated."

Darissa said nothing, but tried to feel the guards' mood, and nudge it to be more favorable. They were mostly bored, and asking a lot of questions might make for a break in the routine—or, Darissa tried to make them think, it might be even duller.

"Royal blood?" the guard asked. He squinted at Marek's face.

"It could be," the other guard said.

"Are you armed?" the first asked. He looked at their waists.

"Not even a belt-knife," Marek said, raising his hands and turning around. Darissa raised her own hands, as well.

"Send an escort, or just let them in?" the second guard asked.

"Oh, let them in." The guard stepped aside. "Good luck. I doubt you'll get an audience with Her Majesty, but maybe someone else can help."

"Thank you." Marek essayed a small bow, and Darissa bobbed her head.

The two of them crossed the stone bridge over the dry moat, then walked through the corridor beyond, past more bored guards, and through the gates into the castle courtyard.

It was all familiar, but subtly different—the chicken coop by the southern wall was a different shape, cobblestone borders had been laid around patches of lush grass, and of course everyone's clothing was in the new modern styles. The steps up to the keep entrance had black iron railings that had not been there before. A woman was hanging laundry, and a girl was feeding the chickens.

As before, Marek did not go straight through the grand entrance, but instead turned aside to the little door on the left—which had been black before, but was now painted dark green. He opened the door, but the two of them were startled by a sudden rattle of armor; the room was not empty. A soldier had been sitting there, his feet up, his helmet off; when the door opened he had dropped his feet to the floor and stood up, grabbing at the hilt of the sword on his belt. "Who goes there?" he demanded.

This man was significantly older than the guards outside, Darissa noticed; his brown beard was streaked with gray, and what little hair remained on top of his head was more gray than brown.

"I'm sorry," Marek said, raising his hands. "I was looking for the queen's audience chamber."

"Well, you..." Then the soldier's eyes widened. He frowned. "Do I know you?" He looked past Marek at Darissa, and his eyes widened further.

"Debren?" Marek said, as he finally adjusted to the ravages of time and recognized the face beneath.

"Yes, Debren," Darissa said. "It's really us. I'm Darissa. We met atop the tower the day the war with Eknera started, remember?"

"But that...you're still young!"

"Wizards," Marek said. "It's a long story."

"You're back! We all thought you were dead!"

"We're back," Marek said.

Debren let go of his sword-hilt and flung himself at the prince. "Oh, your highness, you're back!" He hugged Marek, who smiled foolishly.

"It's good to see you, Debren," Marek said.

The soldier released the prince, then suddenly seemed to realize what an inappropriate thing he had done. He stepped back and said, "My apologies, your highness; I was momentarily overcome."

"Of course," Marek said, slapping him on the shoulder. "That's fine; I'm honored that you're so glad to see me."

"But what...where...why are you back?"

"Because I've come home, of course," Marek said. "And I need to talk to my sister."

Debren's face went pale. "Your sister? The queen?"

"Yes, Debren. My sister, Queen Hinda."

"But I..." His voice trailed off.

"What is it?" Darissa asked. "You can speak freely, I promise."

"The rumors...when you vanished, your highness, there were rumors that your sister had you killed so that she would inherit the throne."

Marek started back. "Really?"

Debren nodded.

"But why would she do that? My brother Evreth was still alive, and ahead of us both in the succession. Besides, nobody killed me—you can see I'm not dead."

"I see, but..." Debren swallowed. "Prince Evreth died the day you vanished, your highness. He was murdered by one of Mad Abran's assassins. Some folks said that an assassin had gotten you, too. Queen Hinda said you had run off with Mistress Darissa, so you wouldn't have to ever be king, but there were rumors that she knew more than she said."

It was Marek's face that paled now. "Oh," he said. "I knew...we had heard, while we were away, that Hinda was queen, so I knew Evreth was gone, but not when, or how it happened."

Darissa was listening to this with interest, and a growing suspicion that Princess Hinda had hired a wizard, rather than an assassin.

There was a moment of awkward silence. Then Marek squared his shoulders and said, "Regardless of any such rumors, Debren, I wish to speak to the queen. Where can I find her?"

"She's holding court right now, your highness," Debren replied, pointing at the door at the back that Darissa knew led to the huge throne room.

"Well, then, let us request an audience," Marek said. "If she *does* mean us harm, she can scarcely murder us in front of the whole court."

"That's right," Debren said, his grim expression softening. He turned toward the big door.

"Wait," Marek said, putting a hand on the man's shoulder again.

"Yes, your highness?"

"Before we go in, tell me—and tell me the truth, Debren, don't try to tell me what I want to hear. What sort of queen has Hinda been?"

Debren hesitated, and Darissa pressed silently at his thoughts, urging him to speak.

"Well, not bad," Debren said. "She isn't a *tyrant*, or anything. But she's a little harsher than your father was. She isn't deliberately cruel, or unfair, but pleas for mercy don't often work, and she doesn't listen to advice much, and she's not as generous as old King Terren. Some say she thinks she has to prove she's hard and strong because she's a woman; maybe that's it."

Darissa remembered her own brief encounters with Hinda, and found this assessment easy to believe. Marek did not seem inclined to doubt it, either.

"Show us in," he said. "And have the herald announce us."

Debren nodded, then looked at Darissa. "What name should I give for you?"

"Can you just say, 'Prince Marek and companion'?"

"No," Marek said, before Debren could reply.

"No?" Darissa asked. "Why not?"

The prince turned to face her, and to her astonishment knelt before her. "Darissa," he said, "if you will permit it, I would have you announced as my betrothed."

Darissa stared at him, feeling his love and determination. Her mouth opened, but no sound came out. She swallowed, and tried again. "I would be honored, beloved," she said. She felt a giggle bubbling up, but held it down long enough to add, "After all, we have been together for forty years; I think that's a long enough courtship." Then the laugh escaped.

It took a few minutes to compose themselves, and then for Debren to relay instructions to the courtiers in the great hall. They stood in the door, looking out at the vast pillared hall, and waited. Darissa could see the queen seated upon the throne at the far end, slumped to one side and looking bored, while people whispered around her.

Then the herald stepped to the front of the royal dais and announced, "Your Majesty, I give you his highness, Prince Marek of Melitha, and his betrothed!"

Queen Hinda sat bolt upright as Marek started marching down the length of the room, Darissa a step behind his right hand. As her brother came close enough for her to see his face, she leapt to her feet and screamed, "Marek!" She took two steps forward, then remembered who and where she was.

Marek smiled, and quickened his pace. Darissa felt a wave of astonishment from the dozens of people in the hall, and hurried to keep up with the prince.

Then Hinda raised a hand and called, "Stop!"

Startled, Marek stopped, and Darissa almost collided with him. She felt the amazement around them turn to confusion.

"We will speak with these two in private," the queen announced. "Chamberlain, what space is available?"

"Ah..." The chamberlain, caught completely off guard, took a moment to gather his wits, but finally said, "The lilac chamber would be suitable, your Majesty."

"Good," Hinda said, turning on her heel. "Bring our guests to me there, immediately." She vanished through a door at the back of the dais.

Guards seemed to appear out of nowhere at either side, but none of them actually touched either Marek or Darissa; instead they simply marched along as Marek led the way out into a corridor, then along the passage to a beautifully-painted door, each panel adorned with pictures of lilacs.

A guard opened the door and ushered them inside, but he and his companions did not enter; they took up positions in the passageway outside.

The wallpaper in the room beyond was the color of fresh lilacs. The draperies in the three windows and the upholstery on the dozen chairs were embroidered with lilacs, as well. Whoever had decorated the place had clearly believed in keeping a consistent theme.

Hinda was already seated at one end of a table, and she motioned for Marek and Darissa to sit, as well. She was smiling broadly, an expression Darissa had never seen on her face before, and judging by his reaction, Marek did not find it comforting or familiar, either.

Where the two travelers had aged scarcely a month in their forty-year absence, Hinda's face seemed to show every day of that time. She was white-haired and wrinkled, her features sagging, though she did seem to still have all her teeth.

"You're back!" she said, as soon as Marek had settled onto his chair. "Did my agent find you?"

"Your agent?" Marek asked warily.

"I sent a man to locate you and bring you home," she replied. "At his last report he had tracked you to the home of some Ethsharitic nobleman called Lord Landessin."

Darissa was watching the queen closely, and sensed no attempt at deception.

"*You* sent him?" Marek asked. "He did not say that."

"You spoke with him?"

Marek shook his head. "No, we never saw him. We were warned that someone was hunting us, and our friends thought it was an assassin."

Hinda's smile dimmed. "Friends? What friends?"

"Our friends in Ethshar of the Spices."

"How could…" She stopped. Then she continued, "How could you have friends? You were a statue."

"You *knew* that," Marek said.

"Yes, I knew that. I told you, I had sent someone to find you, and he got that far…"

"I think you knew before you sent anyone after us," Darissa said.

Hinda stared at her. "I am your queen, girl," she said. "Watch how you speak to me."

"And I spent five years as an apprentice learning to perceive what is in a person's heart, your Majesty. You knew all along."

"*Did* you, Hinda?" Marek asked.

The queen stared at her brother, all trace of her earlier smile gone.

"You hired the wizard, then," Marek said.

"I was trying to protect you!" Hinda exclaimed. "Evreth had died, like Terren—word came at the victory celebration, but Dad said we should not tell anyone that night, so as not to ruin the celebration. Evreth had been murdered by one of Abran's men out of sheer spite, waylaid on the road. I heard the messenger tell Dad, and I think I went a bit mad. I ran to Lirilin, the wizard I had hired, and told her to cast the spell. I didn't want to lose *all* my brothers!"

"Why didn't you have her turn us back once peace was restored?" Darissa demanded.

Hinda was so intent on her brother that Darissa was not sure she had even heard the question, but Marek said, "Answer her!"

"I…I didn't dare! I was afraid of what Dad would do, how he would react if he found out I was responsible."

"And you didn't want a rival claimant to the throne," Marek said.

She stared at him for a second, then exclaimed, "No, I didn't! I admit it, Marek—you never wanted to rule, you *said* as much, you hadn't been trained for it, you never wanted anything to do with running the government! And you didn't know how to lead an army—you *would* have been killed, just like our brothers, if there was another war! So I kept you safe and out of the way, you and your whore…"

Darissa reacted to that without thinking; her body did not move, but the queen nonetheless felt a sharp slap across her face.

"My *beloved*," Marek said coldly. "And now my betrothed."

"But that's another thing!" Hinda said, a hand to her reddening cheek. "She's a *witch*—you can't marry her! You're a prince!"

"I *will* marry her," Marek said. "If I must renounce my birthright to do so, then I will. As you just said, I never wanted the throne."

"But you can't *do* that!" the queen protested. "You're my heir! You're all that's left of our family; you *must* take the throne!"

Marek paused at that; Darissa could sense his mood changing from anger to pity. "What?"

"You're all that's left!"

"You never married?"

"Married *who*? I couldn't marry a commoner, it was politically impossible even if I found one I wanted, which I did not. I needed a king or a prince from another kingdom, and we've fought wars against half our neighbors, and marrying the wrong one would anger the others, and...and I didn't *want* any of them. The kings and princes around us who weren't already married and were anywhere near my age were all repulsive, and most of them weren't interested. Oh, I considered it anyway, I sent emissaries and secret envoys, but even the ones who didn't refuse outright rejected the role of prince consort—they would be *kings* of Melitha or nothing, and I would no longer rule my own realm. I would not accept *that*."

"No, of course not," Marek said, and Darissa felt a thread of bitter amusement beneath the pity.

"That was why it became so urgent to find you!" the queen said. "I wanted to revive you once our father was gone and I was firmly on the throne, but the wizard said the statue had been stolen, and...and I admit it, I did not really try to recover it. I thought it would be safe enough, wherever it was. But once I knew I could no longer hope to bear children even if I did find someone to sire them, I needed *you* to take the throne when I die. We need an heir! Without one, there will be wars, and Melitha will be destroyed."

Marek stared at his sister. Darissa could feel the intense tangle of his emotions—love and hate and pride and disgust and more. From Hinda she felt hope and despair and anger and guilt.

Then Marek said, "I will marry Darissa. If that means I cannot inherit the throne from you, then so be it—I will do my best to negotiate a peaceful transition to whatever nation may claim Melitha."

"But you *can't*," Hinda said. "Don't you think I've tried? Trafoa and Bhella will never agree to anything Kanthoa and Eknera will accept. There *will* be a war if there isn't a clear heir."

"Then name one—one of your advisors."

"No, please, Marek, don't *do* this! That won't work, no one would accept it. You know that."

Darissa saw that Hinda firmly believed that, and what's more, she knew why. Hinda knew that she was not loved and trusted enough for her choice to be accepted once she was gone. She knew that her court was made up of rivals and enemies vying for favor and position, not allies working together for the good of the kingdom. She was not happy about this, nor proud of it, but she knew it and acknowledged it to herself as her own failure.

But only to herself. She would never say it aloud.

"Then I will be king when you are gone, and Darissa will be my queen," Marek said calmly, refusing to yield.

"You *can't do that!*" Hinda shouted, almost in tears. "The Wizards' Guild will not allow it! *At best* they will depose you; more likely they will kill you both. No magician can be a king or queen, or consort to a king or queen; you know that!"

"Marek," Darissa said, "you do not need to marry me. I will be your mistress, and you can marry some princess who will bear your heirs."

Marek turned on her angrily, perhaps the angriest she had ever seen him. "No!" he said. "I will not do that. That would not be fair or kind to you, or to this imagined princess or our hypothetical children! To live knowing your husband loves another, and that you exist only to produce heirs—what sort of misery is that? To grow up knowing your father only tolerates your mother out of political expedience—what sort of childhood is that? And to have you dismissed as a mere toy, rather than my beloved equal? I will not do that! You accepted my proposal of marriage, and I will not withdraw it. I love you, Darissa, and I will marry you, and if the Wizards' Guild does not approve, may demons take them all!"

"Marek, brother, please!" Hinda said, reaching out toward him. "You can't marry a witch! This isn't Klathoa!"

For an instant there was silence, but then Darissa said, "Then I won't be a witch."

This time the silence lasted longer as the siblings turned to stare at her.

"But you *are* a witch," Hinda said.

Darissa raised her chin. "I am a witch's *apprentice*," she said. "But after forty-five years, I have not been made journeyman—what sort of a witch is *that*?"

"But...that forty years..." Marek said.

"Is forty years," Darissa said. "My master still lives, but has never approved my promotion. Clearly, I am a *failed* apprentice and will never be a witch."

"The Wizards' Guild will not be fooled," Hinda said.

"The Wizards' Guild owes us a favor," Darissa replied. "For what we did in Tazmor, if nothing else."

"Can you give up your magic?" the queen asked.

"No," Darissa said.

"Hinda," Marek said, "I am going to marry Darissa. Then, if the Wizards' Guild has no objection, I will be your heir to the throne of Melitha. We will argue that despite her magic, she never completed her apprenticeship and is therefore not a witch. We will argue that the existence of Klathoa and the Vondish Empire demonstrates their willingness to make exceptions. If they agree, I am your heir; if they do not, then you'll have to find someone else. Perhaps…" He looked at Darissa. "Perhaps we will have a child who can inherit the throne."

Darissa smiled. "I would be happy with that," she said. "I've been preventing it, but if I am no longer to use my magic, that's an easy place to start."

Hinda looked frustrated and lost, but then she gathered herself together. She rose to her feet, raised her chin, and pointed a hand at the two of them. "I will accept this," she said.

"You have no choice," Marek said.

"Do not interrupt me! I am still the Queen of Melitha. You struck me, apprentice, and for that you should die, but I know…"

"My hand did not touch you," Darissa interrupted. She could feel that Hinda was on the verge of collapse, that she was barely holding herself together, but she was not going yield to the woman who had stolen forty years from her. If Hinda tried to punish her, she would find out that witchcraft *could* harm people, even if witches almost never used it that way.

"Your magic did, child!" But then the queen sagged. "And because I have wronged you, I will pardon it. Now be still, while I make a decree."

The lovers exchanged glances. "We can always leave if we don't like it," Marek said.

"Fine. Go on, your Majesty."

"I hereby give you permission to wed, and to remain in Melitha. I name my brother, Prince Marek, as my provisional heir, and require you to make what terms you can with the Wizards' Guild in this regard. We will announce that you have been under a spell all these years, cast by a wizard in the pay of one of our foes in the war we were fighting when you vanished. There will be *no* mention of my own role in your enchantment, or this agreement is void. Our entire conversation here today did not happen—neither of you will say anything of it to anyone but the three of us. I ask you, Marek, to study government to the best of your ability, so that you might be a good king when I am gone. I ask you, Darissa, to refrain from making use of your magic in public, and to refuse any attempt to promote you to journeyman. Do you accept these terms?"

The pair exchanged glances again.

"I do," Darissa said.

"Then I do, as well," Marek said, "though we still have much to discuss in private, sister."

Hinda relaxed. "I know," she said. "I know. I'm sorry. But for now, let us go announce your safe return and welcome you home."

Marek rose, as did Darissa—and only then, belatedly, did Darissa realized they had remained seated in the presence of the queen, which was a serious violation of court etiquette.

Marek knocked on the door, and the guard outside opened it, and the three of them marched back to the great hall to spread the joyous news of Prince Marek's safe return.

CHAPTER FORTY-SEVEN

MORVASH OF THE SHADOWS

10ᵀᴴ OF NEWFROST, YS 5238

The door of Erdrik's house was broken open and hanging from one hinge; apparently Tarker *had* come up from underneath the house, and then smashed its way out in pursuit of Zerra's carpet. On Ithinia's advice, Lieutenant Fullan and his soldiers had prevented anyone from entering the house, or even going near it, while they waited for matters to be resolved elsewhere.

The men on guard recognized Morvash, though, and after a brief discussion allowed him past. He marched up the steps and pushed the ruined door aside.

Karn, his uncle's senior footman, had accompanied him, while Zarek, Gror's coachman, waited with his vehicle; now Karn hesitated on the steps.

"Oh, come on in," Morvash told him.

The two men made their way inside, where they were immediately swarmed by several chairs. Papers and nicknacks that had been piled on shelves and tables were now strewn on the slate floor of the entryway, presumably knocked there by Tarker's passage; several of the papers were damp, the ink smeared, and Morvash guessed that rain had blown in through the open doorway. He shooed the chairs away and led Karn further in.

The fire on the hearth in the parlor did not light when they entered the room; Morvash guessed that some of the house's magic had died with its master, or perhaps merely been disrupted by the demon's violent entrance and exit.

That entrance had evidently been made through the dining room floor; the polished wood had been smashed upward, leaving a five-foot hole. Splinters and broken bits of board were scattered throughout the room, and the table had been thrown against the north wall. The chandelier was intact but had lost most of its candles; the sideboard was where it had always been, but the brass bowl was on its side and the platters out of position.

Leaning carefully, Morvash peered down into the hole and saw the familiar cellars, but with a gaping hole in the stone floor.

Karn stood beside him, looking down. "Was it like that before, sir?"

"No," Morvash said. He grimaced. "I think this house will have to be torn down; I don't think it's safe." Not, he thought to himself, that it ever was really safe.

"I see," Karn said, stepping back from the hole.

The kitchen seemed undamaged, and unchanged, and Morvash studied the connecting passage, trying to determine whether there was a seam between the World and some other place. If the kitchen really was in another reality that might make demolishing the house more complicated. He had been meaning to check this for months, but had never gotten around to it.

He ran his athame along the wall of the passageway without finding any discontinuity, but then he came to the doorway joining it to the dining room and had a sudden glimpse of a dusty, empty closet, and the top of a cellar stair that did not run straight, as the visible one did, but turned a sharp corner. *That* was the division.

That sort of magic was *far* above his abilities; he would leave it to Ithinia and the other Guildmasters. He turned and headed for the stairs.

The upper floors showed less immediate damage; the demon had evidently not bothered to come up here, since by the time it burst through the floor downstairs Karitha had already been flown away. Morvash walked slowly along the gallery, looking it over.

The brazier he had used for Javan's Restorative was still there; the remaining jewelweed was strewn across the floor, and the peacock feathers had toppled. The window where he and his companions had climbed onto Zerra's carpet was still open, and the floor below it stained where rain had blown in. A broken rod dangled above one window where draperies had been torn down to serve as improvised garments.

All the statuary was gone, of course, and the place looked bare and desolate. There was no sign of the cat that had been a soapstone carving before Morvash cast his spell; he supposed it had gotten out the broken front door and was living in an alley somewhere.

The alcove at the north end of the gallery was not the one that Morvash had seen during his months of preparation, but the one that had appeared when Erdrik was released. He tried the vault door, but it was locked.

Karn cleared his throat, reminding Morvash that he was there. The wizard turned.

"Those are mine," he said, pointing to the ingredients from his spell. "In fact, anything you find in this room is mine. But most of my things are in the bedroom back there."

"Which bedroom, sir?"

"I'll show you." As they walked, he added, "The food in the kitchen is mine, too—anything that hasn't gone bad."

Half an hour later the two men had gathered all of Morvash's belongings, and had begun loading them into the coach when a woman approached them. She was not quite young anymore, but by no means elderly.

"Excuse me," she said.

Morvash stopped shoving a box of assorted supplies onto the seat of the coach. "Yes?" he said, straightening up.

"Are you Morvash of the Shadows?"

Unsure what to expect, Morvash warily said, "Yes."

To his astonishment, she flung her arms around him and kissed him on the cheek. "Thank you!" she exclaimed.

"For what?" he asked, baffled.

"You saved my brother! He spent thirty-five years as a statue, and now he's back!"

"Oh," Morvash said, blinking. "Which one was he?"

"Radler the Difficult," she replied. "He was just a boy, eleven years old. I was nine."

"Oh," Morvash said again. "I think I remember him." He was one of the ones Ariella had been unable to hear.

"You have to let us thank you! Please, come see us when you can—we live in Eastwark, on North Eastwark Street, two blocks from the wall. Come to dinner!"

"Maybe when I have the time…"

"Please! It's the least we can do." She reached for her belt. "And I know we can't pay you the full fee, but please accept this." She pulled an unbroken round of silver from her purse and held it out.

Morvash wordlessly accepted the coin, still trying to comprehend what was happening.

"North Eastwark Street," she repeated. "The house on the corner has a shrine to Blusheld, with a bronze bowl for flowers, and we're the next house west."

"Thank you," Morvash said, still holding the silver.

"If there's anything else we can do for you, just tell us!"

"Of course," the wizard said, and then immediately thought that was a stupid thing to say.

The woman apparently did not; she just grinned, released him, and walked away, smiling back at him over her shoulder.

Morvash watched her go, then looked at Karn.

The footman remarked, "She thinks you're a hero, sir."

"Well, it's good to know someone appreciates what I did."

"Sir, I have heard what some of our house-guests said about you. Your efforts are very definitely appreciated."

"Oh," Morvash said. He wondered whether he was blushing; he felt as if he might be. He shoved the box into place and said, "Come on, let's get this stuff back to my uncle's place."

They made the trip back to Lord Landessin's mansion without incident, though once or twice Morvash thought he heard his name spoken, and some of the people on the streets seemed to be staring at the coach even more than usual.

They had just brought the first load into the house when Gror intercepted his nephew. "Any problems?" he asked.

"No," Morvash said. He hesitated, trying to decide whether to mention the woman on the street.

"Good, good," Gror said, not noticing the hesitation. "Because it seems you have a dinner engagement."

"I what?"

"A messenger came while you were out. You are requested—not invited, *requested*—to dine with Ithinia of the Isle at her home on Lower Street tonight."

"Oh," Morvash said. "She must want to know what happened to

Erdrik."

"I'd guess she wants more than that," Gror said. "But you'll find out soon enough."

Neither of them mentioned any possibility of refusing the request; turning down Ithinia would be unwise, and they both knew it.

Accordingly, as the sun was sinking behind the western rooftops Morvash found himself knocking on the Guildmaster's door beneath the careful scrutiny of two gargoyles. A servant of some sort—Morvash was unsure whether the man was a butler, a footman, a housekeeper, or what—ushered him inside and led him to the dinner table.

Ithinia was already seated. "Thank you, Obdur," she said. "Please sit, Morvash."

There was only one other chair at the table, so there was no question of where; he took his place and looked around uncomfortably.

The room was large and elegant without being extravagant, and Ithinia obviously liked white—the walls and half the furniture were white, as well as the Guildmaster's robe. A place was set before him. Morvash pulled in his chair and looked at Ithinia expectantly.

"Obdur will bring the soup in a moment," she said. "But let us get directly to business."

"Of course, Guildmaster," Morvash replied. "I suppose you want to know what happened to Erdrik."

Ithinia waved that aside. "I already *know* what happened to Erdrik," she said. "His pet mountain stepped on him. Zerra was here this afternoon; I know all about your adventures in Tazmor. Unless you think there is some relevant detail Zerra might have missed?"

"Ah...probably not," Morvash said. "But then what *is* our business?"

"You brought thirty-odd statues back to life," she said. "I want to know all about them."

"Ah...why?"

Ithinia's expression darkened, so before she could reply Morvash quickly added, "I can better choose what to tell you if I know your reasons."

"I see your point," Ithinia said, her face softening again. "Fine. I want to know what, if anything, the Guild should do about these people. Who enchanted them, and why? Are any of them a threat? What about the wizards who petrified them—should we take any action against any of them? I want to know everything you can tell me about all these people."

"Oh," Morvash said. He would have stammered, unsure where to begin, had Obdur not reappeared at that moment bearing two bowls of soup. As it was, the conversation was interrupted until both diners had tasted their soup and declared it satisfactory.

When Obdur had left for the kitchen again, Ithinia put down her spoon and said, "Well?"

"Well, to begin with, the statue I had *intended* to restore to life was Prince Marek of Melitha and his paramour, Darissa the Witch's Apprentice…"

Through the entire meal, Morvash listed the people he had rescued, giving what details he could remember. He pointed out that there were several he had never identified, as Ariella had been unable to communicate with them and he had fled the area before he had a chance to get to know them. He also explained that he had detailed notes about the others, the known ones, but had not brought them because he had mistaken the purpose of Ithinia's invitation. He described the situation at Lord Landessin's mansion, where about half the revived statues were still his uncle's guests. And he pointed out, as Obdur brought out the final pot of tea, that he had sent the four wizards directly to Ithinia.

"Yes, they came to see me," she acknowledged. "You need not concern yourself further with them. These others, though—tomorrow I will have my representatives visit your uncle, and interview his guests. I hope you will lend them these notebooks you described."

"Of course, Guildmaster!"

"Good." She picked up her teacup and leaned back. "I notice that while you admitted to rescuing Karitha the Demonologist and saving her from her demon, you have not said what became of her. Zerra brought her back from Tazmor; where is she now?"

Morvash hesitated. "She set the demon against Erdrik's dragon," he said.

"I know that."

"She has promised to give up demonology."

"Has she?"

"Yes."

"Nonetheless, she killed a member of the Guild."

"And she spent seven years as a statue."

"The penalty for murder is death, as I'm sure you know."

"But she isn't the same person now that she was seven years ago!"

"Actually, she *is* the same person, finally, after a seven-year interruption."

"But she's changed!"

Ithinia sighed and set down her cup. "Morvash, you are dodging the question. Where is she?"

Morvash realized that he would not be able to hide the truth indefinitely. It would be best, he decided, to answer, before Ithinia got angry. "She's one of my uncle's guests," he admitted.

"He has not delivered her to Lord Borlan?"

Morvash shook his head. "I convinced him not to."

"Does he plan to harbor a fugitive indefinitely?"

"Not exactly, no. He's sending her to Ethshar of the Rocks to work for my father."

Ithinia's eyes opened wider. "And how does *that* work?"

Morvash explained the position Gror had offered Karitha.

When he had finished, Ithinia considered silently for a moment, then said, "Let us consider this. This Karitha killed a wizard. You are offering, as mitigating factors, that it was at least partially in self-defense, as Wosten was already preparing an attack on her; that she spent seven years in a state of petrifaction, deprived of all her senses but hearing, and that this constitutes an adequate punishment for her crimes; and that she performed a valuable service for the Guild and the World by turning Tarker the Unrelenting loose on Erdrik's ridiculous monster. You therefore propose to send her into exile, and to ensure that she no longer practices magic, rather than see her hanged. Do I have this right?"

"Yes, Guildmaster."

"And what does Lord Borlan think of this?"

"We had not intended to tell him she is still alive."

"Hmm. I understand you collected your belongings from Erdrik's house today."

This abrupt change of subject threw Morvash for a moment, but at last he nodded. "That's right," he said.

"What sort of condition is the house in?"

"It's…there's a huge hole through the cellar and up into the dining room, and the entire house was battered. I don't think there's any practical way to repair the damage."

"Really?" Ithinia said, staring at him over her tea. "*Really?*"

"I don't… I don't understand."

"Morvash, *what* spell did you perform in that house a couple of sixnights back?"

"Javan's…oh."

"That's right. We could put it all back the way it was. But now that we know what happened to its owner, I'm not sure we should."

Morvash turned up empty hands. "It's not for me to say, Guildmaster. I paid no rent this month, so my interests there are done."

"And you have no sentimental attachment?"

He shook his head. "Not really."

"Then I'll decide for myself after I've had more time to consider. As for your friend Karitha, make sure she understands that if she ever sets foot in this city again, or troubles any Guild member in Ethshar of the Rocks, she will either die or find herself spending the rest of her life in some form even less enjoyable than that of a statue. And I agree that Lord Borlan need not know she is still alive."

"Thank you, Guildmaster! You're very generous."

Ithinia grimaced. "Mostly, I prefer to not be bothered worrying whether this is entirely up to Lord Borlan, or a Guild matter, or what. Your mitigating circumstances do have some validity, at that, and I generally prefer to err on the side of mercy. Now, finish your tea before it gets cold."

CHAPTER FORTY-EIGHT

HAKIN OF THE HUNDRED-FOOT FIELD

29TH OF NEWFROST, YS 5238

Hakin watched the crowd outside Grandgate, the farmers and merchants selling their wares, the city folks coming out to buy, the travelers arriving from elsewhere, with only moderate interest. The thrill of being in Ethshar of the Sands, instead of his home city of Ethshar of the Spices, was definitely wearing off, but today, according to the magicians, should be the day.

Then he heard screams in the distance, and his heart began racing. He jumped up on the stone bench at the base of one of the towers and stared up the road to the north.

Something black, something bigger than a human, was coming down the road, coming fast, carrying an immense gray stone on its back.

That was it. That was Tarker, bringing the first piece of the dragon to be killed.

"It's coming!" he bellowed to the guards. "Clear the way!"

As arranged, dozens of guardsmen began dragging people out of the demon's path, and shouting at everyone else to move aside. Runners dashed through the gates into the city, to make sure the entire route was open—across Grandgate Market, half a mile up Gate Street, right at the fork onto Harbor, left at the fork onto Quarter Street, across Circle Street and the inner plaza and through the northeastern portal into the Palace.

Hakin jumped off the bench and ran through the gates himself; he wanted to be with Tarker when it reached the Palace, and he was fairly sure that even weighed down by that huge rock the demon would move faster than he could, so he needed a head start.

He dashed up Gate Street, but slowed at the fork, looking back over his shoulder.

Tarker was there, but farther back than he had expected. The demon did not appear to be running all-out. Hakin hesitated, then waved. "Tarker!" he called. "It's me!"

The street had been cleared, but there were soldiers and civilians watching from the streets on either side; they murmured and stared.

The demon came trotting up to him, then stopped, all four of its arms holding that chunk of stone. Hakin could see one face was smooth, and carved with gigantic scales. "Hakin of the Hundred-Foot Field," Tarker said. "Why are you here?"

"To make sure everything goes smoothly, and you don't hurt anyone."

"Then guide me to the place that destroys wizard magic."

"Of course! It's this way," Hakin said, pointing up Harbor Street. "Come on, I'll show you."

"Good," Tarker said.

"Could you find it by yourself?"

"I cannot smell it. I followed the scent of Ederd, Fifth of that Name, Overlord of Ethshar of the Sands."

"Ah. When he heard you were coming he decided it would be safer not to stay in the Palace."

"I knew he had moved."

"Yes. Well, then I'll guide you." Hakin began marching briskly up Harbor Street at the demon's side.

"How is it going?" he asked as they walked. "Have you smashed the entire dragon?"

"No," Tarker said. "I have immobilized it by removing portions of its wings and legs, but I have not smashed all of it."

"But you're bringing a piece of it here already?"

"I wish to leave it able to communicate until I am certain this system you suggested will work."

"I guess that makes sense."

"Why are *you* here, Hakin of the Hundred-Foot Field?"

"That isn't really my name anymore," Hakin said. "I haven't lived in the Field since the day we met. I'm just called Hakin of Ethshar now. Anyway, I'm here to help you, and to make sure nothing goes wrong. I'm working for the overlords now—mostly Lord

Azrad, but sometimes I work with Ederd or Wulran. I run errands, whatever they need done. They sent me here because I know you better than anyone else. They wanted someone you would talk to if there were problems."

"Good," Tarker said.

That surprised Hakin, but he tried not to show it.

The two marched on in companionable silence, through the fork onto Quarter Street.

"A path was ready for me," Tarker said, as they caught sight of the palace dome directly ahead.

"We knew you were coming," Hakin said. "The wizards have been keeping an eye on you."

"I am not accustomed to human cooperation."

"It's kind of a new thing for everyone," Hakin agreed. "We all want that dragon dead, though. Ever since that idiot Erdrik brought it to life, people have been hoping you could kill it for us."

"If the magic can be destroyed as you told me, I will kill it. But it will take several years."

"Oh, we know that! Karitha is counting on it, in fact."

Tarker raised its head and sniffed. "Karitha the Demonologist is not in this city," it said. "She is fifty leagues to the northwest."

"In Ethshar of the Rocks, last I heard," Hakin agreed.

"When the dragon is entirely dead, I must return to her to be released."

That's actually something we were wondering about," Hakin said. "What happens if she dies *before* you finish killing the dragon?"

"Then completing its death will release me."

"You can't go without killing it, even if she's gone?"

"No."

"Well, *that's* a relief! And *how* long do you think it will take to kill it?"

"I have been unable to accurately assess the total mass of stone, and I have not yet seen the mechanism that destroys magic in operation, so I cannot be exact, but I estimate between thirty and ninety years."

"That's a pretty wide range."

"I cannot be exact."

"Fair enough. After all, it took a few hundred humans two hundred years to carve the thing in the first place."

They were approaching the Palace, and four guards were waiting; as they crossed Circle Street the guards pulled open the big doors.

"The central area, under the dome, would be best," one of the soldiers called; then the four of them scattered.

Hakin headed for the door, but halfway across the plaza Tarker suddenly stopped and dropped the chunk of stone; it smashed to the pavement, scattering shards of broken slate.

"It's dead," the demon said. "I can feel it. There is no wizard magic in this place. This is just stone now." It turned and began trotting rapidly back across Circle Street to Quarter Street.

"Wait!" Hakin called, running after it. "Where are you going?"

"For the next piece," Tarker said, and then it was running too fast for him to keep up.

Hakin stopped, baffled, and walked back to the plaza.

The chunk of stone was sitting as motionless as...well, as a stone, Hakin thought. As he stared at it the four guards came up.

"Is it safe?" one of them asked.

"I think so," Hakin replied.

"I thought it was bringing the rocks *into* the palace," another soldier said.

"So did I," Hakin said. "No one bothered to tell me that the magically dead area extended out this far."

"Now what?" a third asked.

"Now I need a hammer and chisel," Hakin answered.

One of the guardsmen signaled to another, and one man ran off, while the other three remained.

By the time the soldier returned with the requested tools a crowd had gathered, but no one had dared to touch the big gray rock the demon had delivered. Hakin recognized a few faces, but did not acknowledge them yet; instead he accepted the chisel and set it against a tiny crevice he had spotted, then swung the hammer with all his strength.

The stone cracked.

With a second blow, a chunk came free and tumbled to the pavement. Hakin handed the tools back to the soldier who had brought them, then picked up the fallen piece. It was roughly triangular, perhaps two inches thick and not quite a foot in its longest dimension.

He hefted it.

It looked and felt exactly like ordinary stone, and quite dead. He turned and carried it carefully away from the palace, watching it for the slightest hint of movement.

He could see no change.

Hakin raised his gaze, and spotted Mereth of the Golden Door in the crowd, as she had said she would be. He brought her the rock.

"Here," he said. "Is this alive?"

She took it, and said, "I'll know by tomorrow." Then she turned and headed home.

Hakin watched her go, then turned to the crowd and announced, "All done. Nothing to see here. The demon won't be back for several days, and it's just a big rock from a mountain up north. The demon's under a binding spell to bring the entire mountain here, piece by piece."

He heard the murmurs but paid no attention; he didn't care what these people did now. He started up Quarter Street, back toward his inn.

The next morning he, Mereth, and half a dozen other magicians and minor officials gathered in the Lady Investigator's hearing room, which was very intentionally *not* in the Palace, but in a nearby building. Mereth had brought the broken-off chunk of stone, and she set it on Lady Sarai's table.

"It's dead," she said.

"Of course it is," someone said. "It's a rock."

Lady Sarai glared at the official who had spoken, then turned her attention back to Mereth. "You're sure?"

"Absolutely," the wizard said.

"So bringing it out of the dead area did *not* restore the immortality spell?"

"It did not. I didn't think it would. Wizardry doesn't work that way."

Sarai seemed to relax. "Good!" she said. "Then we don't need to leave that boulder where the demon dropped it." She gestured to the guard by the door. "Get it cleared away! We'll need the space for the next one."

"It's a good thing it stays dead," Hakin remarked. "You couldn't begin to *fit* the entire dragon into the Palace and plaza."

"That's still hard to believe," Lady Sarai said.

"It's an entire *mountain*, my lady," Hakin said. "Believe me, its head alone is bigger than the Palace."

"And the demon is going to deliver the entire thing here, piece by piece."

"Yes."

"What are we going to *do* with all that stone?"

"Double the city wall, perhaps? Pave every street in the city? Build quays?"

Lady Sarai sighed. "I'm sure someone will come up with an idea," she said, "but fortunately, that isn't my problem."

"At least there are plenty of expert stone-cutters available now; they're looking for work in the Baronies of Sardiron," Hakin said with a smile. "And they're very familiar with this stone, since they're the same people who carved the dragon it the first place. Of course, except for Pender, they don't speak Ethsharitic."

"It's easy enough to teach them," Lady Sarai said. "And we won't need that many, with these pieces coming one at a time."

"Will you still need *my* services?" Hakin asked.

"Perhaps not, but I will leave that up to the overlord and the Wizards' Guild," Lady Sarai replied. "Having someone the demon trusts may still be useful."

Hakin nodded.

Everything seemed to be working out. Karitha was safe for the next few decades—probably for the rest of her natural life—frightening arms buyers in Ethshar of the Rocks. Tarker would be busy for a very long time, but would eventually be able to go home. An entire mountain was going to be delivered to Ethshar of the Sands, but slowly enough to be manageable.

Hakin was very glad that Tarker had not found a way to convince the dragon to walk or fly close to Ethshar of the Sands, to save the demon the trouble of carrying pieces all the way from the Northern Deserts. Having that monster in an inhabited area would not be good.

And he was glad that all those years ago he had been brave enough to stand up and ask the demon what it wanted in the Hundred-Foot Field, because it had been his relationship with Tarker that had led to his present well-paid job as errand boy and troubleshooter for the overlords and the Wizards' Guild.

He hoped all his other companions had been as fortunate.

CHAPTER FORTY-NINE

MORVASH OF THE SHADOWS

7TH OF SUMMERHEAT, YS 5240

Zerra sent the carpet in a long, slow loop before bringing it in to land, and Morvash looked the dragon over carefully.

He suspected that it could still move if it wanted to; Tarker had indeed broken both its wings, but the damage to its legs did not look very serious, and Morvash knew that creatures brought to life by Ellran's Immortal Animation could bend and flex in completely unnatural ways. That meant that it didn't *want* to move.

Tarker was chipping away at the tip of its right wing, using the iron drill as an oversized chisel and driving it into the stone with the big sledgehammer. Morvash waved to it, but the demon did not respond.

At last Zerra brought the carpet down to earth, hovering a foot or so above bare dirt and sparse clumps of grass directly in front of the monster's face. Morvash clambered off and stood facing the creature.

The dragon's eyes focused on them, and it spoke.

"You two? Why have you come?"

Morvash staggered back as the sound of its voice shook the earth. "I wanted to talk to you!" he shouted.

"You are not here to tease or torment me?"

"No!"

"Then speak; what would you have of me?"

Morvash hesitated, knowing that what he was going to say might sound insultingly stupid, but at last called, "I wanted to be sure you were all right!"

The dragon's head had been resting on the ground, but now it lifted up so that the creature could look down at Morvash.

"*I am being slowly murdered, and you know this,*" it said. "*How can you ask whether I am 'all right'?*"

"I...I wanted to know whether there is anything we can do to make it better for you!"

It cocked its head and studied him. "*I don't believe I understand what you are offering.*"

"Well...I want to make sure you aren't feeling any pain."

"*I am not. Was it not your fellow there who told me I am incapable of feeling pain?*"

"Yes, I know," Morvash said. "I just wanted to be sure she was right."

"*I believe she was, if I understand the word's meaning. The demon's pounding feels no worse than a gust of wind, and is far less troublesome than that fool I found in my ear when I first awoke.*"

"That was the wizard that created you!"

The dragon made a noise that Morvash thought would have been a snort had the creature been capable of exhaling. "*He did me no favor. As you said, I am far too large for this world. I am allowing this demon to destroy me because you were right; I should never have existed.*"

"I'm sorry! I...I am not happy to have condemned you to this slow death," Morvash said.

"*Oh, I don't mind. Do not think I am like you in my wants and interests. I have agreed to let the demon destroy me because I have no reason to refuse.*"

"You...agreed?"

"*We speak sometimes, the demon and I. That is the price I ask for holding still, that it take the time to talk to me. On one such occasion, early in our acquaintance, it explained to me the concept of an afterlife. It assures me that humans can continue to exist in another form after they die, as ghosts or spirits. Perhaps I, too, will be reborn into a more appropriate world when it has removed me from this one; perhaps I am as immortal as the spell that created me would claim. I decided I would take that chance. In truth, I have little to lose.*"

"You talk to it? Even though it's killing you?"

"*I do. I wish to understand this world I am in. But alas, it is no part of this world, either, and cannot help as much as I might*" *hope*."

"Are you lonely, then?"

"*I think I might be. I am not sure*."

"I… Perhaps I could visit sometimes, or bring others. I think I could even ask a dragon by the name of Aldagon to stop by."

"*That might be interesting*."

"Or I could put you to sleep with a spell, so that you… If you want."

"*Oh, I prefer to remain awake. I enjoy watching the sunrise. But thank you. And visitors would be welcome*."

"I have… There are these four gargoyles that your creator made, as practice for making *you*. He made six, but only four seem to be alive. I could bring them to stay with you. The house they lived on is gone."

"*That would be interesting. Thank you*." It tipped its head in the opposite direction. "*For someone who was determined to see me dead, you are being surprisingly kind*."

"I never want anyone to suffer. I have made it my business to find people who have been turned to stone and restore them to life—I've been hunting for statues that used to be human. I take other curses off people, too. That's what I want to do, to help people. When I was here before I was so afraid of how many people you could hurt that I didn't think about how *you* felt; I'm sorry."

"*I understand*." Then it turned its attention to Zerra, still seated on her carpet. "*And do you have anything to say*?"

"No," she shouted back. "I'm only here because he paid me to fly him here."

"*I see*." Then it turned its attention back to Morvash, but he could think of nothing more to say.

"I'll bring those gargoyles," he said, as he reached for the carpet.

And then he and Zerra were airborne, bound for Ethshar.

EPILOGUE

Although no public explanations were ever given, some seven assorted wizards scattered all across the World, all of them old and powerful, disappeared abruptly over the course of the year following Erdrik's reappearance. All were known to have been conversant with petrifaction spells of one sort or another, and any inquiries about them were greeted with assurances from the Wizards' Guild that everything was under control.

Word went out that a wealthy collector in Ethshar of the Spices was seeking any and all life-sized works by the famous Lamumese artist Varrek the Sculptor, and would pay generously for them.

The Wizards' Guild, after some discussion behind closed doors, accepted the legal fiction that Darissa was not a witch. In any case, there was precedent for allowing witches in government in places as varied as Klathoa and Ethshar of the Rocks, under certain circumstances, so it was agreed that the Guild would look the other way in this instance. The failed apprentice married Prince Marek and became Princess Darissa, and eventually, some years later, Queen Darissa, consort to King Marek of Melitha, and mother to Prince Nondel, Prince Terren, Princess Zerra, and Princess Ithinia.

Gror and Morvash were eventually able to either restore all the former statues who had taken refuge in Gror's mansion to their homes, or settle them into new lives, though it took almost two years before the last was gone. Most of them were able to adjust to their situation in time. Even Thetta, no longer a dancing girl but a baker, eventually decided she did not need to kill or mutilate herself—she found that ugly clothing and a bad haircut were enough to deter unwanted attention, and that she enjoyed baking at least as much as she had dancing.

In addition to several fees, Morvash received a great deal of favorable free publicity from the people he had rescued. Gror benefitted from the reflected fame; his business thrived. He also found himself the holder of an exclusive license to trade with the royal family of Melitha, which proved reasonably profitable despite Melitha's notable lack of industry.

Morvash became known as an expert on breaking curses—his expertise in curses, which he had never particularly appreciated, allowed him to live up to this reputation, since of course he knew how to remove every curse he could cast. He learned to perform Javan's Restorative more reliably, and over time restored several more enchanted people to their natural forms.

Karitha kept calling herself "the Demonologist," but never again summoned a demon. Her major task was to stand behind Morrin's chair and look menacing, and she became quite good at it, even after she married a swordsmith and bore five children. She did eventually recover Tarker's lost secret name by hiring a wizard who used the Spell of Omniscient Vision to watch her writing it down in the first place, back in 5231, but kept it in reserve.

Erdrik the Grim's remains were found and given a proper pyre; the Wizards' Guild wanted to be *sure* he was dead this time. His house on Old East Avenue was carefully disassembled and carted away, the wards and other spells were removed, and the furnishings, animated and otherwise, were auctioned off. Morvash acquired the animated copper kettle, though he sometimes regretted the impulse that had prompted him to do so, and made good on his promise to deliver the four animated gargoyles to the northern desert where the dragon lay.

Pender opened a jewelry shop on Gaudy Street in Sardiron of the Waters, where he specialized in dragon-shaped charms and gems suitable for enchantment. His mysterious background and his ability to speak Ethsharitic attracted a relatively sophisticated clientele.

And even after losing almost three dozen of the finest pieces, Lord Landessin's sculpture collection remained unrivaled.